Advance Praise for
Fragments of Light

"Michèle Phoenix skillfully explores the strength and resiliency of the human spirit but also its heartbreaking limits. Brimming with expertly researched wartime details, *Fragments of Light* abounds with poignancy and insight."

—Susan Meissner, bestselling author
of *The Last Year of the War*

"Michele Phoenix's *Fragments of Light* is a luminous portrait of men and women grappling with the past in a brave attempt to forge a different kind of future. From page one, I was all in. Ceelie's anguish and hope, Darlene's spunk and pain, and Cal's courage and conviction—all of it combines to create a story as beautiful as it is heartbreaking. In short, I loved this book!"

—Lauren Denton, *USA TODAY* bestselling author
of *The Hideaway* and *The Summer House*

"Michèle Phoenix is a novelist who has chased the truth about World War II and D-Day, and she has made it come to life. Michèle has made sure that this novel is historically accurate. She was right with the jumpers on D-Day. Her literary ability brings out the emotions of the reader. As a D-Day Airborne participant, I recommend this novel with enthusiasm. Everyone should read it."

—Staff Sergeant Thomas Rice, WWII Veteran, 101st Airborne

"*Loving can be just as brutal as it is beautiful.* Michele Phoenix weaves this truth through every strand of the stories in her novel *Fragments of Light*. As the title suggests, there are no easy illuminations on the path of healing. Cancer attacks more than the body. War destroys more than flesh and bone. Not all heroes welcome the attention, and not all husbands are up to the challenge. Women find the most unlikely sources of strength, and the best families defy definition."

—Allison Pittman, bestselling author of *The Seamstress*

"A compelling story across time of love, loss, and what happens when tragedy strikes. In *Fragments of Light*, Ceelie and Darlene forge a beautiful friendship that brings healing, forgiveness, and a chance for new beginnings. Written with depth and understanding, this story offers readers a wonderful journey spanning from war-torn World War II France to a battle for love in our time."

—KATHERINE REAY, BESTSELLING AUTHOR OF *DEAR MR. KNIGHTLEY* AND *THE PRINTED LETTER BOOKSHOP*

"An immersive and unforgettable treatise on the power of love in all of its manifestations. The past and present blur in this exceptionally researched portrait of humanity in the midst of turmoil and great divide. Deeply personal and beautifully humane, Phoenix once again asserts her power as one of the most moving and lyrical voices in inspirational fiction."

—RACHEL MCMILLAN, AUTHOR OF *THE LONDON RESTORATION*

"It's not often a story moves me as *Fragments of Light* has. With a rare and honest voice, Michèle Phoenix weaves a story of heroes from yesteryear and also those from your neighborhood—each with hearts of valor—as they endure the fight of their lives. *Fragments of Light* braids together the dark and light of history and the human soul, both through the lens of restoration and hope."

—ELIZABETH BYLER YOUNTS, CAROL AWARD-WINNING AUTHOR *THE SOLACE OF WATER*

"*Fragments of Light* [is a] compelling narrative that alternates between past and present, asking the reader: What length would you go to defend freedom and repair the fragments of shattered lives broken by war and illness, by misunderstandings and assumptions? But with enough wry humor sprinkled throughout to keep the reader chuckling even in the midst of pain."

—KATHLEEN M. RODGERS, 2019 MWSA WRITER OF THE YEAR FINALIST AND AUTHOR OF *THE FLYING CUTTERBUCKS*

Fragments
of Light

ALSO BY MICHÈLE PHOENIX

The Space Between Words
Of Stillness and Storm

Fragments
of *Light*

MICHÈLE PHOENIX

THOMAS NELSON
Since 1798

Published in Nashville, Tennessee, by Thomas Nelson. Thomas Nelson is a registered trademark of HarperCollins Christian Publishing, Inc.

The author is represented by MacGregor Literary, Inc.

Interior design by Phoebe Wetherbee

Thomas Nelson titles may be purchased in bulk for educational, business, fundraising, or sales promotional use. For information, please email SpecialMarkets@ThomasNelson.com.

Scripture quotation is taken from the King James Version. Public domain.

Publisher's Note: This novel is a work of fiction. Names, characters, places, and incidents are either products of the author's imagination or used fictitiously. All characters are fictional, and any similarity to people living or dead is purely coincidental.

Library of Congress Cataloging-in-Publication Data

Names: Phoenix, Michèle, author.
Title: Fragments of light / Michèle Phoenix.
Description: Nashville, Tennessee : Thomas Nelson, [2020] | Summary: "From D-Day to present-day, two lives are irrevocably changed by the decision to chase brave or to run away from it"-- Provided by publisher.
Identifiers: LCCN 2020008274 (print) | LCCN 2020008275 (ebook) | ISBN 9780785232056 (trade paperback) | ISBN 9780785232063 (epub) | ISBN 9780785232070 (audio download)
Subjects: GSAFD: Christian fiction.
Classification: LCC PS3616.H65 F73 2020 (print) | LCC PS3616.H65 (ebook) | DDC 813/.6--dc23
LC record available at https://lccn.loc.gov/2020008274
LC ebook record available at https://lccn.loc.gov/2020008275

Printed in the United States of America

20 21 22 23 24 LSC 5 4 3 2 1

For Tom Rice—WWII veteran and first-person historian.
Thank you for embodying the valor and
humanity of those who fought for freedom on
one of history's darkest and brightest days.

For Deb—my fellow fighter and friend.
Thank you for praying peace over me on the night I
learned I had cancer and for waging your own battle with
the grace, joy, and faith that are your defining traits.

Prologue

I was dreaming about carousels the night the sky got
loud. Like the one Sabine drew for me that time I asked
her what a fair was like. The white wooden horses
with brown manes and gold saddles looked like they
were running, but she told me it was just the carousel
turning. I'd never seen one for real before, but Sabine
was seven years older than me and she could remember
things from before the Germans came.

"We'll see one soon, Lise," Papa had promised me.
When I asked him how soon, he'd kind of hunched a
shoulder. Then he'd leaned in and touched my hair like
you pet a dog. "Maybe really soon." His voice had the
fairy-tale softness I liked.

I believed him that day, but I didn't believe
him anymore after a lot of months went by and the
Germans were still in the village down the road. And
I guess I really stopped believing I would ever see a

carousel on the day I turned six and the gendarmes took Papa away. Two policemen and a German soldier rode up to our cart on their black bicycles when we were in the village trading leeks for beans. Papa got pale when they asked for his name. They accused him of being in the *résistance* and he told them that it wasn't him, but the big policeman said someone had seen Papa talking with people in the cemetery after curfew. He yelled at Papa that he was a traitor and that the only place for traitors was Hitler's camps in Germany. He was smiling and sweating when he looked at the people standing around us, like he wanted to make sure they were paying attention.

The gendarmes handcuffed Papa's hands behind his back while the German officer watched. Sabine and I didn't know what to do. Old Albert was standing behind us and I could hear him growling really low. He took a couple steps toward the policemen, but Papa told him to stop. "*Albert, non.*" He said it really sharp, like when he'd tell the dogs to be quiet.

Albert stepped back and put a hand on my shoulder. I heard him whisper to Sabine that she should take me home, but we didn't want to leave Papa. He kept repeating that he was innocent, that they couldn't take him away. It was just the three of us since Mum had died and we needed him at home. That's what he told the gendarmes. When the German barked something at them and pointed his chin down the road, Papa started to scream, but they didn't seem to hear him even then. The gendarmes were French like us, but he called them *boches* anyway, the word we were never supposed to say around them.

I ran to Papa before Albert could stop me. I squeezed him tight around his waist and begged him not to leave, like I could keep him with us if I just hung on long enough. The German yelled something again and I felt Albert's hands on my arms. He kept saying that I needed to let go. There was something shaky in his voice. It scared me so much that I didn't fight him when he dragged me back to my sister.

Sabine grabbed me and I could feel her arms trembling around me. She pleaded with the gendarmes to change their minds. She said we needed Papa with us, since Albert was so old and our farm was so big. She kept saying that they had the wrong person and he wasn't a *résistant*. She looked around at the villagers like she wanted them to help, but they just looked away or stepped back.

"I beg of you," she said to the biggest gendarme, tears on her face.

He didn't answer her. Instead, he grabbed Papa and turned him around toward our village friends. "Be warned," he shouted. "This is what happens to traitors!"

Papa's face was white and hard as he passed in front of us, with the two gendarmes and the German soldier pushing their bikes behind him. But there was something sad and scared in his eyes. "*Prends soin d'eux*," he said to Albert. Take care of them. Albert nodded and stepped in front of me when I tried to follow Papa down the road.

We didn't say anything on the way home. Sabine went to the kitchen and sat at the table. Albert stood in the doorway like he didn't know what to do. I went to my sister and leaned in so she had to look at me,

3

and I asked her when Papa would be coming home. She just closed her eyes. I asked her again when we were making stew from the green beans we'd gotten in the village and the rabbit Albert had trapped. She still didn't answer. I probably asked the same question a hundred more times that same afternoon, louder and louder. And at the end of the day, when I asked Sabine again before going to bed, I saw red blotches spreading on her neck. She slapped my face and told me to just . . . stop . . . asking.

Then she looked really surprised and stared at her hand for a minute. I didn't know what to do, so I just stood there until she said, "I'm sorry. Lisou, I'm sorry."

Her voice was sharp and hoarse at the same time, but when she used my special name, I knew she wasn't really mad at me. She kissed my cheek where the skin still stung. She kissed it lots and said she was sorry again. Then she held me away from her and looked hard at my face. Her grip on my arms felt really tight.

"We're going to be fine." I could tell she was talking to herself. She squinted her eyes shut for a long time, then she blew out a breath and her lips trembled like a loose rubber band. "The German work camps . . ." She shook her head and I could see tears teetering on her eyelashes. "I don't know when Papa is coming home." She covered her face with her apron, the one Mum used to wear, with the square pocket and the daffodils. I could see her shoulders shaking.

Albert was old but he was strong. He kept the farm going after Papa went away, even after the Germans moved in, maybe two months later. They turned up with their horses and one fancy car and told us they were going to live with us. Albert said they should go back to the village and leave us alone.

They beat him up bad.

So we moved out of the upstairs bedrooms and into the apartment off the kitchen, where Aunt Sophie used to live.

On the night the sky rumbled, I could barely hear the Germans' boots running down the steps and out the front door. It was so loud, it felt like it was coming from underneath the ground. I sat up and looked around. The shutters were closed, but something orange shining around the slats made shadow-ladders on my wall.

I tiptoed to the window. Normally the air would smell like dew and Mum's lilacs and manure and ocean salt. But it just smelled like shooting that night. I could hear the big guns going off again and again in the battery the Germans had set up in a field behind my friend Lucien's house.

I undid the latch that kept the shutters closed. Then I poked a finger into the opening to make the crack just big enough to look through if I tilted my head sideways.

The sky was bright over by the beach where we used to go before they took Papa away. There were all kinds of reds and yellows, and a glow on the ground like bonfires burning. I stepped back from the window and shook my head to make sure I was awake. Then I pinched the skin on the inside of my elbow just to be really sure.

The rumbling was getting so loud that the floor shook under my feet. I peeked through the crack again and looked up, way up past the tip of the roof. It looked like a thousand giant, black trout swimming in the sky. It was so much like magic that I didn't really hear the booming coming from the village anymore.

"Lise!" Sabine was standing in my doorway when I turned around. "Come-come quickly," she said, motioning for me to hurry up.

I grabbed my blanket from the bed and my tiger too. He was ratty and nearly bald and one of his eyes had popped off a long time ago, but I knew where we were going and it felt safer when he was there with me.

My sister took me under her arm and steered me down the stairs toward the kitchen.

I asked her, "Did you see the planes?"

"It's the Allies," she told me as she took a lantern from a high shelf and lit the wick. She tried to smile but didn't quite manage. "They're coming to help us."

All of a sudden Albert was there too. He yanked hard on the metal bolt that kept the door to the root cellar closed.

"Are you going to hide with us?"

He shook his head, pulled the heavy wooden door open, and motioned for us to go down the three steps into the cellar. "I'm going to watch for the Americans." He grumbled it like he wasn't scared at all. "They'll need to know where the Germans are."

"Be safe," Sabine whispered. She stared at him, then she pulled the door closed.

I didn't like the cellar. Even though it was carved out of a dirt bank on the back side of the house and wasn't really underground, it still made me feel like I couldn't breathe right. Albert had lined the walls with bushels of twigs when the Germans weren't watching. "It'll keep the bullets and shrapnel out," he said. But on nights like this, it didn't feel like anything would keep the shooting from getting to us.

I went over to the stack of potato bags on the side wall and sat down. The crates on the dirt ledge above me were empty, but I still kind of remembered when they'd been filled with apples and carrots and potatoes.

Sabine rattled the bolt into place, the one Papa had put on the inside of the cellar door. Then she turned toward me. I thought she looked frightened, but I could see something strong on her face too. Maybe even something happy, like when you know you're going to have the deer Albert found in the woods for supper, but you can't let the Germans know.

An explosion rattled the empty jars in the basket on the ground next to me. I wondered if a bomb had fallen on someone I knew in the village ten minutes down the road. Like Lucien and his family. They didn't have a cellar like we did.

Sabine jumped a little at the noise and put a hand on her chest. "They won't bomb us," she said. "They're after the battery and we're too far away. They won't try to hit us."

She looked at my face, then came over to sit down beside me. She wrapped an arm around my shoulders and kissed the top of my head. I looked up at her and got worried when I saw the look in her eyes.

"Are we going to die?" I hadn't meant to ask the question out loud.

Sabine took a deep breath and let it out, loud and long. "No," she said like she was still trying to believe it. "No, we are not going to die."

Part 1

Chapter 1

Winfield, IL
Modern Day

I woke to the sound of beeping and whirring machines. Faint pink light stole around the blinds spanning the huge window that looked out over a horseshoe-shaped courtyard, its terraced vegetation manicured to appear natural and wild. I felt the inflatable wraps on my legs fill with air and press my calves, as they had every few minutes during the night.

I'd woken each time, a bit disoriented by the "good stuff" still feeding into my veins from the IV pole next to my bed, and looked around the room, as I was now, trying to get my bearings. The night nurse's name on the whiteboard. The remote on the mattress next to my right hand. The bathroom door just far enough away to remind me of my post-op weakness.

It felt like there was a weight on my chest. Inside it. Around it. The zip-up garment keeping everything—whatever was left—in place felt both stabilizing and stifling. I pulled the blanket back a little and looked down, taking in the two drains extending from each side of my rib cage and the unfamiliar flatness. Every glance since I'd woken from surgery had been preceded by fear and followed by a strange sense of relief and lostness. Relief that it was over. That my shower-time grieving was done and the operation that would alter my life—in ways I still couldn't fully understand—was no longer something lurking in the future.

And lostness. The destabilizing sense that I'd been changed in subtle and overwhelming ways during those five hours in the operating room. There was a deep-rooted disquiet too—the kind that hums on the edge of consciousness, whispering, "You'll find out" in a tone that is both threat and promise.

I pushed myself up farther against the inclined mattress, winced at the discomfort in my pectoral muscles, and opted for an ungraceful scoot instead. My legs and glutes still functioned well, but everything above my waist felt pummeled and encased.

I sighed. Closed my eyes. Breathed as deeply as I could without pain.

"Are you sleeping or picturing yourself in a bikini on a Hawaiian beach?"

A head of teased-high, pink-tipped gray hair poked around my hospital room's door.

"If it's the latter . . . honey, dream away. I'll come back some other time." Darlene's stage whisper held a smile—the kind that borders on outright laughter. It wasn't just a tone of voice for her. It was the way she lived her life.

She made a production of quietly closing the door and tiptoed toward the bed. "Don't tell the nurses I snuck in!"

I glanced at the digital clock mounted on the wall next to the TV. "What are you doing out and about before seven a.m.?"

"Got my Zumba in a bit, but wanted to see how you fared overnight first. Besides," she added, waving away her rule breaking with a slim hand, "the nurses know me. They wouldn't kick out the human equivalent of a therapy dog."

She winked and pulled the computer stool closer to my bed.

Her white sneakers squeaked on the linoleum floor as she turned to perch her tiny frame on the seat. Her peekaboo leggings and figure-hugging Nike shirt likely hadn't been designed with a seventy-six-year-old woman in mind, but they looked—in all their sparkly pink-and-gray splendor—as if they'd been custom-made for Darlene.

She glanced at the drains extending from my sides, then looked up at my face, lips twisted in disapproval. "I'll gladly donate my entire estate to the inventor who can make those tubes obsolete."

I tried to smile. "How about you donate it to someone who can make the surgery itself obsolete?"

She sighed and tilted her head to the side, taking a good look at my face. I saw her features soften as she leaned in to touch my arm—firm, but gentle. "Tell me how you're feeling, Ceelie."

Darlene had ushered something that felt like confidence into Room 268 on the post-op floor of Central DuPage Hospital. Survivors carried that with them, I'd found—the aura of possibility and overcoming. It's what had first drawn me to her when we'd met in the waiting room of the Breast Health Center downstairs nine weeks earlier, both of us wrapped in pilling cotton robes, enveloped by muted colors, soft lighting, and barely audible elevator music.

She'd been sitting by the coffee station when the nurse led me in and left me with, "I'll come back for you once the doctor's had a chance to look at your images."

"That's code for 'Just sit here and stare at a magazine page you're not really reading while we figure out if you should be worried or not,'" Darlene whispered.

I lowered the *Vanity Fair* I'd just picked up and looked across the waiting room at the petite woman with the cotton-candy hair and vibrant, almost indigo eyes. Her makeup was the epitome of 1980s chic—all purples and blues and stark lines. Her skin showed her age, but her eyes belied it.

"Not your first rodeo?" I asked, tamping down the nervousness that always—despite my positive self-talk—seemed to overwhelm me on these yearly visits.

"The nurses are on my Christmas card list. Does that answer your question?"

My smile felt less strained this time. "Every year—*every year*—I tell myself that it's just a routine check," I said, letting some of my anxiety show, "and that millions of women go through this without anything bad coming of it, but still . . ." I shook my head. "I sit in this room that's clearly designed for optimism and calm, and it's all I can do not to write an obituary in my mind."

Darlene laughed and pointed at the speakers in the corners. "You think Elton John knew that his watered down Muzak would be the backdrop to so much mammography angst?" She extended her hand as she moved to the chair next to mine and said, "Darlene Egerton." I felt a weight lift. There was something humanizing about sharing names.

"Cecelia—Ceelie—Donovan."

"Nice to meet you, Ceelie Donovan."

Twenty minutes later, the nurse who had performed my mammogram reentered the waiting room. "We just want to get a couple more shots from different angles," she said in a friendly tone as she ushered me back into the hallway lined with exam rooms.

I could hear sympathy under the practiced cheer of her voice.

Just over two months later, Darlene sat next to me again and, by mere proximity, seeped comfort into my post-operative uncertainty.

Her voice was softer than usual when she said, "The worst is over. All that waiting and imagining. Now you know what kind of pain you're dealing with. And it's not as bad as you thought, right?"

I nodded and blinked back tears.

"You've got this, sweetie. Every day is going to be different. There may even be one or two when it feels like you're slipping back instead of making progress—I had a few of those. But you're in good medical hands. The best. And you're a fighter."

She must have seen something in my expression. Her smile faded and she sat back. Moments passed before she spoke again. "Tell me."

The tears that had been threatening since I'd woken began to fall. I hunched a shoulder and winced. I wasn't distraught. I wasn't terrified. I was . . . daunted. And so very disappointed. "Dr. Sigalove said I'll probably need chemo."

Darlene's pencil-fine eyebrows went up. "Didn't she tell you going into this that the surgery would be enough—?"

"They found another tumor," I interrupted her, needing to get it out. "One that didn't show up on the mammograms." I took a breath and let it out slowly.

Darlene sighed. "So . . . chemo."

"I might have gotten a pass with the small tumor they knew about, but this one . . . She said it could change things. A lot."

Darlene sat up straighter on the stool and projected such bold optimism that I felt it bridge the space between us. "So you don't know for sure."

"No, but Dr. Sigalove—"

"Lesson number one in being a survivor," Darlene cut me off, "do not—I repeat, *do not*—borrow on tomorrow's worries. Do today." She put on her retired-high-school-teacher face. "Repeat that."

I'd grown accustomed to the exercise. "Do today," I dutifully repeated.

She gave me a hopeful look. "Dr. Sigalove didn't tell you for sure about chemo because she doesn't know for sure about chemo. They'll figure it out when they get pathology back, but until then . . .

Don't borrow." She squinted into my face and leaned in a little. "Repeat."

"Don't borrow." There was something spirit-lifting in the words. After a pause, I added, "You had chemo, right?" So much for not borrowing.

I could tell she didn't like the question, but she answered it anyway. "I did. And if the Chicago marathon I'm running next month is any indication, I'm fairly certain I lived through it."

Surprise took my mind off of myself for a moment. "You entered a marathon?"

"October 13. Starts at Grant Park and goes all the way to the 31st Street Beach. But I plan on finishing my race at the Jackson Boulevard Starbucks."

I felt myself frown. "Isn't that . . . like . . . two blocks from Grant Park?"

Darlene winked at me. "Sure is. Now—tell me when that husband of yours is coming in to see you."

Nate. Encourager. Perspective-giver. In-demand contractor prepared to sacrifice a job or two—or three—to care for me.

When I'd gotten back from my mammogram appointment that first day and told him about the repeat images followed by an ultrasound, he'd sat next to me on the couch and listened. Then he'd dragged me out to a nearby forest preserve for a walk in the sunshine.

When I'd gone back to the hospital two days later for a biopsy, he'd sat next to me again and held my hand, talking to the doctor and nurses calmly—steadying my nerves with his attentiveness to me and kindness to others.

When Dr. Sigalove's office had phoned to tell me they had my results, I'd waited for Nate to come home before returning the call. He was sitting beside me—solid and still—when words like *invasive*, *margins*, and *prognosis* entered my vocabulary for the first time.

In the weeks that followed, he lay next to me night after night as I grappled with an appalling new reality, consumed by impossible what-ifs and what-nows.

In ways I couldn't quite define, my diagnosis had altered our relationship. More than two decades of marriage had dulled our conversations and dampened our impulses. Our lives' orbits had started off intertwined, but with time had imperceptibly drifted onto parallel paths. The shock of cancer—the waiting and absorbing and researching and decision making—had forced our trajectories back toward each other before we'd fully realized how far they'd strayed.

Nate had gotten me a vintage Crosley record player for our anniversary, five weeks after the dreaded call from Dr. Sigalove's office.

"So . . . the traditional gift for twenty-four years is supposed to be musical instruments," he'd explained as we sat on the floor in front of the fireplace washing pizza down with beer—a tradition that had begun at about two a.m. on our wedding night in a hotel off the Magnificent Mile.

I stopped chewing and flashed him my attaboy smile. "You did some research, Nate."

"I did. But since neither of us is likely to pick up the saxophone at this point in our lives, I figured we could settle for playing classics on this old gem instead."

He smiled and handed me an LP.

"Weezer?" I shouldn't have been surprised. When we'd discussed what song we'd use for our first dance during the weeks leading up to our wedding, I'd brought "Endless Love" and "Now and Forever" to the table, and he'd tried to convince me that Weezer's self-indulgent "The Sweater Song" was appropriate for that kind of occasion.

On the night we celebrated twenty-four years of marriage, he said, "It took me a week of negotiating on eBay to get this vinyl."

I wanted to enter into the festive mood with him, but my upcoming surgery had been the deafening subtext of every conversation since my diagnosis, and I couldn't quiet it now.

As the album began to spin on the turntable, I said, "Nate, can we talk?"

"We've done nothing but talk. Tonight, we dance."

"You didn't marry me."

He looked at me as if he hadn't heard me clearly. "Come again?"

"You didn't marry two-weeks-from-now me."

He dropped his head for a moment. I vaguely noticed that he was past due for a trim, his usual crew cut softening into graying brown curls. His shoulders were broader now than when we'd first met. His skin more lived-in and leathery from exposure to the elements on his construction sites. "Cee . . . come on." I thought I heard a trace of exasperation in his voice, but his brown eyes were just as solidly calm as they'd been since the phone call that had upended our lives.

I couldn't blame him for feeling frustrated. We'd had this conversation a dozen times, but I needed to have it again—to be sure he understood how this surgery would change me. And probably us.

I forged ahead. "You married someone—you *chose* someone— who was all woman. All her body parts accounted for and functional."

"Cee, I didn't marry you for—"

I put up a hand. "Let me finish. Please?" When he nodded, I went on. "I know we've already talked about this. But I just—" I took a deep breath and looked him in the eyes. "I need you to tell me again that you get how different I'll be. How . . . rebuilt I'll be."

He opened his mouth to say something, but I shook my head. I needed to say it all. "The reconstruction—it's going to take months to finish it. And when it's done . . . There will be scars. There will be nerve damage. There will be discomfort, and—I probably won't look or feel like the Ceelie you married. I guess I need you to know that I'll understand if . . ."

I couldn't put into words the fears that had slithered their way into my courage as surgery day approached, eroding it so subtly that I was just beginning to identify the dread. Years ago I'd given up on becoming a mother—infertility forcing me to relinquish what I'd always considered a foundational piece of being a woman. We'd decided together to try treatments and, after multiple failures and devastating miscarriages, I was the one who'd finally decided I was done—with the treatments and all the alternatives we'd discussed for having children. I simply didn't have it in me to take on the uncertainty and risk of adoption or surrogacy. And I told myself that it didn't really matter—that my life was full with other things that were just as validating of my femininity.

In the intervening years, I hadn't allowed myself to question the decision. I'd focused on my career and told myself that it was fulfilling enough, that kids would only have hampered the aspirations that had brought me such professional joy. But I'd still felt a twinge of uncertainty every time I'd seen Nate playing with our friends' children. I'd chalked it up to hormones and chosen to focus instead on the stability of the life we'd built together.

With a double mastectomy just thirteen days away, the twinges I'd felt years ago were crawling back to the surface again—the sense that my womanhood, already diminished by my inability to have children, was facing an amputation that would erase it for good.

Our intimacy had subtly changed since my diagnosis. What had become more perfunctory than passionate in the last decade or so had suddenly taken on a sad sort of intensity—the sense that every touch was the acknowledgment of inevitable change, the image-altering lessness that felt as threatening to me as it was life-preserving.

The Weezer vinyl spun on the record player. "I just need to be sure you understand, Nate," I said.

I'd caught him looking at me a couple times over the past few weeks, as we got ready for bed, his eyes lingering on my breasts, as if he too was wondering who I would be without them. Something similar flickered in his eyes as he considered what I'd asked. It morphed into hesitation. Then resolve.

He turned his attention back to the Crosley and gingerly lowered the needle onto the vinyl.

I stifled sudden anger as the song began with its ridiculous banter. "I'm serious, Nate."

He held up a hand and watched the record turn, waiting for his cue. The lines around his eyes seemed deeper than they'd been a month ago as he looked up at me again, mouthing the words of Weezer's song, coaxing me to join in and bopping a little to the rhythm. At any other time, I would have found his awkward moves endearing. "'If you want to destroy my sweater,'" he crooned, his eyes and smile on me, "'hold this thread and walk away.'"

"Nate."

He winked and held a hand out to me. "'Watch me unravel—'"

"Nate!" My voice was sharp enough to cut through his best intentions.

The needle squeaked as Nate lifted it off the LP. I saw his shoulders sag. His voice was rough with frustration when he said, "I understand, Ceelie." He looked at the ceiling and let out a loud breath. "I've gone to your appointments with you, I've watched the videos, I've read the articles." He looked at me, eyebrows drawn. "I know what's coming. I know it's going to be hard—really hard. I know it's going to take a while. I know all that. But we have two weeks, Cee. Two weeks before everything we've been planning for happens. Can we *not* dwell on it every moment of every day until then?"

I wanted to let it go. To drop the topic and find the box of old records I'd stored in the attic and sit on the floor while we played them all. "What if this changes everything?" I asked instead.

A taut silence stretched between us. I stared at his face as if it could reveal our future. He looked down at the still-spinning record.

"I told you it won't." There was something steely in the words.

I felt myself frowning as trust wrestled with uncertainty. I wanted to believe that the same forces that had kept us together all these years—through miscarriages and IVF treatments and career upheavals and all the ebbs and flows of marriage between two very different and stubborn people—would serve us again as we faced what lay ahead. In that moment, despite the misgivings that had wreaked havoc on my sleep and sanity since my diagnosis, I *chose* to believe it. Because I needed to in ways that took my breath away.

"I'm sorry, Nate."

"It's not your fault."

"We're going to get through this." I nodded in affirmation of my own words. "We're going to get through this," I said again, just to be sure.

Nate placed the needle back on the record and held out a hand. I stepped toward him and he brought my palm to his chest, anchoring it there with warmth and promise. I could feel his heartbeat—steady and slow. He cupped the side of my head with his other hand, and the roughness of his skin tugged on strands of my auburn hair as he caught the tears on my cheek with his thumb.

"Nate . . ." There was so much more I still wanted to say. I just couldn't seem to find the words for it.

He wrapped his arms around my shoulders and drew me closer to the solidness and sureness of his frame. There was a faint smile in his voice when he said, "Hey, Cee—shut up and dance."

Just two weeks later, Darlene sat near my bed on the day after my surgery. "Nate took a couple days off work. I'm sure he'll be here soon." She nodded and hopped off her stool, moving to the window to lift the blinds. The sun was rising over Winfield. It tinged the treetops in the distance with hopeful hues.

"Congratulations," Darlene said. "It's a new day and you're breathing." There was something bracing in the words.

She stayed a few minutes longer, then sashayed out the door with a wiggle of her cubic zirconia–clad fingers and a pointed "Don't borrow!" tossed in my direction.

I sank lower on my bed, adjusting my position for the least amount of discomfort, and watched the sky lighten as I waited for Nate to arrive.

Chapter 2

THE ENGLISH CHANNEL
JUNE 6, 1944

Cal closed his eyes and tried to picture home, but the images felt out of reach. The roar of the plane, the lurching and banking, the boom of anti-aircraft fire—it all felt overwhelming. He patted his flight jacket, unable to feel the papers he'd tucked into an inside pocket, but somehow calmed knowing they were there.

The jumpmaster, First Lieutenant Reid, a short, wiry man with a voice like a bullhorn, squinted into the chaotic night, then turned to take hold of the electronic communication receiver that hung on the fuselage wall next to the jump door. He yelled into it, addressing the flight crew in the cockpit, but Cal couldn't hear him above the pummeling maelstrom of sound.

Whatever the flight crew said back to Reid didn't ease the hard-edged concern on his face. He turned toward the stick of seventeen paratroopers perched nervously on their metallic bench and motioned to them that they were getting close.

Adrenaline and dread dueled in Cal's mind. He had no idea what the hours ahead would hold, but he was certain they would change the world.

In the days preceding Operation Overlord, Cal's squadron had tried to pass the rare free time they were given by playing cards in a large hangar filled with hundreds of cots, or by predicting which of the squad would be the first to earn a battle scar. It was a morbid form of bravado that served the dual purpose of acknowledging the danger ahead and feigning nonchalance. A fearless private first class by the name of Buck Mancuso, they'd decided, would be the most likely to ignore common sense and beat his comrades to a visit with the combat medic.

A preacher's son from Mentor, Ohio, Buck had brought a reckless streak to the unit's training and downtime, receiving more warnings and reprimands than anyone else in the platoon. He'd gotten his nickname from the pellets of buckshot lodged in his chest-one close to his heart-souvenirs from a childhood game of Cowboys and Indians that had nearly taken his life. He liked to point to his scars as proof that the "namby-pamby sissies" they'd be facing off with in France couldn't possibly hurt him.

When the GIs had made their dire predictions about his early injury on the evening preceding the launch of the Normandy invasion, Buck had yelled, "Not if I see the lousy Krauts first!" Something manic

had flickered in his eyes as he'd pretended to mow
down a row of Germans with a machine gun, yelling
obscenities.

He'd still been rattling off threats eight hours
later, as the paratroopers made their way to the
plane. Their briefing had been long and sobering,
the meticulous outline of their mission riddled
with the gaping holes of unpredictable factors—
enemy preparedness, countermeasures, and unknown
emplacements.

By the time the men had suited up and strapped on
well over a hundred pounds of ammo, guns, demolition
packs, and rations, most of them had needed help
getting up the ladder to the troop carrier.

They took off from Upottery Airfield three planes
at a time, then circled until all the C-47s in their
series had assembled at five thousand feet into nine-
ship formations. As they neared the coastline, they
merged with planes flying in from other parts of
southern England, then dropped to fifteen hundred
feet to cross the Channel under cover of darkness—a
wave of more than eight hundred thundering aircraft.

Cal's pilot turned off the navigation lights as
they left the coast. They'd be flying without radio
contact too, to avoid detection from the Germans
far below. This was a stealth operation of massive
proportions, and the fate of Europe—possibly the
world—depended on its success.

Cal breathed deeply and reviewed in his mind the
dioramas of Normandy the paratroopers had memorized
in the hours leading up to the invasion of France—
the beaches along the northern edge of the Cotentin

Peninsula, the landing zones they needed to reach, the Wehrmacht's known anti-aircraft emplacements on the coast and inland, and the strategic supply routes they were tasked with clearing.

When thick clouds obliterated the horizon, Cal knew that the planes in his group, crippled by radio silence, would drift out of formation, each cockpit crew now flying blind on instruments alone. And when flak and tracers lit the sky around them, he assumed that the wild, evasive action the pilots had to take to protect their human cargo would further dismantle the planes' configuration.

Down the bench from Cal, PFC Deering knelt and crossed himself three times before the plane lurched from a nearby flak explosion, sending him sprawling onto the floor. He struggled to get up again under the weight of his equipment, and Cal had to leave his seat to help the seventeen-year-old back to his. White-faced and wide-eyed, the young man clasped his knees with shaking hands, then leaned forward and threw up, his terror far stronger than the anti-nausea pills the troops had been given before boarding their planes.

The jump light turned from white to red. Every man onboard knew exactly what that meant. The lead C-47 in the formation had crossed the *T* that the Pathfinders, sent ahead of the invasion, had laid out far below in amber lights.

They'd be jumping in eight minutes.

The plane's evasive maneuvers, the explosions of flak, and the scream of tracers were an assault on the paratroopers' senses, but they were all business when First Lieutenant Reid held up his two thumbs, a cue that instantly brought them to their feet. When he gave them the bent-finger signal to hook up, the men clicked their static lines onto the anchor cable running the length of the fuselage.

Reid went to the front of the plane and tested the last troop's line, then checked the rest of his equipment. One after the other, each man in the stick did the same for the paratrooper ahead of him.

Standing behind Cal, Buck gripped his shoulders with adrenaline-fueled zeal, screaming, "Here we go!" into his ear at the top of his lungs. "Hellfire and brimstone!"

At nineteen, Buck was two years younger than Cal, and his impetuous gusto was more coltish passion than measured force. He'd arrived at Fort Benning eager for battle and had quickly grown frustrated with the duration of the training that had preceded their deployment. One particularly intense fit of rage over latrine protocol had landed another trooper in the clinic and Buck in the slammer overnight.

But for all his failures, Buck was a formidable fighter. He'd outrun, outjumped, outshot, and outsmarted every man in the platoon during training on two continents. He and Cal had been deployed to different places after Fort Benning, but they'd been reunited months ago in England, as the land, sea, and air assault neared.

Though their appearance was as different as their personalities—Buck short and compact, Cal tall and lanky—they'd become unlikely friends, Cal's calm and rational demeanor a mitigating influence on Buck's impassioned impulses.

As they waited for the jump light to turn green, Cal yelled over his shoulder, "See you down there!" He tried to infuse enthusiasm into the words, though he knew Buck wouldn't be able to hear them over the cacophony of sound thundering around them. Perhaps sensing the sentiment, Buck smacked his helmet and let out a war cry.

Lieutenant Reid's face turned tense as he leaned over to glance out the jump door again. A muscle worked in his jaw. He leaned toward the cockpit and yelled into the receiver again. When he turned back to the paratroopers after a brief exchange, his expression was set and Cal knew why. The engines were racing, their pitch higher than normal, which indicated excessive speed for a jump. And he could only assume that the stomach-turning dives they'd taken to evade German fire had brought them dangerously low.

As the C-47 lurched to the right, the soldiers reached for anything they could grab to steady themselves. The plane banked and dove again, then righted itself. Now Cal could hear stutters interrupting the engines' roar.

Reid gripped the handle next to the jump door with white knuckles. There was a thin trail of blood running from his hairline to his jaw.

The light turned green, and he pushed several bundles of gear and provisions out the door, then pressed the button that released more bundles hanging from the bottom of the plane, making it jolt upward as their weight fell off.

All seventeen paratroopers plus Reid had ten

seconds to be out the door, but another burst of anti-aircraft fire erupted off the left wing as Cal's turn came to jump. It made the plane jerk to the right, launching him forward. In a flash, he found himself pinned across the jump door, his body on the outside, legs bouncing against the fuselage, while his right arm and shoulder were still inside the plane. The power of the 140-mile-per-hour wind anchored him there as his ankle packs tore off and the men who had been standing behind him jumped past in quick succession.

With his neck bent at a painful angle and his chin pressing into his chest, Cal could see some details below him. A structure burned off to the east. Canons fired. Small lights attached to equipment bundles floated down around him. And somewhere in the distance-too far in the distance for him to see-Cal knew Drop Zone C lay out of reach.

It all crossed his mind in a fraction of a second. The fear. The assessment. The resignation. With the ground too close, landing would be treacherous at best-that's if he survived the artillery fire arcing into the sky.

A plane plunged by, its wing on fire, its tail severed. The heat coming off it brought Cal back to reality. As dangerous as the jump was, staying with his plane was much more of a risk. Summoning every ounce of strength he could muster, he used his body as a pendulum, swinging up and out, gaining just enough rotation to pull his arm free. Then the prop blast caught him and he was falling. His chute deployed, released by the static line, and pulled him up hard.

Cal looked down, forcing his mind off the flak

exploding above him, trying to see something-anything-that looked like a safe place to land.

He could see nothing but fog and indistinct terrain as he drifted sideways, the green silk of the canopy above him miraculously intact. The few lights he'd spotted while hanging from the jump door were out of sight now and the ground was coming up fast.

He grabbed a handful of the webbing connected to the parachute's shroud lines and tried to turn himself around, knowing on an instinctive level that the next few seconds would make the difference between life and death. The maneuver failed, hampered by velocity and lack of time.

Cal was vaguely aware of skimming a rooftop. His head jerked back as his helmet connected with something solid. There was only one name in his mind before the world went dark. He said it out loud.

"Claire."

Chapter 3

I rang the bell. I rang the heck out of that bell. I rang it until the voices down the hall stopped cheering and started asking me to stop ringing the dang bell.

Completed Treatment was engraved on the brass plaque above it. And as I took in some of the faces celebrating with me—nurses and techs who had become mainstays during my chemo days—I felt something unfurl. I thought it might be hope. Or maybe it was future plans. The months that had been metronomed by visits to the Cancer Center, where soothing colors contrasted with the beeps of machines dispensing life-saving poison, were over.

I was bald. I was chunkier than I'd ever been. I was tired and still growing into my new "bosoms," as Darlene called them, but I was done. The nausea, the fatigue, the blood draws and delayed treatments and pep rallies from caring nurses—all behind me.

Darlene hadn't been able to come for the big moment, but she'd given me a bright-red shirt with *Perky, bald, and cancer-free!* written on it in all caps.

"Not pink?" I'd asked when she handed it to me over a hamburger and fries the week before.

"Pink is for sweet people. But red? That's for fighters like you

31

who take on cancer with cold-blooded courage and show it who's boss."

I was fairly sure the description was an overstatement—what with the hours I'd spent, on several occasions, pouring out my frustration and pain to her in rants and tears—but I appreciated the sentiment. "I'll wear it with pride."

"And you'll puff out your chest too—brand spankin' new as it is. Own your victory, Cecelia Donovan. You've earned it."

"Did you get the whole bell-ringing?" I asked Nate as we were leaving the hospital. His sole job for the day had been videoing the moment, then whisking me away for a malted chocolate shake. The late-January chill wouldn't keep us from our tradition.

"The next county over caught the bell-ringing, Cee."

He'd been patient. Patient and strong and kind—in a painstaking, let's-get-this-done way. Only on a couple occasions could I remember him getting short with me or expressing something less than full-bodied support. He'd shaved my head when fistfuls of my thick auburn hair had started falling out toward the end of October. He'd researched natural remedies for the side effects of my treatment and been there with me through the vomiting, the out-of-whack emotions, the changes of course—over and over again. And he'd somehow made our cancer-tinged Christmas a gentle, meaningful occasion. He'd endured it all with a steadfastness that shouldn't have surprised me. I'd always known that I'd married a good man, and he'd proven it to me all over again.

"So . . . Hawaii or Switzerland?" I said once we were in the car. I'd refused to plan any celebratory travel until the last treatment was over. There had been too many surprises from the moment I was diagnosed, and I didn't want to jinx my dream trip by expecting it to happen on a predetermined schedule. I turned in my seat. "Hawaii has beaches, but the sun on my hairless scalp . . . not sure that's wise. Switzerland, on the other hand. Mountains. Lakes. *Chocolate*."

Nate nodded and steered the car into the left-turn lane. He pulled into our usual spot next to the Shake Shack without commenting.

"Nate?" I realized how little he'd said all day. I'd been so focused on all the lasts that were yielding to new firsts that I hadn't really noticed the remoteness of his disposition—even during the now infamous bludgeoning of the chemo bell. He'd videoed the milestone, but looking back, I could recall neither smile nor encouraging words. Just his quiet presence on the outskirts of the high fives and attagirls swirling like confetti in the hall.

"Honey." I leaned forward a little to try to meet his gaze and laid a hand on his arm. "Are you okay?"

For a long moment, he said nothing. Then, "I'm done."

"We're done." I nodded. I closed my eyes, let my head fall back, and laughed, reaching out to squeeze his arm in excitement and relief. "Nate! We're done!"

He turned in his seat and carefully removed my hand from his arm. "I told myself I'd see you through it." His voice was thin, like he was out of breath. "And I—" He looked at me then. Right into my eyes. I realized with a jolt how long it had been since his gaze had been that direct. "I saw you through it, Cee."

I felt my lungs constrict as a trickle of dread ran down my spine. "Nate . . ."

He straightened and faced forward, gripping the steering wheel too tightly. "I—I need to breathe. Not Hawaii, not Switzerland. Not a friggin' malted shake . . ." A muscle in his jaw clenched as he sucked air in through his nose. "I need to breathe," he said again, a tremor in his voice.

I tried to still the thoughts ricocheting in my mind.

"What are you saying . . . ?"

"I need out." Just like that. Flat voice. Flat gaze.

I looked at him and tried to swallow the shock and unasked questions clogging my throat.

"Okay, so you need a break," I said, inwardly begging for that to be all this was. Him needing to get away. A day. Maybe a week.

His headshake was nearly imperceptible. I couldn't speak. I could barely breathe. Something impenetrable descended over his form and countenance. The look on my husband's face was hard and merciless and stunningly sure. "This is what we're going to do."

I bit my lip as my stomach clenched in disbelief and my lungs froze. The voice. It wasn't his. It was too cold to be Nate's.

"We're going to go in there and get you your shake." His words had a stony undertone. "Then I'm going to drive you home and get my stuff." He turned the engine off. "We can figure out the details later, but, Ceelie . . ." He glanced at me, and I saw something that looked like hard-earned freedom in his eyes. "I'm done."

We never got the milkshake.

Nate's declaration on the heels of the day's monumental high was too much for my mind to process. I felt it shutting down, a spectator to my own mental break. I could hear Nate talking, but his words were garbled and slurred. He shook me by the arms and spoke so loudly in front of my face that I could feel his spittle, but nothing registered.

We drove home. He came around the car to help me out. Or to evict me. That's what it felt like. When I didn't get out of the car—not out of stubbornness but from sheer lack of strength—he said something about my drama getting old and stalked into the house. I sat there. For a couple minutes. Or maybe a lot longer.

The walk up the front steps felt overwhelming. My skin tingled and I couldn't seem to take in a full breath. There was a large duffel bag by the door. *That was fast*, I thought. Nate was pulling jackets and baseball caps out of the hall closet and stuffing them into another bag when I walked in.

He looked up. There was purpose on his face—maybe even excitement.

"I'll get a room at the La Quinta for now," he said, pausing only briefly on his way to the living room. "You can reach me there if you need anyth—" The words seemed to bring him up short. Habit. No longer necessary.

I sank into the wingback chair and shook my head. Tears blurred my vision. "Nate."

He looked up at me for a moment, then went back to unplugging his record player. The one he'd bought for our anniversary. The one he'd played music on the last time we'd danced. He set it aside with a handful of LPs. "I wanted to wait. Really, Cee. I planned on waiting longer. But . . ."

I could feel myself frowning, trying to make sense of this brutal turnabout. A hand went to the turban that covered my head. "We talked about this. The hair and the"—I swallowed hard—"the surgery. You told me it wouldn't change how you—"

"But everything else has changed!" He looked surprised at the volume of his own voice. I hadn't heard Nate yell at me that way before. Not with such disdain.

"Please don't do this," I whispered, wondering how the day I celebrated victory had turned into the day I lost my future.

Nate went to the desk in the alcove off the living room and started pulling out papers and blueprints—the work he'd started bringing home when I'd been at my worst. He was moving more slowly now, as though he was running out of steam.

He put down the leather messenger bag he'd been filling and sat on the armrest of the couch, taut and gaunt. He was quiet for a moment. Then he murmured, "I need to do this. I need out—away."

"But I'm better. The cancer—"

"It's not just the cancer," he said through gritted teeth, every syllable loaded with frustration. "It's . . . I don't know. It's everything."

"Nate . . ." I shook my head. "I thought—I felt . . ." At a loss for words, I just stared at him, praying he'd understand what my mind couldn't formulate. "We've been better. I know we grew apart a bit, but . . . it's been better. Right? Especially since the diagnosis. We've been good." I said it loudly. To convince Nate. To convince me.

He ran tense fingers through his salt-and-pepper hair. "I've tried to convince myself—us—that we are. But we're not. You have to see that too. We might be better, but 'better' is a long way from 'good.'"

I shook my head. "Relationships change. People evolve. We can get back to good again."

He stood and stared at the floor for a moment. Something that looked like regret crossed his face just long enough for me to wonder if I'd imagined it. "I've pushed through, Ceelie. I've done all I can for as long as I could." He closed his eyes as if the enormity of the milestone was finally hitting him. When he opened them again, they fastened on mine with chilling clarity. "I didn't want to do this now. Not this way. But . . ." He tucked the messenger bag under his arm and walked to the door to pick up the duffel. "I'm done."

Chapter 4

I sat in the house for two days.

When I wasn't in the wingback chair, I was sleeping on the couch. I went to the kitchen on occasion for a yogurt or some fruit, then I went back to the living room on wooden legs and sat some more.

I couldn't talk myself into going upstairs to the bedroom. Not even to change my clothes or shower. I couldn't bring myself to face the pictures on the dresser, the half-empty closet, the unmade bed—vestiges of a marriage that had felt strong enough to endure my surgery and treatment.

So I sat. I steeped in the silence. I let the shock and disbelief and upheaval torment my waking moments until my body escaped into sleep. But they were still there when consciousness returned, a gut-shocking, humiliating, dismantling force I couldn't seem to shake.

At the end of the second day, I stood and found my purse. It was sitting by the front door, where I'd dropped it after our aborted Shake Shack trip. My phone was in the front pocket. It took courage to click the home button—once I connected with the world again, I'd have to speak the words my mind still couldn't entirely fathom. Nate left me. Nate . . . left me. Nate. Left. Me.

There were too many texts to count. Congratulations on the end of my treatment from friends, from random coworkers. There were missed calls and voicemails. Two from my boss, Joe. Six from Darlene.

Those got my attention.

Darlene never left messages—it was a red line for her. "I'll talk to you and I'll talk to your husband, but I will *not* talk to that dang robo-voice on your phone."

I let my head fall forward and focused on breathing through a panic I didn't fully understand. Without listening to the messages, I hit Call Back and waited for my friend to pick up, but it was a male voice that finally said, "Hello?"

"Um . . . I'm sorry. I must have—"

"Were you trying to reach Darlene?"

"I— Yes."

"This is her phone."

"Oh." My mind was still too muddled to engage in small talk. "Can I speak with her? This is Ceelie."

I heard a sigh. "Ceelie. She's been wanting to talk to you. This is Darlene's son."

"Is she okay?"

There was a pause. "I think it would be good for you to come over."

"Right now?"

"When you can."

Something in my body understood before my mind did. A jagged dread lodged in my veins. Clawed at my synapses. I could almost hear it pleading, *"Please, no!"* as if it knew I couldn't take much more.

I glanced at myself in the full-length mirror next to the front door. Disheveled. Gaunt. Hunched over and pale. But *Perky, bald, and cancer-free!* still screamed from my red shirt. I borrowed—what had Darlene called it?—"cold-blooded courage" from the words and, with concern for my friend hastening my steps, headed for the bedroom.

Darlene's house was a small Tudor on a quiet street in Geneva, just fifteen minutes from my home in Saint Charles. Her old, turquoise PT Cruiser sat in the driveway—a custom paint job, she'd proudly informed me—and icicle lights still framed the recessed front door. It opened before I reached it.

"You must be Ceelie," Darlene's son said. Concerned. Relieved. Though he was a few inches taller than his mother, there was no denying their resemblance. Same small frame. Same high cheekbones. Same direct gaze. His hair was dark blond, but just as unruly. He held out a hand. "I'm Justin."

He stepped back to usher me inside. "What happened?" I asked, following him down the hall.

"She's been feeling under the weather for a while—which was news to me, but you know how she is. She took a fall a couple days ago and injured her hip. When they did a CT scan . . ." He paused at the end of the long hall that led to the living room doorway and motioned me inside.

"Don't hog the guest!" Darlene's voice was loud, but more breathy than usual.

I stepped into the room, where an alarming number of garden gnomes perched on bookshelves, end tables, and an upright piano, and tried not to show my dismay when I saw my friend.

"But the hair looks good, right?" Darlene said with a small, weary smile, apparently spotting the shock I'd attempted to hide. She sat on the reclining portion of her couch, her legs covered by a crocheted blanket.

Justin's voice came from behind me. "Things you don't find in

39

the model-son handbook: teasing mom's pink hair while she recovers from a fall."

Darlene laughed. Then she let her head fall back and inhaled a long, deep breath.

I took a step toward her, trying to school the emotions overwhelming my control. "Darlene . . ."

She patted the spot next to her on the couch. "Sit."

I did as instructed and took a good look at her. Her face was pale under her pink and blue makeup. The lines seemed more deeply creased than usual and, though her trademark feistiness was in her eyes when she turned her head to look at me, there was weariness there too.

I remembered the texts and missed calls on my phone and guilt overcame me. "Darlene . . ."

She waved away my unspoken apology. "Hush now."

"I'm so sorry I didn't call you back or . . . or text. If I'd known . . ."

She sat up straighter and carefully adjusted her legs on the footrest in front of her. "Honey, that wasn't me calling. Why would I expect you to get on the phone with me when you're busy celebrating the end of Drip 'n' Drain?" It's what she called chemo—the IV treatment followed by the inevitable intestinal discomfort. Justin ducked out of the room just as she was saying, "I'm guessing my boy might have used my phone to summon the troops, when said troops should have been on a plane to . . . what was it? Sweden?"

"Switzerland." I turned more fully toward her. "Tell me, Darlene. What's going on?"

She pursed her lips and looked back at me. Then she reached out a hand to give mine a squeeze. "Turns out my version of the Drip 'n' Drain didn't take."

I'd known as I drove from my place to hers that this was the news I'd receive. Still, my stomach dropped as I felt my breath catch. "It's back?"

Darlene squeezed my hand again. "In the hip and femur."

"Oh, Darlene . . ."

"No. Not 'Oh, Darlene.'" She pushed herself up straighter and winced a little. "They're going to start me on radiation—that oughta get rid of some of the pain—and a newfangled drug to slow the progress."

I tried for a strong voice. "You'll beat this again. I know you will."

The smile she gave me somehow managed to be whimsical, strong, and grave. "Honey, I've beat this thing twice. It's back to tell me my winning streak is over. But I'm fully planning on going out strong."

I wasn't sure what that would look like. I'd seen others die of the disease—my own mother from ovarian cancer—and couldn't envision a "strong" exit under similar circumstances.

Justin materialized next to me with two cups of coffee. "Yours has the high octane stuff in it," he said, handing one to his mother and the other to me.

"Of all my children, you're my favorite," she declared dramatically, then she winked at me. "A little Baileys is good for ailing bones, right?"

Justin left the room again.

"When did he get here?"

"The day I fell. The hospital called him—against my wishes, I might add—and he hopped in the car and made it here from Madison before they were done with all the poking and prodding."

Though Darlene had talked about her only child before, I'd never met him until now. "Is he taking good care of you?"

She nodded and sipped her coffee, rolling her eyes a little in approval. "Too good. He has firm instructions to move me into a darling little nursing home I've found so he can go back to his life in Wisconsin."

From what she'd mentioned before, I knew that life included a second wife Darlene didn't particularly appreciate—a feeling that was apparently mutual—and a career in the insurance industry.

"Darlene . . . isn't it a bit too soon to be looking for a nursing home?" I couldn't picture this woman with the vitality of a twenty-year-old confined to such a diminishing place.

She set her cup on the console behind the couch and smiled for a moment before speaking. "This isn't a rash decision, honey. I've been looking for a place with a good Zumba class for months. This—what do the French call it?—this *contretemps* didn't exactly come as a surprise." She hunched a shoulder. "The pain's been there for a while. I knew what it was. Doesn't take a genius, right? I just opted to live around it for as long as I could before . . ."

She took a deep breath and smiled. "I've been ready for it. And now it's time for me to take a bow. However—" She smiled in an enigmatic way and wiggled an eyebrow. "There's one more thing I need to do before I fly off to the land of milk and honey. And by milk and honey, I mean Milk Duds and honey-glazed donuts. I've got an order pending with whatever angel's guarding those pearly gates."

Her willingness—her readiness—to die stood in stark contrast to everything I knew about this feisty, fearless fighter. "This doesn't sound like you, Darlene."

"The Milk Duds or . . . ?"

I sighed and shot her my I'm-serious look. She countered it with one of hers. Then I saw her expression soften as she scrutinized my face. "We can talk about me later," she said after a moment. "Tell me."

I felt a flutter of resistance. "Oh, there's nothing much to—"

She interrupted with a laugh. Some of the old Darlene was in it. "Honey, you have a lot of really impressive skills, but putting on an act does not figure among them."

"Darlene . . . ," I tried again. My mind still hadn't fully recovered from its two-day pause.

"Tell me." Her tone was firmer this time.

I wrestled with myself, desperately needing to tell someone about Nate, but determined to protect my friend from worrying about me too. "It's nothing," I murmured. "Nothing for you to be concerned about anyway."

She gave me the look that always preceded a pseudo-magical reading of my mind. "Nate?"

I looked around the room, inventorying the garden gnomes that lurked on every surface. There was one that seemed strategically placed under a lamp. He stood there, smiling as if he was enjoying the spotlight, a giant brick clutched to his chest.

Delaying the inevitable, I said, "What's with the gnomes?"

She laughed. "That's a skillful dodge, my friend." Her eyes on me were loving and compassionate. "I'm going to answer your question, but don't you think we're not circling back to mine." She waved around the room at the collection of brightly painted, pointy-hatted figurines. "Angus and I started collecting them—what—twenty years ago? Maybe more. We saw them in gardens over in Germany when we took a Rhine cruise and liked them so much we brought a bunch back with us. And of course, because I'm such a restrained person, we just kept on collecting these little guys and little ladies who tickle my funny bone."

"Clearly."

"They were all over the yard for years, to my neighbors' displeasure," she went on. "Right around the time Angus—bless his heart—passed on, I decided that a little bit of cheer might do me some good, so I brought them all inside. The neighbors considered throwing a parade. It was just for a little while . . . That's what I told myself. But the longer they lived in here with me, the more accustomed I got to their company, and the thought of banishing them back out to the yard again was just unbearable."

From the kitchen, Justin said, "Only to her. I've been plotting their banishment for years."

She caught me looking at the brick-holding gnome. "My plastic surgeon's assistant got him for me when she found out I had this collection. Construction Gnome is what they officially call him, but we named him Masto-Gnome on account of how my post-surgery chest felt."

I shook my head. Oh, to be able to find the giggle in the grim, as Darlene always did.

"He's also a reminder to build something on the rubble of all of this." She glanced down at her chest and winked. "The surgeons did it, right? Built these jaunty B cups on what was left of saggy me. I vowed to do the same with my future—right there in my pre-op room." Darlene reached for my hand again. "And you, my dear, are a bright and shining star in my reconstructed life."

I blinked back tears. Tears of gratitude. Tears of confusion and devastation.

"Now." Darlene gave my hand a firm squeeze and held the pressure, drawing my eyes to hers with the intensity of her stare. "Tell me what's going on."

I didn't know how to put words—out-loud words—to the unthinkable. Not when the first person I was going to share them with had just declared that her life was drawing to a close. But with her hand still pressing mine, I articulated the reality that had paralyzed me for days. Looking down—away, anywhere—I said, "Nate left me."

A sob bubbled from my lungs to my throat and I swallowed hard to hold it down.

Darlene released my hand and said nothing. She said nothing for so long that I glanced up, wondering if she'd heard me. Her eyes were closed. Her lips were pinched. Her hands were clasped so tightly in her lap that her knuckles were white.

I let the silence stretch a little longer, listening to the slow, deep breaths entering and exiting my friend's lungs, and was about to say her name when her eyes opened again.

"It is a very difficult thing for a spontaneous person to keep from blurting out obscenities when something this unjust happens to a friend." I thought I heard a tremor in her voice. Her eyes were shiny with emotion. "So forgive me for choosing my words very carefully, my dear. I know you love that husband of yours and wouldn't want me to speak ill of him, but he's an—"

The word she used to describe Nate had the dual effect of making me feel loved and making me smile in spite of the agony of his abandonment. Yes, I loved my husband—but the person who had left me so suddenly seemed to have earned Darlene's epithet.

"He just . . . walked out," I said.

"When?"

"Monday. After I rang the bell at the Cancer Center." I told her about the Shake Shack, Nate's almost casual statement that he was done, the way he'd packed up a few basics like he'd thought it all through in advance.

"No explanation?" I could see the skin of her throat turning redder, as if her disbelief was a physical ache.

I shook my head. "He needs out," I said. I heard the acid in my voice. "And he said he's been wanting to leave for a while. He just . . ."

"Wanted to bless you with his two-faced presence while you were going through cancer-hell?" Darlene suggested.

"I guess."

"Coward."

"I think he views his staying in a different light—a heroic gesture for his ailing wife. And leaving . . . Maybe he sees cutting himself loose as his just reward."

"Ceelie." There was such kindness and sadness in the word that it brought tears to my eyes. I blinked them away. Crying felt too much like surrender. "I'm so sorry, sweetie." She paused. "What do you need?"

Her question prompted me to consider the future again. It felt bleak.

"I don't know," I said honestly. "It's hard to think any further ahead than right now."

"Not surprising, given what your 'right now' looks like. Did he say he wanted a divorce?"

"Not in so many words. But he made it pretty clear that's where we're headed." Panic gripped my lungs. "I just . . . I keep trying to figure out what I need to do next. About the house. About our finances. Telling our friends. Everything. I felt like I was finally getting my life back and now . . ."

"The ignominy of it all."

I nearly smiled at the word. Nearly. But there were too many dark and weighty unknowns spinning in my mind. "I was supposed to go back to work after our celebration trip." The memory of my dream vacation wounded me. "Joe told me I didn't have to right away, but I planned on it as soon as I felt physically able."

"Work" was a bit of a misnomer. The *Saint Charles Sentinel* had always been much more than that for me. I'd walked in off the street looking for a summer job between college graduation and what I thought was going to be a stellar career in Pulitzer-level writing. After three weeks temping in the classifieds department and just as many conflicts with the managing editor—two of which I'd won—he'd called me into his office for what I'd assumed would be a peremptory firing. Instead he'd said, "Listen, the pay isn't great and we might not be around a year from now, but you've got something, kid. Not sure what it is, but I'm pretty sure we need it."

He was probably still scratching his head all these years later. With a degree in literature and criminology—which I'd naively thought would fuel that Pulitzer—I'd gone from the classifieds to marketing to associate editor and on to the position I now held, which nobody—Joe included—could accurately define. The plaque on my door said Editor in Chief, and though I spent my days overseeing the smooth operation of the paper, brainstorming articles with our stalwart journalists, holding interns' feet to the fire, and shielding Joe from the minor and major frustrations of running a publication, my role still felt nebulous to me.

"Ceelie?" Darlene brought me back to the present. "You were saying . . . about your job."

"Right." I felt hesitation tugging at my consciousness. As much as I craved going back to my career, envisioning the workload felt draining. "Joe told me I'm welcome to return anytime, and I know I need to get back in the saddle, workwise. I was planning on it—excited about it even. But with Nate leaving . . ." They were bruising words. "I just can't think straight right now. If I have to pack up the house and move out . . ."

It was just one of the scenarios I'd tried not to contemplate as I'd sat virtually motionless for two days.

Darlene was plotting something. I'd seen the look before. Squinty eyes and a far-off stare. The occasional bob of her pink-tipped head.

"Okay," she finally said. "Here's what you're going to do."

Under normal circumstances, I wouldn't have let anyone dictate my next step. But on this day, having a drill sergeant bark orders felt like a healing thing.

"First, you go back to work when you're ready, but you tell Joe that it's going to have to be part time for a while until things settle. I met the man on one of my visits after your surgery, and I can tell he cares about you. That he can't say 'breast' or 'cancer' without twitching isn't something we'll hold against him, right?" She winked. "Honestly, sometimes getting back in the saddle lifts us just enough to get a better perspective on things."

"You're right," I said, realizing at that moment how much I

missed the feeling of satisfaction at the end of a long day. I craved the rhythm of working again. And a part-time arrangement felt less daunting than launching back into the usual twelve-hour shifts.

"I need routines," I said, desperately trying to bolster my resolve. "I need to feel productive. I need—" I caught myself. Those were the needs I'd inventoried when life had been regimented by medical appointments, but what I really wanted—needed—in that moment, was a husband who hadn't been run off by my cancer. And apparently, by me.

Darlene sat in silence. I could see the emotions playing over her face. Sympathy. Frustration. Anger.

"Maybe there really was something wrong with our marriage." I hated saying the words. "Even before cancer."

"Ceelie—"

"I was so caught up in other things. Nate mentioned it sometimes. Even when I was home. The calls from Joe, the deadlines. Maybe I just didn't see it."

"Hogwash."

"And then the cancer. I thought he was doing okay with all of it—with the craziness of the last few months—but . . ."

"Don't you go down that rabbit hole, Ceelie. Do marriages struggle? Yes, absolutely," she said. "Of course they do. And when you add disease to the mix, it gets even trickier, for sure. But that dope—that saint-in-his-own-mind-only—has dishonored himself by throwing in the towel."

I felt grief wash over me again with crippling intensity.

"Do you have a lawyer?" Darlene asked.

I hadn't even contemplated the fact that Nate and I shared the same one. "I guess I need to get one."

"Mine'll take good care of you." She called toward the kitchen. "Find Sue Jones's number in the address book under the phone, will you?"

A shuffle in the kitchen indicated that the message had been received.

"Sue's a good woman. She'll make sure you don't get steam-rolled any more than you've already been."

"Thank you, Darlene." I fought to keep my voice from breaking as I considered a future that loomed unpredictable and challenging. I couldn't wrap my mind around the new reality imposed on me—inflicted on me by my husband's decision to leave.

"And remember," Darlene said, interrupting my thoughts, "when you feel like you're ready for an extracurricular assignment, I might—just might—have a proposal for you." She smiled in her inscrutable way. There was something wistful and excited in it. "It's just a little something I want to sort out before, you know, hopping the twig."

I'd gotten so caught up in my own predicament that, for just a moment, I'd forgotten that my friend—my stalwart champion—was facing a battle for her life. That she could so casually discuss death felt like a physical blow. "Darlene, 'hopping the twig'?" I heard the dismay in my own voice.

She laughed and gingerly moved her legs off the footrest, motioning for me to get her walker from across the room. "Beloved son," she called dramatically toward the kitchen. "It's time for you to accompany your momma on another tinkle trip."

There was a smile in his voice when he replied, "Yet another item you don't find in the model-son handbook."

Justin helped his mom to her feet and stayed at her side as she pushed her walker toward the bathroom at the end of the entryway hall.

"I'll come by again tomorrow." I had to say it twice, as my first attempt had been muted by unshed tears.

"I look forward to it," Darlene replied, wiggling her fingers at me over her shoulder. "This dying thing ain't for the faint of heart, but it sure will be more fun with the right kind of company."

I let her words settle for a moment and considered the kinds of death present in that space. Her life. My marriage. Hope itself, it seemed to me.

I swallowed past the lump in my throat and tried to summon up the courage just walking to my car required. The rest of it—calling Joe, hiring a lawyer, determining the posture I'd take on the road to divorce—I'd deal with those later.

Chapter 5

Cal regained consciousness hanging from a tree thirty feet above the ground.

He swam back to reality through a swirl of disjointed memories. The roar of planes flying wing to wing across the Channel. The flashes of orange light, bright and terrifying, through the open jump door. The wail of wounded C-47s plunging toward the Channel.

He had no way of knowing how long he'd hung there, but he suspected from the pain in his neck when he raised his head that he'd been immobile for a while.

As awareness returned, his feet came into focus first. Then branches. Then the ground below him.

He moved his arms and legs just enough to scan for pain. There was nothing he could identify as a wound or broken bone, only the aches and abrasions of having been snagged on the doorframe of a plane, then crash-landing in what appeared to be a large oak tree.

Artillery fire cracked through the fog. Not near, but close enough. Adrenaline surged back. Cal felt it flood his bloodstream and stiffen his muscles. He looked up, squinting into the early-morning darkness,

and saw that his canopy was caught on the upper
branches of the tree, glaring evidence to the enemy
that a paratrooper had landed there. He needed to get
down-fast.

Cal briefly considered his options. The parachute's
lines were too tangled to allow him to swing toward
the center of the oak, and he didn't think he had the
strength to hoist himself up to the thicker branches
above him. Coming to a quick decision as staccato
bursts of gunfire rang out in the distance, he
released the gear he could reach and watched it drop.
Then he pulled the M2 switchblade from the double-
zippered pocket at the neck of his jump jacket, took a
deep breath, and cut himself free.

Cal realized that he'd misjudged the distance to
the ground as he was falling. The base of his helmet
bounced off a large branch as he plummeted, and his
brain erupted in a bright flash of light. He landed
hard on the gear he'd dropped moments before and
stifled a yelp as his leg bent and buckled under
his weight. A half-dozen injuries in his high school
football days had taught him to distinguish between
broken bone and torn tendon. He suspected this was
the latter.

Cal tried to sit up, but the spinning in his head
made him collapse again into the damp grass. He took a
breath and squinted hard against overwhelming nausea,
reaching for his Garand semiautomatic and bringing it
to his chest. From his prone position, he could see the
broad building he'd skimmed before getting hung up. It
looked like a small castle and stood just fifty feet
from him, its windows dark. He knew this was occupied

France, and there was no telling whether its occupants, if any, were friend or foe.

Cal also knew he needed to get to cover before assessing his next move. He scanned the space around him and felt the world tilt again as he turned his head. Swallowing the bile that rose in his throat, he set his gaze on a grove of small trees another fifty feet away and, with what felt like his last ounce of strength, began to crawl toward it, dragging his gear behind him, trying to ignore the pain and dizziness that hampered his progress.

He was nearly there when the spinning in his head overwhelmed his efforts. Letting out a soft groan, he pushed himself onto his back to rest for a moment, a finger on the trigger of the Garand at his side.

Looking back, he wouldn't be sure how long he lay immobile, praying for the waves of vertigo to pass. It was the sound of approaching footsteps that finally snapped him from the veil of blackness descending over his mind. Fueled by adrenaline, Cal forced himself onto his side, arching his back and craning his neck as he aimed his Garand above his head toward the sound coming from somewhere near the oak tree.

"*Non! Non! Non!*" Hushed words. Outstretched hands.

Cal squinted up toward the voice. It took him a moment to take in what he was seeing. He'd expected German Wehrmacht. Instead, this was a girl, her expression tense and her words urgent.

"I am a friend," she whispered in accented English, motioning with one hand for him to lower his weapon. She took a step toward him. "I am a friend."

Cal lowered the Garand just a fraction in surprise, then raised it again, his mind too tense to trust what she was saying. She looked like a teenager. Maybe thirteen or fourteen. The movements of her small, thin frame were quick and lively. But there was something world-weary in her hazel eyes, something courageous in the set of her jaw as she stared him down.

"*Américain?*" the girl asked, still standing where she'd stopped.

Cal nodded but kept his rifle leveled.

There was nothing overtly threatening about the young woman in the blue button-down shirt and long, beige skirt. Her gaze was direct and unflinching as she said, "I am Sabine." She motioned toward him, indicating that she wanted to come closer. The pain in Cal's neck and ankle came back into focus as he moved his finger off the trigger and dropped his hand onto the grass. He realized he had no choice but to trust what he saw in the girl.

Sabine hurried to his side when he groaned. She knelt next to him, scanning his body for evidence of an injury.

"You are shot?"

"I don't think-" His voice was so hoarse that the words were barely audible. He cleared his throat and tried again. "I don't think so."

Sabine nodded. "You must come inside." Her voice was soft and lilting despite the seriousness of the circumstances. "The Germans-*les boches* . . ." She made a face and glanced toward the gate in the stone wall behind her. Cal looked too, realizing that neither the wall nor the fields beyond it had been visible when he landed. The fog was lifting.

"They are not far," Sabine continued. "You must get up-quickly."

Cal looked up. "My chute-"

"I will get it." From the confidence in her voice, Cal knew she somehow would. She stood and held out a hand to help him up. "First, sit."

"I have to get out there," Cal said, pushing himself upright, the gunfire in the distance a call to arms. The world spun and he shook his head to try to clear it. "Gotta get out there," he murmured again, closing his eyes against a crippling dizziness. The pain at the base of his skull became a stabbing throb. There was a rushing sound in his ears, and darkness tinged the edges of his consciousness again. He felt Sabine's hands lowering him back to the ground and berated himself for his weakness.

She leaned in to look at him more closely. "Your head," she said. "Did you hit it?"

Cal remembered the sharp whack as his helmet had made contact with a branch during his fall from the tree. "I think so. After I cut myself loose." He suspected he'd hit it earlier too, when he'd first gotten hung up in its branches.

Sabine glanced up at his parachute. "You were high. Too high."

"Yeah, I figured that out on my way down." He attempted a smile, but even that seemed to increase the pain that extended from the nape of his neck to the space behind his eyes.

The girl released the chinstrap on his helmet and

gingerly lifted it from his head. She ran her fingers over his scalp, then checked them for blood. There was none.

"Nothing serious, right?" Cal said.

She gave him a look before saying, "You stay here." Then she scurried off.

Cal felt the darkness in his mind overtaking conscious thought.

"*Non-non-non!*" She was back, but he had no idea how long she'd been gone. "You stay awake." She shook his shoulder. "Mister GI! You stay awake."

"Cal." The effort of speaking made him stifle another groan. "My name—"

"Cal," Sabine repeated after him, the name somehow shortened by the crispness of her French pronunciation. "Let us help you now."

From his position, all he could see were two sets of feet next to Sabine's, one in muddy wooden clogs and the other in small, well-worn, ankle-high boots. It hurt to turn his head, but Cal forced his gaze up nonetheless. An elderly man wearing a dirty beret, his face gaunt under a few days' beard growth, scanned the woods and fields around them, his posture tense, his vigilant eyes a startling shade of pale blue.

Beside him, a younger girl—maybe seven or eight—stared at Cal through heavy, chestnut-brown bangs with something that looked like awe. Somehow she perfectly matched the stained boys' overalls and scuffed boots she was wearing.

Sabine took a hunting knife from her pocket and handed it to the younger girl, saying something to her in clipped, urgent French. Cal watched as she galloped toward the tree, took hold of one of its thick, lower branches, and heaved herself onto it.

"We must move fast," Sabine said. "Lise—my sister—she will cut down the parachute."

The old man leaned over to open a makeshift stretcher on the grass. He moved around Cal's head and slid his hands under his shoulders while Sabine grasped his legs at the knees. "*Un, deux . . .*" he counted, his voice gravelly. On three, they lifted Cal onto the stretcher, which was little more than a piece of oiled canvas stretched between two hand-hewn poles. He was surprised at how easily Sabine managed his weight. He was six foot one and a solid 180. Still, she and the stooped man in clogs lifted him as if he weighed no more than a child.

Cal caught a glimpse of the young girl as they rounded the corner of the small castle, its circular tower reaching into a brightening sky. She'd already unhooked the top of his canopy from the high branch it had gotten snagged on and was using Sabine's knife to cut through the lines trapping it in the tree.

"She is our little monkey," Sabine said. "She will get your parachute."

Chapter 6

I was taking a midday nap upstairs, about two weeks after Nate walked out, when I heard the front door open. Grabbing my phone and tapping nine-one-one on the keypad, just in case, I tiptoed out of the bedroom. Nate was halfway up the stairs when I rounded the corner. His face fell.

After a few moments of overfull silence, I said, "What are you doing here?"

"I didn't think you'd be home."

I wasn't sure what to say to that. Explain that I'd fought cancer for several months and was still recovering my strength? It seemed self-evident.

"Why are you here?" I asked again. There was an edge to my voice.

"Just need to get a few more of my things."

I fought the urge to ask questions. To plead. To demand answers. I fought the urge to slap him too.

Instead, I stood aside and let him pass, then I retreated downstairs on unsteady legs and went through the motions of making a cup of coffee.

"I'm heading south," Nate said from the kitchen doorway on his way out. The suitcase we kept on the top shelf of our walk-in closet was in his hand. It looked heavy. "That project my crew's working on . . . the cabins."

I closed my eyes and breathed for a moment. The project Nate was referring to was a dream job he'd bid on and won just before my diagnosis—a community of vacation cabins on the edge of Rend Lake, just north of Marion. It would allow his company to earn steady income during the brutal winters of northern Illinois. Because of my cancer, he'd opted not to oversee the build—the largest his company had ever undertaken—and had sent his foreman to head up the project instead. I'd tried to convince him to go, at least for a few days at a time, since it was only six hours away. Darlene would accompany me to my treatments and he'd be able to go back to doing what he loved. But he'd insisted that I came first.

That he was heading south after all felt like confirmation that our marriage was truly beyond repair. The emotions welling up in me surprised me, and I wondered if I'd been, on some indiscernible level, still hoping that Nate's decision could somehow be reversed.

I tried to keep my tone neutral when I finally found my voice. "Okay." I couldn't look at him. I focused on the coffee I held instead and tried, by sheer willpower, to stop my hands from shaking.

"They've run into a snag with the developer, and I'm . . ." Nate trailed off mid-sentence. I felt his posture change. "I've spoken with Bruce."

My heart sank. Bruce Watkins was our lawyer. Correction— Bruce Watkins was Nate's lawyer now.

"He'll keep things moving while I'm gone."

Silence. It was all I had to give him.

"It'll be two months, maybe a bit longer, before I'm back. The library renovation starts in April, so . . ."

"Are you done?" I glanced up at him. The determination on his face was a wounding thing.

"I just wanted you to know that I'm leaving town and that Bruce will be getting in touch with you. There'll be stuff to sign."

Stuff felt like an insulting word. Something rebellious fluttered in my chest. "I'll sign the divorce papers when I'm ready."

"Cee." He frowned, looking at me as if he didn't understand my reticence to make our split official. "This doesn't need to be complicated."

Humiliation and rage tightened my throat and sent shivers down my spine. "Really?" Sarcasm—the broken, helpless kind—oozed from the words.

There was something brittle in the tension between us. A muscle worked in Nate's jaw. Nothing in his expression even hinted at remorse.

"I'll give you a heads-up if I have to come over again before I take off," he said.

I shook my head. "You need to leave your key and go."

He seemed surprised. "Leave my . . . ?"

"Your key. Please leave your key and go."

"Cee, this is still my house too."

I tilted up my chin and looked at him full-on for the first time since he'd arrived. "You forfeited the right to waltz in here and make demands the day you waltzed out."

He hung his head for a moment. "I could have done things differently."

I let the words and their futility hang there. When he said nothing more, I finally whispered, "Please leave."

He turned and went out the door.

The adrenaline that had kept me together while we were talking dissipated so fast that I sank to the floor, my hands over my face, my body shaking in its core, and let out a howl of pain and disbelief. The tears I'd mostly quelled in the days since Nate's departure finally poured out through the fissures in my strength, wrung from the fabric of the dreams I'd had for us. My sobs were nearly voiceless—lung-strangling, muscle-clenching, and gut-wrenching. Devastating.

A creaking floorboard brought me up short. Nate stood in front of me again, but I couldn't look up.

"I forgot my stuff," he said, reaching for the handle of the suitcase he'd packed.

"Go away, Nate."

Without another word, he left.

He took his key.

I called Joe the day after my encounter with Nate and told him that I was ready to step back in, but that I'd have to work reduced hours for a while.

"Listen, if all you do is keep the interns from asking stupid questions, I'll pay you overtime for part-time work," he'd grumbled.

It felt good to have a reason to get up five days a week. I usually headed home around two, but if Joe caught me looking weary, he ordered me to "get the heck outta here" earlier.

I hadn't heard from Nate since he'd left for Rend Lake, except for the occasional impersonal text about documents and deadlines. Every one of them was a gut punch. Every one of them went unanswered. The lawyer Darlene had found for me kept repeating that there was no hurry signing anything, but I could tell from her tone that she didn't understand. My husband had left. He'd filed the paperwork. What could I possibly gain from delaying the inevitable?

I wasn't sure either.

Most of the time I managed to convince myself that I was okay, but there were milestones that reminded me of how very much I'd lost. Moving into my new apartment was one of the hardest.

I'd made the decision almost on a whim after Nate had come by that day. Living in the house, I could almost feel the fragments of my illusions crunching under my feet as I moved numbly from room to room. Our house on Harbor Lane was the symbol of an existence I'd thought I knew. A figment I couldn't stomach anymore.

Though I was told I'd have up to six months to pack up and find another place, I woke up one Monday morning certain that living there was sucking the life out of me. The cost of paying rent elsewhere seemed a small price to pay for escaping the memories saturating our home. I called a Realtor that afternoon, found the new place on Thursday, and partially moved into it a week later. It was a comfortable, small, recently renovated, but affordable loft in downtown Saint Charles. The sandwich-and-tea café downstairs was a popular hangout, but it closed early on weekdays, so my evenings at home were quiet.

Most of my things—most of *our* things—were still in the old house, but I figured I'd deal with packing up our lives when they were officially severed. Whenever that would be. Until then, I'd have the loft. And Nate had no keys that would allow him entry.

Chapter 7

Darlene arrived right on time on a cold, early-March afternoon—she always did. She was mobile again, thanks to physical therapy, capable of walking unassisted and climbing stairs as long as she took them slowly. "You okay?" she asked as I adjusted the cushions on the couch and settled into them. I was eight days out from my final reconstruction surgery, and sitting upright for too long still made me a bit uncomfortable.

"Just shifting some weight off the incisions," I told her. These permanent implants were a huge step up from the expanders I'd called boulder-boobs, but they were taking some getting used to.

It felt like the last few months had been a crash course in "getting-used-tos." I'd done my best to mitigate what discomforts I could—like sleeping on my back, for the first time in my life. Wearing loose, layered clothing to hide the stages of reconstruction. Spending far too much money on a couple of lifelike wigs before I even started chemo, but turning to more breathable turbans when hormone-induced hot flashes made the wigs feel too hot.

Only recently had I tried wearing my golden-brown layered-bob wig again. Darlene had given me a few pointers to make it feel less stifling and taught me to apply the false eyelashes I'd been given at a "Look Good, Feel Better" event at the Cancer Center. It had all seemed like too much work during the worst days of my treatment, but with my energy returning, looking like my old self again had become more of a priority. It felt good to go out in public without feeling the stares—some compassionate, some curious, some oddly hostile—of the people I crossed paths with.

I tugged a bit on the edge of my wig and looked at Darlene, alarmed by the weight she'd lost since starting radiation. Treating the tumors on her hip and femur had helped with her pain, but aiming the beams through part of her abdomen to get to the right spots had caused such bad nausea that she'd contemplated quitting.

"How's the zapping going, Darlene?"

"Like giving a ninety-nine-year-old a facelift," she said, not for the first time, as her memory seemed to be failing along with her body. "Doesn't do a whole lot of good in the long run, but it sure feels like a teensy bit of control over the tyranny of time."

"You look good." She didn't. She looked sick. And the hair she'd now tipped in bright purple did nothing to counteract the yellow pallor of her skin.

"Sweetie, I love a good compliment, but only when it's honest."

I tried for a smile. "You look . . . alive?"

She laughed—a tinkling sound that felt death-defying. "Yes!" she said, a finger spearing the air. "Yes! That's the kind of compliment I can get behind."

Something warm and bruising overwhelmed me.

Darlene's eyes locked with mine. Her laughter fizzled away. Though our lives had been intertwined since our chance meeting in the mammography waiting room, we'd expressed our love for each other more in deed—in time spent and conversations had—than in outright statements. But as we sat in my loft that afternoon, the looming end of her life struck me with such potency that I couldn't *not* say the words that defined our friendship.

"I love you, Darlene."

"I know you do, sweetie," she said. There were tears in her eyes and mine. She smiled through them and raised an eyebrow. "I feel like I should get over there and give you a hug, but those chicken cutlets are so fresh, I'm afraid I'd hurt you."

"There'll be plenty of time for that," I said, wanting to sound hopeful.

"Actually . . ." Darlene's voice trailed off. Her gaze didn't. It was steady. Sure.

I felt the breath freeze in my lungs. "What are you saying?"

"I'm going to be getting a bit of an upgrade at Sunny Cove." She pinched her lips briefly. "Turns out it's time for me to call in hospice care."

"Darlene . . ."

"It's gone to my lungs. A couple small spots right now and not too debilitating, but . . . Don't know why I thought it wouldn't happen to me."

I had trouble believing that the woman sitting in front of me, the woman who still zipped around town in her PT Cruiser against medical advice, using her left foot to work the pedals, was suddenly needing end-of-life care.

"I know, right?" Darlene said, reading my thoughts. "Here I was thinking that I was beating the odds, that the Big C had given up when my bones got zapped, and now they tell me it's metastasized again. And likely in the lining of my spine too. They wanted to do an MRI to be sure, but why bother? That's what I told them. You don't find out hell is real and go to extremes to figure out if the devil is too. Hell's enough. That's what I told them. Hell's enough."

The silence that stretched between us was full. Full with realization. Full with the preciousness of life. Full with Darlene's acceptance and my rebellion.

"Will you need to move out of your studio at Sunny Cove?"

"Not yet. Hopefully not for a while. Hospice sounds ominous, but it's just the next step in getting more appropriate care. We're filling out the paperwork now and they'll start the extra pampering in a week or so."

She smiled. I tried to smile back but found myself incapable of it.

"You'll be needing to come to me, once you're up to it," Darlene finally said. "No more driving for this girl—doctor's orders. I might actually have to obey them this time."

"Darlene . . ."

"But my car—Melba." She put on the dramatic, effervescent tone I loved so much. "That turquoise testament to flaunting vehicular norms and living life unleashed—I want her to be yours."

I didn't know what to say. I opened my mouth to protest. Then I closed it. The Corolla I drove was a hand-me-down from Nate. For a moment, I contemplated how much it felt like living life *leashed*.

"You know you want it," Darlene said in an enticing voice, leaning forward with a sparkle in her eye.

It felt inappropriate to be so casually talking about taking her car. She must have seen the conflict on my face.

"I saved my pennies for months to get Melba her custom paint. And I've probably invested ten times that much just keeping her ticking all these years since then, even when my longsuffering mechanic told me to just walk away. That's how important she is to me. And I want you to have her and drive her."

I hesitated only briefly. "Okay." Saying the word out loud felt like admitting my friend's death sentence was real and imminent.

"Okay," she repeated, a broad smile deepening the lines in her face. "And you and Melba will come visit me, right? It'll do me good to know she's in the parking lot."

"I'm so sorry, Darlene." Tears stung my eyes again. This was a conversation I'd known was coming, but hadn't contemplated having so soon.

"Ech," she said, waving her hand. "They tell me I may still have months, but . . . I think it's time to stop defying the beast and start respecting it."

I caught a fleeting glint of sadness in her eyes, quickly replaced by something that looked like hard-won serenity.

"I know it's a stupid question, but is there anything I can do?" I asked. "Other than take your car out for joyrides?"

"Actually . . ." Darlene seemed to hesitate.

I caught the seriousness in her voice and felt myself straighten. There was so little I could offer to ease her circumstances. Whatever she needed, I wanted to do. "Tell me," I said, turning her favorite phrase on her.

"It's just that it's so much more than joyrides and visits."

"Darlene."

She held my gaze for a moment before reaching into the giant tote she called a purse and pulling out a brown envelope. Then she looked at me with something like determination on her face. "Remember the day you told me about Nate?"

"Gnome Day?"

She smiled. "Yes, Gnome Day. I think I mentioned that there was one thing I needed to figure out before my not-so-early demise."

I tried to think back to that day in her living room, but it was all a blur. "I don't think I remember . . ."

"Of course you don't, sweetie. You had a couple things on your mind."

"What do you need?"

"You said you've always wanted to be an investigative journalist, right?" Darlene opened the envelope and slid its contents out onto my coffee table. There was a yellowed picture and a handful of envelopes tied together with a ribbon.

Somewhere in the far recesses of my spirit, I sensed that they would alter the course of my life.

Chapter 8

Sabine and the old man carried Cal up the steps and through the broad front doors. A couple dozen people, ranging in age from infant to elderly, their faces gaunt, their eyes haunted, crowded the castle's tall entryway. Most of them sat on the floor with their backs against the wall or on the wooden steps of a staircase extending off to the right. Some seemed alert and watchful, while others held rags to bleeding wounds or lay on the mosaic tile, pale and listless. A couple of the younger men stepped forward in a protective way and stared as Sabine and her companion carried Cal through the foyer.

As they approached the tall, ornate doors leading to another room, a woman pushing a small child behind her skirts moved into their path. She unleashed a torrent of machine-gun-fast words on Sabine, clearly distraught and furious. Her eyes were wide and panicked as she gestured toward the front door, motioning for them to take Cal back outside.

Sabine's grip tightened on Cal's stretcher and her eyes flashed with anger. She retorted with equal vehemence, undeterred by the fact that she was probably ten years younger than the woman confronting her. When her challenger snapped back, Sabine took a quick step toward her, jarring Cal's stretcher and exacerbating the ache in his skull. *"Non!"* she said so forcefully, eyes ablaze and jaw set, that the other woman visibly flinched.

Sabine stood there a moment longer, scanning the room, returning the glares of some of the foyer's occupants until the last of the resisters averted their eyes. Only then did she nod in the old man's direction and push through the doors of the adjoining space.

"She is afraid that you bring danger here," she whispered to Cal as they carried the stretcher into what appeared to be a living room where a dozen more haggard and wary people were gathered. Some of them shifted out of the way as Sabine and the old man moved to an alcove surrounded by windows covered in tar paper. A couple lengths had come loose and flapped lightly in the breeze blowing through a broken pane of glass.

Cal scanned the room and its occupants, looking for anything or anyone suspicious. The space itself felt as weary as the ragtag group it harbored. It had probably once been grand and stately, but its wallpaper was peeling in the corners now, its parquet floors were dusty and buckled in some places, and its furniture looked faded.

A young mother nursed her baby while a toddler slept in her lap. An elderly couple huddled close, hands clasped, foreheads furrowed. Two teenage boys watched Cal with suspicion and seemed coiled to leap at the first sign of trouble. A handful of adult men stood guard at every window, peering around blackout curtains and tar paper, holding primitive weapons—pitchforks, shovels, and lengths of metal.

"They are from the village down the road," Sabine said after lowering the stretcher to the parquet floor. She blew a stray tendril out of her eyes, then paused to secure it with one of the combs holding her straight, brown hair back from her face. "When the planes started flying over, these people came here. We are far enough from the village and our walls are thick and strong. They had nowhere else to go."

Cal tried to focus. "The fighting—where is it?"

Sabine jutted her chin toward the courtyard out front. "Six kilometers that way," she said. "On the other side of Aubry-en-Douve." She caught herself. "If there is still a village there." Sadness darkened her wide, hazel eyes, but only for a moment. Squaring her shoulders, she shooed a young couple off the banquette in the alcove and got down on her haunches next to Cal.

"First, we must take off your uniform," she said, all business. "If they come back—the Germans. You must look like one of us or we are all in danger."

Cal's head was still throbbing, but that got his attention. "Wait. 'Come back'?"

Sabine nodded. "They have been staying in our home. Upstairs. They left a few hours ago, when the *débarquement* began, but they could come back again."

She caught Cal's change of expression and raised her chin in a gesture of defiance. "We did not invite them here. We did not welcome them. We are not *collaborateurs*," she said with vigor.

"I didn't–"

"They forced us to let them live here because we have a large house for the Kommandant and stables for their horses. And because it was just me, my sister, and Albert here."

Sabine began to unbuckle his harness, but Cal pushed her hands away. "I can do that."

She gave him a look and sat back while Cal raised his head and fumbled with the buckles of the jump gear still strapped to his body. Nausea overcame him before he'd made much progress, and he lowered his head back onto the stretcher's canvas, letting out a long, steadying breath.

Sabine raised an eyebrow when Cal made eye contact with her. "I can help you," she said with something that sounded like disapproval. "Or you can be stupid and make yourself sicker."

Cal stared at the ceiling and tried to tamp down a burst of frustration. He'd expected enemy fire. He'd expected the brutality of battle. He'd trained for months in anticipation of this day, and his inability to do the simplest thing, let alone stand and raise a weapon, was bruising.

Reading his silence as assent, Sabine released the remaining buckles and clips. She started to unzip Cal's field jacket, and he reached out, startling her. Exasperation flashed in her eyes. "I am fourteen. I am not a child," she said with a hint of petulance. "I have seen men's underthings."

Cal shook his head and regretted it instantly, as

it reignited his pain. "No, it's not that. I'm just trying
to say thank you."

He saw something soft come over the teenager's face.
Then something proud. "We help our liberators," she
said, glancing up at the people around them. "Not the
occupiers. It's what good French people do."

"Where are the Germans now?" Cal asked.

"Still in the fields behind the village, probably.
They were there all night, shooting at the planes and
defending the . . ." She frowned, searching for words.
"The place where the big guns are. The Américains-your
people-they want to take it from the Germans."

"A battery?"

She leaned forward to start unbuttoning his shirt.
"Yes, the battery. That's where the most fighting is
happening near here. But we have heard there is much
more in other parts of the Cotentin."

Cal knew that was true. The plan had been for
the invasion to be so multifaceted and vast that the
Germans wouldn't know where to focus their defenses.

"How do you speak English so well?" he asked
Sabine, his voice hoarsened by pain.

"My mother was from England. She died three years
ago. I haven't spoken the language very much since
then, but . . . I remember enough." She turned toward
the old man and said, "Albert," motioning for him to
come nearer. He gathered the gear scattered around the
paratrooper and headed out of the room with it.

"The Americans. Have you seen them?" Cal asked.

She shook her head. "Not me. But when the fight for
the battery started and people ran away-ran to here-
they saw American fighters."

"I've got to get back out there," Cal said, attempting and failing once again to sit up.

Sabine shook her head. "If you cannot sit, you cannot fight. Not yet. First, you must put on different clothes so you don't look so American if the Germans see you. That is what you need to do now, because you are a danger to all of us."

The door to the living room burst open, and an exuberant Lise strutted in, her arms full with the remnants of Cal's canopy. "*C'est fait!*" she declared, striking a victorious pose. Her thick bangs were damp with sweat and stuck to her forehead as her eyes darted off Cal and settled on her sister, clearly expecting validation for her efforts.

"*Bravo, Lisou,*" Sabine said softly.

The girl's exuberant smile, missing a front tooth, seemed a sharp contrast to the direness of the circumstances. Albert reentered the room and handed a bundle of clothes to Sabine without a word. Then he took the green nylon from Lise's arms and strode out again.

"He will bury it outside," Sabine explained to Cal. "With your uniform and your things."

"No," Cal said. "You can bury the parachute and harness, but I'm going to need my gear."

"We will see."

He reached out and grabbed her hand. "I'm going to need my uniform, my rifle, my ammunition, and my gear," he said more forcefully.

Sabine hesitated, then nodded imperceptibly. Her gaze glanced off her sister, who still stood in the entrance to the living room, and settled on the villagers who had been watching their interaction in silence. "But I will not endanger my people to preserve your things," she said in a low voice. "We will hide them in a safe place until you're strong enough to leave."

Sabine helped him out of his shirt and into a wrinkled beige button-down. To his surprise, she seemed to blush a little as they worked together to pull on a pair of stained work pants. It was the only time he'd seen her act her age since she'd found him in the backyard.

Sabine handed the bundle of Cal's clothing over to her sister with instructions.

"Wait!" Cal said as Lise scurried toward the door.

"I told you. She will hide it," Sabine insisted.

"Inside jacket pocket. Left side. There are things in there I need to keep on me."

She translated for her sister, and the girl took some envelopes and a small, worn picture out of the pocket he'd indicated. She handed them over, standing as far away from Cal as she could. Then she turned and ran out of the room.

Chapter 9

I reached for the aged picture Darlene had handed me and held it close to read the faded inscription in the margin underneath it. One word: *Daddy*. It was a sepia-toned snapshot of a man in a plain T-shirt and a baby girl in a lacy dress. He held her in the crook of his arm, and she looked up at him with just a hint of a smile on her face.

"Your dad?"

Darlene nodded. "Callum McElway. I found it in Mother's Bible—years ago now. It was tucked into the pages."

I glanced at the picture again. "You haven't talked about him."

"I had my reasons."

"Care to share them?"

"Let's start with this: he was a feckless husband and a deadbeat dad." Her expression wasn't much softer than her words. She took a deep breath and went on. "Honestly, I never knew much about him. Never wanted to. 'Feckless' and 'deadbeat' didn't exactly fill my daddy-void, but they did make it more of a seething than a yearning thing, which felt like a less maiming condition." She reached for the bundle of letters she'd brought and undid the ribbon that held them together. "Then I got these three years ago. Of course, I didn't read them until just recently."

I took the papers she extended to me. Six envelopes. Handwritten addresses.

"Four from Mother, Claire McElway, spanning about eighteen months," Darlene explained. "And two from his mom, Lucy, my paternal grandmother, I guess. Sent from Missouri."

"Tell me what you need, Darlene."

She sighed. "I'm actually not sure where to start. I never knew much more than bullet points about my father. He married Mother on a whim right after they met, then shipped out to England. She found out she was pregnant a few weeks later and had me while he was still overseas. He fought in World War II, then came home when I was about six months old. A hero—that's what Mother called him." Darlene looked up at the ceiling for a moment, as if she was bringing the details back into focus. "He left us two months after that, so I have no memories of him except for that picture. It was in a frame on the mantel as far back as I can remember, before Mother took it down to keep it in her Bible." She raised an eyebrow. "Charming-looking rogue, isn't he?"

"Agreed. Even by modern standards." I took in the details. Dark hair. Strong jawline. Slightly hooded eyes.

"Every so often, I'd catch her pausing by the fireplace, when she didn't think I was looking, and laying a hand next to the picture. Like she was paying her respects or, worse, missing him." Darlene looked at me. "It bothered me—for reasons my young mind didn't fully understand."

"His eyes look . . ." I shook my head, unable to put words to the expression on Callum's face.

"My father was a paratrooper who dropped into France on D-Day, 1944. He came back"—Darlene made air quotes with her fingers—"a 'troubled man.' That's what Mother called him. I translated 'troubled' to mean impulsive and irresponsible. But I had nothing to base that on.

"I have a vague recollection of Mother trying to tell me about him. Sometimes at bedtime. Or when we went for walks in the park on Sunday afternoons. And I remember getting mad when she did. Just this deep feeling of—I don't know—anger. Rebellion. Resentment, maybe. I didn't want to hear about him. He'd left us, and I didn't feel he had a right to intrude on what was left of our family anymore."

Darlene laughed softly and shook her head, her eyes on nothing, remembering. "I had an overdeveloped sense of justice for one so young, don't you think?"

"It doesn't surprise me at all," I said, my eyes still focused on the picture I held. Curiosity stirred in parts of my mind I hadn't tapped into in recent months. It felt invigorating.

"There was one day—I must have been ten or eleven. Mother had been sick for a while, in and out of the hospital with a case of pneumonia that hung on for weeks. Maybe that spooked her a bit. I remember her sitting me down and telling me that it was time for me to listen. That this man I didn't want to hear about was part of my history and that I was the only one who'd be able to pass it on."

Darlene looked at me with a bit of sheepishness. "I yelled at her to be quiet. Can you imagine? In that era, for a child—a *daughter*— to behave that way toward her mother. I remember her looking shocked. Tears in her eyes. But they sure didn't keep me from screaming that I hated the man in the picture and that I never wanted to hear about him ever again." Darlene took a deep breath and blew it out. "Overdeveloped sense of justice—underdeveloped sense of compassion.

"Mother cried, but I didn't care. We'd been through so much— so much. Living hand-to-mouth and putting up with the stigma of being a single mother. If my father had *died* in the war, we'd have been deserving of kindness and compassion. But my father had walked out, and that was an entirely different scenario in those days. That's why I started telling my school friends that he'd been killed fighting the Nazis. Darn well convinced myself that was fact too, for a while."

She paused for so long that I had to prompt her to go on. "Darlene?"

She smiled a bit wistfully in my direction, as if coming back to the present, and continued. "You may have figured out by now that I was a bit of a dramatic soul, even then. So—that night Mother was so intent on talking about Dear Old Dad? I grabbed his picture off the mantel and tossed it in the fireplace. There was no fire in it, mind you, which took the wind out of the sails of my grand gesture, but it still felt good to hear the frame's glass break. Then I stormed upstairs and yelled a few more things through my bedroom door. None worth repeating."

"So what you're telling me is that you were a compliant, quiet child."

My friend smiled a bit sadly. "When my mom tried to talk it out later that evening—still crying—I told her that I never wanted to hear about my father again. I put all the venom I could muster into calling him a 'mean man,' which isn't exactly stinging repartee, but felt satisfying to my abandoned-little-girl heart. The picture never went back on the mantel after that."

There was a fine sheen of perspiration on Darlene's face, something that had become more common since she'd started the immunotherapy she was taking. She patted the sweat away with thin, shaking fingers. "I suspect that's when it found its way into the pages of Mother's Bible."

I looked at the picture again—focusing on the man's posture and expression. There was nothing that indicated "trouble," except maybe for the tentativeness of the smile he directed toward his daughter.

Darlene reached for the snapshot and held it up to the light coming in the window across from the couch. "I already knew he was a soldier, and those letters you're holding tell me he trained for a long time to fight in Normandy." She pursed her lips and frowned. "Then he came home, tried the husband-and-father thing, and I guess he decided that he wasn't much for domesticity and nurture. That's what I've told myself all these years. Fatherhood must have been boring to him after fighting the bad guys, so he took off. Mother said he loved me. I remember that much. Mostly because it exasperated me. But she also said he didn't leave a note or any explanation when he took off. So much for love, right?"

I struggled to form a precise picture of Darlene's story from the scattered details I was hearing. "She never tried to track him down?"

Darlene shrugged. "Not to my knowledge. Those were different times."

"You never asked her for more information—even when you got older?"

"I think I've established that I hated the man sight unseen. Hate is one of those stubborn forces that time can't always soften. Mortality, on the other hand . . ."

Darlene's dire reality seeped into the moment. "So that's why you're digging into this now. Because you're sick again?"

"Still," she corrected. "Because I'm still sick. And because of those." She pointed to the letters on my lap. "They're so full of . . . This is going to sound corny, but they make him sound kind. Committed. A far cry from the scenarios I conjured up over the years. Besides, as Mother said back when she was fighting pneumonia, I'm the only one who can pass on that part of the family's story and, well, the vultures are circling."

I moved across the room to sit next to my friend. I took her hand and clasped it firmly between both of mine. "I love that you're doing this, Darlene," I said. "It shows courage. And I think the timing's just right."

"Pshaw."

Something struck me. "His mother—your grandmother," I said, remembering Lucy McElway's name on the return address of two of the envelopes. "Surely she would have wanted to keep in touch with her granddaughter even after your father left."

Darlene nodded. "My thoughts exactly. There may be five hundred or so miles between here and her place in Missouri, but wouldn't a first-time grandmother have found a way to make the trip at some point, regardless of her son's involvement? It's a mystery I could have cleared up three years ago, when I got the letters Mother sent to him. But I was still too stubborn to look at the dang things. I just stuffed them in a box with other odds and ends and tried to forget they existed."

She reached for an envelope, gingerly parting the edges to pull out what was inside. A smaller, yellowed piece of paper slid onto the floor as Darlene unfolded one of the letters her mom had written to Callum. She wiggled her finger for me to retrieve it and found the passage she wanted to read.

"*'We've received a few pieces of mail for you, Cal.'* This is my mother writing to her man," Darlene explained as an aside. "'*I'm enclosing a letter from a Rhoda Bishop, of Kinley, that arrived just yesterday. Darling, I'm sorry. I know this will come as a shock to you. From all you've said of your mother, I know you loved her dearly, and to lose her while you're still so very far away . . . I had hoped to introduce her to our baby when you returned, on that trip to your hometown that we've dreamed of together. My heart aches for you, my love, and for all that will not be. I know your mother died loving you as much as you loved her.'*"

Darlene lowered the letter and looked at me, an eyebrow raised. "So she died while he was deployed."

"*February 22, 1944,*" I read from the faded obituary cut out of a newspaper. "'*Survived by her son, Callum Ian McElway, and predeceased by her husband, Callum Lorne McElway.'*"

I handed the obituary back to Darlene and watched her insert the two items back into the envelope. "That doesn't leave a whole lot of loose ends, does it."

She pursed her lips for a moment. "It certainly doesn't."

"Darlene," I said, realizing I hadn't asked an obvious question. "How did you get these letters?" I looked through the envelopes again, fascinated by the neat penmanship and their survival all these years.

"That, my dear, is where fate comes in," she said, energy replacing the contemplation that had softened her voice. "Or dumb luck. Destiny. God. Whatever you want to call it." She adjusted her position on the couch and the grimace she tried to hide reminded me again of the grim news she'd been given. "It started with a call from this woman in Normandy," Darlene began, launching into a tale that took a few minutes to unfold. The woman worked for La Belle Génération, a French nonprofit devoted to flying D-Day survivors back to the place where they'd contributed to freeing Europe. "She called me out of the blue three years ago and asked if a Claire McElway still lived at my address. I told her Claire McElway had died a couple decades ago, but that I was her daughter and this had been her home. She told me her name was Maribeth and that she had in her possession letters written by Claire McElway to a certain Callum McElway back in 1944. That got my attention."

Maribeth had explained to Darlene that they'd been found in an historic building in a small Norman village during a renovation project. Workers replacing damaged parquet boards had discovered the letters hidden under the floor.

"And this woman, Maribeth, sent them to you?" I asked, the mystery quickening my senses.

Darlene nodded. "First, she asked me if my father was still alive. When I told her I sincerely didn't know, she asked if I'd like to have the letters and if she could help me do some research to try to track him down. Initially, I said no to both. I'd long ago accepted not knowing the coldhearted man I imagined my dearly departed father to be. And the chances of him still being alive all these years later? Slim to none. But then I recalled my mom's words about my responsibility to preserve our family's history, as unappealing as it may be. That's what changed my mind."

"So she sent you the letters."

"Yes. But no research. That's what I told her. I'd let her know if a day came when I wanted to know more."

Darlene sighed. She closed her eyes for a moment, as if reliving the deliberations that had brought her to this point. "When I first got them, I just stashed them away. But it turns out the third go-round with cancer can make a person take stock. So I got them out of the old shoebox a couple months ago. I was drawn in by Mother's words—the way she spoke of their relationship. I may never know what happened after the war, but what came before certainly felt real, the way she told it. I didn't even read the letters from Lucy until just a couple weeks ago—probably because I was scared my grandmother's words would make me feel sorry for the old deadbeat dad."

She smiled in a way that made me think her opinion had started to change. "I was what you'd call reluctantly intrigued. So I used my legendary technological skills and tried to sign up for one of those online ancestry services, but they lost me at 'Please pick a username.' Then I emailed my old friend Maribeth, who it turns out had gone ahead and done a little search of her own back when she found me, and she informed me that Cal's military records went up in smoke in some big fire in Saint Louis in the seventies.

"So I called up Kinley, Missouri's post office, since it's on my grandmother's return address. I was hoping somebody there could tell me if any McElways were still around."

"It's almost like you wanted to learn more about your dad, Darlene," I teased.

She rolled her eyes at me. "That immunotherapy treatment must be making me soft."

"What did you find out?"

"Well, a lovely lady informed me that there are no longer any McElways registered there. And then she refused to tell me anything else—confidentiality or whatever. So I turned my attention to obituaries, which, granted, isn't the most optimistic approach to locating the missing. Found lots of McElways. One Callum Lorne from Kinley, in fact—my grandfather, it turns out—but no Callum Ians." Her eyes got a bit wider and she repeated, "No obits for a Callum Ian, Ceelie. Not anywhere on the Googlewebs."

I felt myself frown as I considered the possibilities. "Wait . . . you don't think—" It seemed inconceivable. "You don't think Callum McElway could still be alive somewhere?"

She hunched a shoulder in a nonchalant way, but there was intensity, even excitement in her eyes. "Maybe. He'd be well into his nineties, but . . . maybe?"

Something childlike came over her face. Something expectant and uncertain. "So I'm thinking . . ." Her voice trailed off. She shook her head and seemed to search for her next words. "Ceelie, if he's still alive and I could meet him, if I could figure out who he really was—who he really is—before I . . ." She squared her shoulders and fixed a determined gaze on me. "I've been angry at him my entire life. Even when I was thriving, there was this deep-down acid that bubbled under the surface every time I thought of him. I want to die acid-free. And I want to honor my mother by doing so." She raised an eyebrow. "Seems like a worthy last wish, right?"

I looked from her face to the yellowed vestiges of a bygone era still in my hand and felt curiosity and compassion stir. "What can I do?"

She pointed at the letters and said, "You told me you started out wanting to be an investigative journalist. Well, I want you to keep these letters. Give them a look. And if you're still game once you've had time to think it through—I'd like you to consider launching a search for a World War II veteran by the name of Callum Ian McElway."

It felt like a lot. On the heels of the surgeries, the chemo, Nate's departure, and the move out of our house. I wondered when—if ever—life would feel predictable again.

But this was Darlene. This was my friend and champion, the only person with whom I didn't have to muzzle the memories, disappointments, or grief because she wanted to hear it all. Ugly and sad and angry and raw.

And she was dying.

There was so little I could do for her, so little that might ease the pain that lay ahead. I owed it to Darlene to at least try.

"Okay," I said.

My seventy-six-year-old, terminally ill friend squealed. Then she giggled and punched the air like a high school football player. "I knew you'd come through for me!"

We smiled at each other for a long moment.

"You sure you're up for this?" she finally asked, her smile slipping a bit. "His trail will be cold as Finnegan's feet."

"I'll do what I can. How's that? I'll dust off that journalism degree, think like a detective, and hunt down whatever information is still out there about the man in that picture." I tried to sound confident, though I knew the odds were against me. "And when my post-op drains come out in a couple weeks, I think I might take a quick trip to Kinley, Missouri," I said. Then a thought so irrational that I didn't dare question it popped into my mind. "But I have one condition."

"Name it."

"You're coming with me."

Chapter 10

The tension in the castle was palpable. Few spoke above a whisper. Fewer yet dozed. The distant bursts of gunfire and the concussion of mortar shells exploding kept Aubry-en-Douve's refugees on high alert.

Those who had been most hostile at the time of Cal's arrival seemed to have lost some interest in him in the handful of hours since he'd been carried inside. Their eyes and ears, their very spirits, it seemed, were fully trained on the world outside the castle. They exchanged glances as planes flew over, with less frequency now than they had in the early hours of Operation Overlord. They listened for the wail of falling bombs or other ominous sounds outside the thick, stone walls. They took turns at the windows, peering around blackout curtains and through holes in the tar paper.

The more time he spent under the same roof as the terrified people of Aubry-en-Douve, the more protective Cal felt of a population that had endured so much for so long at the hands of the Nazis.

Sabine had applied some kind of poultice to the base of Cal's skull, and he was able to sit up again, though the edges of his vision still felt a bit soft. He'd gotten Albert's attention, communicating as best he could through sign language, and the old man had left his position by the living room window to join him. Now he sat hunched over the low table between them, drawing a rudimentary map with charcoal on the back of one of the warning leaflets that had been dropped by the Allies over Normandy before the invasion.

Cal peered intently at Albert's sketch, determined not to let lingering pain and dizziness prevent him from planning his next move. Based on the drawing, Cal estimated that he was about ten kilometers west of Sainte-Mère-Église, a town he clearly remembered from the map he'd memorized before departing England. More importantly, the castle stood some twenty kilometers from Carentan, whose access roads were essential to securing the area and routing Nazi forces. He'd head that direction as soon as he could and had to assume he'd intersect at some point with other soldiers who had, like him, dropped far from their landing zones.

"*Les Allemands*," Albert said, his voice gruff and barely above a whisper. He made a Heil Hitler salute, followed by a shooting motion.

"Yes," Cal said. "The Germans will be everywhere." He waved his hands over the map to show that he knew they'd cover the whole territory.

Albert mimicked getting low and scanning his surroundings.

"Yes, I'll be careful. I'll watch for them."

"Careful," Albert repeated in an accent that would have been comical under other circumstances.

"Can I keep this?" Cal asked, folding the hand-drawn map.

Albert nodded, pushing his chair back and reaching for the hunting rifle that was never far from his side. Sabine took Albert's vacated chair as he left the room and handed Cal a cup of steaming tea.

"Drink," she said.

"Yes, ma'am." Cal pointed his chin toward the door, immediately regretting the motion as it made nausea stir again. "I'm surprised the Germans let Albert keep his rifle."

"They didn't," Sabine said. "It has been wrapped in old sheets and buried in a corner of the barn since the Nazis arrived. They will kill him if he is found with it."

"Brave man," Cal mused.

Something that looked like pride crossed Sabine's face. "He has been waiting for years to fight back. Living occupied is . . ." She searched for the right word. "It has been an *insulte suprême* to men like Albert, men who oppose Hitler's regime but could do nothing more than bow down to the Germans if they wanted to keep their families safe."

Cal took a sip of the tea she'd offered him and couldn't mask his disgust. For the first time since he'd arrived, he heard Sabine's laugh. It was rich and honest. "*Fenouil*," she said. "Fennel, I think, in English. For your dizziness."

"It tastes like licorice and hay," Cal mumbled, sniffing the steam coming off the liquid.

Sabine reached into the pocket of her skirt and handed him a hunk of dark bread. "You need to drink and eat. If you are going to go out and fight . . ." After some hesitation, she continued. "But you know you do not need to fight. You are just one man—one injured man—and there are thousands of *boches*. In homes. In churches. In the fields and the forests. They are everywhere and you are just one man with an injured leg and head."

"I'll be more than one man when I find my guys out there."

"The Germans know this land. They have been here for many years. They know where to hide and where you and your people will hide too."

Cal sipped the tea again and took a moment to consider the odds against him. Before they could discourage him, he said, "I have to try. I have to do something."

He wasn't sure whether it was approval or misgiving that flashed across Sabine's face. Probably a combination of both. "First, you must feel better."

Lise entered the living room and came to lean against her sister.

"*Tu vas tirer sur les Allemands?*" she asked Cal.

Cal looked to Sabine for a translation. "Will you shoot the Germans?" she said.

Looking into the little girl's wide, brown eyes, he answered, "I will." Something almost imperceptible in him flinched at the admission. Killing another human being had until then been a theoretical thing. He knew it would become reality in the hours that followed and understood on a visceral level that the first kill would take something from him. But he wouldn't question it, just as he hadn't questioned the operation that had left him stranded near Aubry-en-Douve. He would kill without hesitation to stop Hitler in his tracks.

"If you see Otto, do not shoot," Lise said in halting English, her brown eyes wide with pleading. "He is nice. He is scared of you."

Cal looked at Sabine. "Otto?"

"He is one of the Germans who has been living here. The youngest of them, I think."

"Wehrmacht?"

Sabine nodded. "Lise is still able to see the humanity in people who do not show it well."

Cal looked at the younger sister and hesitated before answering. "I can't promise—"

Lise interrupted him. "Please."

"Lise. We cannot ask Cal to . . ." She paused, deep in thought, before looking at Cal again. "He was not cruel to us. Not like the others, but he was—how do you say it? In French, it is *rigide*. Very *rigide*. Wanting to impress his superiors, perhaps. We could tell he did not want to be here, but when the Kommandant gave orders, he was the first one to obey." She looked at Lise and smoothed her hair with a gentle hand. "Lise told me there were times when she saw him being sad, but I did not see that in him. I saw only an enemy soldier."

"He was nice sometimes," Lise insisted to Cal. "But he does not climb trees," she said. Her disapproval was clear on her face.

Sabine drew her sister closer and swept her bangs out of her eyes. "Lise sees a friend in everyone."

"I'm guessing you can't, given what you've been through," Cal said.

"I am not seven, like Lise. The way I see the world is not so innocent." She looked around the room at the exiled population of Aubry-en-Douve and shook her head. "They have starved us. They have stolen everything from us. They have lined up villagers and shot them in the square in front of their children because they thought they were working against them. Without any proof. They just . . . shot." She looked directly at Cal as something soft came over her face. "They took our father to a work camp in Germany because they thought he was in the *résistance*. There was nothing we could do."

"So that's why it's just the three of you."

Sabine nodded and glanced at her little sister. Lise was looking down, but Cal could see tears suddenly filling her eyes. Sabine wrapped an arm around her shoulders and drew her in to kiss her cheek, but Lise pulled free and hurried out of the room, head low. Sabine watched her go. "They came for Papa more than a year ago. And then they came back months later and told us they would live here with us. They took it all when they moved in—our house, our food, our horses. Everything."

"Did they harm you?" Cal could feel something protective stirring.

Sabine shook her head. "They weren't really cruel—not the ones who lived here. Just preoccupied and unhappy. They rarely spoke to us, except for Otto. He speaks English like we do, so when we didn't understand what the Kommandant wanted, he translated for us."

"How long have they been here?"

"More than one year. We had no choice. They would have shot us if we refused to house them. To serve them. So we did. We cooked and cleaned and sewed for them. We ate black bread and soup because they took all the better food. We tried not to make them angry and we waited for the Allies, the *Américains*, to come."

A gunshot rang out instantly panicking the castle's occupants, just as Cal was about to ask another question. Women screamed and men barked orders. Cal bolted upright and squinted hard against renewed dizziness, realizing in a flash that the sound hadn't been the crisp clap of a military-grade weapon, but the more sloppy concussion of a hunting rifle.

Sabine's face blanched as she looked toward the windows facing the courtyard. Cal leapt to his feet, urgency overriding caution, and heard as much as he felt a crack in his injured ankle. Pain shot up his leg, but he ignored it, a surge of adrenaline coursing through his bloodstream. He took two steps toward the entryway as the distinctive burst of a semiautomatic split the air, but his exit was blocked by the crush of townspeople rushing into the living room.

Sabine grabbed a hold of the back of Cal's shirt and pulled him up hard, stepping in front of him with eyes wide and jaw set. The girl pointed with a shaking hand at the people now cowering in the far corner of the room, a handful of the men in front of the women and children, eyes fixed on the door. "You go stand with them!" she said fiercely. "Remember, you are not American! You are not American!"

She snatched the envelopes extending from his shirt pocket and looked around for a place to hide them. Then she froze and looked toward the door. Her face turning impossibly whiter, she whispered, "Lisou" so softly that Cal barely heard her.

There was screaming outside now. The raised voice of a man shrieking orders penetrated through the windows. Then another round of gunfire.

An elderly woman stepped forward to take the letters from Sabine's shaking hand and returned to the alcove, bending low to stuff them into the crack between two warped floorboards, but Cal's mind wasn't on his precious possessions anymore. It was on the voice, distorted by hysteria, hurling expletives with orders to "Drop it now, you—"

Cal recognized it instantly. "It's okay," he barked at the villagers, holding his hand out, palm down. "It's okay!" he said again, more urgently. But at the sound of the front door bursting open, the men still raised their pitchforks, as if they'd do any good against a military rifle. Cal stepped in front of them, waving his arms this time, "No—it's okay! It's okay!"

The living room door crashed back on its hinges and Albert stumbled in, followed by a paratrooper whose face was partially obscured by dried blood. Before Cal could get a word out, the GI caught sight of the combat-ready villagers. He shoved the old man out of the way and raised his Garand, crouching in anticipation of the salvo that would eliminate the threat.

"No!" Cal yelled.

The other American froze.

"Holy mother of-" He lowered his rifle and cocked his head to the side, as if he wasn't sure of what he was seeing. Then his bloodied face split into a gap-toothed smile. He let out a wild howl and yelled, "Cal McElway! What are you doing in this Kraut-infested hellhole?"

Chapter 11

I didn't bother to knock on Joe's office door. I walked right in and struck a confident pose. Ten days had passed since I'd told Darlene that I'd search for her father, and I was a woman on a mission. "I need time off," I declared, hitching my chin up a notch.

Joe leaned back in his faux-leather chair, making springs creak. He contemplated me with eyes that held both frustration and kindness. "Ceelie . . ."

I'd grown accustomed to Impatient Joe, Dictatorial Joe, and Borderline-Friendly Joe in our years of collaboration, but Sensitive Joe still made me—and him—uncomfortable. "It's not so much time off as the chance to go on an assignment."

"An assignment?"

"Yes. Or I can resign and pursue this on my own time."

He raised a bushy, salt-and-pepper eyebrow. "So this is blackmail?"

I pasted on my best employee-of-the-month smile. "I'd prefer to keep my job, but . . ."

"We need you here."

"And I've been here for going on twenty years. A few days, Joe. A week, tops. That's all I'm asking for."

He leaned forward again and propped his elbows on the desk, pointing with his chin for me to sit in the chair across from him. Joe wasn't a nice man, not in the traditional sense of the word. He was driven—driven enough to keep a regional paper circulating where other publications had failed. He was old-school in his approach to business and relationships: work hard, say little, and prove your mettle.

Given the limited curb appeal of those traits, it was no surprise that he'd seen in my more gregarious personality a useful addition to his small but sturdy paper. My greatest contribution to the company had been pulling it kicking and screaming into the twenty-first century, adding a digital element to our reach, and hiring a millennial or two to man our social media accounts. The mere mention of Twitter still made Joe cringe, but now that we were the fourth largest paper in the state, I knew he saw the benefits of "selling out," as he put it.

Though most of our content was regional, we didn't shy away from the global, but covered it from a perspective that made it feel local. We reported on political, social, and economic events, but with a painstaking devotion to cutting out the superfluous and pointing out—per Joe's oft-repeated question—why it should matter to our readers. His motto, since starting the paper in his parents' basement nearly forty years ago, had been "Entertain, Educate, and Elevate." To the extent that our readership covered more than two hundred thousand households, the approach had been effective.

"Is this about Nate?" Joe didn't understand or employ subtlety. Before I could answer, he put up a hand. "What with your . . . challenges . . . and Nate's decision. Is that what this is about?" He held my gaze for a second or two, and when I didn't immediately respond, took off his glasses and made a production of wiping the lenses with the tip of his tie. Joe had never been good with loaded silences.

I opted for truth. "It's about Darlene. Remember her?"

"I remember her," he said, shifting in his seat. Of course he did.

My mind flashed back to an awkward encounter in the days following my surgery. *"Breast cancer,"* Darlene had said, a bit too loudly, after Joe had tried to find a euphemism for the disease during the three and a half minutes he'd spent in my home. *"Repeat after me. Breast. Cancer,"* she'd said again, leaning toward his flushing face.

"She needs me to track down her father, a World War II veteran by the name of Cal McElway," I now told Joe. "He left when she was young and she needs to know what happened to him." I shrugged, hoping it looked nonchalant. "So you can fire me or you can give me some time off. Either way, I'm taking my high heels and chutzpah and hitting the road."

"High heels and chutzpah, huh?" It was a phrase I hadn't used in years, not since my early days at the *Sentinel* when everything I said was a plea for recognition. I sat up straighter and looked him in the eye. "I told Darlene I'd try."

"So you make a few calls."

"We did. We called every McElway within a hundred-mile radius of his hometown. All dead ends. Turns out his branch of the family was pretty small and insular, and after they scattered . . . radio silence," I said.

I could tell he was running numbers in his mind. "Your guy would be well into his nineties by now."

"There's no obit on record—I checked. And if we could at least find a neighbor or someone back home who knew him . . ."

"So you're going to drive around until you stumble across a WWII veteran's trail?"

"I have a couple leads. And I'm a reporter. I investigate for a living. So, yes. But without the 'stumbling' part."

"You're killing me, kid."

I could hear the hesitation in his voice. "It could make for a great human-interest story. You know our readers love that kind of thing."

Joe frowned and didn't bother to address the fact that I hadn't written an investigative piece in years. He tapped the rim of his glasses on the pages of the article he was editing longhand—always longhand—and didn't look up for a while.

"The seventy-sixth anniversary of D-Day is this June," I added as the thought came to me. "It's the perfect tie-in—we feature a long-form essay about a lost local veteran to mark the occasion. People love WWII fare."

"Except the veteran isn't from here."

"Okay, but his daughter is."

Joe said nothing for a moment.

"Come on, Joe," I pleaded.

He seemed to be contemplating the frustrations of running the company without me again. "What's the hurry?" he finally asked.

"Darlene is dying."

That got his attention.

"Her cancer's back. It's in her bones and her lungs, maybe in her spine too. There's no time to put this off until it's convenient, Joe."

He let out a loud breath. "Three days," Joe said.

"One week if necessary?"

He put his glasses back on and adjusted the papers in front of him. I sat there waiting for him to grant my request. "You sure about this?" he asked, not looking up.

"I need it, Joe. Darlene needs it."

"One week." He sighed. "Not a day more."

I put a hand to my chest and felt my heart pounding. "If I didn't think it would scar you for life, I'd hop over this desk and hug you."

"Number one, you haven't hopped in years. And number two, 'hashtag MeToo,' Ceelie. Keep your grubby hands off me."

I laughed. The brightness of the sound surprised me.

"One week," I said as Joe pushed his glasses higher, picked up his pen, and went back to editing his article.

My doorbell rang late in the evening, three days before Darlene and I were set to leave on our quest to find Cal. I glanced out the window and down into the street, then stepped back. From the second floor, all I could see of the person standing at the door was the top of his head. It was all I needed.

For a moment, I contemplated pretending not to be home. Nate would ring the doorbell a couple more times and be gone.

Or I could suck it up and answer the door.

I had discovered in the weeks since Nate's abrupt exit from our marriage how many emotional forms abandonment could take. It morphed in an instant from grief to anxiety, from immobility to hyperactivity. It cloaked itself in numbness only to erupt in irrational fury the next moment. Nate had taken the most important relationship of my life from me. He'd taken my friendships too, as those who loved us both seemed paralyzed by the fear that spending time with one of us would look like choosing sides. He'd taken my sense of certainty, the illusion of permanence that had lent a sort of foundational stability to my life. He'd taken my ability to trust myself, my confidence in my instincts and perceptions. I'd been so sure—so sure—that what we had was not only resilient but finally growing stronger.

Nate's abandonment still ran through my days like a barely perceptible current, a subtle and persistent burn that reminded me at every turn of how stupid I'd been and how angry I still was.

With resentment fueling that moment of courage, I walked over to the intercom next to the loft's door. As broken as I felt, I wanted to prove to Nate that I wasn't.

"What do you want, Nate?"

There was a beat of silence, then, "Can we talk?"

"We're talking now."

"This is important."

"Write a note to my lawyer. You have her address." There was something both satisfying and mortifying about giving in to infantile impulses.

"Ceelie . . ."

"I can't think of anything we need to talk about. If this is about the financial disclosure, I'm working on it. It just takes a while to itemize twenty-four years' worth of assets and income."

"Please let me in, Cee."

"No."

The silence this time lasted so long that I went to the window again. Nate was still there, hands in his pockets, head hung low. Something in his stance weakened my resolve. I went back to the intercom. "What's this about?"

"I'd rather discuss it face-to-face."

I pressed the unlock button almost in spite of myself. The door downstairs clicked open and shut again. Nate's footsteps on the stairs to the loft were a familiar rhythm. They stopped on the landing outside the door.

He looked shorter. That was my first thought upon seeing him up close. He wore his old leather jacket over grungy jeans and a lived-in hoodie. His construction uniform. But none of that registered as much as his stature. This was not my sturdy, six-foot-something husband standing there looking at me. His features seemed sunken, his shoulders less square, his frame less solid. I took satisfaction in the vaguely haunted shadow in his gaze.

When I stepped aside, Nate walked in. He paused for a moment, taking in the small space. His eyes lingered on the large, sculpted-metal depiction of mountains hanging above the secondhand couch I'd bought at a Red Cross store. It was the only decorative piece I'd taken from our home, because it affirmed to me that someday, somehow, I'd make it to Switzerland.

"Why aren't you down south?" I asked.

"I needed to see you. To tell you what I've been thinking since . . ."

"Since what?"

"Since the last time I saw you."

The encounter flashed through my mind. Nate finding me at home when he'd come back to get more of his stuff. Packing his suitcase. Announcing he'd be spending a few weeks on the Rend Lake build. Me losing it after he left and Nate walking back in to find me devastated, wailing with loss and grief.

"What happened to the cabin project?" I said.

"It's moving along without me." He took another step or two into the room, then stopped abruptly and turned to me. "I didn't feel like this could wait." He took a deep breath. "I think I made a mistake."

I racked my mind for what he might mean. "With the paperwork?"

"With us."

Something odd tingled down my spine. It wasn't anger. It wasn't hope. It was a jagged sort of energy that left me feeling like an already precarious moment was about to become maiming.

I inhaled and held my breath for a beat, hearing the blood pounding in my ears. Then I let it out and looked Nate straight in the eyes for the first time since he'd arrived. "You can't be serious," I said. There was gravel in the sound.

Nate opened his mouth to speak, then closed it again. He hung his head and shook it, hands on hips, visibly tense. "I've been thinking—" he began in a hesitant voice. That alone got my attention. Nate wasn't hesitant. Ever.

"I'm happy for you," I interrupted. "While you've been thinking, I've been moving out of our house, having more surgery, figuring out how I'm going to afford living on my own, and finding out my friend is dying."

Nate was still looking down. A faint flush colored his cheeks.

"So I'm not sure what this is really about, Nate." Anger slashed through any semblance of civility. "But if you're here to process out loud or find closure or . . . whatever . . . you've come to the wrong place."

He stared at the metallic wall hanging for a moment, as if he was trying to understand what I'd said. It struck me how awkward the scene must have looked—the two of us standing just inside my door, Nate's hands in his pockets now, my arms crossed in front of me, neither looking directly at the other.

"Darlene's dying?" he finally asked.

I didn't want to discuss it with him. My friend's illness was a grief too intimate to share with this man who had severed our oneness. "That's none of your business anymore."

He looked at me. "I still care."

"Forgive me, but my lawyer's bills indicate that you don't."

We stood in silence a while longer, stuck in the no-man's-land between the coolness of the entryway and the warmth of the living room.

"It's been . . . ," he began. He looked up at the ceiling and let out a long breath. "I was angry," he finally said, something sincere in his tone. "Not at you. I'm not sure at what, actually. I said things . . ." He shook his head as if to clear it. "I've been thinking, a lot, and I guess I want to . . . I just want to talk."

Cynicism chilled me. This man who seemed to be reconsidering the decision that had upended my life had not just walked out on me. He had brutalized my reality.

A part of myself I couldn't control—the impulsive, idealistic part that wanted to believe in miraculous outcomes—fluttered its way to the edges of my consciousness, spoiling my anger with "what-ifs" and "maybes." I couldn't trust it. Truth be told, I blamed it for the illusions that had left me so eviscerated. I'd finally disavowed its lies and futile hopes.

"You want to talk?" I said to Nate, as the bile of pent-up anger seeped into my voice. "You were angry and you've been thinking and you want to have a chat about what? Leaving me? About telling me you were tired and outta here while we sat in a parking lot? You want to talk, Nate? After not saying a single word to me in weeks, except for that time you came home hoping I was at work? We're this close," I said, holding up my fingers an inch apart, "to finalizing a divorce you dumped on me when I was still neck-deep in cancer recovery, and now you decide you want to talk?"

He said nothing as my words struck him, all sharp edges and disbelief. Then a thought that had been hovering at the periphery of my consciousness for weeks struck me again with aching clarity. "There was someone else, wasn't there?" I said before I could stifle the impulse.

I'd known Nate long enough to recognize the flash of shock in his eyes, quickly replaced by unnerving sincerity. I ignored it.

"Was it Julie?" The name surprised me. I hadn't intended to blurt it out. I hadn't even considered the role she might have played in Nate's departure until that moment.

He frowned and shook his head. "Cee . . ."

I'd only met Julie once. She'd started her five-month stint as Nate's interim administrative assistant just weeks before my surgery, and she'd been behind the desk facing the office door when I'd dropped by for lunch one day. She was younger than me—probably in her late twenties. I'd commented on her thick eyelashes and she'd let out a warm, round laugh and told me they were on sale at Walgreens. She was the epitome of the all-American girl. Soft and fresh and sunny. Nothing like me—not pre-cancer-me and certainly not the post-cancer incarnation of the person I used to be.

"Why didn't I see this before now?" I said, more to myself than to Nate.

"I have no idea what you're talking about, Ceelie. She's a temp.

Nothing more." A frustrated edge was creeping into his voice. "How can you even think that?"

I wasn't hearing him. Not in any way that mattered. Every insecurity I'd carried around since adolescence—since the infertility and cancer that had followed—was roaring at me more loudly than reason. The movie playing in my head was so real that the confused expression on Nate's face, the disbelief and discomfort in his tone, couldn't dissuade me.

"So it didn't work out with your perky secretary and now you're crawling back to second-best?" There was venom in my voice.

"That's not what this is," Nate said, tortured and intense. "Nothing ever happened with Julie. Never even a hint of anything."

"And you expect me to just—" I stopped myself. I didn't have it in me to explain to the man I'd married how impossible it had become for me to believe anything he claimed, no matter how forcefully he said it.

I walked the few steps to the console just inside my door on unsteady legs and pulled its drawer open. The wedding ring I'd dropped into a plastic organizer, alongside batteries, spare keys, and rubber bands, glinted in the light from the still-open door. I picked it up with shaking fingers, fighting the nausea clawing at my gut.

"Please leave, Nate," I said, holding it out to him. "I believed you once. What was it you said back then? Oh yeah. 'I do.' That's what you said. So don't expect me to believe anything you feel like saying to me now."

"Can you at least let me try to expl—?"

I reached for his hand and pressed the ring into his palm. Then I stood back and averted my eyes. "Just go."

Nate opened his mouth as if he was about to speak. Instead, he turned without a word, walked down the stairs, and let himself out.

Chapter 12

"That was close!" Buck leaned against the wall by one of the front windows, weapon in hand, grinning at Cal as if they were players on a football field reviewing their game. He'd survived their jump with just a cut to his forehead and, now that Sabine had cleaned the dried blood from his face, looked no worse for wear.

Cal hobbled over to a chair and lowered himself onto its armrest. "Glad you recognized me before you started shooting," he said, the pain in his ankle coming into focus as adrenaline subsided.

Buck jutted his chin toward the courtyard. "Saw the old coot with a rifle out there and figured nobody here was up to any good." He glanced around the room, taking in its faded grandeur. "How'd you end up in a castle while I was trudging thigh-deep through swamp water, you lucky mongrel?"

"I landed in a tree out back," Cal said. "The 'old coot,'" he added, emphasizing Buck's terminology, "dragged me and my busted ankle to safety after Sabine found me."

Buck leered. "The girl who cleaned me up? She's a looker, that one."

Cal shot him a glare. "She's a kid."

He knew Buck wasn't listening. The same battle-thirst that had defined the paratrooper during training was coming off him in waves. There was something manic in his eyes.

Buck scanned the room's occupants with an enthusiastic sort of suspicion-the kind that dared anyone to step out of line. They returned his stare with equal wariness. This American who had held one of their own at gunpoint would not easily gain their trust.

"How d'you know these people are friendlies?" Buck asked Cal, apparently unfazed by the cool reception.

"I wouldn't be sitting here if they weren't."

Buck left his position at the window and a villager stepped in to take it. There was a renewed sense of foreboding in the castle, as if his appearance had reminded its occupants of how very unprotected they were. He lowered himself onto the couch across from Cal and dropped his boot-clad feet onto a delicate coffee table with a thud. Then he reached for the bottle of Calvados Sabine had left after using it to clean his wound. He took a swig and let out a loud, satisfied breath. "These Frogs sure know their way around booze," he said, contemplating the amber-colored apple liquor as he settled back against the striped upholstery of the antique furniture.

"How'd you get here, man?" Cal asked, still stunned to be sitting in a room with someone he'd last seen leaping out of their C-47 under punishing fire.

"Dumb luck! That jump was like buckshot, right? By the time we landed, we were so scattered there was no way we'd regroup. So I just kept on moving and hoped the fighting would wait for me."

"I'm guessing there's plenty left for you," Cal said, his smile devoid of humor.

"Gonna get me some Nazi scalps." Buck's grin turned into a full-on smile as he raised his semiautomatic and took aim at the wall. "Line 'em up and mow 'em down." He pretended to shoot, making gunfire sounds as he blasted whoever he was seeing in his mind.

"Buck!" Cal snapped, conscious of the townspeople looking on.

The paratrooper lowered his weapon and brought the bottle to his lips again, eyeing his audience. "You really sure about 'em?"

"They took me in, didn't they?"

"Took your uniform too," Buck noted, nodding at his civilian clothes.

"So I'd blend in if the Germans come back. You should probably change too."

"That's what the girl said . . . right before I told her to shove off." He frowned. "Wait. Did you say, 'if the Germans come *back*'?"

Cal weighed his words before speaking. "They requisitioned this place for their HQ a few months ago." When Buck frowned, he added, "The way Sabine tells it, there was nothing anyone could do about it."

"Where'd they go?"

"Took off for the battery last night and haven't been back. Not sure if we took it, but it sounds like we put up a good fight."

Buck leaned forward to slap Cal's leg, making him wince. "Come on, man. Enough pussyfooting around—we've gotta get back out there and give those Nazi punks what they deserve!"

"I know," Cal said, his voice somber. "I was planning on leaving tonight. Maybe head toward Carentan and hope to intersect with some of our unit on the way there." He hesitated, frowning in frustration. "But if I can't put any weight on my leg . . ."

Some of the enthusiasm went out of Buck's posture. "That bad?"

"I thought it was a sprain, but I don't know."

Buck took another swig from the Calvados bottle, then held it up to peer at the half-liter that remained. "How's this?" he said. "I'm gonna give you until the last drop of this Kickapoo Joy Juice. When it's gone, so am I. And if your bum leg lets you, so are you."

Cal's helplessness felt like just one more wound. A few hours before, when he and Buck had been on the plane dodging flak over the Channel, he'd imagined that he'd be neck-deep in battle by now. He wanted to fulfill the mission he'd trained for. He wanted to engage the enemy alongside his comrades and bring an end to the reign that had terrorized Europe. But in his state, he wouldn't run into battle, he'd hobble. The handicap felt like failure, an affront to all he'd become in the nearly two years since he'd reported to Camp Toccoa, then gone on to train at Fort Benning.

"Still don't like the looks of that one," Buck said, jutting his chin toward Albert, who had just entered the living room with Sabine and Lise.

"I believe he feels the same way about you," Sabine murmured as she walked past Buck on her way to Cal. She instructed him to sit in the chair, and he winked at Lise as he lowered himself from the armrest to the seat. But the girl's brown eyes were on Buck, defiant and fearless. "You can tell your sister this is one of the good guys," Cal said to Sabine.

"Anyone who holds a gun on Albert is going to have to prove that." She smiled a bit tightly. "We found her in the cellar. She ran there when she heard the shots." She cast a quick glance in Buck's direction. "I will be happy when there is no more reason for French children to hide."

"Have you heard any more about what's going on out there?"

"We know for sure that the battery is in American hands," she said.

Cal cringed as his friend let out a howl of victory that reverberated in the silence of the castle, startling some of its occupants. "A star-spangled touchdown!" He bolted upright and brought his hand to his temple in a dramatic salute.

"But Germans have been seen all around still," Sabine continued, aiming a disapproving glare at Buck. "They have not run away. The Americans are fighting them, but it's small battles, not big ones."

Cal said to Sabine, "If you can stabilize my leg, we'll head out later."

She looked out the window. "It would be better for you to leave when it is dark. The *boches* have been here for months. They know the roads and the land. You don't."

Sabine finished unwrapping Cal's ankle. It had turned a darker shade of mottled red since he'd stood on it, and though the bandages had contained the swelling, it began again the moment they were off. She gingerly moved his ankle side to side, and Cal jerked back from the pain.

"You cannot fight if you cannot walk," Sabine said.

Cal didn't like her assessment. "I have to," he said firmly. "I didn't fly over here to sit in an armchair and listen to the fighting going on down the road. And if I stay here, I endanger all of you. This"—he pointed to his injured leg—"is no reason to put civilians in the Nazis' crosshairs."

"We are not scared."

He looked from Sabine's resolute eyes to Albert's unyielding expression. Then he let his gaze settle on little Lise. She gave him a tentative smile. "And you," he said, leaning in a little. "Are you as brave as your sister?"

The girl pulled herself up to her full height and declared a resounding, "*Oui!*"

Cal chuckled and held up his hands. "I believe you!" He paused. "How old are you, Lise?"

"I am seven," she answered, saying each word carefully, her English as clipped as her French.

"You speak good English."

"*Pas vraiment.*"

"Not really," Sabine translated. "She was young when our mum died and we always spoke French with Papa."

"Sabine, do you know where your father is?"

She shook her head. "There has been no word since

they took him away. We do not even know if he is still-" She glanced at her sister. "We do not know if our father will come back. But Albert has been . . ." She shook her head, as if her vocabulary was too limited to express what she wanted to say.

"He's taken care of you."

"He is our friend. He worked with my father and now-he is our friend. If he had not been here . . ."

Cal shot a glance at the older man. His wrinkles were deep and he stood slightly stooped, but there was something of a warrior in the calm, intense energy he radiated.

"Now"-Sabine reached into the broad pocket in her apron and took out bandages and a small medicinal vial-"we must try to get your ankle ready for combat."

Cal sighed. "You really think I'll be able to stand on this thing?"

The young woman frowned. "I will do what I can so you can do what you came for."

"Whoopin' them Krauts!" Buck yelled.

Sabine shot him a disapproving glare. "That bottle," she said to Cal in a low voice. "We use the Calvados to disinfect wounds, and we were not able to save much of it after the Germans came here. Your friend must not drink it all."

"I'll send you more when the war's over, little lady," Buck said loudly to the teenager, raising the bottle in an ironic salute before bringing it to his lips again. "Good stuff." He wiped his mouth with the back of his hand. "You have any more of this?" he asked Albert.

The old man stared back without a word.

"What—are you mute or something?"

"He does not understand English," Sabine said.

A flush crept up Buck's neck. He got off the couch and swaggered toward Albert, stopping inches from his chest. "But I bet he got along fine with the Germans, right? Thick as thieves when they were hangin' out around here, right?" He shoved the old man, but Albert caught him by the front of his jacket and jerked him close enough that they were nearly nose-to-nose.

"Albert, *non!*" Sabine gasped.

Cal was on his feet immediately, limping over to push the men apart, then spearing a finger into his friend's chest. "Knock it off, Buck!"

A muscle clenched in Buck's jaw. He swatted Cal's hand away and kicked a wooden footrest across the room.

Cal turned toward Sabine and Albert, hands outstretched in apology. "He doesn't mean any harm," he said, but even he could hear the uncertainty in his voice. Buck's histrionics were nothing new, but there was something even more frantic and fractious roiling in his friend that day, something that felt dangerous.

Buck took another swig of Calvados. "Relax, man," he said to Cal. "Just tryin' to figure out who's really on our side."

"Keep this up and we'll lose the friends we have," Cal said softly. He motioned for Buck to hand over the bottle and was surprised to find that it was nearly empty.

As Buck threw himself down on a nearby couch, Cal lay a hand on top of Lise's head and nodded, as if assuring her that Buck wouldn't be bothering Albert again.

"I will bandage your foot now," Sabine said.

Cal hobbled back to the chair and she knelt in front of him, propping his foot on her lap. She handed the small vial and a rag to Lise, who soaked the cotton fabric in pale-yellow liquid.

"Nettle and dandelion to make the swelling go down," she explained to Cal, taking the cloth from Lise and lightly wrapping it around his still-discoloring ankle and foot. "I will place these thin pieces of wood on the sides and hold them there with bandages. Tight. It will hurt." She tried to smile, but her efforts fell short. "If it works, you will be able to move your foot up and down, but it will not bend sideways again."

"How do you know how to do this?"

"The Germans—they made me work at their clinic for a while. Until they discovered I could not do that and cook their meals too." She shot Cal an ironic look.

"Were they . . . ?" Cal struggled to find the right word.

Sabine said, "They were not cruel to us, because we didn't give them reason to be." She began wrapping his swollen and bruised ankle, pulling the bandages nearly unbearably tight. "But they were not good either. We could not move freely, even if family needed us. All of us, we have lived under their boot. Not enough food. Never enough food. No possessions they could not seize. No freedom." She looked Cal directly in the eyes. "More than four years living as prisoners in our own country. Our own home. It was—how do you say it? *Un enfer.*"

"Hell?" Cal guessed. He could see the depths of it darkening Sabine's expression.

"Yes, hell." She agreed. "And when they went to fight last night, they left more hell behind them. Our barn is filled with the dead horses they could not leave for you Americans to take."

Cal frowned. "They shot their own horses?"

"Theirs and ours." She glanced toward Lise. She was sitting with an elderly couple across the room, bringing smiles to their faces as she talked in her animated way. "Lise hasn't seen the horses yet. She doesn't know. When she does . . ."

Cal tried to imagine what the family had endured and again felt something protective descend over him. With no adequate words coming to his mind, he simply said, "You've been through so much and you're still so young."

She attempted a smile. "It is nearly over," she said. "But we will not soon forget. We will *never* forget," she amended, blinking away tears.

"Thank you, Sabine," Cal said, though the words seemed insufficient. "For taking the risk of bringing me inside when you found me. For fixing me up. You've been . . . Thank you."

Sabine shrugged. "My father taught us to treat good people like family. Family is worth taking risks for. He would have done the same."

Cal reached into his shirt pocket and realized most of the items he'd carried over from England weren't there anymore. "Do you know what happened to my letters?"

"Your . . . ?"

"The letters. You took them out of my pocket when we still thought Buck was the Germans coming back."

She frowned. "A lot was happening. I think . . . I think someone took them from me to hide them." She seemed to be trying to recall the details of the brief but intense moment. "Maybe Sylvie. I will ask her if she has them."

"I'd appreciate that. Those letters . . . they're important to me." He reached deeper into his pocket and relief swept over him as he found the small picture that never left him. "You were talking about family," he said, holding it out to Sabine. "This is mine."

The fourteen-year-old took the picture from him. "This is your . . . ?"

"My wife, Claire." Saying the words was at once a comforting and a devastating thing.

Sabine peered closely at the black-and-white snapshot. "She is very beautiful."

"That's the day we got married. Right before I took off for England. What we didn't know then–" Cal hadn't spoken the words out loud before. He'd wanted to, but he'd feared that they'd somehow heap an even heavier burden on his fight for survival. "What we didn't know then," he tried again, "is that she was expecting."

Sabine looked at him, confused. "Expecting what?"

"A baby," Cal said, realizing the term might not be familiar to the young French woman. "She was expecting a baby."

"You are going to be a father?" It was the first bright smile he'd seen since he'd landed on French soil.

114

Cal felt one of his own spreading across his face. "I'm already a father," he said. His own words stunned him. "She was born nearly six months ago, when I was at Ramsbury. Claire and Darlene . . ." He swallowed past the emotions tightening his throat. "They're my life." He shook his head, keenly feeling the distance between them, the dangers ahead, and the frightening prospect of never being able to hold his infant daughter. "They're everything," he said, his voice soft with yearning. With hope. With dread.

Sabine frowned. "You must see them soon," she said emphatically.

"There's a war to fight first." Determination and frustration dueled in Cal's mind.

"Then right after. As soon as it is over. Daughters need a father." Cal saw something sad descend over the teenager's face. She blinked hard as tears rose in her eyes. "Daughters need a father," she said again. Then she sat up straighter, handing the picture back to Cal.

"I'm sorry, Sabine," he said. "I'm so sorry your father isn't here. You and Lise . . . you've been so brave."

"We did not have a choice." Something steely dropped over her momentary show of emotion, a resolve, Cal suspected, born of untenable grief and a ferocious determination to live in spite of it.

Suddenly getting back to business, Sabine motioned for Lise to join her. The seven-year-old held the splints in place while her sister applied a second layer of bandages to Cal's aching ankle.

"Whaddya gonna do for me?" Buck asked from the couch, his words slightly slurred. "I got a few boo-boos and I bet a kiss or two would make them all better."

"Buck!" Cal's voice was sharp. "I told you-knock it off."

As if sensing the nature of Buck's comment, Albert stepped closer to Sabine and leveled a hostile stare on the American soldier. His hands were in his pockets and his stance was casual, but from the hardness of his expression, Cal could tell he was coiled to strike.

Sabine stopped wrapping and said, "Albert" under her breath.

"You want a piece of this GI, old man?" Buck asked, sitting up straighter.

"Albert," she murmured again. "*Ignore le.*" Albert held her gaze for a moment. He nodded but did not step away as Buck lay back and stared at the ceiling.

"I'm sorry," Cal said quietly as she got back to work on his ankle. "Buck's . . ." He sought the right word to describe his comrade in arms. "He talks tough, but he's not a bad person."

"He is rude," she whispered, dismissing his explanation.

"Yes," Cal agreed.

A moment passed. "Is your head feeling better?"

With all that had happened, Cal had nearly forgotten about the dizziness that had plagued him after his fall from the tree. He moved his head side to side and took stock. "I think so. Still a bit woozy if I move too fast, but yeah, I think it's getting better. Good enough to get out there if my leg will hold me."

Sabine ripped the tail end of the final bandage down the middle and tied it in a knot around his calf, inspecting her handiwork with approval. "We will replace the oils every two hours until you leave." The look she gave him was direct, devoid of hesitation. "When you are ready, we will return your uniform."

Cal glanced over to the couch, where Buck had fallen asleep. Memories of the months they'd spent in training flooded into his mind and it struck him in a fresh way that he was on French soil, that Operation Overlord was underway, and that there was still a war to wage to break Hitler's hold on Europe.

Military pride and a deep sense of duty inflamed Cal's imagination once more and heightened his drive to join in the fight. Looking around at the haggard townsfolk who had already endured so much-at Sabine and Lise and dozens of others still confined to the castle-he felt a warrior's spirit surge in him again.

"We'll head out after midnight," he told Sabine.

Chapter 13

I shall review the things we know, from most certain to most obscure," Darlene declared.

We'd just left I-55 and were traveling west on I-44, over halfway to Kinley, Missouri. The car's tires clunked over the seams in the pavement in rhythmic monotony. Convincing Joe to let me go, it turned out, had been the easiest part of the negotiations. Darlene's medical team had been outright hostile to the idea. They'd reluctantly relented only after we'd had a lengthy sit-down together. I'd promised to break the nine-hour trip into two days, to be on the lookout for any signs of medical crisis, and to get immediate help if and when they manifested. And Darlene had vowed that she'd tell me the moment she felt unwell. Her oncologist had finally let us go with a smiling but terse, "Have fun, but not stupid fun."

As for Justin, Darlene's son, she'd opted to leave him completely in the dark. "He'll have a conniption if he gets wind of our little excursion. His ignorance is our bliss. We'll tell him when the trip is over."

We hit the road in my car—as Darlene's Melba had over two hundred thousand miles on her—armed with little more than a handful of yellowed letters and an intrepid spirit. There hadn't been much margin in my life to do in-depth research before we set off, as I'd wanted to devote as much of my time to the *Sentinel* as I could before leaving, but I'd done what I could in my after-work hours, relieved that my stamina finally seemed to be coming back. Though my expectations were somewhat tempered by the scant information we brought to our search, my travel companion's were not. Everything about her appeared to have revived in anticipation of the adventure. Her voice was stronger. Even her coloring had improved.

She held my phone in her hand and summarized the Wikipedia page I'd pulled up during our last pit stop. "Kinley, Missouri. Population just under five hundred. Farming community. Nearest hospital is in Bolivar, about thirty miles away. The boonies, in other words."

I tried to concentrate on the details she was reading and failed. For three days, I'd attempted to put my encounter with Nate out of my mind so I could fully enter into the excitement of this trip with Darlene. For three days, I'd told myself that I'd made the right move by asking him to leave, that I'd shown strength and resolve more than anger and contempt. For three days, I'd tried to shake off a gnawing bitterness that had grown more acidic with each recollection of Julie's name. I hadn't succeeded. All the positive self-talk I could muster hadn't eased an intensified sense of lessness and loss.

"It's buzzing again," Darlene said, snapping me out of my morbid reverie, holding the phone out so I could see Nate's name on the caller ID. "Are we going to answer it this time or see if he leaves a message?"

"Message." She didn't know that there had been a dozen other attempted calls since our encounter in the loft. Just hang-ups—no voicemails.

Darlene sat in silence for a while and I wondered what she was choosing not to say. Then she glanced at the screen. "Hey, it looks like he got a clue and left something this time." She held the phone up for me to see. "Tell me how to get to it and I'll play it for you."

"I don't need to listen to it now," I said.

She heard the petulance in my voice and didn't reply.

"I can see you pursing your lips, Darlene. And I've known you long enough to know what it means."

She hesitated a moment. "It's just that if there's something urgent . . . an accident or your house burning down. You'd want to know, right?"

"You pick the oddest moments to turn into a pessimist."

I tried to tell her how to find the voicemails on my phone, but the device seemed incapable of recognizing her touch. "Maybe I'm already a ghost and I just don't know it," she mumbled.

I pulled over, tapped the phone a couple times, and put it to my ear, not realizing that the Bluetooth connection was activated. Nate's voice came over the car's speakers. "It's me." I reached for the controls on the stereo, but Darlene swatted my hand away. "Been trying to get a hold of you . . . guess you know that. I didn't want to text, but I can if that's what you'd prefer. Ceelie—" I froze. My name on his lips felt like an intimate thing. "I'd like for us to talk. To explain what happened—and what *didn't happen*." He sighed. "I know you don't owe me anything, but will you give me a few minutes? Please." There was a long pause, long enough for me to think that was the end of his message. Then he added, "I know I'm in no position to ask for you to talk to me again. But if you've got it in you, hit me back?"

The car's engine idled as we sat by the side of the road. I tried to will my heart to stop racing and my hands to stop shaking. After a couple minutes passed, Darlene said, "Well, he's got a lovely voice. I'll give him that."

I knew she was just trying to fill the silence, but the statement rankled me. "But a pretty dismal marital record."

Darlene reached over to pat my arm. "No one's denying that, dear."

I put the car in drive and pulled back onto the road. The tone of Nate's voice had gotten to me. I'd grown used to Defensive Nate, Standoffish Nate, and plain old Cold Nate in the months since he'd walked out, but he'd sounded sincere on the phone and I hadn't braced myself for Vulnerable Nate. I recognized the hint of a softening in my spirit and rebelled against it, squaring my shoulders and squinting at the empty road ahead.

"What do you think he wanted?" Darlene asked. She'd taken the phone back from me and was furiously swiping and tapping on the screen. "And how do you get back to that Wiki page on this darn thing?"

Nate's voice came through the car's speakers again. "Hello?"

I panicked. A quick glance at Darlene confirmed that she was panicking too. "What did you do?" I mouthed at her, ignoring another "Hello?" from Nate.

"I must have pushed the wrong button trying to get back to Wikipedia," she answered in a frantic whisper, loud enough, no doubt, for Nate to hear.

"Ceelie, are you there?"

I took a calming breath. "Tell him I'm driving."

Darlene did as instructed.

"You realize I can hear you, right?" Nate's voice filled the car.

"Tell him I can't talk right now."

Darlene conveyed the message.

"I've done something you need to know about, Cee," Nate said quickly, as if he wanted to get it in before he was disconnected.

From my peripheral vision, I could see Darlene staring from the phone to me as if she'd been complicit in a crime. "Do I hang up?" she whispered.

"Please don't hang up." Nate's voice was rough.

I pulled over again and took the phone from my friend, switching off its Bluetooth. Darlene motioned toward her door, eyebrows raised. I shook my head. This would be brief. No need for her to step out of the car.

"Can this wait?" I asked Nate. The hardness in my voice felt satisfying.

"I actually have you on the phone, so no, I'd rather say this now, before you go silent again. I don't blame you for avoiding my calls—I don't—but can you just give me a few seconds?"

I closed my eyes and fought the impulse to hang up. But I knew Nate. He would only call again. And again.

"Make it quick. We're somewhere in Missouri and running out of daylight."

"What are you—?" He brought himself up short. "Doesn't matter. Here's why I'm calling."

Darlene adjusted her position. She feigned discomfort, but I knew it was a pretext for leaning close enough to hear Nate better. I pressed the phone to my ear and let my head fall back against the headrest.

"I fired Bruce," Nate said.

"My condolences."

"And before I did that, I put the divorce proceedings on hold."

"You did what?"

"I hit pause. I hit it pretty firmly."

"Why in blue blazes would he—?" Darlene began in full voice from the passenger seat. I put out a hand to let her know to stay out of this conversation.

There was the trace of a smile in Nate's voice. "Darlene, could I ask a favor of you?"

The tone. The humor. Persuasive Nate. Charming Nate. The man I used to know.

Darlene suddenly blanched. "Hang up, Ceelie," she said with authority, waving a finger for me to do as instructed.

I felt myself frown. "What do—?"

"Hang up," she said again.

I was so taken aback by the order that I froze, torn between obedience and utter confusion. Seeing my inability to respond, Darlene took the phone from my hand and poked at its screen until, in exasperation, she dropped it into the glove compartment. She snapped it shut with more force than necessary as my surprise gave way to consternation. "Darlene! What the—what on earth?" I stammered.

"I recognized that tone of his," she said. "All buttery and syrupy and come-hithery. Dangerous—that's what it was. And if you'd seen your face getting soft and mushy. Honey, mark my words. I saved you from yourself."

"I was not getting 'soft and mushy.'" I tried to inject confidence into the words, but they came out sounding defensive.

We sat by the side of the road a moment longer, engine idling. The sun had arced toward the horizon, tinting the greenery around us with a warm, amber glow. Darlene stared at me, not a hint of remorse on her face, and all I could hear were Nate's last words. *I put the divorce proceedings on hold.* They filled my mind with a tangle of anger, frustration, and morbid curiosity.

"He's pausing the divorce," I said softly, more to myself than to anyone else.

"Yes. But you can't go falling all over yourself running back into his arms based on that statement alone."

I couldn't help but picture Julie smiling up at us as we'd left Nate's office for lunch that day. "I'm not running back into his arms, Darlene. Nate Donovan is dead to me."

I was surprised by the sharpness of my words, but I'd felt the flutter of something hopeful as Nate spoke. Something disloyal to my pain. Prone to weakness. I would not be softened by a traitor's change of heart.

I wasn't sure in that moment who I loathed more—Nate or the version of me that had trusted him so blindly.

"Here's a new motto for you," Darlene said. "Repairing something well requires more time than it ever took to break it. Repeat."

I shook my head, my thoughts too muddled to parrot what she'd said.

"However long it took for your marriage to break, you've got to give it at least that much time to Humpty Dumpty itself back together again," Darlene said. "Anything less would be foolish."

"I'm not going to be repairing anything." I liked the clarity of the statement, but it left me feeling oddly bereft.

"Then it was the right thing to hang up when you did."

I shook my head at the memory. "Correction," I said. "*You* hung up when *you* did."

"You think it surprised him?" she asked with a giggle.

I blew out a breath. "Oh, I'm confident it did."

"I did like his voice," Darlene mused after a few moments of silence.

"Now who's going soft and mushy?"

"I'm not. Voices can be deceptive. I'm just saying that he *sounded* sweet."

"He had a—" I stopped myself. Saying anything remotely positive about him felt like betraying myself. "He had a sweet side," I finally admitted. "The Nate I used to know—he was sweet and kind."

"Well, honey, at least now you know what he's been wanting to talk about. And now you have some time to get your thoughts together before you chat again. That sappy look on your face scared the heck out of me."

"It wasn't sappy."

"It was sappy-adjacent."

"I'm not going back to him, Darlene," I said softly, putting the car in gear and pulling onto the road again.

"Are you mad at me?" Darlene asked after we'd driven in silence for a few minutes.

"Everything's fine." I glanced at her. She was staring at me squinty-eyed. "Could you get my phone back out of the glove compartment? We're getting closer and I need the GPS."

She did as instructed. I took the phone from her and brought up the navigation app.

"Truly good men are as rare as rocking horse poo," Darlene declared a little while later, reaching over to pat my leg.

I couldn't help but laugh. "You have a way with words, my friend. It's a bit on the dramatic side, but you sure get your point across."

Darlene shrugged. "Angus liked to call it my Zsa Zsa Gabor. I could make a hangnail into a national catastrophe."

"Do you miss him?"

"Every day." She leaned her head on the headrest and added, "But at nights I'm quite content to sleep in a snore-free zone."

As Darlene drifted into silence, I took inventory of the emotions still clanging around in my head. There had been something different in Nate's voice. Not the hardness of the day he told me he was leaving. Not the sullenness of our two encounters since then. Something honest and unnerving.

The pain of his rejection still echoed in the crater of his abrupt departure. I felt it swell in intensity as I replayed his statement in my mind. *I hit pause. I hit it pretty firmly.* The echo grew sharp edges as my mind bent toward hope.

I would not. I could not. The risk was too great, the hurt too crippling, the devastation still too raw.

Chapter 14

Sabine led Cal to the formal dining room on the other side of the foyer.

"I thought this could help," she said, motioning toward the far wall.

Cal's eyes widened with interest as he stepped toward the communications hub the Germans had set up in the wood-paneled space. There were two radio transceivers, a small switchboard, and a handful of other instruments Cal vaguely recognized.

"If you can fix them, maybe you can use them to contact your colleagues."

Cal would have smiled at her terminology if his mind had been on Sabine, but it was on the devices in front of him. Every piece had been rendered useless. Cables severed. Registers and keys shattered.

"They must have sabotaged their own equipment before they left," he muttered, his hopes of communicating with American forces dashed.

"No." She paused, something guilty in her expression. "We came in here after the Germans left and it was all *intacte*, but Albert said . . ." Her voice trailed off.

"What did Albert say?"

"He said he would need to destroy it all so they can't use it against the Allies if they come back. But maybe you can fix it?"

Cal leaned in to see if there was any chance of repairing the gear. With insufficient time, no spare parts, and few adequate tools, there was no way he could rebuild the damaged comms before his planned departure. He sighed, shaking his head. "Well, he did a good job, I'll give him that. A little premature, but effective."

As they went back to the living room, Cal noticed that he was walking a bit more easily, a testament to Sabine's nursing skills.

Buck was still asleep on the couch when they reentered the living room, a crumpled, unkempt version of the ruthless soldier he thought himself to be.

"It is nearly dark now," Sabine said to Cal, motioning toward the transom above the window facing the backyard, where daylight had taken on sunset hues. She accompanied him to the alcove and they stood there, holding back a curtain to watch for any movement in the fields beyond the castle. Under other circumstances, the lush green pastures extending north toward the Channel would have captivated Cal with their peaceful beauty, but to his fighter's mind, they were a minefield of potential traps and dangers.

"*Tu pars?*" Lise asked from right beside him, something that looked like worry on her face. "Are you leaving?" she tried in English.

Cal nodded and lightly flicked her nose. "In a little while. Got to go get the Germans, right?"

She shook her head. "You need to stay with us."

Sabine bent down and, Cal assumed for his sake, spoke in English to her sister. "We will be fine," she said, a smile softening her features. "Cal will fight the Germans and liberate our country and you, me, and Albert, we will be fine."

"But if Papa doesn't come back . . ."

Sabine frowned. She glanced at Cal, then traced down Lise's cheek with her fingertip. "If Papa doesn't come back, we will find a way. Cal has to be a soldier now. It is who he is."

He lowered himself onto an upholstered bench next to the window. "Tell me what you're going to do when the Germans are gone," he said to the little girl.

She looked up at her sister, as if asking for permission. Sabine shrugged and smiled. "I'm going to ride a carousel," Lise said with great enthusiasm, pronouncing the last word the French way. "Papa said he will take me."

Sabine squeezed Lise's shoulder. "We will make sure you see your carousel, with or without Papa."

As sadness descended over the girl's face, Cal said, "Maybe you can come to America and I'll take you to the State Fair. There's a merry-go-round there that'll knock your socks off."

The girl frowned and tilted her head sideways, then looked from Cal to Sabine. "*Mes chaussettes?*"

Her confusion made Sabine laugh. It was a light and warm sound. "She is wondering why you mentioned her socks in relation to a carousel," she said to

Cal. Then she switched to French to explain the expression to her sister. Turning back to Cal, she added, "Some things in English do not translate well."

"*Mais j'veux aller voir celui de Bayeux,*" Lise said.

"She wants to see the carousel in Bayeux. That's the one our father told us about."

"You can do both," Cal said. "Bayeux first and then the Missouri State Fair. How's that?"

Lise asked him a question in French, eyes wide and expectant, and Cal looked to Sabine for a translation.

"She wants to know if she can see the Liberty Statue too."

"The Statue of Liberty?"

She blushed a little at her mistake. "Yes–the Statue of Liberty."

Cal turned his attention to Lise. "If you come visit me when all of this is over, I'll take you to New York so you can see her for yourself."

"New York?" Lise asked, the freckles on her nose crinkling into an excited smile.

"You, me, and the Statue of Liberty. It's a date."

Sabine looked at Cal disapprovingly. "She will never forget, you know. She will dream about this every night and tell me about it every morning until it happens."

He held his hand out to Lise. "Shake on it?"

Lise placed her small, cool hand in his and shook hard. Her fragility and vivacious strength moved Cal in a way that surprised him. Something tender and vigilant welled up in him. It felt visceral and primal. And somehow more frightening than the battles ahead. Cal looked at Sabine. "There's something in my field jacket—the zippered pocket in the front, right by the throat. Could you find it?" When she hesitated, he added, "It's for Lise."

Sabine left the room without a word, and Lise plopped down on the couch next to Cal, earnestness on her face. "When you see a German, ask if his name is Otto. If he says yes, you do not shoot. Okay?" She leaned in a bit closer, looking Cal directly in the eyes. "Okay?"

"Lise . . ."

"Otto is my friend."

Cal wanted to reason with her. He wanted to convince her that the German was part of the machine that had destroyed her country and her life. But he realized that at her age, she'd have few memories of France before the Occupation. This child with the luminous brown eyes had only known oppression, and from its depths had summoned up compassion for one of its enforcers.

Cal blinked away unexpected tears. The confidence in Lise's gaze made him feel more like a man than he had when he'd jumped out of a careening plane into enemy territory.

"You're a brave girl," he said to her.

Her head bobbed in agreement. "*Ouaip!*" she agreed, beaming from the compliment.

"Ready to go get us some Nazis?" Buck said from right behind him. He was standing so close that Cal could smell the liquor on his breath.

"You'd best sober up before we head out."

Buck smiled sloppily, his eyes unfocused and his helmet askew. "Lesson number one for shooting while drunk," Buck said in the tone of a lecturing professor, "aim for the middle one." He let out a guffaw and stumbled back into Sabine as she reentered the room.

"Is this what you wanted?" she asked Cal. A silver coin lay in the palm of her hand.

"Who'd you steal that from?" Buck slurred.

"It belongs to Cal," she answered as she passed him, barely glancing in his direction.

Buck frowned and pointed at his friend. "Keep an eye on that one, pal. Wouldn't put it past any of these frogeaters to try and rob their rescuers."

He moved unsteadily to the couch and collapsed onto it, falling nearly instantly into a deep, liquor-fueled sleep.

"Your friend is a *crétin*," Sabine said lightly, eliciting a giggle from Lise.

Cal smirked and said, "Listen, I don't speak French, but I'm inclined to agree."

He took the coin from Sabine and held it up for Lise to see. "This is a silver half-dollar." When she looked confused, he added, "Money from America."

Sabine translated for her sister and she nodded in understanding.

"It was made in 1916, about a year before my pops came to France with the Corps of Engineers."

Sabine stopped mid-translation. "I'm sorry, the Corps of . . . ?"

Cal tried for simple words. "The part of the army that helps to repair bridges and roads and builds hospitals and . . . lots of things. Pops was sent to France to do that, and before he left, my mother sewed

this into the hem of his uniform." Cal turned the
coin over for Lise to see its design. "Can you tell who
this is?"

Lise leaned in, scrunching up her nose in
concentration. Then her eyes widened. "*La Statue de la
Liberté*?"

Cal smiled at the awe on her face. "This coin is
called Walking Liberty. My father brought it back from
the war, and can you guess why my mom gave it to me
too before I left?"

Lise thought again, but it was Sabine who answered.
"Because liberty can't be stopped," she said. Her eyes
flickered up to Cal, then back to her sister. "Because
when liberty starts walking, she will reach her
destination. Lise"—she waited for her sister to look up
at her—"this coin is hope. It tells us that Cal and—"
She hesitated, glancing at the couch. "Cal and Buck
and their friends will win."

"I want you to have this coin," Cal said to the
child. He smiled as her face lit up with excitement.

"For me?"

"Absolutely. Because things might still be hard for
a bit, but liberty will win." He held Walking Liberty
out to the girl, but Sabine took it from him.

When Lise protested, she said, "Just for now, Lise."
She wrapped the coin in a handkerchief and dropped
it into the pocket of her apron. "Tomorrow or the day
after, when this is all over, I will give it back to you.
But for now, I don't want you to show your American
present to anyone."

"But I'll get it back?" Lise asked, frowning.

"You'll get it back."

Cal looked from Lise to Sabine. "Your father would be proud of his daughters."

Sabine pulled Lise close and her little sister wrapped her arms around her waist. "We miss him now," Sabine said simply. "But we will miss him much more when the war is over, if life must go back to normal without him."

Cal was about to say something about hope and resilience when he saw Sabine's face go white. Her eyes were fixed on a spot in the field beyond the castle's perimeter, where a stone wall intersected a pasture. Her body tensed as she leaned forward, her hands on the windowsill, to squint into the darkening night.

Cal followed her gaze and felt his lungs freeze. Three soldiers, crouching low, were stealing toward the castle.

Unaware of the danger, Lise leaned in close to the window and seemed to recognize something familiar among the silhouettes outlined against the still-reddened sky.

Her face lit up. "Otto!" she yelled.

Chapter 15

A little over an hour later, we turned North off I-44 toward Kinley, Missouri. Wide-spaced farm houses stood well off the main road into town, the distance between them decreasing as we drew closer to the diminutive hub of the farming community.

Main Street was a two-lane road with twentieth-century commercial buildings on both sides, their brick facades and flat roofs the epitome of small-town America. The occasional misfit structure interrupted the lineup of storefronts, some of which were boarded up. There was a barbershop, a Dollar General, a tavern, and just past the old mercantile, a wooden chapel that had seen better days.

Judging by the cars parked along the town's only street, it was safe to assume that at four p.m. in Kinley, the tavern was the place to be.

"Two Yankee women walked into a bar in the far reaches of the Ozarks . . . ," Darlene muttered under her breath as we approached the front door, making me laugh despite some nervousness.

A dozen pairs of eyes shifted from the Nuggets game on TV as we entered. We paused long enough for our eyes to adjust to the darkness. Pulled shades covered tinted windows, and muted lighting only barely illuminated the tavern's low ceiling and checkered, linoleum floor. There was one elderly man at the bar, stooped over a beer, his eyes unfocused and his expression vacant. Several other men sat at tables facing a large TV whose cables were duct-taped to the wall.

Some of the patrons turned back to the game when I stepped up to the bartender, Darlene in tow, but others continued to openly stare. I heard a drawn-out, "Look what them cats dragged in" from somewhere in the back corner, while an ESPN announcer detailed the fast break that had resulted in an impressive dunk.

"Help ya?" the bartender asked. Not, "What can I serve you?" I guess we didn't look like the happy-hour type.

"I'm hoping you can." I fished around in my purse for the brown folder that held Cal's letters. "I'm a journalist with the *Sentinel* in Saint Charles, Illinois," I began.

The same voice from the dark corner of the tavern yelled, "Fake news!" loudly enough to startle me.

The bartender cracked a bucktoothed smile. "Welcome to Kinley, population five hundred, social skills zero."

I squinted in the direction the voice had come from and heard a snort and a couple chuckles as a glass or two were raised in my direction. I reminded myself that I'd wanted an adventure that would take me outside my comfort zone. Kinley appeared to be mission accomplished.

Turning back to the bartender, I tried for a more friendly approach and held out my hand. "My name is Cecelia, and this is my friend, Darlene."

"So nice to meet you," Darlene said brightly, reaching across the bar to shake his hand.

He wiped his palm on his faded jeans and shook. "Devon."

"Can I ask you a couple questions, Devon?"

"Won't even charge you for my answers."

"I'm doing a story on some letters that belonged to an American GI. They date back to the Second World War, and these two," I said, opening the manila folder to reveal the letters, "were sent from Kinley. I'd love to find out if there are any relatives who still live here and might want to see them."

"What's the name on 'em?" Devon asked.

Things had gone quiet around the tavern and I sensed all eyes on me again. I cleared my throat. "Callum," I said. "Callum McElway. The letters I have"—I picked one up and showed Devon the return address—"are from his mother, Lucy McElway. The address is Mud Creek Road, but I can't find it on any maps, so . . ."

I sensed movement to my right, caught a hint of beer breath, and turned to find a man craning his neck to see the letters. He was tall and gangly, and his gray hair lay flat on one side of his head. Pulling a pair of readers from the pocket of his denim shirt, he leaned in, his dentures clicking in his mouth. When he'd gotten a good look at the envelope, he held out a hand. "Jesse. Town historian."

Someone in the back corner guffawed and crowed, "Self-proclaimed and proud of it."

Jesse's eyes were on me. "Callum, you said?"

Something bright zinged along my veins. "Yes. Callum McElway."

Darlene leaned in close and whispered in my ear. "Warning, Will Rogers—this boy might be a half-bubble shy of plumb."

Jesse said, "Went by Cal, if I recall. Bit of a local hero to my pop's generation." The hairs on my arms rose. But my expectations sank again when he shrugged a shoulder and said, "Haven't heard that name since I was a kid." He looked over his shoulder. "What would it be—sixty, seventy years?" A couple of men grunted their agreement from the shadows. "The old McElway homestead is out past Foggy Acres. Not lookin' very good, but standing."

"On Mud Creek Road?"

"I'm guessin' that's just what the family called their laneway," the bartender said. "Not someplace you'd find on your fancy phone maps."

Darlene stepped closer to the man named Jesse. "Does anyone still live there?" I heard the hope in her voice.

"Nope. Not since I can remember. Ain't nothin' there now but the fallin' down house and an overgrown yard. Last I saw it, the barn roof'd caved in too. Neighbors might be able to tell you more, though. Look for the yellow house 'cross the creek from the McElway place."

Darlene looked at me and I nodded agreement to her unspoken question, shoving the letters back into the envelope. "The homestead," I said to the bartender. "How far out of town is it?"

"Just a click or two as the crow flies. But I wouldn't go out there this time a day 'less I had a good reason and some snake repellent."

Darlene leaned in and turned up the wattage on her smile. "Devon, my friend."

"I'll draw you a map," he said.

The bartender's drawing and instructions were landmark-based and detailed. "Turn left past the shelter with the blue rain barrels. Then right again after you pass the Cooper house with the rusted-out windmill at the end of the lane."

And there it was. With daylight fading, the house seemed absorbed into the hills and fields behind it, a revenant barely visible from the end of the driveway.

"You think this is it?" Darlene asked softly. I couldn't tell whether the grit in her voice was fatigue or emotions.

"Sure looks old enough to have been standing seventy-some years ago."

We bumped over the potholed, unpaved laneway that led down what I assumed was Mud Creek Road to the front of Lucy's home and stopped a fair distance from the house, a fallen tree preventing us from driving any farther. The barn—what remained of it—stood just to the left of the house, a little farther back, its roof caved in. One broad door hung sideways on broken hinges, and I could see the grille of a tractor just inside.

When we got out of the car, Darlene stood motionless for a while, her eyes on the home her father had likely lived in. I wondered about the thoughts running through her mind and should have known that my friend would speak them without my prompting.

"What are the odds that he's still living in there? A kindhearted recluse with a lapful of cats, maybe. Or an ornery old geezer with Jack Daniels in one hand and a rifle in the other?"

I came around the car to stand by her, taking in the modest, two-story structure. Though the siding might have been a shade of white once, there was little left to show for it. Just the remnants of peeled and mildewed paint. Many of the windows were broken, some of them boarded over, and a tattered curtain rested across an upstairs sill.

"Looks pretty deserted to me," I said, an eerie feeling trickling up my spine.

"I'm trying to picture it like it would have looked back then."

I let the silence stretch as Darlene slowly scanned the space from the house to the barn.

"I bet there was a garden out there." She pointed toward an over-grown patch where something that looked like the handle of a well's pump rose above the weeds. "They'd have used that to water their vegetables, right? Green beans, carrots, pumpkins in the fall . . ." Her voice trailed off. "Can you picture a little boy playing in the yard right off the front steps? Lucy hanging the laundry over there."

"Yep," I said softly. "I can picture all that."

She nodded. Then she shook her head. "Or maybe it was some-thing entirely different. A derelict family on a derelict farm."

"The letters, though," I hinted.

Darlene looked at me. "Lucy loved him." It was a statement of fact. "I just can't picture in my mind how he went from being loved that way by his mother to—" She didn't finish her sentence, but I knew what she meant. Callum's abandonment of his only child seemed an offense to the idyllic scene she was envisioning.

"Let's get a bit closer," I said. I picked up a stick with one hand and held an elbow out for Darlene to grasp.

"What's with the twig?" she asked.

"Snake repellent."

She laughed at that. "City girl."

I walked carefully through the tall weeds between the car and the front door, swinging the stick like a divining rod and keeping Darlene close. When we got to the house, I put some weight on the bottom step leading up to the front door to test its solidity.

"Follow my lead," I said with a bit of trepidation, unwilling to see my friend get injured but fully aware that she would not be kept out of her father's home. "Step where I step and if I fall through, stop moving." I tried to infuse some laughter into the words, but there was something foreboding about the old McElway homestead and it was affecting my nerves.

"Copy that," Darlene said, adrenaline livening her words.

I walked up the steps, testing each one, and she followed close behind, hugging the railing to avoid putting weight in the middle of each plank. A chair, its wicker seat long scavenged by animals, sat forlornly in a corner of the porch, and a smattering of weeds grew through the gaping spaces between rotted floorboards. I tried to gauge the distance between support beams and walked on those, conscious of Darlene, whose hands on my waist told me she was following instructions.

By the look of the cobwebs spanning the doorframe, I assumed no one had entered the house in a while. The tattered screen door creaked as I pulled it open. The front door beyond it was locked, so I put my hand through its broken windowpane and found the deadbolt.

When we stepped inside, a feeling of time standing still washed over me. It wasn't completely dark yet, but I still pulled out my iPhone and turned on its flashlight.

"Look over there," Darlene whispered behind me.

I followed her pointing finger. To our left was a living room. A green corduroy sofa and a delicate, floral upholstered chair stood against two walls. Stuffing protruded from holes in the couch's cushions, wounds I presumed had been inflicted by nesting rodents. The faded print of a sunset over water hung askew above a long radio cabinet that doubled as a sideboard. Just a few odds and ends were scattered around the room—a candle bent sideways from the heat of past summers, a newspaper holder, a curio cabinet—vestiges of the life that had once been the beating heart of the McElway home.

"What's with you fancy folks and trespassing?"

The sharp voice barked at us from just outside the front door, making my heart skip a beat before it began to race. I thought Darlene might have torn a muscle twisting toward the sound like a thief caught red-handed. A middle-aged woman in rubber boots and a coat pulled on over green-striped pajamas stood just outside the door. The flashlight she held in one hand was trained on us, but it was the old pistol in her other hand that brought me up short.

"I'm so sorry," I said hurriedly. "We were told this was the McElway home and we were . . ." The details seemed too lengthy to explain. "I'm so sorry," I said again. She was pointing the pistol at the ground, and I didn't want to give her any reason to raise it.

I looked over to see Darlene squinting toward the doorway with a hand over her heart. Ever the peacemaker, she attempted a smile, but it was more strained than she probably realized. "You nearly gave me a heart attack sneaking up on us like that!" she said.

"Darlene." She clearly hadn't seen the gun.

"I've called the police," the woman said gruffly, her voice like muddy gravel. "It ain't right for people to go snooping around somebody else's property." She raised the pistol to waist level, trained in our general direction. That got Darlene's attention.

Her hands shot up like she was trapped in an old western. "I'm his daughter," she blustered, her smile slipping. "I'm Cal McElway's daughter." She cleared her throat and added more persuasively. "We're not trespassing, we're . . . we're visiting."

"Say that again?" the woman said, the grit in her voice ominous.

"We think my friend's father grew up in this house." I tried to sound calm and reassuring. "We were hoping—"

She cut me off. "You don't say."

"We went by the Kinley Tavern and—what was his name?" Darlene looked at me.

"Jesse."

"Yes, Jesse. He told us this is where my father's family lived before I was born."

The pajama-clad woman lowered her pistol as a delighted smile spread across her face. Then, in a voice that sounded an octave higher and a decade younger than it had moments before, she said, "You don't say."

I stepped toward her. "Do you know anything about Cal?"

"I do," she answered, smiling at Darlene. "But it's gettin' awful dark out here. Why don't we hop over the crick to my place and chat about your daddy over a cup of tea?"

Chapter 16

"Get down!" Cal barked, grabbing Sabine and Lise's arms and pulling them into a crouch. Aubry-en-Douve's residents appeared to shrink into themselves, fear and defeat on their faces.

An elderly woman began to walk in circles, her hands on her head, looking upward and wailing in a broken voice. When two of the younger women tried to calm her, she started to scream, a shrill flurry of words Cal couldn't understand. Other villagers spoke up, pleading with her to be quiet.

"*Arrêtez!*" Sabine yelled, taking a couple steps forward. The people crowded into the living room's far corner instantly fell silent. The fourteen-year-old spoke in rapid-fire, terse syllables, her voice low. Cal could see the fear in her eyes, but her expression was intense and persuasive.

"*Tous d'accord?*" she finally asked. Cal had learned in his few hours in the castle that *d'accord* was an expression of agreement. The woman who had been wailing moments before said something combative and a couple of the villagers spoke up to silence her.

"*Tous d'accord?*" Sabine asked again, more firmly this time. There were nods and murmurs, some of them hesitant, from the people of Aubry-en-Douve.

Sabine blew out a breath and seemed to brace herself before turning to Cal. "Otto is with them," she said. "If I speak to him, I might be able to . . ."

But Cal wasn't listening. "Get the women and children somewhere safe," he interjected before she'd finished her sentence. Then he turned to the couch, where Buck lay in an inebriated stupor. He picked up his friend's Garand.

Sabine translated, but some of the villagers had already started to move. Women and men pushed children toward the kitchen, uttering words that sounded brave, but the glances they exchanged reflected the gravity of the circumstances.

Several of the townsmen, Albert among them, stood to the side of the windows with their backs against the wall. Cal motioned for them to scan the fields from their vantage point. "Tell me how many there are. Yes?" he said, interpreting his words with his hands. One of the men nodded and translated for the others.

Lise pulled away from Sabine as her sister propelled her out of the room. "*Ils vont tirer sur Otto?*" she asked.

All Cal recognized in the French was "Otto." Sabine responded in English. "They are not going to shoot Otto," she said firmly, eyes on Cal.

Lise was unconvinced. Taking a step toward the men guarding the windows, she launched into a barrage of French, the anguish on her face deepening as her voice got louder.

Sabine put a hand over her sister's mouth and said something that made her go silent. Lise's eyes were wide and teary as she looked up at Sabine. "*Tu promets?*" she asked.

Sabine nodded. "I promise you, Lise. I will do what I can to keep Otto safe." Then Sabine grabbed one of the women leaving the room and motioned for her to take Lise to safety.

"*Non!*" Lise screamed, pulling her arm away. Sabine tried to pacify her again, but Lise would not go without her sister. Sabine finally picked her up and carried her from the room.

Cal moved to the wall by the alcove that gave onto the backyard. He glanced at Albert, who shook his head. The Germans hadn't come any closer. They were biding their time, probably scanning the area for any sign that the liberating forces had arrived before them.

Cal was vaguely aware of movement and turned to find a dozen women reentering the living room, Sabine in the lead. "There are too many of us," she said, a tremor in her voice. "The children are safe, but . . . we will wait together." Her hands were clasped in front of her, and Cal wondered if it was to control their shaking.

"The kids?"

"In the cellar," Sabine said. "As many as could fit. The rest are in Aunt Sophie's quarters. The older ones will watch the younger."

Cal nodded, the responsibility for so many lives a nearly physical ache. He checked the magazine on Buck's Garand. "I need my rifle," he said to Sabine. When she frowned, he added, "There are at least three of them. We need all the firepower we can find."

"No." Sabine's statement was sharp and unequivocal. The townspeople gathered against the rear wall of the living room looked on with heightened emotions.

The teenager squared her shoulders and stared Cal in the face, speaking fiercely. "We cannot shoot." She looked at the villagers huddled behind her. "There are too many innocents here."

"What do-?"

She didn't let him finish. "We must let the Germans come in," she said, nodding as if she was coming up with the plan as she spoke. "Otto will not harm us. I know he will not! Let them come in and see who we are. Let them take what they want and leave again. There is no need for shooting."

She'd uttered the last sentence with so much conviction that Cal actually paused long enough to consider it. But it was a ludicrous idea at best. And at worst, suicidal.

"Sabine . . ."

"I know Otto," she repeated.

"This is not the Occupation," Cal said, each syllable clipped. "This is war. Who you know doesn't matter anymore."

She raised her chin and faced off with him. "What we begin with fire will end with fire."

Cal was stunned. "If we let them through those doors," he said, pointing toward the entryway. "If we let them walk in without resistance, there's no telling what they'll do!"

"Otto is not a threat," she insisted.

"The gun he's carrying tells me otherwise." When Sabine hesitated, Cal said again, "I need my weapon.

Buck and I need to be armed to defend you and your people."

"It would put every person in this castle in danger," she answered with so much sureness that Cal felt anger quickening his pulse.

"They're in greater danger if we're defenseless!"

She looked at the men standing near the windows, only Albert holding a single-shot rifle. "We will do what we must. Only if we must."

Cal took a step toward her, but she was already on the move, her eyes on Buck, whose liquor-fueled sleep hadn't been interrupted by the commotion around him. She began to shake him by the shoulder. "Wake up!"

"What are you doing?" Cal asked, torn between incredulity at Sabine's naivety and confusion at her focus on Buck.

"Wake up!" she said more forcefully when Buck merely groaned and shrugged off her hand. There was urgency in her voice now. Something more frantic than Cal had heard before. She pulled his legs off the couch and yanked him by the arm into a semi-sitting position.

"What the—" He warbled an expletive and squinted at Sabine. Then he reached out and grabbed her by the neck of her shirt, pulling her down so swiftly that she lost her footing and fell awkwardly across him. "If you touch me one more time," he sneered, his face mere inches from hers.

"Buck," Cal spat. When his friend didn't respond, he strode across the room and grabbed him by the hair, exerting enough force for Buck to let go of Sabine and look up at Cal, enraged and confused. What he saw on Cal's face brought him up short. A glance around the room seemed to sober him up in an instant. "How close are they?" he asked, reaching for the weapon he'd kept at his side since the moment he'd arrived. "Where's my gun?" he demanded.

Sabine shook her head, determination on her face. "You cannot fight. You must leave the room," she said. "You are in uniform. If Otto-" She stopped and started again. "If the Germans see you, they will shoot before they ask questions. The women. The children . . . You cannot be seen." She pointed toward the door. "Go. Go hide upstairs."

"If you think-"

"Do as she says," Cal interrupted, surprising even himself. Everything in him was coiled for battle, the pain in his leg eclipsed by the urgency of the situation. He'd already run a dozen scenarios in his mind, every single one of them involving his and Buck's weapons. The thought of letting German soldiers enter the castle unchallenged still felt reckless. Possibly deadly. But something in Sabine's stance and conviction had gotten through to him, overriding his military training. The frightened teenage girl who should have been hiding in the cellar with the rest of the town's children was defying him-defying logic-with too much certainty to ignore. She knew Otto. He'd lived in the castle for months along with her family. And if she thought they could resolve this without harming civilians . . .

Cal leaned in close to Buck's face. "If we fight, we'll be risking every one of their lives."

"This is what we came for, pal!"

"You must be gone when they enter," Sabine said to

Buck, her chin jutting out, her eyes blazing. "You must go upstairs now."

"Hide away like a sissy while the Krauts are attacking?" Buck exclaimed, incredulity on his face.

Out of the corner of his eye, Cal saw Albert step away from the window he'd been guarding, his eyes on the GI defying Sabine's orders. There was a threat in his stance.

Cal hesitated only a beat, conscious that the Germans outside could make their move at any moment.

"Go!" Cal said, giving his friend a rough shove toward the door.

"Are you out of your bloody mind?"

Now that Cal had made his decision, he was in no mood to equivocate. He handed Buck his Garand and pointed out the door. "Go upstairs. Lay low. And if things down here get out of hand . . ." He jutted his chin toward the weapon.

There had been rebellion and disbelief on Buck's face. It suddenly turned into disdain. He spat at Cal's feet. "You're a coward!" he said. "We trained for this! We trained for this!" he repeated with venom. "To kill the stinkin' Nazis. Period. And you choose these peasants over-"

Cal grabbed Buck by the back of his neck and yanked him forward. "We will kill anyone who tries to lay a hand on these people," he snarled. "But we'll do everything we can to avoid a bloodbath first. Understood?"

Buck stared at Cal for a moment. "Why aren't you hiding too?" he finally asked, squinting at his friend through unfocused eyes.

"Because I'm in civilian clothes, and . . . these

people aren't soldiers. Someone needs to stay with them in case this gets out of hand."

"Let me!"

"You're drunk, Buck. And you're in uniform."

"*Ils sont dans le jardin*," Albert mumbled from the window, his expression tight. The villagers murmured and huddled closer, reaching for each other as danger drew nearer.

"They're in the garden," Sabine translated for Cal.

"Go!" he ordered Buck.

"If they come anywhere near me . . . ," his friend said through clenched teeth.

Cal looked over his shoulder at the terrified villagers. "If things take a turn, we'll be counting on you," he said. "Now get out of sight. And, Buck . . ." He paused, then repeated the words his friend had used before. "We trained for this."

The two men stared at each other for a moment, then Buck, still a bit unsteady, turned and stormed out of the room.

Cal was so focused on Buck that he was barely aware of Sabine marching to one of the windows that faced the fields. Before he could do anything to stop her, she threw it open.

"What are you—?" Cal reached her in two strides and pulled her out of sight against the wall.

But she wasn't listening. Before he could finish his sentence and without the slightest hesitation, she turned her head toward the window and yelled, "Otto, it's Sabine. There are only villagers here!" in a voice as clear and calm as he'd ever heard.

Every person in the room froze.

149

Chapter 17

S ee that porch light over there by the water tower?" Brenda asked
as we gingerly took the stairs down from the McElway porch.
"That's where we're headed."

The water tower was barely visible, silhouetted against the remains of an early-spring sunset. But the porch light shone boldly in
the deepening night.

"Why don't you drive your car around and I'll meet you there.
I've been jumping the crick for years, but I can tell by your foot-
wear that you're not the hopping type."

"I like her," Darlene said as we returned to the car.

"I'll like her better when my blood pressure goes back to normal," I muttered.

"Might need to get into my luggage for a clean pair of undies,"
Darlene agreed, smiling. "What are the odds of running into the
neighbors when the next house over is a quarter mile away?"

The sign above the front door read *Welcome to Foggy Acres.*
Brenda stood underneath it as we drove up to the farmhouse, and
Darlene said, "How the heck did she get here before us?"

We'd talked in the car for a minute before I started it, but it
didn't seem long enough for Brenda to have beat us to the front door.

"Get a lot of fog around here?" Darlene asked as we climbed the steps.

"Nope. Foggy's our last name."

"Really?"

"I told my husband he'd have to change it if I was going to marry him, but . . . fifty-one years, three kids, seven grandchildren, and two great-grandsons later, I guess I've gotten used to the darn thing. Tea or coffee?" she asked as she opened the front door for us. "And you might as well get your things out of the car now, if you're going to spend the night."

That took both of us by surprise. "Oh, we saw a Days Inn outside Bolivar and thought we'd head back there for the night," I said.

Brenda propped a fist on her hip. "Well, that would be mighty silly when I've got two empty bedrooms upstairs with clean sheets on the beds."

Darlene and I exchanged glances. Nobody knew where we were. These were perfect strangers. And although Brenda seemed friendly, we'd both lived in the city suburbs long enough to distrust an act of kindness.

"I'll throw in a homemade breakfast," Brenda said. "Tom makes a mean omelet." She smiled as if we couldn't possibly resist.

It was Darlene who finally said, "It'll sure beat the motel's prefab fare."

Tom seemed not in the least surprised to learn that two strangers would be spending the night. As soft and rumpled as the recliner he sat in, he greeted us with a handshake, then put his earphones on again and turned back to the TV hanging above the family room's mantel.

"He'll resurface in a couple hours," Brenda said. "The NFL draft's on and with those things on his ears, he might as well be in Las Vegas with Roger Goodell. Let's us ladies retire to the drawing room," she said with an affected posh accent.

Minutes later we were sipping herbal tea in an all-season sunroom off the kitchen. Darlene and I sat on a plastic-covered couch. She'd abstained from broaching the topic of Cal McElway until that point but clearly couldn't wait any longer.

"Did you know my father?" she blurted halfway through Brenda's description of recent weather and the impact it would have on crops.

"Darlene has some questions," I interjected wryly, hoping our host wouldn't be offended by her bluntness. I shouldn't have worried.

"I was waiting for you to bring it up. Didn't want to seem too forward. This isn't coincidence, you realize," she said, wiggling her finger at the two of us. "This is a divine appointment. I've had this gut feeling all my life that something surprising would come from the ruins of the McElway place." She leaned forward and smiled at Darlene. "Now, you tell me what you know and then I'll tell you what I know."

For the next few minutes, Darlene gave Brenda an overview of what had led us to Missouri, leaving out the contentious relationship she'd had with her dad's memory and her recent diagnosis.

"Wait," Brenda interrupted at one point. "You're telling me that Cal stayed with you and your mom for just a couple months after he came back before leaving again?"

"No explanation given. Just up and disappeared." Darlene shrugged, but the gesture was far from casual. "Just one of the many reasons I'm wanting to know more," she said.

Our host shook her head. "That doesn't jibe with what I know of Cal McElway . . ."

"Or with my late mother's recollection of the man," Darlene said. "I've been putting off hunting for him for nearly three years, but something told me now was the time." She glanced in my direction and I smiled my encouragement. "I need to know if by some miracle he's still alive. We haven't been able to uncover anything that tells us he died. No obituary. No death certificate. I was wondering—almost hoping—if someone here knows where he went, where he is now."

"I'm so sorry." Brenda seemed genuinely contrite. "I wish I could tell you that he's living in a retirement home down the road, getting three squares a day and telling war stories, but . . ." She raised her hands in a helpless gesture. "All I know about Cal is a few memories from childhood and the legend my mother built around the man."

I patted Darlene's knee and told Brenda, "Whatever you can tell us will be more than we already know."

"Well . . ." She frowned, then she smiled at Darlene. "I just don't know where to begin. I grew up hearing about him, so he's just always been a part of my life. When we were little, my brother and I used his old barn as a jungle gym. 'Callum McElway would not appreciate your trespassing,' Mother would yell at us from the other side of the creek. And sometimes at bedtime she'd spin tall tales about the hometown hero who'd gone off to join the army and stormed the beaches of Normandy. She's the one who wrote him when his poor momma died."

"Rhoda Bishop?" I felt a small thrill as our stories intersected.

Brenda was taken aback. "Well, yes. Yes, that was her name."

I hurried to the entryway, where I'd left my purse, and came back with the brown envelope. I'd found the letter Brenda's mother had sent to Claire for Cal when he was in England. Brenda covered her heart when she saw the handwriting. "Where did you find this?" Her voice was hushed with emotions.

"Your mom sent it to my mother's address in Geneva, Illinois," Darlene said, the glint of excitement in her eyes. "And then my mother sent it on to Cal. It was found with five other letters in some kind of mansion in France."

"This here is a piece of history," Brenda said. We waited in silence as she unfolded the yellowed piece of paper. "'We found her in her bed,'" she read. "'The Good Lord took her peacefully while she *slept, probably dreaming of her heroic boy.'"* Brenda blinked back tears and smiled at us. "Mother was always a bit of a poet."

Darlene leaned forward on the couch next to me, making the plastic squeak. "I'm thinking my father might have come back here after he left us."

"He sure did," Brenda said. Darlene took in a quick breath but let Brenda go on. "I would have been five or six at the time, but it was big news. Huge news. Watching over the farm after Mrs. McElway passed became sort of a family thing. I was too young to remember most of the details today, but I know my parents took in their livestock and harvested their crops. There was nobody else to do it.

"The way my mom told it, Cal came wandering back completely unannounced one day. August or September, I think. She saw light coming through the windows and went over to check on the house. Found him living there like it was the most natural thing in the world. Looked like he was going to put down roots too . . ."

I glanced at Darlene as Brenda paused in her retelling. There was something tight in my friend's expression. I tried to imagine what could be going through her mind. Cal hadn't just "wandered" back to his old life in Kinley, as Brenda had so casually put it. He'd walked out on a wife and a daughter in Illinois without explanation, leaving them to question his departure for the remainder of their lives.

"He got right back to it," Brenda continued. "Fixed up the place, got his cattle back from us. Dusk 'til dawn work getting the old place up to speed again, especially with that injured arm. Bob—that's my baby brother—and I would loiter over there when we could slip out from under Mother's radar. He had a dog. Can't remember its name. Huck, maybe. Some kind of shepherd mix that seemed to like our company. Besides, it just felt good to hang out with a war hero, right? We worshipped the ground he farmed on . . ."

"What was he like?" Darlene asked.

"Hard to remember much. We were kids and he was an adult, so . . . I guess he was kind. That's what strikes me when I think back. He never shooed us home or acted like we were a nuisance, which we likely were. Answered all the questions we had. Let us bottle-feed the calves. When Father broke his foot, Cal jumped in and helped us out. No questions asked. Fair return, right?"

I was trying to connect the man Brenda was describing with the "deadbeat dad" Darlene had resented all her life. "Did he stay?" I hesitated to ask, but the words had to be spoken, and I suspected Darlene would have trouble uttering them. "Did he . . . find a wife? Start a family?" I felt more than I saw Darlene flinch.

Brenda laughed. "Probably not for lack of options. An army vet returns home and holes up in his mom's old place. Quiet. Hardworking. Easy on the eyes. I'm guessing every girl in the county wondered if she could domesticate that man. But no. He wasn't around long enough to put down roots."

Darlene looked from Brenda to me and back again. "Wait—he didn't stay?"

"Heavens no! The way my mom told it, he was just getting the old farm back to rights when he disappeared again. The house looked like he'd been raptured. Food in the fridge. Paper by the chair. Just no Cal McElway to be found. That was—what—maybe November that same year. He couldn't have been home more than two or three months."

A grandfather clock ticked in the corner of the sunroom. None of us spoke for a moment.

"He just . . . left?" Darlene finally said.

"Poof!" Brenda confirmed. "Nobody really noticed until Veteran's Day. Armistice Day, back then. He was supposed to be honored for his service in the county parade. The mayor had to come out here himself to talk him into it—Cal wasn't much for public spectacle. But he never showed up."

"And no one went looking for him?"

"Oh, we sure did. Bunch of the townsfolk came out to help with the search. Figured he might have gotten hurt out in a field somewhere or had some kind of accident. Maybe come up against a bear—we used to have more of them back then. It just didn't make sense for him to disappear with a barn full of livestock and a dog tied to the front steps. Unless he'd harmed himself. That scenario didn't come to mind until I was a lot older, but . . . as withdrawn and solitary as he was, and with whatever he went through during the war . . ." She hesitated before going on. "I wondered if there was something self-inflicted that happened there."

"So it stayed a mystery?" I asked, just to be sure I was understanding Brenda's story.

"Never heard from him after he disappeared. We took in his animals—again—and tended the farm, just like we had after his momma died. For a while, we kept an eye out when we were riding in the fields and pastures, wondering if we'd find remains or something. I can remember going over to the house with Mother one day, maybe a week after he disappeared, to clean out the fridge. 'Don't want the kitchen stinking when Cal comes home,' she said. Or something along those lines."

"But he never did," Darlene said.

"He never did. I guess—" When she looked at me, I nodded for her to go on. "I guess that could explain why you didn't find an obituary. If he did pass away way back then, but a body was never found . . . and with no family around to miss him . . ."

Tension pulsed across the distance separating me from Darlene. She sat ramrod straight with white-knuckled hands clasped in her lap. Her eyes were laser-focused on Brenda, her lips pressed together.

Brenda continued, a bit of discomfort in her voice now. I could tell she wanted her news to be more positive. "After a couple years, it didn't make much sense to keep the old farmhouse in shape."

"It's been abandoned ever since?" Darlene asked, her voice a little hoarse.

"We treated it a bit like a shrine. Nobody wanted to tear it down. Nobody wanted to buy it. I think my father took ownership of the land after a while. Some kind of abandonment law. But we didn't want to touch the house. Just in case, you know? My mother believed Cal might still come back until the day she died. There was just something so . . . alive in the old place."

"I'd like to see it tomorrow," Darlene said. "In the daylight."

I patted her knee to let her know we would.

"Of course!" Brenda seemed energized by the suggestion. "The only people who've been in there since Tom and I took over Foggy Acres are looters in fancy cars looking for abandoned treasure. Can't tell you how often I've had to tramp over there and threaten them away."

"The revolver is a nice touch," I said.

Brenda laughed. "That old thing? It's a collector's item. Dates back to the Civil War or thereabouts. Couldn't fire a shot if I begged it to." Her smile faded as she looked at Darlene. "How about I show you to your rooms so you can rest a bit?"

It was obvious that the day had exhausted Darlene's dwindling supply of energy, so we finished our tea and thanked Brenda for taking us in.

Tom tore himself away from the draft long enough to carry our bags upstairs. "Maybe he'll put down some plywood over at the McElway place tomorrow," Brenda told us as we said good night. "Those floors have seen better days and I wouldn't want either of you to fall through. Breakfast at eight okay?"

I looked at Darlene. She merely nodded.

"That'll be fine," I told our hostess.

I followed Darlene into her room after Brenda had gone back downstairs. She perched on the edge of the quilt-covered bed and looked at me. The usual spark had gone out of her eyes. She seemed smaller. Reed thin. Weary.

I sat next to her.

"Not what we hoped to hear, right?"

She shook her head. "I'm not sure what I expected but . . . I guess it was something more than nothing."

"We know he came back here," I said, hoping that gleaning that much information from Brenda's memories would fill in one of the blanks. "We know he was kind to the kids next door. We know he had a dog—that means he had to be good people, right?" I smiled and hoped she'd mirror it.

Her attempt was half-hearted. "Hard to imagine that someone remembered so positively would be capable of leaving his wife and daughter for . . . what? Country life?" She shook her head. "You'd think if he could care for his livestock, he could care for a baby."

"It's hard to reconcile the two," I admitted, pressing her hand between both of mine. "But we tried, right? We packed our bags and hit the road and drove across state lines and got a few answers about the man."

"But we'll never know what became of him," Darlene said after a brief silence. "His old bones could be out in these fields somewhere or he could have gone off and started a life with someone else under a different name. We'll never know."

I couldn't think of anything to say, so we sat there for a while listening to an owl hooting in the distance.

"You need to get some sleep," I finally said, releasing her hand. "It's been a long day and I'm under strict orders to give you time to rest." I lifted her bag onto a chair and unzipped it. "I'll bring up a glass of water so you can take your pills. And I'm right next door if you need anything."

I left her sitting on the bed and went down to the kitchen for water.

Chapter 18

Sabine strode to the front door with surprising calm and confidence. Cal heard it open as he stepped toward the group of people crowding into the living room's corner. The men had come forward to stand in front of the women and were braced for a confrontation. Albert pressed his rifle into Cal's hands along with a few cartridges, a dire foreboding in his expression, indicating to Cal that he should take the lead if things got out of hand. Cal nodded and ducked to the back of the group, dropping the cartridges into his pocket and stashing the gun under the wide seat cushion of a banquette, where he could easily get to it if needed. Then he found a spot among the men in the front row.

Sabine's voice reached them from the entryway. She sounded more disapproving than terrified, and Cal had to remind himself that she was only fourteen.

"Otto," she called in English. "I know it's you. We are mostly women and children. Innocent people, not soldiers. Please—just take what you need and leave us unharmed."

In the silence that followed, all Cal could hear was the frightened breathing of the people around him—women and men alike shaken by the uncertainty of what the next moments would hold, their minds undoubtedly on the children hiding in the root cellar just a few feet away.

"Otto!" Sabine called again.

The voice that answered came from somewhere outside the northeast corner of the room.

"Do you have weapons?" It was a male voice—a young one. And it had a heavy German accent.

A tingle of pure terror coursed through Cal's body. Terror that he was virtually unarmed. That a young girl was managing the volatile situation. That the people crowded around him were easy prey for soldiers on the run after a stinging rebuke on land and in the sky.

"We are unarmed," Sabine said, an almost imperceptible tremor entering her voice.

"Stand back." The thick German accent added a threat to the words.

Silence buzzed inside the castle's walls for interminable moments. The sound of boots on the stone front steps finally broke it.

"Please, Otto . . ."

"*Zurück!*" a deeper voice than Otto's barked.

"Stand back!" Otto echoed in English, the only language he and Sabine had in common.

Sabine backed into the room, her hands out as if to prove she was no threat. "Go over there!" Otto ordered, the syllables hard and sharp. He jutted his chin toward the huddled villagers, his eyes alert and piercing as he trained his rifle on them.

Sabine moved closer to the group, but stopped and turned before she joined their ranks, a small, inconsequential bastion standing between her people and German guns.

There were three of Hitler's Wehrmacht in the room now. Otto stood facing Sabine, his gun directly aimed at Albert, as if the old man was the one he expected to fight back.

The other two walked the periphery of the room. One appeared to be about thirty and the other closer to Otto's age. But the look in their eyes was the same Cal had seen in Buck's-a potent brew of lust, courage, and recklessness. They checked the living room for threats, moving curtains aside and pointing the muzzles of their Mausers into the space behind furniture. Cal froze as they approached the banquette, but they didn't check under the cushion where he'd hidden Albert's rifle.

Otto scanned the terrified group of villagers. "You said there were children." His accent was thick. His tone unyielding.

"They're in the cellar," Sabine said, sounding conciliatory. When Otto's face darkened, she hastened to add. "We didn't know if . . . We wanted them to be safe."

"Go. Get them."

"You cannot hurt them." There was dread and pleading in Sabine's voice.

"Get the children!"

"Please, Otto. They have done nothing. They are innocent! Lise-you know Lise. She has done nothing to you or to your comrades."

A muscle in Otto's jaw clenched and his gaze narrowed dangerously. "Get everyone into this room. Now," he ordered, his voice low and ominous.

It was all Cal could do to remain still as Sabine took a step toward the young German. The other two had stopped searching and now stood on either side of him, their focus entirely on the men and women exhibiting both courage and terror.

"Promise," Sabine said. "Promise you won't hurt them, Otto."

He gave an almost imperceptible nod.

Sabine hesitated. Cal could see the turmoil on her face. He wanted to act . . . to do something, *anything*, to prevent the children from becoming part of the standoff. It took every ounce of self-control he possessed to stifle the impulse to take on the soldiers threatening the people of Aubry-en-Douve. But he knew that any wrong move would only escalate a situation that still stood the chance of being resolved without shots fired.

Sabine left the room, her steps now more shuffles than strides, as if her body were weighed down by the risk she was taking.

The eldest of the soldiers mumbled in Otto's direction, "*Unsere Funkanlage.*"

"*Esszimmer,*" Otto snapped. He nodded toward the dining room on the other side of the entryway, where Cal had seen the destroyed communications apparatus. He assumed that the soldiers, separated from their unit during the battle for the battery, had come back to use the radios to communicate with their command.

The oldest of the soldiers pushed through the

children reentering the room, Sabine in the lead, and disappeared from sight.

Lise took one look at Cal and rushed to him, squeezing between him and the man to his right. She pressed into his back, arms around his waist, as if he was her last hope, and a furious protectiveness came over him. The rest of the children ran to the adults they knew, who took them into their arms in a futile attempt to shield them. Following her sister, Sabine came to stand beside Cal.

"Get behind me," he whispered low enough that no one but her would hear the words.

"*Non*," she whispered back.

The German who had gone to check on the equipment stormed back into the room, unleashing an angry tirade that made Otto and the younger soldier bristle. "What have you done?" Otto demanded, pointing his rifle at Albert, then Sabine.

She held her hands up, half apology, half self-defense. "I wasn't . . . We didn't—"

The older soldier stepped forward so fast that Cal didn't have time to intercept him. He backhanded Sabine and sent her sprawling to the parquet. Lise screamed and tried to go to her sister, but Cal pushed her back behind him as Albert lunged at the soldier who had laid Sabine out. The German shot him in the shoulder before he'd taken two steps, but the old Frenchman staggered forward and knocked the Mauser out of his hands and across the floor as he fell.

Without thinking, Cal rushed the other Wehrmacht and knocked him down with a fist to the side of the head, then leapt for the rifle he'd hidden in the banquette. He was vaguely aware of French people bending to tend to Sabine and Albert. Of the German retrieving his gun and discharging it into the villagers, hitting at least one of them.

Cal swung around and leveled the hunting rifle at him, shooting him in the chest.

There was open sobbing among the women now and screams from Lise, who was fighting restraining hands in her desperation to reach her sister and Albert. Otto, his voice shrill with panic, yelled, "*Halt!*" and "*Stehen bleiben!*" while he wildly swung the muzzle of his weapon from side to side, seemingly too terrified to pull the trigger.

As Cal reloaded, the soldier he'd decked earlier rose to his feet, unstable from the blow to his head, but still able to hold and aim his rifle. There was no time for hesitation. No time to evaluate possible outcomes. Cal shot the German before he was fully upright, the impact in his chest and neck spinning him sideways and back.

It only took a couple of seconds for Cal to reload, but they felt agonizingly long.

"Cal, *non!*" Lise screamed, her voice hoarse with anguish, when he finally turned his rifle on Otto.

Otto's Mauser shook in his hands. His face was ashen and his eyes kept darting from the girls to the German soldiers lying at his feet.

"Put the gun down, Otto." Cal saw surprise briefly replace the horror in the young man's gaze when he spoke to him in English. "This can end here. Right now. Just put your gun down."

Otto shook his head, confusion on his face, and

tightened his grip on the weapon now trained on the center of Cal's chest.

"Please do not shoot," Lise sobbed. "Please, Otto . . ."

The soldier glanced at the child with whom he'd lived for months. At Albert, who lay motionless but conscious, a red stain spreading across his shirt. Then at Sabine.

"Otto." It was all the fourteen-year-old said. Her chin trembled with barely suppressed emotions as she stared up at the young man.

Cal waited, barely breathing, his finger on the trigger, forcing himself not to pull it. Not yet. Not when the greater threat had been eliminated and there was still a chance of avoiding more loss of life.

Something that looked like indecision passed over Otto's face. The muzzle of his Mauser began to drift off Cal, but he seemed to catch himself and brought it up again, his pinched lips, drawn eyebrows, and narrowed gaze a mask of fierce but frightened determination.

The room around them seemed to dim in Cal's mind until all he could see was the young soldier's face and the shaking hands holding the Mauser. "You don't want to do this," he said softly. He heard the rasp of steely resolve in his own voice and hoped Otto heard it too.

After what felt like an eternity, the German's posture changed almost imperceptibly. He swallowed hard, took a small step back, his eyes on Cal still determined, but something broken in their depths. When he began to lower his rifle, Cal followed suit. Slowly. Steadily. Cautiously.

Lise pried her arms free and threw herself down between Albert and her sister, wailing her anguish.

"*Vas-t'en!*" Sabine spat at the German soldier, covering her bruised cheek with one hand and squeezing Lise's shoulder with the other. "Leave!" she shrieked.

Otto took a step toward the door, his eyes haunted as he watched Lise trying to stem Albert's bleeding with her hands.

For just a moment, Cal thought the standoff would end there. Their guns were nearly down and the fight seemed to have gone out of the young Wehrmacht soldier.

Then he heard Buck roar.

Part 2

Chapter 19

Darlene seemed determined to be cheerful at breakfast the next morning. She came downstairs in full makeup, her hair teased and sprayed, and a brave smile on her face. But even Tom's famed omelet couldn't dispel the disappointment I could glimpse when her defenses were down.

An hour later, Brenda and I stood next to my car. Darlene was already in her seat, a notebook in her hand, scribbling rapidly.

"Thank you for answering what questions you could," I told our host. "Are you sure you don't mind if we take a look inside the old house again?"

"I want you to. Tom was over there first thing this morning putting down big sheets of plywood. If you stick to those, they'll distribute your weight and cut down on your chances of landing in the crawl space under the house."

"That was kind of him."

Brenda's smile was nostalgic. "He's not much of a talker, but he sure looks out for people."

A sad sort of envy hummed somewhere in the back of my mind. "You're a very fortunate woman," I said.

"I know that now." She laughed. "Didn't always, mind you. But all these years later, when the frustrating stuff has settled into normal, it's easier to see the treasure in the trash."

It was my turn to laugh. "Is that a local idiom?"

"It's a Foggy Acres idiom—and I stand by it!" She gave me a hug, then stepped back. "You want the keys to the old McElway place or are you happy to let yourself in like you did last night?"

I felt myself blush a little. "We really didn't mean to trespass."

"Sure you did. Difference is, you belonged there. It's the antique scavengers I have trouble with."

"Do you get a lot of them?"

"A few every year. Caught one young couple sneaking out to their car with a couple bags full of pewter and a cookie jar. Another woman thought she'd serve herself to Lucy's old china."

"Did you ever think of cleaning out the house?"

Brenda shook her head. "It's like I told you last night. We thought he might come back. And then—then we figured out he probably wouldn't, but it still felt wrong to intrude on his space." She saw my confusion. "Listen, people in these parts are equally sentimental and superstitious. It's not really conducive to progress, but it sure is sweet. And as long as I live here, Cal's house will live too."

"I'm so grateful, Brenda. If we'd found nothing at all, I'm not sure what it would have done to Darlene."

"Well, anything Darlene sees that she'd like to take—it's hers, obviously. Aside from rodent nests and water damage, it's pretty much the way Cal left it. Didn't feel right to go poking around in there."

I thanked Brenda again and got into the car while she walked around to the other side. Darlene lowered her window and Brenda reached in to give her shoulder a squeeze. "You take whatever you want over there, okay? It's all your daddy's stuff. Just don't go up to the bedrooms. Those stairs are too rickety to risk it."

A couple minutes later, we stood on the porch of the McElway homestead for the second time in twenty-four hours. I reached through the broken windowpane to open the front door. Brenda hadn't lied. There were several lengths of plywood extending from the porch through to the kitchen, and more leading into the living and dining rooms.

"We need to walk on the plywood," I said to Darlene.

"Okay."

Her tone concerned me. It was flat and listless. "Are you feeling okay?"

She looked away, but I saw the tears coming to her eyes.

"If you'd rather not look around—"

"No," she interrupted. "I've just—I've been documenting what we found out talking with Brenda last night . . . and what we didn't. It just feels so . . ." She tried to shake it off, squaring her shoulders and taking in a deep breath. "Never mind me. We came to find out more about my father and since this was his place, we'd be fools not to look around."

She attempted a smile and I reached out to give her a hug, but she held up a finger like she was chastising a child. "If you so much as touch me, I'm going to start crying and ruin my makeup, so hands off, Ceelie Donovan!"

After a moment of surprise, I burst out laughing and gave her a hug anyway. She laughed too, through her tears, then declared, "Let's scavenge the heck out of this place." We moved toward the kitchen, careful not to step off the boards Tom had put down for us. The hardwood underneath them still cracked and creaked. A staircase extended up to our right, its roses-and-greens wallpaper faded to pastels.

Something scurried and Darlene yelped and pointed. "Critters!" My eyes snapped to the kitchen, where a Formica table and yellow-painted cabinets seemed to reflect the morning sun. It sifted through dirty windows that faced the rolling hills beyond the farm. A mouse climbed up the peeling paper in the corner of the room and darted through a hole near the ceiling.

I caught myself tiptoeing as I approached the cupboards, most of them gaping open. In one of them, there were still cans of chicken soup and peas from another era. Salt and pepper and spices in another. Boxes of noodles and toothpicks. Cleaning products cluttered the space under the sink. A mug and two plates sat on the drainboard.

"Rural Missouri, the recession, two world wars, and decades of looters," Darlene murmured behind me. "I'm not holding my breath for a silver flatware set."

"There still might be some collectibles," I said, taking a tin of cinnamon off one of the shelves. "I've seen this type of thing at flea markets."

Darlene took it from me. "It's a bit late in life for me to be starting a junk collection." She pursed her lips and thought for a moment, her eyes on the cinnamon tin. "And here I thought all I'd gotten from him was a lifetime of resentment."

"That's a little dark," I said sarcastically, hoping to lighten the mood.

She ignored my statement. "Let's look around upstairs."

Brenda had warned us about the staircase, and one look at the partially decomposed steps confirmed her misgivings. "Uh . . . we'd be crazy to even attempt it."

"Uh . . . ," she mimicked, "you're in Missouri hunting for a guy who hasn't been seen in seventy-six years. We passed crazy two hundred miles ago."

She had a point. "It really doesn't look safe, Darlene."

Shoving me aside, she said, "Let me go—I'm on borrowed time anyway."

"Darlene!" I was horrified. Then I saw the sparkle in her eye and knew I'd been had. I looked at the dilapidated staircase and the moth-eaten carpet runner that spanned it. I really did want to scrounge around upstairs, but . . .

"How about you walk on the very outside edges of the steps, where the nails or the glue or whatever makes them stronger, and then when you get—"

Footsteps creaked on the porch outside the front door. Darlene whipped around and nearly lost her balance. I reached out to steady her just as Tom's voice said, "Figured you two might get a hankerin' to head up to the second floor." He looked at us through the empty frame of the screen door. "I brought something over to make it safer."

"Tom," Darlene drawled, suddenly sounding like a Southern belle, "I could just kiss you."

He seemed embarrassed by the offer.

Two minutes later, without many more words spoken, he'd extended an aluminum ladder from the small landing at the base of the stairs, turning it sideways to lean against the railing that ran the length of the walkway between rooms on the second floor.

Tom climbed the ladder with a hammer and proceeded to knock out several rungs beneath the railing. He looked down at me. "Big enough for you to pass through?"

"I'm a bit insulted by the question, Tom."

We handed a few sheets of plywood up to him, requisitioned from the kitchen and dining room, and he pushed them through the hole he'd made, laying them out for me to walk on. "You can shift them around if you need to," he said as he descended the ladder again.

I thought he was putting far too much confidence in my adventurous spirit.

"I'm going up too," Darlene said.

"Darlene—no, you're not."

She planted her fists on her hips and raised her eyebrows at me in a defiant way. "Are you telling me that I can't go exploring in my own father's house?"

I smiled as sweetly as I could. "One, you weren't so inclined to call him your father an hour ago. Two . . ." I hesitated. She was a survivor gazing down a rather short track to the end of her life. I didn't want to deprive her of anything joy-giving, but I didn't want to see her further diminished by an injury either. "I'm younger. I'm stronger." I pushed my luck. "I have catlike reflexes."

"Sheesh." She rolled her eyes.

"Let me go up. I'll take pictures. And you and Tom can wait down here with nine-one-one pre-dialed into your flip-phone in case I wander off the plywood and crash through the floor."

She considered the proposition for a moment. "If you see anything worth more than forty-nine cents, bring it down for me," she said.

Tom nearly smiled.

There were three rooms that extended off the long hallway. The plywood Tom had put down extended into one of them, so I entered it first. It was filled with boxes, small pieces of furniture, bags of linen, and frames leaning against a twin bed—post-empty-nest storage or something of the sort.

It was in the room next door that the eerie feeling of trespassing on sacred ground shivered across my skin again. I moved the planks of wood as I went, directing them to the places I wanted to see. I had started to sweat under my wig but didn't let it deter me. A moth-eaten cardigan and a few shirts hung in the open closet of the second bedroom. Sheets and blankets were still on the double bed, as if someone had just pushed them back to get up, and a pair of wool slippers protruded from under the box springs.

The dresser near the broken window had three drawers, all

swollen and warped from exposure to the elements. I got the first one open with a little effort. Nothing there. There were a few undershirts and socks in the second one. Work pants in the last. I moved to the desk, testing exposed floor joists before putting my weight on them—Tom's plywood system was functional, but far from user-friendly. There was nothing significant in the desk either.

A few wall hangings decorated the space and a stack of magazines that had seen better days sat on the floor next to the bed, but the room felt spartan. I had to remind myself that it had last been inhabited in 1944 by a man whose life was simple and whose priorities were surely not the esthetics of the home.

I stood in the middle of the room and took a few pictures, berating myself for expecting to find something there that would explain Cal to me. I just so deeply wanted Darlene to have answers. But there seemed to be nothing in the house other than the discarded vestiges of a life rendered mute by absence.

Darlene called from the base of the stairs, as if reading my mind. "You uncovering any treasures?"

"Not much."

"Well, hurry up and find something," she said. "Tom and I ran out of things to talk about roughly ten seconds after you climbed that ladder."

Imagining Tom's discomfort made me smile. "Can you manage a couple more minutes of scintillating repartee?" I asked.

She didn't answer me directly, but I heard her say in the most natural way, "So, Tom, what do you think about those sissies in Congress?"

I picked up the pace, as much for Tom's sake as for mine, and repositioned the plywood to visit the last bedroom. I was anxious to get on the road. We had about four hours to drive before stopping outside Hannibal for the night, and Darlene wanted to visit a couple historic locations we'd passed on the way to Kinley.

The last bedroom felt different from the other two. It faced away from the morning sun and the tattered remains of floral curtains were pulled across two windows, darkening the space. While the rest of the house was more austere, this space seemed to still have a soul. I felt goose bumps rising on my skin.

The bedroom I assumed to be Lucy's was furnished with modest pieces—a wardrobe, a simple oak rocking chair. The bed was made, and a crocheted bedspread, eaten away in spots, hung nearly to the floor. Just inside the door, a pink-shaded lamp and a couple framed photos stood on a maple dresser. I lifted them toward the light shining dimly through the curtains. Then I peered more closely.

In the first black-and-white snapshot, the same man I'd seen in Darlene's baby picture looked younger—maybe sixteen or seventeen. He wore dark pants with a light-colored, button-down shirt tucked into the high waist, its sleeves rolled up. He stood in front of a barn door, laughing directly into the camera's lens, holding a disgruntled kitten in one hand, while another cat clawed its way up his sleeve and yet another huddled close to his neck. The bright delight of his smile had not faded with the ink of the picture, and I wondered if the devil-may-care, all-male aura young Cal exuded had been one of the traits that had attracted Claire.

The second picture seemed older. The quality was grainier and the printing a muddy, dark brown. It featured a car that looked to me like an old Model T. A young man stood next to it, one foot propped on its running board. A softly smiling woman sat in its open door holding an infant wrapped in a blanket. It was an idyllic scene that spoke of birth and family. Darlene would love it.

I took a few pictures on my phone. The vase perched on a deep windowsill, undisturbed after so many years. The delicate vanity near the window—a yellow enamel hand mirror and matching hairbrush on its dusty surface.

Before heading back downstairs, I made my way to the plain,

pine nightstand, where another small, framed photo next to a stained glass lamp had caught my eye. I lifted it toward the light coming through the curtains and felt my breath catch.

Cal wasn't smiling in this one. He looked into the camera with gravity, the straight lines and angles of his military uniform accentuating his broad neck and strong jaw. His eyes, shadowed by the brim of his visor cap, were startlingly intense.

I opened the drawer of the nightstand and froze.

For a moment, I wondered if my mind was playing tricks on me, but there was no denying the reality of the envelope that lay at the bottom of the drawer, the handwriting on it crisp and stark. I reached for the letter and held it for a moment before raising it into the dim sunlight. Lucy's name was on it. The return address was Ramsbury, England, and the name of the sender was Callum McElway.

Chapter 20

Discomfort seemed to be coming off Tom in waves when I rejoined him and Darlene downstairs.

"Find anything?" she asked, expectant.

I held out the three framed photos and the yellow mirror and brush set I'd taken from Lucy's vanity. The letter was in my jacket pocket. I'd show it to Darlene later, when we were alone and able to process it. "Pictures," I said. "And a few of Cal's mother's—your grandmother's—things."

She seemed to hesitate before taking the frames from me. Her hands were shaking as she looked at each one.

"Are you sure it's okay for us to take these?" I asked Tom.

He'd collapsed the ladder and was heading for the door. "This is your family's house." He tipped an imaginary cap and left.

Darlene and I sat in the car for a few minutes and looked at the pictures. She dusted each one with a Kleenex and stared as if they might hold the information she needed—something to connect her to the heart of the man who had left her when she was still too young to remember him.

"You think this is Lucy and Cal Senior?" she asked.

"That's what I assume. And your dad in her arms."

"They look like a normal family, right?" The question sounded more like frustration than endearment. "Mom and dad and baby boy."

She moved the picture of Cal and the kittens to the top of the stack. "And again," she murmured. "The smile. The happy-go-lucky, farm-boy pose." She glanced at me, then looked back at the picture again. "I thought I'd feel something—some sort of mystical connection if I stared at these long enough, but . . . How in the world did he go from this to . . . ?"

I could see her shoulders tensing, her eyes laser-sharp on the photos.

Reaching over the console, I lay a hand across hers and suggested, "How about we take a breather?"

"I don't need to breathe." There was something petulant in the way she said it. It didn't sound like Darlene. It hadn't been lost on me that her moods had been erratic for the past few days, starting shortly before we'd launched off on our trip. Given how tired I felt, I wasn't surprised that the journey, along with the emotional weight of what we were trying to uncover, was taking a toll on her.

"Okay," I said calmly, "but thinking about something different for a bit might do us both some good."

She pulled her hand out from under mine and placed the picture of Cal in uniform on top of the stack in her lap.

"How about we put on that audiobook?" I suggested, wanting to give Darlene's emotions a reprieve. "We can talk about all of this when we get to the motel. Are you okay with that?"

Her gaze didn't waver from the photo of her father.

"Darlene?"

Still nothing.

I put the car in gear, entered our motel's address in the GPS, and drove back down Mud Creek Road.

Dinner was a somber affair. I picked up salads at the Denny's next door to the Travelodge and hoped putting something in Darlene's stomach would improve her mood. It didn't.

We sat on her bed when we were finished eating and looked at the pictures again. I tried to draw her into a conversation by commenting on what her grandparents were wearing and the antics of the kittens using Cal as a climbing wall, but the woman who had been an insatiable talker since the moment I'd met her in the Breast Health Center seemed to have run out of words. She just stared at the pictures and chewed on her lower lip.

"There's one more thing I found in Lucy's room," I finally told her.

I went to the chair where I'd dropped my jacket and pulled the envelope addressed to Lucy out of its inside pocket. "This was in her nightstand," I said, handing it to Darlene. She squinted up at me, still preoccupied. "I was holding on to it because I didn't want to just skim it while we drove down the road. It feels like something special that deserves our full attention."

Darlene turned it over in her hands. "From my father?" I nodded. "To my grandmother?" She seemed to be having trouble connecting the dots in her mind.

"Yes. Written in January, 1944—five months before D-Day."

"Have you read it?"

"Nope—I was saving that honor for Lucy's granddaughter." I smiled. She didn't smile back.

Darlene took the letter from the envelope and unfolded it. "Why am I so nervous?" she asked.

"Do you want to wait?"

She shook her head. Then she took a deep breath and looked at the paper. "Pretty bad penmanship," she said just above a whisper.

"Spoken like a former English teacher."

She read the letter out loud, stumbling a bit when it was hard to decipher the words Cal had written more than seventy years before.

Dear Mother,

I'm writing to you from a bunk in a hangar in South England, surrounded by the snoring and sleep-talking of roughly three hundred men. We've been in Ramsbury for six weeks, and there's a buzz in the air. Something big is coming. We can feel it. Although it doesn't seem to be keeping anybody else awake, it sure is on my mind.

The days are long here, but the blisters, the bruises, and the endless drills are okay by us. If we can show those Nazis a thing or two, it will be worth the aches and pains . . . even the sleepless nights. We have no idea when our marching orders will come, but we'll be ready when they do.

The fellas are great. They're eager to get to fighting. We listen to the news every evening in the mess. Liberty continues to march forward, as you told me she would. She is upright and proud, and I carry her with me. I'm not sure how a ragtag bunch of guys like us will live up to her call, but we'll keep trying as long as we can, in whatever way we can. It's a strange thing knowing that the fate of the world depends on our success.

Now for the big news: you're a grandmother! Claire was going to send you a telegram and I hope she did, but just in case it didn't reach you . . . Her name is Darlene Marie and she was born on January 4th. The way Claire tells it, she's big and beautiful and healthy. Most days it's hard for me to really grasp that I'm a father. It feels so strange and out of reach, but I love her already, sight unseen. I can't wait to be able to hold her when all of this is over. Keep praying, Mother. I don't want this war to take being a dad from me.

Thank you for writing. Reading about the farm and life there feels like another world. I miss you every day. Huck too. Give him an extra rub for me and keep your best prime rib on ice. No one knows how fast things will happen, but I will come home and bring my Claire and our baby girl with me. I promise you that. It's time for you to meet them both. I know you'll love them as much as I do.

I must stop now and try to sleep, since there are only four hours left before a new day begins. I'll write again soon.

Lady Liberty marches on,
Cal

When she'd finished reading the two-page letter, Darlene flipped it over and read it again, silently this time. Then she delicately laid it in her lap along with the pictures we'd found in Cal's home. "Humph."

I didn't know what to say. I'd hoped the letter would humanize Cal in some way—put flesh and bone and personhood on the framework of what we already knew. In my mind, it had. The words he'd used to speak of Claire and his daughter had revealed some of his heart, but Darlene clearly didn't share my point of view. "Care to elaborate?" I said.

She frowned and quoted from the letter. "'I know you'll love them as much as I do.'"

I tried for an encouraging expression as I met her gaze. "That's kind of sweet . . . right? He sounds like he was truly thrilled to be a dad."

"And yet, just a few months after meeting me for the first time . . ."

"Yes." I acknowledged the contradiction but didn't want to let her dwell on it. "Darlene, we may never know what happened. Why he left. But . . . can you at least take some comfort from knowing that he wanted you? That he loved you and couldn't wait to meet you—"

"But he did. He did meet me. And the man who couldn't wait to hold his baby walked out of her life without so much as an explanation three months later. How do you square that little detail with the words in that letter?"

I wasn't sure how to respond. This indomitable woman whose positive outlook had buoyed me throughout my battle with cancer and Nate's sudden departure appeared to have lost her trademark optimism. While I'd been elated to have found anything at all in Lucy's home—a tangible connection with the father she'd lost—it seemed to have only exacerbated the frustration I'd glimpsed in Darlene, in lengthening bouts, over the past two days.

"This place is starting to feel like a crypt," she finally said, contemplating the photos and mementos spread out on her bed. "So much for answers."

"We did get some answers," I said, trying to gently contradict her statement. "Think about it. We found your father's house, met a neighbor who knew some of your family's history, then went back and got ourselves some treasures from his place. Who would have thought any of that could happen when we set off on this trip?"

She frowned and continued to stare at the objects on her lap.

"And we found a letter—a sweet, sincere letter—in which he talked about you. That's something to feel good about, right?" I tried to piece a story together that would hold some comfort for his suddenly belligerent daughter. "Maybe he did love you, Darlene. Maybe he and Claire truly were happy for a while. And then maybe something happened—"

"Maybe he was a jerk," Darlene interrupted. "It's easy to sound sweet in a letter."

I was taken aback. "Or maybe the war—something he experienced over there—broke him, somehow, and that's why he left. He may not have been thinking straight when he—"

"Abandoned me?" she interrupted again. "When he disappeared in the middle of the night and stayed away for—what—months before he got mauled by a bear or shot himself or whatever happened to him in Kinley? Maybe the war hero didn't have it in him to be a husband and father. Maybe he got bored. Maybe all he wanted was to get back to his blessed farm where his only responsibilities were cattle and crops. Maybe it was that *easy* for him to walk away."

The veins in Darlene's neck stood out as she got angrier. Her voice was razor-edged and cold. "Maybe when the neighbor kids came over to play, it triggered nothing in Dear Old Dad about the child he'd left behind. The daughter he claimed to love." She swiped at the pictures and sent them flying off the bed onto the floor. "Maybe dying somewhere out in the fields with no one to recover his body was exactly what he deserved. He may have helped free France, but he was a coward on the home front."

Darlene was visibly shaking—not just her hands but, it seemed, the center of her being.

I swiveled to get a better look at her, stunned and worried by the vitriol pouring out of her. "Darlene?" I leaned in and tried to catch her eye. "Look at me, Darlene. I get it. I get that you were hoping for more."

"He was a—" The word she used was crude and shocking. Her voice loud. Brittle. She raised the crumpled letter in her fist and shook it at me. "My father was a heartless monster and he can rot in hell."

"Darlene!" My own voice was sharper now. Sharp with dismay and concern. I grabbed her arm and tried to pry the letter from her hand, but she fought me with surprising force. At my wits' end, I finally yelled, "Darlene—stop it!"

I thought she'd heard me. She suddenly became very still. Then her eyes rolled back and she fell sideways on the bed, her body racked with spasms.

"Darlene!" I reached out and found her rigid, every muscle taut and quaking. "Darlene!" Fear exploded in my mind. The color had gone from her skin. Her jaw was set, her eyes half-open and unfocused. Her arms and legs and core jerked and quaked.

I didn't know what to do. Adrenaline surged, turning my blood to ice, then fire. I staggered to the front door and found my jacket. My hands were shaking so badly that I struggled to reach into the pocket for my phone. I rushed back to the bed with it, frightened that Darlene's shaking would topple her onto the floor. Then I dialed nine-one-one.

Chapter 21

The ambulance raced ahead of me, lights flashing and siren wailing. I tried to keep up but found my reflexes and processing hampered by fear.

The paramedics had arrived within five minutes of my call, as the fire station was just a block from our motel. They'd quickly assessed that Darlene was at the tail end of a seizure and administered something that made her stop shaking. Then they'd loaded her into the ambulance and were now speeding toward the Hannibal Regional Hospital.

My arms felt leaden on the steering wheel, frozen by shock and a gut-level terror that I was going to lose my dearest friend. Just as powerful as my concern for her was the realization that I was utterly alone, far from home, and facing an overwhelming crisis.

If Darlene died . . . I tried to reject the conjecture before it anchored, but the prospect of losing my friend overrode my defenses. Responsibility added its weight to debilitating fear. If Darlene passed away under my watch. If I had to make last-minute medical decisions on her behalf. If I was the one who, by default, had to call her son and tell him his mother had succumbed to whatever it was that had made her lose consciousness . . .

Tears sprang to my eyes and I blinked them away, focusing on the ambulance speeding toward the Hannibal hospital. I berated myself for the stupidity of inviting an ailing woman on a road trip that had taken us so far from her medical team. "Please," I whispered into the silence, chilled by what I'd witnessed and what I couldn't predict.

I parked my car not far from the ambulance bay and watched them push my friend's gurney through whooshing, automated doors, then I went to the registration desk on unsteady legs. A young nurse assured me that someone would come get me when Darlene was stabilized. I found a chair and sat there, barely breathing, surrounded by the crisis of a dozen other families, mind-numbingly isolated and afraid.

On an impulse, I reached for my phone.

No. I couldn't.

I put the phone away and waited.

Five minutes passed without an update. They felt like hours. As my anxiety increased, so did my desperation for contact with anyone who knew me well enough to understand the depth of the dread crippling my thinking.

I reached for the phone again and stared at the name in my contact list.

Need dueled with resolve.

Need won.

The phone only rang twice on the other end. "Hello?"

I'd thought reaching out would be the hardest part, but finding words proved more challenging yet. "I didn't know who to call," I finally said, emotion roughening my voice.

"Ceelie?"

"I . . . Yes."

I could picture Nate frowning. "What happened?" he asked.

"Darlene is . . ." I swallowed past the sob I'd been restraining since the medics had loaded her into the ambulance.

"Ceelie."

"She's in the hospital." I took a deep, stabilizing breath and tried to put coherent thoughts together. "We were in our room at the motel in Hannibal and she—she started to seize and passed out and . . . I don't know what's wrong with her. Nobody's come out to tell me anything."

There was a brief pause. "What do you need?"

I realized this was why I'd pushed through my misgivings and called my soon-to-be ex-husband. He was a problem solver. A doer. And I felt paralyzed with worry and uncertainty.

"I don't know," I told him. "I just—I needed someone to know what's going on in case . . ."

"Does she have family?" Nate asked.

"I'll call her son when I know something more. He doesn't even know we're here." It was hard to believe that we'd been walking around Cal's old house just a few hours earlier.

"They'll want her insurance card."

"I already gave it to the front desk." The tears I'd been trying to stem ran down my cheeks. "I just—I just needed somebody to know what's happening," I repeated.

"Just take it one piece of information and one decision at a time. You're strong, Ceelie. You've got this."

"I don't feel strong."

There was silence on the other end of the line. Then Nate said, "Would it help if I drove out there? It's probably just four or five hours from here. I can come right now if . . ." His voice trailed off.

A slideshow of our encounters since the day he'd walked out played across my mind, each frame a reminder of the evisceration of my world. "No," I answered his question. "I shouldn't have called. I'm . . ." I stared at the ceiling for a second and tried to recapture my resolve. "Force of habit," I finally said. "I'll be fine. I'm sorry I bothered you."

"Ceelie, you didn't—"

I disconnected the call and put the phone back in my pocket, shaking my head at my stupidity. What had I been thinking?

Then I braced my elbows on my knees, covered my face with my hands, and let my worry flow.

"We're taking her back for a CT now. She hasn't fully regained her faculties, but is awake and talking." The man looked too young to have a job, let alone be a neurologist. He'd come out to update me about forty-five minutes after they'd taken Darlene back.

"What do you think happened?" I asked, relieved to finally be speaking with someone who might have answers.

"We're not sure, but it looks like a mini-stroke or TIA—that's short for transitory ischemic attack. She's taking a while coming out of it, though, and that's a bit unusual. So we'll get the scan done, just to make sure there isn't something else going on, and I'll be able to tell you more once that's over."

"A lot of people have TIAs, right? They're not too serious . . ."

"They're not uncommon. We typically send the patient home pretty quickly and follow up with blood thinners to prevent a repeat performance," he explained, his voice low. "But sometimes TIAs can be precursors to a bigger stroke, so we're erring on the side of caution and making sure we don't miss anything."

"When can I see her?"

"As soon as she's back from imaging. I'll send someone out for you."

Nearly an hour passed before a sweet, red-headed nurse invited me to follow her through automatic doors and down a busy hallway. Darlene looked frail and pale against the white sheets, dwarfed by the medical equipment around her.

"I'll be back in a little to check on her," the nurse said with a compassionate smile. Then she left the room.

Darlene's eyes were open. I went to the bed and took her cold hand into mine. Her eyes shifted in my direction but didn't quite reach me. "Darlene, I'm right here," I said, leaning over and raising up just enough for our gazes to meet.

"Messed up big-time," she said. The words were misshapen, uttered through barely moving lips.

"You didn't mess up, Darlene."

She squeezed my hand. "I—sorry."

I leaned in close and saw her eyes slowly focus on my face. I tried for a comforting and hopeful expression. "You're in good hands. They've run some tests and will let us know as soon as they have results."

"Jus—tin."

"Justin?" She squeezed my hand. "Do you want me to call him?" Another squeeze. "I was going to wait until we have more answers."

"Call . . ."

I took out my phone and found the number he'd given me after Darlene injured her hip.

"This is Ceelie, your mom's friend," I said after he picked up. "I don't want you to worry, but we're in Missouri and she's had an . . . episode."

He was instantly concerned. I answered his questions as best I could and assured him that her doctors were optimistic and that I'd call again once I knew more.

"Do you think I should head out there?"

I hesitated. What I'd witnessed back in the motel room certainly seemed like something serious enough to warrant Justin's presence. I just didn't want him to make the trip until we were sure of what we were dealing with. I said as much to him and he asked to talk to Darlene.

"She may not be able to speak very well," I cautioned him. Then I turned on the speaker and held the phone up to her ear.

"What have you gone and done now, Mom?" Justin said with a smile and concern in his voice.

"Messed up big-time," she said again. The words sounded somewhat clearer to me.

"Listen, I'm going to be tracking with Ceelie, but if you want me to come now, say the word."

"No—need."

The odd-shaped words must have frightened him. "I'll be there in a few hours. If I leave now, maybe by morning."

"No." This time the word was clear.

"I want to, Mom. If anything happened—"

"Don't bor—row," she mumbled.

I smiled despite the dire circumstances and said to Justin, "I'm guessing you're familiar with the phrase."

He sighed. "I am."

Darlene tried to form a word a couple times before it finally came out. "Re—peat."

"Really, Mom?"

"Re—peat."

"Don't borrow," Justin said.

Darlene said, "Goo' boy."

Justin signed off with his mother and I turned off the speaker. "I'll let you know the minute I have more information," I said to him.

"Do you think I should come now?" There was an anxious edge to his voice.

"I don't know what to tell you. She's doing better than she was a few minutes ago. Her speech. Her focus. If she keeps on improving . . ."

"Okay. I'll have a bag packed just in case. If there's no significant improvement or medical verdict in a couple hours, I'll be on my way."

Darlene said something I couldn't quite understand after we hung up. I leaned closer. "Say that again?"

"Told you it would be an ad—venture." A slight smile curved her lips and a trace of the old Darlene was in it.

"You outdid yourself this time, my friend."

Chapter 22

Darlene continued to improve over the hours that followed. She had some weakness and lack of coordination on her left side and her speech was still impaired, but her clarity and muscle function were getting better by the minute. A doctor I hadn't seen before came in halfway through the night to give me an update. The scan had shown that she'd indeed had a small stroke and that this probably wasn't the first one. More importantly, it had revealed a lesion on the frontal lobe of her brain. Small. Potentially benign, but with her recent medical history, likely serious.

"I can't be certain the mass caused the stroke, but I do know that without the TIA, it might not have been found for a while. We can certainly keep Darlene here and do some more testing to determine what it is, but . . . maybe we should get her well enough to go home and let her own doctors take it from here."

I went out to the waiting room to call Justin and get a cup of coffee.

"What are you two doing in Hannibal anyway?" he asked once I'd filled him in on what I knew.

"Well . . . ," I began.

"No need to sugarcoat it. My mom is known for two things:

impulsivity and a total disregard for potential consequences. Whatever it is, it won't surprise me."

I attempted a light laugh, but my nerves and emotions were still too raw for it to sound authentic. "We drove to Missouri in search of her father," I finally said. "She found some letters of his a while back and—long story short—she decided someone needed to visit his old home in Kinley to find out if he was still alive. When she asked me if I'd be willing to make the trip, I was the idiot who figured she should come along too."

"My grandfather?"

"Yes."

"The man whose name alone can shut down a perfectly good conversation?"

"That's the one."

I heard him sigh. "After all this time . . . ," he said. "She never spoke to my grandmother about him. Or to me either. It was always, 'That doesn't matter anymore' or 'All in the past, Justin, all in the past.'"

I heard his frustration and tried to soften my revelation. "I think her last diagnosis—her prognosis—kind of threw her for a loop. It was the perfect storm, really. Someone sends her letters written to her father when he was in Normandy, her doctors tell her the cancer had spread and . . . Well, you said it—'impulsivity and a total disregard for potential consequences.' She just wants to learn more while she still can."

I heard him sigh. "Can I speak with her again?" There were equal parts love, concern, and exasperation in his voice.

I walked to Darlene's room and handed her the phone. Her improvement in a few short hours was remarkable. Her color was brighter and her eyes held traces of the fire that defined her.

"I hear you're doing a bit better," Justin said.

"Fit as a fiddle missing a few strings."

"And Ceelie tells me you'll be cleared to travel in a day or two. That sounds like a good report."

"Except for the marble-sized something-or-other on the old brain. Am I a frickin' smorgasbord of medical conditions or what?"

"Language, Mom," Justin said wryly.

I interjected, "The mini-stroke seems to have unchained her inner truck driver."

I heard Justin chuckle. Then there was a brief silence. "What were you thinking, Mom? Going off to who-knows-where on a wild goose chase."

"Seemed like a great idea at the time," Darlene said, not in the least defensively. "But I'll admit I never thought it would land me in the hospital."

"Are they taking good care of you?"

"I think the CAT scan technician has a crush on me."

Justin laughed. His voice held affection and patience as he continued. "So . . . remember how Nana and I would go off to the library together for hours at a time when we visited her?"

Darlene seemed confused by the question. "I— Yes. Of course I do."

"Did you ever wonder why we spent so much time there?"

"My son picks the oddest times for jaunts down memory lane," Darlene said to me. Some of her consonants were still too soft and the vowels too broad, but the eye roll she aimed in my direction was executed with so much flair that it seemed to be more proof of her quickly recovering brain.

"No, I did not wonder that," she said to Justin. "I figured you were enjoying the time together."

"We were researching a man by the name of Callum McElway, Mom."

Her gaze locked on mine. "You were what now?"

"You may not have wanted to know anything about him, but . . .

195

he was a legend to my little-boy mind. And I think Nana loved that one of us was intrigued enough to ask questions."

"Well, I'll be."

"We never did figure out what happened after he left you and Nana, but I've got a binder full of the little we uncovered and the *lot* she remembered."

"Well, I'll be."

"So you've said. See what happens when a person refuses to communicate with her son on important topics?" There was a smile in his tone. And a soft reprimand.

"What exactly did you learn?"

"His rank. Some of his deployment details. There was a fire at the National Archives in the seventies that wiped out a bunch of military records, so we had a hard time getting specifics. Plus, he seemed to fall off the face of the earth after he . . . left. Most of what I know just came from Nana's memories and the documents that came with his medals."

"Medals?"

"Get well. Come back home. I'll tell you everything I know, Mom."

I left them chatting and returned to the lobby for the coffee I'd never poured. The fact that Justin had some additional information about Cal should have been exciting, but Darlene's condition was a greater concern now than the unanswered questions about her father. I sat in a chair and tried to envision a positive medical outcome, but the more I contemplated Darlene's diagnosis, the less likely her survival seemed.

I put my coffee down and rubbed my hands over my face, realizing I'd left my wig in the bathroom back at the hotel. It had been twenty-four hours since I'd showered or looked at myself in a mirror, but it didn't matter to me. Darlene's wellness was my sole, overwhelming concern.

I recognized the footsteps before I opened my eyes. There was something about their cadence and calm that immediately identified their owner.

"Ceelie?"

I hesitated. I breathed in once. Twice. Then I looked up into Nate's face.

Chapter 23

There was an interminable moment when I couldn't conjure up a single rational thought. It was too much for my mind to absorb and process. The shock of his presence in a place where neither of us belonged. The aching relief of his familiar, capable nearness at a time when I couldn't fathom leaning into his strength. The frightening realization that he'd dropped everything to make the trek to Missouri in the middle of the night, and the odd, angry confusion that notion inspired.

I stared at Nate. He stood a few feet away, his hands in the pockets of the camel-colored jacket he always wore for travel. He was unshaven. His hair was longer than it had been in our two decades of marriage. His expression was sincere, somehow both hesitant and sure. He hunched his shoulders. It was a gesture that looked like passive readiness. He was there. He was willing. But he was going to let me take the lead.

I wanted to close the gap between us and wrap my arms around his waist. I wanted to yell at him that he had to go away—that this crisis belonged in my single-woman-world and that his presence was bringing the bile of my broken-marriage-world into an already untenable situation. I wanted to shrink down in my chair and stop being strong and let him make the decisions that would get my friend home without complicating her condition.

"What are you doing here?" I said instead.

"I . . ." He frowned as if he truly wasn't sure of the answer. "I thought you could use some help. When you called—you sounded upset on the phone and . . . I thought you could use some help," he said again.

I knew the civil response would have been gratitude, but I shook my head in confusion instead. "I didn't ask you to come."

"I know."

There was something about his presence that felt diminishing. It filled me with a rebellion that was as deep-seated as it was out of place. I told him, "You shouldn't have come," which seemed a better alternative to, "You make me feel weak."

He nodded and continued to stare at me as if he was trying to read on my face what my lips couldn't formulate. "I nearly didn't. I got out of the car twice before finally hitting the road. I know I'm . . ." He looked up at the ceiling and blew out a long breath. "I realize I'm the last person you want to see, but you sounded like you were in over your head and—I wanted to be here. Just in case I could do something for you. And if I can't . . ." He raised his hands in a gesture that told me he'd leave just as easily as he'd come.

I thought of Darlene. I remembered the seizure. The stroke. The terror of wondering if my friend would die there in that motel room. The doctor's somber assessment. Her broken, confused words. The fear on her face and the need in her grip.

"It was a TIA," I murmured as much to myself as to Nate. "A mini-stroke. But there's something else on her brain. A mass. They don't know yet what it is, but . . ."

"Can they Medevac her?"

I shook my head. "No need, apparently. At the rate she's

improving, she'll be cleared for the drive home in another day or two. But that tumor—it's not good."

"Do you want me to stay and drive her back?"

"I'm still capable of driving, Nate."

"I'm sorry. It's just that you didn't sound like you were a few hours ago."

"So you swooped in like the conquering hero?" Sarcasm dripped from the words, fueled by the terror I'd felt since Darlene's seizure and the utter powerlessness that had followed. "You're good at being the hero, Nate—right up until you're not."

"I came because I wanted to help. Period."

I looked at him then and realized how desperately I was fighting gratitude—the kind that softens sharp edges and enlivens numb emotions. At that moment, it seemed a much heavier burden than hate.

Seconds passed. We still stood facing each other in the waiting room at the end of Darlene's floor. If there were people around, I wasn't aware of them. Nate was the searing focus of all my cells and synapses. "You said you wanted to talk. On the phone two days ago. You said . . ." I straightened a bit and squared my shoulders. "I don't want to talk."

I'd known him long enough to recognize the tensing of his jaw. "I didn't come here to corner you."

His expression was still sincere, but I saw the glint of frustration in his eyes. I suspected my face conveyed nothing but spite. The words I'd stifled every time I'd crossed paths with Nate since he'd so brutally exited my future surged to the surface again. I hadn't spoken them when he'd turned up at our old home to get the items he'd forgotten. I hadn't spoken them when he'd informed me that the divorce papers were about to be delivered. I hadn't spoken them when he'd entered the loft on the eve of my departure, as if his penitent countenance could soothe my angry wounds.

But I chose to speak the words in the waiting room of a hospital in small-town-Missouri. "What part was the sham? That's what I want to know. The part where you married me? The part where you stayed with me for nearly twenty-four years? The part where you carried me—sometimes literally—through a devastating battle with cancer? Or the part where you sat in the car outside the Shake Shack on the same day I celebrated the end of the ordeal and told me you were done?" I watched the words hit home but felt little satisfaction. "I trusted every piece of our lives together, but for the Nate I knew then to become the Nate I know now, some huge part of our past had to be a sham. Which was it?"

He seemed taken aback. I saw surprise cross his face, followed closely by determination, as if this opening, as bitter as it was, was a chance he couldn't let slip away.

"If you want to talk about this now—"

I hitched my chin a notch higher. "I do." The words surprised me, coming on the heels of the statement to the contrary I'd made moments before.

He looked around the waiting room. "We could sit back there—"

"Fine." I swiveled and walked to the corner he'd indicated, where a small table and chairs were surrounded by artificial ferns. I hoped he couldn't see how unsteady I felt.

Nate sat across from me, his hands folded in front of him. Rebellion, need, and rage fought for supremacy, paralyzing my lungs and chilling the blood in my veins. My heartbeat pounded in my ears and I pinched my eyes closed against the panic encroaching on my momentary courage.

Then I met his gaze with what I hoped was a defiant invitation to speak. He dropped his head for a moment. When he looked up again, there was determination and conviction on his face.

"It was all me."

I wasn't sure how to respond. I'd expected a long diatribe about the complexity and toll of the past few months. I'd expected explanations and excuses. I'd expected him to say something—anything—that would give me permission to rant, accuse, and demand. His simple statement left me bereft.

So instead of the monologues I'd been writing in the sleepless nights since he'd abandoned his vows, I said, "Why?"

He blew out a breath and sat back, his eyes soft and regretful as they connected with mine. "I wish I had a good answer. I wish I did. But the fact is—I don't know."

"You seemed mighty sure when it happened."

"I was as shocked as you."

"And yet you said you'd been contemplating it for a while."

"But not as something I'd actually do. I'd envisioned it sometimes, but . . . I loved you."

I laughed. It was a cynical, acrid sound. "What an odd way to show it."

"There's no way of saying this that won't sound . . . infantile."

I wouldn't give him the satisfaction of encouragement. So I sat and waited for him to go on.

He finally said, "I was exhausted."

"Really."

He shook his head. "I know, Ceelie. Believe me, I know."

"What do you know? How stupid that sounds or how selfish that sounds?"

The acid in my voice made him wince. "Both. Stupid and selfish."

"Cruel." I blinked back tears and cursed the fact that anger had always brought them out in me.

"That too," Nate said. He reached for my hand. I pulled away from him. "Sorry." He attempted a rueful smile. "Force of habit."

"I'm familiar with the concept. The last few months have been a master class in 'force of habit.'"

"I . . ." He hesitated. "I panicked, Cee."

"There's no such thing as premeditated panic. The timing might have surprised you, but you made it clear that the decision had already been made."

"Not a decision. I'd fantasized about an escape route. I'll admit to that. But honestly, I never made a *decision* to leave you." He pushed his chair back and ran his fingers through his hair. I remembered the first time I'd noticed the gray lightening his temples. *"My already-hot husband is becoming Clooney-esque,"* I'd joked. Back when I thought we'd be aging together.

Everything about Nate indicated effort. He took a breath and sat forward again, arms propped on the table, intensified purpose on his face and in his posture. "Brace yourself for a deluge of 'stupid and selfish,'" he said.

"Believe me, Nate, there's nothing you can say that will make my opinion of you worse."

He cringed a little at that, but forged on. "Nothing was a sham," he said. "We had our ups and downs over the years, but I didn't stick it out because of some martyr's complex. I stuck it out because . . . because what we built together felt worth staying for."

I couldn't help but roll my eyes. Bitterness gnawed at the essence of my spirit, deepening the wound that had been festering since Nate's departure. "That's not what you said the day you walked out."

There was something courageous in the way he marched on—ignoring the acrimony and anger slithering across from my side of the table.

"We drifted. I get that. Life, careers. We drifted into a routine, and our closeness probably suffered from it starting well before your cancer." Something that looked like defeat descended over his face, darkening his gaze and slackening his jaw. "From the moment you were diagnosed, though, I made a pact with myself and with you. We'd get through it together. Whatever it took—we'd get through it. There was no sham, Ceelie. I wanted to be there with you. I wanted to drive you to and from appointments as often as I could. I wanted to make sure you ate and were comfortable and stayed hopeful. All of that—it wasn't marital martyrdom. It was a choice. A responsibility and a choice."

He seemed to struggle to find the next words. "I gave it all I had." He held up his hands before I had the chance to retort. "You gave it more. I get that. You gave it everything. And I . . . I gave it all I had."

"How kind of you."

"There are no excuses." He let that settle. "There is nothing I can say now that can minimize what I did to you. To us."

"Or that can explain why it's taken you this long to even try," I said.

He looked at the ceiling and blew out a breath. "I did try. I came back from the lake project precisely for that."

I remembered our recent encounter in the loft, when he'd said he made a mistake and I'd sent him packing with my wedding ring.

"You were angry," Nate said. "You *are* angry. And you have every right to be."

A red-and-green foam ball rolled under our table and a little girl chasing it, pigtails bouncing, followed close behind. Nate found the ball and handed it back to her with a wink. She scrunched up her nose in a smile and ran off again.

He watched her go, then said, "The day you ended your treatments—"

"Darlene calls it the Shake Shack Shocker." He seemed perplexed. "She believes a cute moniker can mitigate the awful."

He still looked confused but let it drop. "The day you ended your treatment honestly is a blur to me."

I bit back a retort.

"I remember the bell-ringing and the celebrating, but . . . what

I remember most clearly is this all-consuming . . . I don't know. Exhaustion. Relief that it was over, for sure, but also a mind-numbing combination of freedom and fear."

"You're going to have to explain that."

He frowned. While he tried to organize his thoughts, a voice came over the hospital's PA system calling a code blue on the floor above ours. I only vaguely heard it. It felt like every fiber of my being was trained on Nate while my heart wavered between curiosity, resentment, and the burn of rejection.

"The worst was over," Nate finally said. "That's what the chemo bell told me. The worst was over and you were going to survive. The freedom of that . . . I saw it in you too."

"Right."

"But as we drove to get you that milkshake, this gut-level battle fatigue set in."

Cynicism rose in me like bile. "And you decided that your fantasies of leaving me might as well happen right then and there."

"I panicked," he said again. "Battle fatigue combined with sheer terror."

I was confused. "But you said it—the worst was over."

"Yes. Yes, the worst was over. And I felt like I had nothing left to give. The counselor I've been seeing—"

"Wait—counselor?"

He looked surprised that I didn't know, then seemed to realize how sparse our communication had been. "I've been seeing her for a few weeks—mostly by Skype while I was down south."

This was disorienting to me. I couldn't imagine Nate—pull-yourself-up-by-your-bootstraps-Nate—seeking a counselor's help. "Go on."

"She calls it post-traumatic claustrophobia."

"Cute."

He lifted one shoulder and let it fall again. "Accurate, I think.

It's a fear response, she tells me. And not uncommon in caregivers, whether they identify it or not."

"Get your story straight, Nate. Fear or claustrophobia?"

"Both. Fear that I wouldn't know how to do normal life anymore. Fear that the doctors were wrong and you'd get sick again. Fear that my body and mind would explode if one more crisis or obligation happened to me. All that fear led to this feeling that I had to get out. That I was about to lose it and I had to get away. To stop caring. To stop cheerleading. To stop spending my days trying to ignore or live above or stuff down the terror and stress and dire predictions and life-altering changes that kept happening to us."

"So it's my fault." I felt anger fluttering closer to the surface and breathed deeply to control it.

"It's not your fault. It's cancer's. Cancer and the toll it takes."

"Cancer didn't pack your bags for you."

The words seemed to hit their target. "You're right."

"I didn't see exhaustion or fear. I just saw this brutal, ice-cold determination on your face." I paused. A nauseating bitterness settled in the pit of my stomach. I couldn't help myself. "So did you go straight to Julie or wait a minute before making the leap from your wife to your girlfriend?"

Nate leaned in, elbows on the table between us, and with his gaze boring into mine, said, "Nothing ever happened between me and Julie." Each word was weighted with conviction. "She left months ago—when Agnes came back from maternity leave. *Nothing* happened, Ceelie. Of all the crappy things I've done to you, that's not one of them. You've got to trust me on this."

"Well, she did have a full head of hair and the boobs God gave her." There was no satisfaction in seeing Nate flinch.

"This is *not* about your mastectomy, and it's absolutely not about Julie," he said again, this time even more earnestly.

I hated that I knew my husband well enough to recognize truth when he spoke it. I didn't want to, but in that small part of my heart that hadn't been hardened by abandonment, I believed what he was saying about Julie.

But there was no relief in the realization.

The specter of an affair had fueled an animosity that had kept me from succumbing to my grief. Without it, all I had left was scenarios indicting me.

"It's not about your surgery," Nate said again, as if repeating the words would convince me that my most intimate fears were unfounded.

"You barely touched me afterward," I said, surprising myself, my voice hoarse with defeat.

"I did." The ferocity of his previous disclaimer was gone. He sounded more defensive and unsure.

"Oh, please, Nate. A half-hearted hug and a pat on the back don't count."

He hung his head. For a moment, I hesitated to be any more vulnerable than I'd already been. I didn't want the man who'd left me to have access to my most intimate wound. But I'd already revealed so much that self-preservation seemed futile. "How was I supposed to make peace with my altered self when the person who was supposed to love and want all of me was so turned off by who he saw post-surgery?"

"I wasn't—" Nate stopped himself and seemed to be reaching deep for the words he wanted to say. "I was afraid of hurting you."

I opened my mouth to say something sarcastic, but he went on before I could.

"And—" He paused. "I wasn't sure you wanted me to touch you. It had been weeks, Cee. I could check your incisions and flush your drains any time you needed it done, but when I . . ." He frowned and seemed to struggle with finding the right words. He finally said, "That afternoon at Blackwell . . ."

I immediately remembered the day he was referring to. We'd gone for a long walk at a nearby forest preserve, following doctor's orders to get as many steps in as I comfortably could in the weeks following surgery. By unspoken accord, we'd found the small path we'd called Magic Lane when we'd discovered it years before. It led between bramble bushes to a small, grassy clearing few wanderers knew about. We'd sat close to the stream and chatted. The rare, warm, late-fall day felt so good that we'd eventually laid back, listening to the bird trills and soaking up the heady aromas of earth, grass, and sun.

When Nate had come up on an elbow and looked at me, his finger tracing circles on the inside of my forearm, a sheepish smile on his face, I'd felt a trickle of dread. I was fully aware that my uneasiness was ridiculous. He knew the post-surgery version of me. He'd changed my bandages and been there for every checkup in the early stages of my reconstruction. Yet something in me feared—in a blood-chilling way—that I was not enough. Not anymore.

Despite the assurances with which he'd countered each one of my fears, in the weeks leading up to surgery, about the mastectomy's impact on my femininity, the prospect of being touched by my husband—of having sex with my husband—terrified me.

"You looked horrified, Ceelie," Nate said now as we sat across from each other in a hospital lounge.

I closed my eyes to the confusion in his gaze. The memory was still fresh. So was its sting. I realized in that moment how subtly a life-saving surgery had altered us both.

"I was scared," I said. As the words came out, I realized Nate had said the same thing.

He smiled sadly. "So was I."

As much as I wanted to steer the conversation toward another topic, I heard myself say, "You never reached for me again. Not in that way."

He frowned and shook his head. "I'd gotten the message that you didn't want me to. And—maybe I just needed more time too. To get used to . . . everything." He saw something in my expression and hurried to add, "There was so much going on. In my mind. Between us. I was overwhelmed and didn't know . . ." He shook his head. "I was scared too," he finally repeated.

The intimacy of our exchange—of his eyes on me—suddenly got to me. I felt vulnerable. Exposed. In its urgency to step back from the minefield of our wounded sexuality, my mind leapt back to Nate's abandonment. The horror of the day he walked out and the untenable pain of the intervening weeks came crashing back. Memory relit the anger in me. It was oddly comforting.

"You didn't seem scared the day you left me." The hard edge was back in my voice.

"I was."

"It looked more like disgust. Worse—indifference."

That muscle flexed in his jaw again. "It's the only way I could do it. I had to be completely disconnected or . . ." He closed his eyes for a moment before going on. "That's the thing about the claustrophobia piece of this. I wasn't thinking about our history or our vows or all we'd already been through together. It's like someone was sitting on my shoulder screaming, 'Run! Run! Run!' into my ear and I was too worn out to outscream it. I just ran. I felt like my life depended on it."

So many of the men I'd known before Nate had been unwilling and incapable of expressing the abstract—thoughts, emotions, dreams. One of the first things I'd noticed about him on the day we met, when I was a college student at University of Illinois, was how verbal he was. But even for Nate, the degree of self-revelation I was witnessing was surprising.

"I felt trapped," he finally said. "I realize that now."

"Your 'claustrophobia,'" I said with resounding rancor, "destroyed me."

He nodded.

"At a time when I was finally beginning to feel like I'd have a future." I fought the tears. I fought them hard. They overflowed my attempts to stem them. "Just when I thought we could get back to something resembling normal and breathe a little and hope—together . . ."

"I walked away," Nate completed my sentence while I swallowed past the sob in my throat.

"You didn't just walk away!" I nearly shouted, infuriation erupting from my pain. "You took a hammer to everything I'd hoped for and were gone before the last shard of my obliterated future had spun to a halt."

Nate's eyes shifted to the handful of people who had turned to see where the raised voice was coming from.

"You destroyed me," I said again, more softly this time, allowing my tears to reveal just how broken I felt.

A muscle in Nate's jaw spasmed and he swallowed hard. The sheen in his eyes was not lost on me. "I am sorry, Ceelie." He said it again. "I'm just so sorry."

I dug around in my purse for a Kleenex. "What do you want from me?"

Nate said nothing as I wiped my eyes. I couldn't look at him quite yet, so I got up and went to the nearest trash can to dispose of the tissue. Then I returned to the table and sat across from him. It felt like an hour passed before he spoke, but I knew it had only been a handful of minutes.

"I just wanted to explain," he finally said, his voice hoarse. "It's why I've been trying to reach you. I want you to know that it's not you. It's me. My weakness, my failure, my fault."

I looked up at him then. "You deserted me, Nate. After all those pledges."

He nodded. "I can't take it back. But . . . I had to tell you that it's all me. And that I'm so sorry. And that if it were up to me, I'd want to see what we can recover from the broken pieces of what we were."

This time I let him touch my hand. That's all he did. He reached across the table and laid the tips of two fingers on my clenched fist.

I didn't know what to say. I didn't know what to think or feel either. So I stood and picked up my things. "I need to go check on Darlene," I said quietly.

"Do you want me to wait?" he asked.

I turned and walked back to my friend's room, knowing Nate would stick around a while longer and hating myself for feeling relieved.

Chapter 24

Nurses continued to monitor Darlene throughout the day and progressively removed some of the devices measuring her progress. The TIA's side effects were gone by the time she was discharged, but the mass they'd found on her brain continued to be a concern.

Nate wasn't in the waiting room when we passed through, Darlene in a wheelchair. He'd sent a brief message to my phone.

"Heard the good news. Heading home."

It was as abrupt a departure as his arrival had been, but the collision of my worlds, in addition to the trauma of Darlene's ministroke, was still playing havoc with my thinking and emotions.

The condition of Darlene's release was that we hole up in our motel for another full day before driving the six hours from Hannibal to Saint Charles. We spent the time communicating with her doctors back home, getting an emergency appointment with her oncologist, and setting up an evaluation with the brain surgeon who would follow up from there.

Darlene had barely mentioned the new tumor. When I asked her about it, she told me she had better things to consider—like the color of her next pedicure. So we'd left our room long enough to find a nail place that took walk-ins and she'd spent her time there brightening the atmosphere on an otherwise gloomy day.

"Are you going to tell me about your Significant Scumbag?" she asked as we were driving back to the Travelodge.

"Huh?"

"Your Jerk of All Fails. Your old Ball and Pain. Your—"

There was laughter in her voice, but I still said, "Darlene, are you having another TIA?"

"Just trying to find a way around saying the Nate-word out loud."

I gave her a look. "How did you know he was here?"

"Sent the nurse out to find you and she told me you were engaged in an intense talk with a dashing stranger. That new knob on my brain hasn't grown so much that I can't put two and two together."

"He's not dashing."

"Did you used to think he was?"

I felt myself blushing.

"So he is. You've just lost the eyes to see it. Why'd your Indifferent Other turn up in the thriving metropolis of Hannibal?"

I laughed. It felt good and completely out of place. "You got a lot more of those sabotaged idioms, Darlene?"

"I'm here all night," she said. "How did he know where you were?"

"I called him," I admitted, feeling embarrassed. "After you were admitted. I was sitting out in the waiting room and . . ."

"Absence makes the heart grow fonder?"

"Strokes make it grow more desperate."

She turned in her seat to get a better look at me. "So you asked him to come in your hour of need."

"I didn't," I said. "I called him because I felt like somebody else needed to know what was going on and I was . . . I was scared. And alone. I hung up the minute I realized the can of worms I'd opened. And the next thing I knew, he was walking into the lounge."

I pulled into the parking spot nearest our motel room and turned to find Darlene, penciled eyebrows raised, looking at me. "In a creepy stalker way or . . . ?"

I got out of the car and walked around to open the door for her. "I think it was a 'repentant ex-husband' way."

"Really?" This seemed to intrigue her.

"Really," I confirmed, unlocking the door to our room and ushering her inside.

She said nothing more as she hung up her jacket and propped herself against the stack of cushions on her bed. Then she looked at me with expectancy and said, "Tell me."

I spent the next few minutes walking her through what I remembered of the conversation with Nate. Exhaustion. Contrition. Julie. Some of what he'd said struck me differently as I repeated it to my friend.

"And this leaves you thinking . . . ?" she prompted when I was finished with the retelling.

I sighed. "This leaves me . . . I don't know," I admitted.

"Did he seem sincere?"

"I don't know."

"Did he seem truly remorseful?"

"Again, Darlene, I don't know. I trusted the man implicitly for the better part of my adult life. I trusted him through infertility and career hiccups and cancer. And then the man I married for his dependability and caring heart just—" I couldn't think of the right word to describe the shock of his departure.

"Pulled a Casper." When I looked at her in confusion, she added, "Ghosted you. But not in a friendly way."

"That's some modern terminology you're throwing around there, my friend."

She waved the comment away with comical hauteur. "So—where did you leave things?"

"You mean, after he was done explaining himself? Nowhere, really. He just said he'd wanted to apologize to me now that he understood better what he did and why he did it."

"Sounds like a step in the Claustrophobics Anonymous handbook."

I laughed. The weariness of the last two days washed over me and I lay down on my bed facing Darlene, hugging a pillow in front of me. "When I married him, I thought he was the kindest and bravest man in the world," I said softly. "I never dreamed that my battle with the Big C would reveal him to be so weak."

Darlene tsk'ed at that and shook her head at me. "I haven't been a fan of the man. You know that."

I nodded.

"But I've got to tell you that what he did yesterday doesn't look like weakness to me. It looks like a whole heck of a lot of courage."

Her statement didn't sit well with me, so I let it drop and tried to steer the conversation away from Nate. I looked at my seventy-six-year old friend on the bed next to mine and marveled at the recovery she'd made since the mini-stroke that had temporarily short-circuited her brain. "How much do you remember of your TIA, Darlene?"

"Not much," she answered, squinting as she tried to recall the details. "I remember reading the letter and . . . I guess that's it. Lights out. Next thing I recall is that handsome doctor shining something in my eyes."

I sat up and faced her, cross-legged on my bed. "Darlene, right before you started losing your speech and orientation, you got angry. I mean, really angry. You don't remember it?"

"Who was I angry at?" she asked, confused.

"Your father. And your language got . . ."

She raised an eyebrow at me. "Not Sunday school worthy, I presume."

"You sounded so hateful, Darlene. I actually wondered if the emotions caused the stroke. It just didn't seem like you."

Darlene's eyes had a faraway look. After a while, she nodded and said, "Some of it is coming back." She pushed herself up and frowned, looking down and away. "Mostly I remember the—what's the word for it? The rage, I guess."

"There was plenty of that."

"I remember what it felt like," she said. "This burning feeling in the pit of my stomach. The same kind of thing I remember from all those times Mother tried to talk about my father with me. This boiling-up rage." Her eyes widened. "I did say some choice words, didn't I?"

I smiled. "You did."

"Do you know how often my mom had to wash my mouth with soap when I had my daddy episodes?"

I considered all that had happened in the hours preceding Darlene's seizure. "You had every reason to be upset yesterday. Yes, we found a few treasures, and yes, that letter seemed to indicate that your dad did love and want you . . . but that little girl Cal McElway wounded still hasn't gotten any answers that explain his departure."

Her eyes moved to the bedside table, where the crumpled-up letter I'd retrieved from Lucy's nightstand lay. Something vulnerable and sad came over Darlene's face as a hand fluttered to her chest. "Maybe it wasn't the stroke speaking. Maybe . . ." She hesitated. "Maybe that was the real me."

"Darlene. Of all the traits that define you—"

"But it's in there, Ceelie. All that anger under this cotton candy hair," she said, frowning. "It may not define me, but it sure has motivated me."

"And yet you launched into this hunt for your father. At a time when you should have been sitting back and taking care of yourself, you set off to parts unknown in the hope of uncovering something about the man who gave you life. That doesn't sound like anger, Darlene."

She blinked away tears and reached for the letter, smoothing it out with her hand. "After seventy-six years of doing nothing. Asking no questions. Refusing to entertain the idea that the man was anything more than—" She stopped herself and a rueful, disappointed smile softened her features. "Whoever said 'better late than never' hasn't walked in my shoes."

Chapter 25

We drove up to Darlene's retirement home midafternoon and saw Justin's Explorer in the parking lot outside. Once we'd unloaded her things and installed her in her favorite spot on the couch, Justin sat on a footstool across from his mother and took her hand in his.

"Is this the part where you tell me that you love me but my whims are killing you?" she asked before he'd had the chance to get a word out.

He rolled his eyes. It seemed to be a family trait. "This is the part where I ask you how you're feeling."

"I'm fine."

He stood and reached for his coat. "Good, then I'll head back to Wisconsin."

Darlene laughed. "Oh, stop being dramatic and sit yourself back down," she said, waving for him to come back to his perch on the footstool.

Justin winked at me. "Manipulation works both ways," he said, dropping his coat back on the edge of a chair and returning to his mother's side. "Now—tell me what's been going on, Mom."

I edged toward the door. The trip had been taxing, and Justin deserved some time alone with the woman who'd declined to inform him of her plans and suffered a medical emergency while she was away.

"Do you really think I'm so far gone that I don't see you slinking toward the exit?" Darlene asked, her hand on Justin's arm to pause their conversation.

"I just thought you and Justin might—"

"Nonsense. You were a coconspirator in the whole thing. Might as well stick around for his lecture about going on a road trip with stage four cancer."

Justin flinched a little at the bluntness of her words. "No lecture," he said to her before turning to me. "And I'd love for you to stay. Not as a coconspirator, but as one of Mom's friends. I brought some things along that you might be interested in too."

Darlene's eyes lit up. "That binder you talked about?"

"When you were in the hospital in Missouri suffering from a mini-stroke on a trip you deliberately hid from me so I wouldn't stand in your way? Yes. That's the binder I'm talking about."

Darlene patted his hand and shook her head in my direction. "One of Justin's gifts is embedding recriminations in perfectly civil conversation so you're never fully aware that you're being sermonized."

I moved to a chair across from the couch and sat. Everything in me wanted to go home, crawl into bed, and sleep off the stress of the last three days. I'd been aware before our departure that I hadn't fully regained my pre-cancer energy and endurance, but I had counted on taking things slowly for Darlene's sake. Her emergency had undone all that. I felt weary to the point of tears.

But Justin had information about Cal and, for reasons I still couldn't quite understand, learning the veteran's fate had become paramount to me.

A few minutes later, we all had cups of tea and Justin reached into his backpack for a green, three-ring binder.

"How long have you had that, son?" Darlene asked.

"My whole adult life. Which you spent telling me to shut up about Grandpa," he added when his mom opened her mouth to protest.

I smiled at the love hovering like sun flares over their banter. Darlene made a face but stayed silent while Justin opened the binder.

"Thankfully for both of us, Nana was a lot less hostile to the idea of talking about Cal McElway than you were when I was growing up." He frowned. "I'm not exactly sure when he became such a big piece of our relationship, but it felt like something special she and I shared. I heard some of the stories so many times that I could write them down nearly verbatim by the time I started compiling this collection."

"And when was that?" Darlene asked, mock-offended to have been left out of the bonding.

"College. I took a history class that dove pretty deep into Operation Overlord. It made the Normandy invasion feel like more than just family lore. Then Nana died and . . . I guess I decided that I needed to document what I knew of The Man Who Shall Not Be Named while I still remembered most of the details."

He opened the binder's clip and took a few pages from the top. "Here's a letter that came in . . . July 1944, so just a few weeks after Cal came back." He skimmed the letter and read a portion out loud. "*I am directed to inform you that you are entitled to a Purple Heart in the name of the president of the United States and the secretary of the army for an injury sustained in action against an enemy of the United States on June 7, 1944. The medal is being forwarded to you under separate cover. Sincerely yours,*' yadda, yadda."

Justin handed the letter to Darlene, then took another from the binder.

"And this one," he went on, "informs dear old granddad that he'd also be getting a Silver Star." He held it away from him and squinted at the faded ink. "*Private First Class Callum Ian McElway, 506th PIR. You have been awarded the Silver Star for gallantry in action. Please accept my sincere congratulations on your heroic actions. You have upheld the high standing of the 506th Parachute Infantry Regiment without thought of your personal safety. It is the character and courage of men like you that make the United States Army the powerful fighting machine that it is. You will receive your medal at an appropriate ceremony in the near future.'*"

Darlene's head was up. Her eyes were wide. "Wait, wait, *wait*, son. You're running through this like you've known it all your life—which you have. But give a dying woman a moment to take it in." She looked at Justin, eyebrows drawn together in concentration. "So he was injured. I know that's why they sent him home. How? Where?"

"Bullet through the right arm. Tore things up pretty bad. Broken ankle. Broken ribs. Concussion. Nana never knew how or where it happened."

"And the Purple Heart he got for his injuries—where is it now?"

"Framed on my bedroom wall at home," Justin said with a sheepish grin. "It was one of the items Nana kept in a shoebox in her closet all those years—along with the framed picture she said you made her take down."

Darlene pursed her lips. "We'll get back to that later," she said before turning her attention to me. "You—what do we know now that we didn't before?"

I laughed. "Okay then." I reached for the letter Justin was still holding. The folds in the yellowed paper had begun to tear and the ink was faded, but its contents were pure gold. "Well, we know from this that he was a private first class in the 506th and that he earned two medals." I looked at Justin. "The Silver Star is for . . . ?"

"Acts of gallantry. Something he did that was above and beyond the call, in service of others. Usually demonstrating extraordinary courage."

"A big deal, in other words," Darlene said. The conflicted expression I'd come to recognize descended over her face again.

"Are you okay to go on?" I asked, fearing a repeat of what we'd been through in Hannibal.

"I'm fine."

She seemed okay, so I nodded at Justin to continue.

"It's a pretty high honor," he said.

"And is that one framed on the wall of your boudoir too?" Darlene asked her son.

He laughed. "What, am I a seventeenth-century courtesan now? And no, it isn't. It's in my office."

Darlene threw up her hands and mock-glared at him.

"The medal itself actually came in the mail right before Cal left, along with a citation outlining why he was receiving it. Nana said he'd refused to attend any kind of ceremony, so the US Postal Service did the honors." He flipped to the last page of the documents in the binder and removed a piece of paper in a clear plastic sleeve. "This is where things get murkier," he said, handing it to Darlene. She took one look at it and handed it on to me. It was the top part of a letter addressed to Callum Ian McElway.

The document was marked confidential and had *"Award of the Silver Star Medal"* written across the top of the page.

Only three more lines of text were legible above the charred edges of the partially burned paper. I read them out loud for Darlene. "*'Callum McElway, private first class. For gallantry in action on June 7, 1944, eight miles west of Sainte-Marie-du-Mont. PFC McElway, 506th Parachute Infantry Regiment, with complete disregard for his own safety, in an effort to spare . . .'*"

I looked up. "The rest is gone."

Justin nodded. "Nana found it in the AGA—that's what she called her wood-burning oven—a couple days after he disappeared."

"Abandoned us," Darlene corrected him.

"I'm sure that's what it felt like," he conceded. He flipped through the rest of the pages in the binder. "As I told you on the phone, the rest of his records went up in smoke too—in the Missouri fire. Nana and I did our best to find out more, but . . . well, that was nearly forty years ago—we were dealing with microfiche, not Google. When I was compiling this stuff, just out of college, I called around to find out if there was any trace of him in veterans records, but that was a dead end. And then . . . life happened. I got busy and didn't try again. So the rest of the documents in here are transcripts of Nana's personal accounts, plus printouts of D-Day stories that piqued our interest."

"You were a good grandson to her," Darlene said.

"She was a pretty fantastic grandmother too."

"Even if she did go off on covert library operations without informing your mother of what you were really doing."

He seemed to be remembering their time together. "Every so often we'd be looking at WWII articles, and she'd say, 'That sounds like my Cal.' So we'd print out the pages and she'd retell the story with him as the lead—this grand, romantic warrior risking his life for the sake of others."

He glanced at his mom. "She never said one negative thing about him. In all those conversations. In her mind, he was still a hero and an honorable man. I realize that's not the way you've pictured him."

Darlene frowned and took the charred paper from me. "How could a man be selfless enough to earn a Silver Star and heartless enough to . . . ?"

Justin nodded and pinched his lips together for a moment. "Walk out on his wife and daughter?"

"A daughter, we know from Lucy's letter, that he loved," I said.

Darlene considered my words for a moment before saying, "Correct."

"I'm sorry, Mom. I wish I knew more."

She sighed. "Part of me wonders if it would be easier to just keep seeing him as a monster. Keep it nice and tidy in my mind." She motioned toward the letters and the binder. "All this . . . honor stuff. It just frustrates the heck out of a little girl who spent her lifetime convinced the man was a good-for-nothing—"

"Don't say it, Mom." Mother and son exchanged a small smile.

"I should have been the one listening to her stories," Darlene said after a moment. She shook her head. "I was so determined to blame him that I shut her down. Every time she mentioned his name, I shut the poor woman down."

"I think she understood," Justin said softly. "And honestly, Mom, I'm confident she made sure I knew her stories so I'd be able to pass them on to you when you were ready."

Darlene sat back and fiddled with her wedding ring. It turned loosely on her finger, reminding me that this woman absorbing information she'd resisted most of her life was fighting a battle she wouldn't be able to win.

But behind the fatigue and regret in her eyes, I saw a steely resolve. To ask more. To know more. To extend understanding to her mother even though it came years after she'd died.

"Do you want to take a break, Darlene?" I asked.

She looked at me with troubled eyes, then turned to Justin with a weary smile. "What else did she remember about him?" she said, wincing a little as she shifted her position on the couch. "And maybe just give me the bullet points for now. This ingrate daughter is ready for a nap."

"Wounded," I corrected. "This wounded daughter."

She nodded at that and motioned for Justin to go on.

"She loved him," he said.

"You're such a romantic."

"Mom—she loved him. Every time she spoke about him, there was something nostalgic about it. I kept looking for resentment or frustration. But it's like she knew that whatever drove him away was too big for him to handle."

Darlene frowned, but it looked more like curiosity than frustration. "They met in Chicago, right?"

Justin seemed surprised. "So you do know something about them."

"Cal was part of Mother's story too. Some of it I had to hear if I was going to know my mom."

"They did meet in Chicago. He'd come up from Fort Benning on his last hurrah a few weeks before heading overseas and she was working at the Amertorp factory in Forest Park at the time. Doing her part for the war effort at age eighteen by making torpedoes, while he was preparing to deploy at age nineteen.

"The way she told it, they met at the Servicemen's Center downtown one Saturday evening—this huge place on Michigan Avenue that could hold twenty thousand people at a time. It was a thing of legend in the military, and soldiers came hundreds of miles just to hang out there and drink, or dance with pretty girls while a big band played."

"Enter Claire Asbury." There was something soft in Darlene's gaze.

"Claire meets Cal," Justin said. "They dance. She finds out he's shipping out. They spend the next two evenings together—they're both smitten. He asks her to marry him before he takes off and she amazingly says yes." He smirked a bit sadly. "Your basic 'boy meets girl, boy marries girl, boy goes to war, earns a Silver Star, comes home to a daughter he's never met, and disappears three months later' story."

I looked over at Darlene and saw a pallor to her skin that hadn't been there a few minutes before.

"Time for that nap?" I asked her.

She looked at her son. "Do you mind?"

"You should have taken it before I launched into the convoluted history of Cal McElway," he said.

I got up and retrieved the throw blanket from the back of the couch as Darlene scooted down and got comfortable. "I'm going to head home. So glad you're feeling better, Darlene," I said, draping it over her.

She reached for my hand. "You're a good friend, Cecelia Donovan. I'm sorry I messed up our trip with my stupid TIA."

Justin walked me to the door and opened it for me. "Thank you," he said. "For being that good friend."

I hunched a shoulder. "It's far from a sacrificial thing."

"Even so. You were there when the stroke happened and you got her the help she needed. Plus, you took a road trip with Darlene Egerton. I'd nominate you for a Silver Star too, if I could."

I smiled, but it felt forced. Fatigue had yielded to exhaustion. The lack of sleep, the fear for Darlene, the encounter with Nate . . . All too much too close together. I needed to get home.

I filled Justin in on the appointments we'd made for his mom and assured him I'd drop by in the morning.

As I was turning to walk away, I asked him one more thing. "Your grandfather—did your grandmother have any theories about his abrupt departure?"

He shook his head. "She really had no idea. She knew he was suffering, in more ways than one, but for him to up and leave . . . The way she told it, he never mentioned France after the war—never spoke of D-Day or what he saw over there. He had nightmares. A lot. She said she didn't get good sleep for the months he was home. He couldn't get through a night without waking up in a cold sweat. But—it's that generation, right? He was completely mute about it. No matter how many times she asked. So she just . . . stopped asking."

He scratched his head in a weary gesture and I realized how

heavily Darlene's dire prognosis must be weighing on him too. We'd been so busy chasing the ghost of an army veteran than I hadn't stopped to consider how the end of Darlene's life would be impacting her son. "She loves you so much," I said to him.

He smiled. "I know. For all her stubbornness about speaking of Cal, she was never shy about her feelings for me."

"It must have been so hard for your grandmother to keep her memories to herself."

He hunched a shoulder. "She actually saw some of her husband in her daughter. And she wondered if some of the trauma that had crippled him had somehow been passed down to his offspring. They've done studies about that, you know. And . . ." He shook his head. "The way Mom would rage when his name came up—even as a little girl—Nana knew there was something deep there. It's just that, in those days, nobody knew what to do with it."

"Did Cal rage too?" I asked.

"Not at anybody, to her knowledge. But there were things he did . . . Like disappearing for three days after that letter came telling him he'd earned a Silver Star. She said he was drunk out of his mind when he stumbled home. And then the actual Silver Star was delivered—because he refused to attend the ceremony—and two days later, he was gone. Found the citation and the medal in the AGA when she went to light it. As far as she could tell, he only took the clothes on his back. Left no note. No explanation. Nothing."

"I can't imagine."

"But she had a kid, right? She had to provide for the baby and they didn't have a whole lot of buffer in the bank. So she went back to factory work. It's what she knew. Family members watched my mom and . . . somehow they made it."

The silence that stretched between us was taut with unanswerable questions. When Justin spoke again, it was with a hesitant voice. "The doctors—did they say how bad that tumor is?"

I didn't know how to answer. "It's not good," I finally said on a sigh. "They might need to do a biopsy to figure out what it is, but combined with the metastases to her bones and lungs . . . It's not good, Justin."

He nodded. "Okay."

Tears came to my eyes and I tried to blink them away. "I so desperately wanted to get her the answers we went for. About Cal."

"It's still a pretty gaping wound," he admitted.

I filled him in briefly on what we'd learned from Brenda and answered the questions he had. "Maybe a daughter who grows up feeling so unloved by her father that he could leave in the middle of the night without a second thought . . . and then finds out, like we did this week, that he lived for months just a few hours away without making any contact—maybe that kind of thing anchors at a deeper level than you or I can imagine."

"So you think he died out there on the farm?" he asked.

"All evidence points that direction. And if there's nothing about him in any of the veterans records after 1944, like you said, I'm guessing he did."

He sighed heavily and leaned against the doorframe. "I just want her to die at peace," he said.

The finality of those words crushed the breath from my lungs.

Chapter 26

Justin headed back to Wisconsin a few days later. He'd spent nearly a week accompanying Darlene to her appointments and planning with her for the next phase of cancer's savage march.

She called me anytime she learned a new piece of medical information or had to make another decision, and though the calls were generally brief and cheerful, I still felt their wear and tear on my spirit.

Where fighting my own battle had been a full-throttled rejection of cancer's worst intentions, walking with Darlene through her fight for survival—and her capitulation—had struck me in a completely different way. With my own illness, I'd been the warrior. The decision-maker-in-chief. The strategy-builder and torture-chooser. I was the one who decided to put my body through the ravages of chemo. I was the one who monitored the side effects and let Nate know if I needed medical help. I was the one looking down the road at desired outcomes and potential dangers, weighing the untenable against the unfathomable and choosing to live with whatever consequences my choices yielded. There was fear—a deep-rooted fear—that I would make the wrong decision and suffer through an agonizing end of life. There was anger too—a full-blown rebellion against the disease forcing me to view the future through a grid of "ifs" that felt like Damocles's sword poised above my head, ready to strike.

I'd dug down to my most primal courage during those months and marched through cancer's minefield, clinging firmly to the hope that somehow I'd beat the odds.

Caring for Darlene was subtly different. While my own battle had been a series of laser-focused "next steps," I saw my friend's through a wide-angle lens, a devastating landscape of hazards and dread and loss. There was still fear. There was still anger. But both were couched in a kind of stricken grief that felt debilitating and marrow-deep. I was realizing more clearly every day that one's own survival—one's own overcoming—is a different burden than witnessing the suffering of someone dear and the blistering awareness of what a loved one might still endure.

To Joe's frustration, I cut back on my hours at the *Sentinel* to spend more time caring for Darlene after Justin returned to his job in Wisconsin, as he was unable to miss more work without risking being fired.

Darlene appeared immune to the worry that had slowed my thinking and my planning to a crawl. She spoke of dying nearly as easily as she described the latest episode of her favorite TV show. To me, surrendering for Darlene the stubborn hope that had propelled me through my own battle felt more torturous than any of the treatments I'd endured.

"Stop it, Darlene!" I snapped at her one morning when her laughing account of choosing a casket had eroded the last of my patience, exposing the grief I'd been wearing like a cloak.

She looked at me with surprise, penciled eyebrows raised, from the depth of her La-Z-Boy. She was smaller and frailer than I'd ever seen her, and her mental confusion was becoming more obvious every day. Hearing her speak of the pink satin in her casket had made her death all too vivid in my mind.

"Well, that was a bit abrupt, young lady," she said, crossing her hands in her lap and tilting her head sideways at me. "Care to share where that little outburst came from?"

I hung my head and bit my lip to keep from crying. "I'm sorry."

"Honey, we're well past the pussyfooting-around stage. You said it because you thought it. Now unpack it."

I shook my head and hoped my eyes conveyed remorse when they met hers. "There's nothing to unpack. I'm sorry. I'm tired and I'm scared for you and . . ." Anger—at myself and at the circumstances—bubbled to the surface. I stared at the ceiling and blew out a loud breath before looking back at her. "And you're dying." A lightning bolt of horror shot through me at the words. It was the first time I'd spoken them aloud. "You're dying and I'm complaining about being tired and worried. What kind of despicable person would do that?"

Darlene laughed. It was a lilting, joyous sound, roughened by her body's battle, but still luminous and sweet. "Despicable!" she repeated, laughing some more. She wiped her eyes with the back of her fingers. "Oh, honey, of all the words to use."

She shook her head and considered me for a while. Then she motioned for me to come nearer. I knelt on the floor next to her chair and took the hand she extended. "You listen to me, Ceelie Donovan," she said, her grip tight on my fingers. "You are not despicable. You are not any of the things your mind is accusing you of."

Her face softened before she went on. "You have gifted me with your presence since the moment we met at Central DuPage Hospital. You have stood by me and supported me and brightened my life. You have saved me from myself on more occasions than I care to count, and you have hoped even when I knew it was too late. Ceelie, you have *loved* me. And I know from having loved my mother and my sweet Angus right up to their last breaths that loving can be just as brutal as it is beautiful."

She let the words linger in the space between us.

"I need to talk about dying because it makes it less scary," she said after a while. "I need to go on about the pink satin in my casket. I need to tell Justin what I want in my eulogy and the ladies at St Andrews that I will not allow them to serve cucumber sandwiches at my funeral. I need to imagine out loud running into Cal when I get to the pearly gates, because I hate leaving this life without knowing more about him. Maybe after death is when I'll get my answers. Right? A girl can hope . . ."

"I'll keep trying," I told her. "Even after you're gone, I'll keep trying."

"No need for heroics, sweetie. It is what it is."

She paused and looked at me for a moment. "I know it feels very different to be witnessing death, as you are now, than facing it—which you've done too. Just tell me to shut up when my talking about it gets to be too much." She smiled a bit wryly. "Just maybe do so before you lose your cool and snap at me again."

I bit my lip in remorse. Then I brought her hand to my cheek and contemplated what my friend had said. The beauty and brutality of caring for the dying washed over me in a nearly palpable, heartrending wave. The yearning to make things better. The ache of knowing there was nothing that would help.

I tried for a smile when I looked at my friend again. "I want to be brave like you when I grow up, Darlene."

"Oh, honey, you should aspire to so much more. The way I've lived my life might have had moments of bravery, but what I harbored for decades about my father—that's the opposite of brave."

I gripped her hand more tightly and leaned in close so she'd see the intensity I felt. "You *are* brave, Darlene. You prove it every day."

She cocked her head to the side as if she was considering my words. Then she said, "Turns out the opposite of brave might not be fear." She looked at me with somber certainty. "I think it's resentment, Ceelie. The opposite of brave is resentment."

Two hours later, having finished lunch with Darlene and talked about the weather, her will, heaven, her gnome collection, and the man down the hall who seemed sweet on her—"I sure hope the lad likes short love stories"—I turned her old PT Cruiser onto Colones Lane.

I'd found Nate's address on a document I'd received from his lawyer a week or so before. It was a motion to dismiss. Nate had made it official. From his side at least, the divorce was off.

I pulled over in front of the townhouse he was renting and turned off the engine. It was hard to define the broad, warm, frightening force at the back of my mind that had prompted the detour to Geneva on my drive home, and I wasn't sure what to do now that I was there.

Nate's truck was nowhere in sight. There were no lights on inside the house. After another minute passed, I turned the key in the ignition and pulled away from the curb, nearly broadsiding his F-150 as he turned into the driveway. I slammed on the brakes and Nate jerked his steering wheel, almost driving off the asphalt. He came to a halt at an angle in front of his garage door. We sat in our vehicles, engines idling, for what felt like an eternity. I saw Nate reach up to adjust his rearview mirror, his eyes trained on me.

When he turned off his engine, I did the same. Then we sat there a while longer.

It was Nate who finally exited his truck and strolled down the driveway toward me. I watched, panic gripping me. Everything about him was familiar. His gait. His curious frown. The messy, wavy, graying hair. My mind filled in what I couldn't yet sense. The smell of pine, paint, and drywall on his clothes. Construction dust under his fingernails and in the creases of his neck. I felt his presence as much as I saw it.

He walked around to my door and stood there. I sat immobile. He tapped the window with his knuckle and I rolled it down, keeping my eyes fixed on a spot in his driveway.

"Hi," he said in that baritone that had spoken the score of our twenty-plus years together. There was something perplexed in his voice. When I said nothing, paralyzed by uncertainty, he added, "Would you . . . like to come inside?"

I shook my head. "I'd rather stay here if you don't mind."

He paused. "Okay."

A couple cars drove by. It was a quiet neighborhood not far from the Fox River. Modest and homey. Much like Harbor Lane.

"Darlene is dying," I said.

"I'm sorry."

"I've been spending a lot of time with her."

"I figured you were." The curiosity was still in his voice. He spoke softly. Patiently.

"Cancer sucks." I felt a tear running down my cheek. Then another. "Death is brutal," I quoted Darlene. It made her feel more present.

Nate's voice was compassionate when he asked, "Why are you here, Cee?"

"I hate what you did to me."

He walked around the car and opened the passenger door. He dwarfed the interior with his presence. "I hate myself too," he said. "It was—it was beyond cruel. I know that. And it wasn't me."

I looked at him as tears ran down my neck. "But it *was* you," I told him.

"Maybe. Scared-to-death-me. Exhausted-beyond-sanity-me. Desperate-me."

I nodded. I didn't want to understand. I didn't want to empathize. I didn't want to excuse or justify. But the part of me that was watching my friend die was beginning to differentiate between commitment and terror. Between compassion and self-preservation. Between courage and devastation.

"How can I know that you're still the other Nate? The one I married. The one I . . ." I swallowed the sob rising in my throat. "The one I thought would stick with me in sickness and in—"

"Let me prove it to you." There was a hint of energy in his voice now. Something that sounded like life.

"I can't be hurt again," I said. The sobs I'd been subduing broke through. "You can't hurt me again. You can't walk away. You can't hurt me that way again, Nate."

He seemed at a loss. The sincerity on his face—the tears in his eyes—dueled with something that looked like self-loathing. "I wish I could explain it . . ." He shook his head as if to clear it. "Being out from under the shadow of your cancer felt . . . felt like being alive again. But when the rush faded, I realized that I had nothing left. That we had nothing left. The man who did that, that wasn't me. That was . . ."

I knew my smile was sad and tremulous. "Claustrophobic-you?"

He reached for me—he always had when we were arguing, as if he was trying to maintain connection even when we intensely disagreed. I pulled away. Viscerally unsure and anguished. I fought the weakness softening my resentment and stared at the man I'd trusted for more than two decades.

He read my body language and paused before going on. "That time I went by the house to get some things and you were there . . ."

I remembered it well. Those final moments felt humiliating to me. Sliding to the floor after he had left, pain pouring out of me in tears and moans and unbearable lostness. Nate walking back in to get his bag and finding me there.

"I've always known you're strong, Ceelie. I knew it from the first time I met you. And in all those years before cancer hit . . . The way you got through our poor-as-dirt phase. Pursuing your goals and willing them into reality—no matter what got in the way. Pouring every ounce of yourself into the *Sentinel*. Climbing the ranks. Even making your peace with infertility."

"We made that last decision together."

"We did," he conceded, something sad flickering across his expression. He seemed to pull himself back together and went on. "You were so strong, Cee. You *are* so strong. And we had a good life."

I let the silence stretch between us. I lacked the energy to prompt or question him.

"You were doing your thing and doing it well," he said a minute or two later. "I was doing mine and mostly loving it. Home was the place where our two worlds met, but everything else in our lives felt separate."

Something indefinable stirred in me as Nate spoke. First, there was a sense of agreement—I too had realized even before my illness that we'd begun to drift a little. Then there was the guilt of wondering what I'd missed or just ignored. Close on the heels of that was a mix of confusion and resistance. I didn't know where Nate was going, but I suspected he was about to indict me for the fracture in our marriage. "What are you getting at?"

Nate sighed and held up a hand. "I'm not saying this right."

I tried for a smile and knew I failed. "But points for trying."

He contemplated me for a moment. Then he closed his eyes, frowning, as if he was trying to formulate complicated thoughts.

"Then came cancer," he finally said. "The fear, the—the torture of surgery and treatments." He shook his head. "You needed me. And I stepped up because . . . because I wanted to and because I loved you."

"You know how laughable that sounds, given what happened next, right?"

"I do." When I didn't say anything more, he went on. "For a few months there, it felt like cancer was bringing us back together. And then you started getting better—which was incredible to watch. Your trademark strength came back. You were making plans again."

"So . . . you decided I was well enough for you to walk away?"

He paused for a long moment before speaking again. "Brace yourself. This is going to sound wrong no matter how I say it."

I hitched my chin a bit higher. "Go on."

"I felt unneeded again. It felt like I'd gone from being your husband—your partner in survival—to being your roommate again. The videographer of your happiest moments."

I could feel myself frowning. "What are you saying?"

"When I left you that day and came back for my suitcase—I'd never seen you like that before. Never. Your tears, the—the intensity of your emotions. It got to me. And I started to wonder if maybe I'd read you wrong," he finished.

I leaned in on an impulse. Just a little. Then I caught myself and sat back again. "I've been married to you for more than twenty years. What better proof is there that I was in it for the long haul?"

"I know," he admitted, blowing out a breath. "But that's the moment I realized I'd made a mistake. It took me a while to admit to myself that a divorce was the last thing I wanted—the most egotistical thing I could possibly do. I just didn't know how to walk it back. With all I'd said to you. With all I'd done to you. I don't think I completely understood how deeply I'd harmed you until that day in the old house—or, I guess, how much our marriage meant to you."

"How could you not?" Even before he answered, I realized my own failure—the scant evidence I'd given him, even in the months before my diagnosis, of how much what we had mattered to me. Of how much he mattered.

Nate raked his fingers through his hair. There was frustration in the gesture. "I was a jerk."

"Yes." I wasn't sure what more to say. One part of me wanted to acknowledge the role I might have played in our dismantling. The greater part needed to trust again before I spoke.

"Ceelie." My name on his lips made something flutter in my chest. "Please—let me prove to you that that jerk wasn't me," he said. "It was fear. It was weakness. It was battle fatigue. It was panic . . . It was cancer. But it wasn't me."

I looked into his face through the tears blurring my vision. As he'd spoken, I'd heard his words, but my focus had broadened to encompass Darlene too, and the unbearable weight of her imminent death. It bound my breathing. It strangled my heart. It darkened the corners of my mind until it felt like I'd pass out from the grief.

The intensity of protectiveness, helplessness, and loss Darlene's waning life had engendered in me was so much more than what I'd felt as I'd waged my own fight against the merciless disease. I saw my devastation reflected in Nate's gaze and began to fathom the assault he too had endured. Because of me. For me.

"Prove it to me," I said, shaking with fear and resolve.

He didn't reach for my hand. He sat facing me, immobile, something soft and steely in his gaze. "I'll try," he whispered, his eyes on mine unwavering and true.

Chapter 27

Darlene died in the middle of the night ten days later. It wasn't the brain tumor that took her. It wasn't the metastasis to her lungs. Winston, the Jamaican nurse who had been one of her caretakers, suspected that she'd just allowed her life to seep away. "It's the way it is sometimes," he told me in his sunny, warm accent. "They tell their body that it's time to go and just like that . . ." He brought the fingers of both hands together, then blew on them and let them drift apart. "The spirit leaves. She died in peace, Ms. Donovan. Of this, I am sure."

I hoped he was right.

Though she'd seemed determined, in her final days, to focus on the aspects of her life that were beautiful and memorable, there were still times when Cal's name had come up. But it hadn't been accompanied by the angry outbursts I'd witnessed before. Those had been replaced by a quiet sense of dissatisfaction at not being able to know more.

Our final conversation had been about Nate and the tentative steps we'd taken toward each other. We'd gone to coffee a few days after our encounter in his driveway, but I'd come away from our hour at Starbucks feeling frustrated and hollow. The interaction had been stilted, the questions either too vague or too pointed. The toxic sludge of my illness and his choices roiled in the chasm that yawned between us. I just wasn't sure we could ever find our way across it.

Nate had awkwardly kissed my cheek as we parted on the sidewalk. I'd been walking away when he said, "Maybe it'll be easier next time."

I kept moving and mumbled, "Maybe," over my shoulder.

"Well, it was a good first step," Darlene had told me the next day. "Is that what it was?"

"Listen, you've gone from being married to fighting cancer to nearly divorced and now back to maybe-married in a matter of months. It's going to take some weirdness to get back to normal."

"If we do get back to normal." The hope I'd felt after our conversation in my car had dissipated quickly. The old doubts and anger hadn't taken long to stir again, and I'd lain in bed that night—and every night since—wondering how I could possibly have thought reconciliation was achievable.

Darlene seemed to have no such reservations. She made a check mark in the air with her finger. "First awkward date—done. It'll be onward and upward from here."

I'd had to cancel our second date.

Instead of sitting at a table in a downtown restaurant, I stood at the back of St Andrew's while guests formed a line that curved around the front of the sanctuary. There was no casket. In its place was a table draped in pink satin on which photos of Darlene and some of her favorite objects were displayed.

She'd made the change in funeral plans just a week before she died, and she'd announced it with her usual Darlenian flair. "Why would I want the last image in people's minds to be of dead-me in bad makeup and flat hair?"

She'd opted for cremation and declared that the service celebrating her life would be corpse-free and joyful. Though Justin and the funeral home had followed her instructions to the T, there was still a somber pall over the room. Darlene had lived seventy-six years as a vivacious shooting star and had left in her absence a tangible ache.

The room was filled with people who had brought color to the kaleidoscope of her life—her yoga friends, her bingo buddies, her nurses and doctors, her neighbors, and her former colleagues. They congregated in small groups, occasional laughter piercing through tears and solemn silence as stories of Darlene found new life in the retelling.

I'd done my grieving by her bed after Winston had woken me with a phone call and told me to come quickly. I'd held her hand as the space between her breaths had lengthened, then deteriorated into a guttural rattle. I'd begged her to hang on until Justin could get there. I'd told her that she'd brought joy and beauty to a season of pain. And I'd admitted that I didn't know what I'd do without her in my life.

Then Justin had arrived. He told me to stay when I got up to give him space, so we sat on either side of the tiny, indomitable woman we loved and whispered to her that it was okay to let go.

I'd grieved some more as I drove home early that morning, pulled over on the side of the road, my head on the steering wheel as I tried to catch my breath. And the waves had kept coming as days passed—broadsiding me in the grocery store, on the sidewalk, and in my sleep.

Now Justin stood at the front of the sanctuary, next to the table that held a dozen or more objects meant to express his mother's life and spirit. We'd chosen them together—the brick-carrying gnome, a couple of her favorite pictures with Gus, the Bible in which her mother had kept the snapshot of Darlene and Cal. Justin had asked friends coming to the funeral from Wisconsin to bring two more items from his home. The framed Purple Heart and Silver Star stood on small easels next to Claire's Bible. Parents reunited by the death of their daughter.

I went back to work that Monday and tried to bandage loss with busyness. Joe told me that he still wanted to publish the Cal McElway editorial and I asked him if I could make it about Darlene too. He looked at me over the rim of his glasses. "If it wins us a Pulitzer, you can make it about Donald Duck."

So I'd set to work distilling Darlene's energy and determination into words on a page, describing her single-minded effort to find her father during her waning months and morphing a story about a lost veteran into the account of a daughter's complicated loyalty.

I extended my hours to bring order back to the *Sentinel* and assured Joe that my traveling days were over.

"Fat chance," he mumbled. "Now get out and close the door so I can get some work done."

A week after the funeral, Justin turned up at my apartment.

"I'm on my way home," he informed me, standing in my entryway. He'd stayed in town to take care of the chaos the end of a life precipitates. The will. Darlene's mostly empty but still unsold home. Her funeral bills. Her things at Sunny Cove. He looked weary and relieved to be leaving town but told me he'd be back in a couple weeks to address what he hadn't had time to tackle yet.

"This is for you," he said, handing me a dark-green canvas bag. "Three things Mom asked me to give to you."

I held the bag open and peered inside. Then I reached in and pulled out the brick-carrying gnome. Tears came to my eyes. I placed it carefully on the console against the entryway wall. Claire's Bible was in the bag too. And a small, black urn adorned with flowers painted in gold.

I looked up at Justin. "Her instructions were one urn for me and another small one for you. So . . ."

"Her ashes?"

"I'm sorry," he said. "I know it's a bit—morbid. But Mom wanted you to have them."

I looked at the urn, at a loss for words. "Justin . . ." I tried to smile but knew I fell short. "I'm not sure whether to be sad or horrified or honored."

His smile was as unconvincing as mine. "She said you'd know what to do with them."

"She did?"

"You'll figure it out," he said with the kind of calm assurance that seemed to define him. "When I was little and things would frustrate me, she'd tell me to give time the time it needs. I'm guessing that's true for death too. Right? Give time the time it needs."

I placed the urn on the mantel above my fireplace after Justin left. Then I moved it to the bookshelf in the hall. After an hour or two passed, I took the urn to the laundry room and left it between bottles of detergent and bleach in the utility closet. I turned off the light, closed the door, went to bed, and found it impossible to sleep.

I checked the top shelf in the laundry room the next day as if the urn might have disappeared overnight. I wasn't sure what it was about it that made me so uncomfortable—except that it contained the utterly lifeless ashes of a person who had been the definition of vitality. Or perhaps it was Darlene's assurance that I'd know what to do with them.

I didn't.

I contemplated sprinkling them in the backyard of her home, where memories of Angus and raising Justin still lingered. But that house would soon be sold. I thought of driving them to Kinley and scattering them on Cal's farm, but that felt more like an indictment than closure.

Returning to the living room, I put the urn on the end table by my favorite chair with the ridiculous expectation that it would speak to me when the moment was right. The gnome and Claire's old Bible were there too. Its leather cover was worn and scratched, the gold edging of its pages rubbed off in spots. I picked it up and leafed through it. Darlene had told me that Claire always kept it near her—that it seemed to bring calm to her complicated world.

I bent its soft cover and let the pages flip, catching glimpses of underlined passages and notes in the margins. There was a spot near the middle where the whir of pages paused. I let the Bible fall open. Several verses of the Psalms were underlined, but there was one around which Claire had drawn a bold frame. While the rest of her notes were in pencil, this rectangle was in thick, blue ink and looked as if she'd gone over the lines several times.

"Cease from anger, and forsake wrath."

I closed the Bible and started leafing through it once more to see if it would open to that page again. It did. I held it upside down, gently shaking it by the spine, and when I flipped it over . . . Psalm 37. *"Cease from anger, and forsake wrath."*

I tried to picture Claire, abandoned wife and single mother, preserving her serenity by choosing healing over hatred. Then I thought of Darlene, of the simmering anger that had haunted her joy and singed her spirit for seventy-six years.

I wondered what it would have taken for her to find peace.

Goose bumps rose on my arms as something otherworldly washed over me. I glanced from the Bible in my lap to the urn sitting on the table next to me and heard Darlene's voice as clear as day saying, *"Maybe after death, I'll finally get my answers."*

An overwhelming mandate echoed in the spaces left hollow by

my grief. It was laced with so much certainty that I could not dismiss it and filled with so much purpose that I would not silence it.

"I quit!"

I walked into Joe's office with enough confidence and vigor to flutter the top pages of the stack next to him. It took him an inordinate amount of time to put down his pen, release a long-suffering breath, and look at me over the rims of his half-moon glasses.

"You're not really quitting," he said, gravel-voiced and unsurprised. "You didn't really quit in September. Or in November. Or in January. And you're sure as heck not quitting now."

I tossed a key onto his desk. "Watch me."

He glanced at it and grunted. "That's not your office key."

"Couldn't find it." I ignored his sigh. "But I figured my locker key from Miss Irma's Workout Garage would send the same message."

"For the love of Pete!" he growled, throwing down his pencil.

"Hold your fire," I said, putting up a hand. "Quitting is option number one. Option number two is giving me another week to finish the story about Darlene's father."

He rubbed his forehead and let out a sigh that sounded like a groan. Then he looked up at me. "You're aware that we're functioning on a skeleton staff, right?"

"I'm aware."

"So where do you need to go in such a hurry?"

I spent the next few minutes ignoring his incredulity and negativity. I explained my reasoning and recounted Darlene's frustrated attempts to learn more about the man whose absence had cast a shadow over the entirety of her life.

"I know it sounds harebrained. I know it's spontaneous. But sometimes you've just got to pull a Darlene. When she got a bee in her bonnet, she went for it. She dropped everything and did it."

"She didn't have an employer whose sanity and efficiency were dependent on her actually showing up for work between those hare-brained schemes!"

"I promise it's the last time. Just another week—ten days. And I have this feeling the story will be worth it."

He looked at me over the top of his glasses. Joe had always been a gut-instinct guy. That and hard work had built the paper into what it had become. "Your gut's telling you to do this?"

"It's barking orders like a drill sergeant, Joe."

"And this isn't you just trying to distract yourself from—you know—Nate and Darlene and . . . stuff."

I caught myself smiling. "No, you softie, this isn't about me running away from things that hurt. It's about looking in the last place that still could hold some answers."

"The last time you did something like this, you came back in worse shape than when you left," he said gruffly. He tapped his glasses on the desk and stared me down for a while. Then he said, "When you get back, I'm going on a vacation. To Maui or some other place with palm trees and piña coladas."

I felt excitement trickling up my spine. "Does this mean I can go?"

"One, you're not getting a penny from me. The article you've been working on is good enough to publish as it is, so no more *Sentinel* funds for this trip." He was trying to be harsh, but there was a twinkle in his eye.

"And two?"

He slid my locker key across the table to me. "Miss Irma says she misses you. Maybe hit a treadmill or two when you come back."

Chapter 28

I drove straight to Colones Lane after work. Then I sat in my car for several minutes, taking deep breaths and remembering Darlene's words about courage and resentment.

Nate and I had decided during a phone call after Darlene's funeral that going on dates was an awkward and unhelpful thing. There was something artificial and contrived about meeting at a coffee shop for "casual" conversation after twenty-four years of marriage. He'd convinced me, in his soft-spoken way, that getting together in a more informal context might be a better approach.

I would have stayed in my car a while longer after parking outside his townhouse, but my peripheral vision caught Nate's front door opening. I looked up to find him watching me.

"Thought you might be contemplating dashing before we dined," he said when I joined him on the front stoop.

"I might have been," I said. He stood aside and I stepped in. His home was small, narrow and deep, and sparsely decorated. The only personal touches I could see when we entered the gray-painted living room were his old Crosley record player on a side table and the orange and blue of a Chicago Bears blanket thrown over the back of a tan recliner. Everything else felt sterile and unlived-in. Practical and soulless.

A minute later, we were seated across from each other on uncomfortable chairs, holding glasses of red wine. I looked at his hand and, not for the first time, wondered why he hadn't taken off his ring. I picked at a hangnail and let my eyes skim the room.

"I like what you've done with the place," I said.

He smirked. "Sarcasm noted." Then he added, "I like your new hair."

I let myself laugh and realized how little of that I'd done in the time leading up to Darlene's death and since then. "Uh—thanks?"

"It's coming in straighter, right? I think it suits you."

I put my hand to my head. For the past couple of weeks, I'd begun going out without my wig occasionally, opting for a more natural look now that my hair had gotten long enough to be styled into something resembling a short pixie cut. It was thin, but it was mine.

I was fully aware that there was something mildly defiant in my decision not to wear the wig to Nate's place that day. "It's certainly different," I said.

"I think you look great, Cee."

Trying for humor, I added, "But how do you feel about my chemo poundage? You liking that too?"

His countenance changed. "You are no different today than the day I married you. Not in any way that matters."

I didn't know what to say, so I sat in silence.

"Are you doing okay?" His voice sounded sincere.

"I'm . . ." I hesitated. "I think I am," I finally said, surprising myself.

"Look," Nate said after another silence stretched too thin. "I know it was my idea for you to come over for a no-stress conversation, but I'll be honest—I have no clue what kind of questions to ask."

I tried for a smile. "How do we go from sleeping together for a couple decades to"—I made air-quotes with my fingers—"'getting to know each other,' right?"

He dropped his head and I saw more than heard his chuckle. Then he raked his fingers through his hair and looked up at me with a hint of mischief in his eyes. "Want to listen to some music?"

I glanced toward the kitchen's open door. "You got some pizza stashed away back there?"

He ignored my allusion to our honeymoon tradition and went to the small stack of records propped next to the Crosley. He selected one, removed the vinyl from its jacket, and installed it on the turntable.

The sound of a Rhodes piano blew through the record player's front speaker, followed closely by percussion and Bob Marley's unmistakable voice.

"Going old-school, huh?"

He held out a hand.

"Nate, we've been over this. We stink at dancing."

He'd started stepping side to side to the rhythm of "No Woman, No Cry," hand still outstretched toward me. I couldn't help but smile.

"We also stink at talking these days," Nate said. "Let's do this first and see if it helps."

I rolled my eyes. Nate reached down and cranked up the volume, then held his hand out toward me again. It was thick and calloused and familiar.

I let him pull me out of my chair and stepped easily into his hold. "This isn't exactly rock 'n roll," I mumbled as he turned me under his arm, bebopped around me, and brought us face-to-face again. It felt natural—mindless—to settle my hand in his and bring the other up to rest on his shoulder.

"Hey, Cee," he said, chuckling a bit. "Shut up and dance."

How often had I heard those words? He hadn't ever spoken them in anger. They were an invitation more than an order.

We danced until the song ended, saying nothing, letting the music guide us. When it was over, he held up a finger for me to wait and turned to install another record on the turntable. This time it was the Bee Gees' "Stayin' Alive." I laughed out loud and shook my head. Nate—measured, respectable, calm Nate—began to nod in rhythm and launched into a slightly less than convincing imitation of John Travolta's signature move.

"Nate," I said loudly enough for him to hear me over the thumping disco beat. "What are we doing here?"

Without pausing his choreography, he said, "Don't know what you're doing, but I'm shaking off the nerves and making a fool of myself. Same thing I did the night we met."

I remembered it like it was another lifetime. Me a sophomore in college, in a lukewarm relationship with a junior named Caleb, and Nate already working in construction. We'd met at a place called O'Hurley's, a popular student hangout, and exchanged looks, then smiles, across the busy space. I'd waited for the good-looking guy with the kind eyes to make a move for three nights in a row. On the third, he'd finally gone to the jukebox and pulled up a Bryan Adams song. Then he'd sauntered over to me, inadvertently knocking over a bar stool, and asked me if I wanted to dance.

"This isn't exactly a dancing kind of place," I'd told him, flattered and a bit embarrassed. "And I'm not exactly a dancing kind of girl."

"It's exactly what we decide to make it."

So we'd danced, tucked away in a corner of a dark room where beer, pool, and muted sports channels—not dancing—were the norm. And after a couple more songs and a conversation that lasted until closing time, I'd decided that getting to know this enigma named Nate was worth the odd looks from other patrons.

Twenty-five years later, the last notes of "Stayin' Alive" faded out, leaving us standing in the middle of his living room. The crooked smile that had been on his face for the duration of the song faded too. "I hate this awkwardness," he said. "Trying to be casual when everything's the opposite of it."

"I hate it too."

I could feel the warmth coming off his body as we stood facing each other. I took my hand out of his and stepped back as a ridiculous notion entered my mind and began to take root.

"Nate . . ."

He must have seen something of the surprise and alarm I was feeling. "You okay?"

I shook my head. "I don't think so."

He reached for my elbow. "Do you need to sit down or—drink something? I'll get you some water."

I shook my head again and felt a frown come across my face. "I think . . ." I hesitated. What I was about to suggest was so irrational that I wondered for a moment just how deeply the chemo had affected my brain. But there was something about what I was plotting that felt invigorating and purposeful. Also utterly terrifying.

I squared my shoulders and looked up into his face with what I hoped was certainty and determination. "I'm going to France," I told him.

I saw his expression change from concern to disappointment. I knew him well enough to realize that it sounded to his ears like I was throwing in the towel. "Okay," he said in a flat voice. This time it was Nate who took a small step back.

"I want you to come with me." I quelled the instinct to look around for the source of the voice that had spoken the words.

Nate blanched. "You—what?"

I realized that what was perfectly clear in my mind was probably a monumental question mark in his. "We can't keep manufacturing casual conversations, Nate. I hate it. And you just said you hate it too."

His expression went from dismayed to curious. "Go on."

"We work best in the real world—with activity and goals—not this artificial let's-sit-and-talk-it-out world. So . . . I'm going to France. To see if I can find out anything more about Darlene's dad. And I think we should go together."

Nate cocked his head to the side and smiled. "How much did you drink before driving over here, miss?"

"I'm stone-cold sober, Officer."

He paused. "When do you leave?"

"June 1st."

"That's just over a week from now."

"Yes."

"The library project is just getting underway."

"You have a foreman."

"I do."

"So . . ."

"How long?"

"Ten days."

"France, huh?"

"Normandy." I smiled and tried for a coaxing, Southern accent with mixed results. "I could use a strong man to carry my luggage."

Nate's eyebrow went up. "I think I like it better when you don't use your feminine wiles."

For some reason, that reminded me of cancer. Of surgeries. Of less-than-lifelike results.

Nate caught the emotions. "Yes," he said quickly. It was a simple agreement to something that felt far beyond what either of us could grasp. "Yes, let's go to France."

252

Chapter 29

We barely saw each other for the next eight days. We exchanged texts about Normandy's weather and plans for the trip. We'd agreed to split everything two ways, now that our finances were mostly separate. Nate was in charge of finding a rental car and I'd take care of booking our last-minute tickets. When I was making our reservation at an Airbnb not far from Sainte-Marie-du-Mont, the town mentioned in Cal's Silver Star citation, I had to pick up the phone again and push through my discomfort for the sake of clarity.

"Just FYI," I told Nate, "we're getting a place with two bedrooms."

There was a smile in his voice. "I never assumed anything else."

His easy acceptance of our living arrangements rattled me in an odd way. "Well, I—I just wanted to be sure you understood that."

"I do."

"This is us going on a hunt for more information, not . . . not a . . ."

"Honeymoon? Yep, I figured that too."

"And it doesn't mean I've—"

He interrupted my stuttering. "Can I get back to renting our car or would you like to beat this dead horse for a while longer?"

I went to Nate's place the evening before we left so we could make some sense of the bits of information Darlene and I had collected about Cal. He hadn't been to my loft again—not since the time he'd turned up unannounced and asked if we could talk. Having him in my space still felt too vulnerable.

So we sat in his gray living room and I filled him in on everything I knew, from the medals Cal had received to the woman, Maribeth, who had sent his letters to Darlene.

"Did she ever say exactly where the letters were found?" he asked.

"I don't think so," I said.

"Any chance of getting in contact with this Maribeth?"

I thought for a moment. "Darlene told me the name of the organization she works for, but it's French and I can't remember it."

"They bring veterans over to Normandy for D-Day ceremonies, right?" he asked, reaching for his laptop.

"Right."

"Let me Google groups that do that. Maybe you'll recognize it when you see it."

I did. La Belle Génération was headquartered near Sainte-Mère-Église, and a deeper dive revealed that one of its directors was a woman by the name of Maribeth Coupey, an American married to a Frenchman, whose passion for veterans had led her to found the nonprofit.

Nate reached for the items I'd brought along for show-and-tell. The letters found in France, the pictures from the McElway farm, the citations, and the small, faded photograph of Cal holding Darlene.

"No military records?"

"Only what's in the letters that came with the medals. We do know he loved his mom and his mom loved him. We know he loved Claire and she loved him. And we know he took off for Kinley when Darlene was eight months old and likely died on the farm. It's not much, but it's what we have."

"Hence this trip to Normandy"—he paused and made a production of emphasizing his next words—"*where we will be traveling as companions and staying in separate rooms.*"

I sighed. "Do you know how many times I've asked myself if I was crazy for inviting you along?"

"Flattered."

"No—it's not that." I stopped myself long enough to pick careful words. "Doing this together feels like a good plan. For a lot of reasons. But I don't want you to think it means . . ."

Nate's eyes seemed to cloud over. "I'm not jumping to conclusions, Ceelie. We're going on a trip." He smirked. "Because you need me to carry your luggage."

"No strings. No promises," I whispered.

"No strings. No promises."

"No dancing."

The way he chuckled made me feel off-kilter. "That, I can't say for sure." He opened his laptop again and seemed to turn the page on our conversation. "Okay—let's reach out to this Maribeth and see what she can tell us."

The Charles de Gaulle Airport in Paris was chaotic—dark, poorly signposted, and vast—but after eight hours in tight confines and with my recent incisions sore from immobility, it felt good to be moving and focused again.

We walked for what felt like miles from one terminal to the other to pick up our rental and set off on the *autoroute* toward the west coast of France. Once we left the Paris suburbs, the four-lane highway cut through lush green countryside, where rapeseed and barley fields extended out of sight. Small villages and ruins dotted the landscape, and herds of brown-and-white cows clustered under shade trees in overgrown pastures.

Nate caught me looking longingly at the dilapidated remains of a castle on a hill just off the road. "Want to go exploring?" he asked.

I shook my head. On any other trip, I might have welcomed the detour, but everything in me was focused on Normandy.

Nate quickly learned that sticking to the speed limit made other drivers angry, so he picked up the pace, getting us to the outskirts of Sainte-Marie-du-Mont by midafternoon. Nate slowed as we passed a sign with the town's name inscribed in bold, black lettering.

"*'For gallantry in action on June 7, 1944,'*" Nate said, quoting from Cal's Silver Star citation. "*'Eight miles west of Sainte-Marie-du-Mont.'*"

We'd been surprised by the American flags in storefronts and windows in the towns we'd passed through, but nothing had prepared us for what we found in Sainte-Marie. Nate slowed the car as we drove into the small town. It was built around a grassy central square. A small church stood in the middle of it.

"Nate . . ."

He'd seen it too. He slowed the car nearly to a halt, eliciting a honk from an irate delivery driver. Then he pulled over to the sidewalk, ignoring a no parking sign.

"Nate," I said again, disbelief softening my voice.

We got out of the car and took a few steps toward the church. There were several Jeeps parked on the grass around it. To my uneducated eye, they looked like authentic WWII-era vehicles, painted army green. A collection of small, A-frame tents surrounded the church, and men dressed in American uniforms lounged among them, interacting with a handful of women who were the epitome of the civilians I'd seen in old war photos—their hair curled perfectly, their lips a bold, bright red, and their black eyeliner impeccably applied.

The reenactors didn't seem to be performing for passers-by.

They were carrying on conversations, rolling cigarettes, and tinkering with the engines of their Jeeps.

"You're seeing this too, right?" Nate asked.

"I have so many questions," I said.

I caught him smiling at me. "Looks like you and your high heels and chutzpah are going to get to be war reporters."

Our bed-and-breakfast wasn't fancy, but it was located less than a mile from the historic village and had looked clean and bright in online pictures. A woman who appeared to be in her mid-forties, her streaked blonde hair short and sassy, came out to meet us when we pulled into the graveled courtyard through a narrow gate.

"Welcome to Chez Dany," she said to us in excellent English. "I'm Florence, and you must be Cecelia and Nate?" Her smile was broad and welcoming as she shook our hands, her bright-blue eyes as friendly as her voice. She wore jeans and a long, gray cardigan over a black T-shirt. Looking up at the overcast sky and adjusting the large, multicolored scarf wrapped around her neck, she said, "I hope you brought clothes for all weather. This is Normandy in June—it could be winter tomorrow."

Florence—who instructed us to call her Flo—ushered us to the side of the long, two-story building where a separate entrance was marked "*Visiteurs*." She showed us around the modest apartment. A kitchen and sitting area downstairs. Two bedrooms upstairs flanking a low-ceilinged bathroom that needed remodeling, but whose slanted skylight faced a vast expanse of fields. It was nearly at eye level and cracked open.

"If you look far in the distance," Flo told us in her delightful accent, "you can see a bit of the Channel. That is Utah Beach. A lot of history between here and there. And many travelers at this time of year who want to learn more about the *débarquement*."

"We saw the Jeeps and the soldiers when we drove through town."

Flo smiled. "Most of them are friends. They do this every year around D-Day—live like the soldiers did in 1944. The camp in Sainte-Marie," she said, rolling the *R*, "is small. You should see some others—Camp Arizona has hundreds of actors who sleep in tents and eat and drink like soldiers for days. Everywhere around Normandy is history alive around June 6th."

Nate looked intrigued. "Did a lot happen in this town?" he asked.

"*Oh là là!*" Flo exclaimed, throwing her hands up. "There is a road between here and the beach," she said, pointing out the skylight again. "You can't see it from here, but it goes from Sainte-Marie to Utah. That is the road the GIs took when they landed." She made a jumping, then a walking motion with her fingers. "They came by landing craft, and those who didn't die kept walking and arrived at this town." She pointed to the courtyard. "They went right past my gates. My mother—" She paused long enough to cross herself. "My mother, Dani, was a child, just five or six. She stood out by the street, holding her apron in front of her like this, and the Americans on foot dropped chocolate and chewing gum into it when they marched by, with their tanks and their GMCs following." She raised her hands again and took on an ecstatic expression. "She had never tasted anything like that before. Never! So—yes, a lot happened around Sainte-Marie. *Parachutistes*—paratroopers, yes? Infantry. German snipers in the church tower. Fighting in the fields and around the hedges. A lot," she said again.

Something that felt magical zinged in my mind. I looked at Nate and could tell he was getting caught up in it too.

Chapter 30

The offices of La Belle Génération were on the lower floor of a stone building in Saint-Martin-de-Varreville. We arrived mid-morning, after a breakfast of coffee and croissants.

"Say that name three times fast," Nate said as he maneuvered the Opel Corsa we were driving into a narrow spot beside the village church. I was still getting used to the smallness of Normandy, and this town was no exception. It featured one main road, a church, and a cluster of homes spanning several eras. Some looked like they'd been there a few hundred years, and others stood out like garish reminders that progress marches on.

Maribeth opened the door before we reached it and greeted us warmly. She looked to be about forty, and enthusiasm radiated from her voice and smile. We exchanged pleasantries for a few minutes, us filling her in on what we'd learned about Cal and her bemoaning the fact that she hadn't been of more help.

"The months before our D-Day celebrations are a blur of activity—we're a small organization and with just three of us doing the planning for the nine World War II veterans returning this year . . ." She brought her hands to her head, where a bright-green headband held back a riot of curly, graying brown hair, and made a face. "I have no doubt that we'll all get through this in one piece, but I could use about six more hours in every day."

I glanced at Nate. "And then the two of us show up to suck more time out of your schedule."

She brushed my concerns aside. "You are precisely the type of people for whom I'll willingly make time. My heart is for veterans." She motioned toward the walls of the small office space, placarded in framed pictures of elderly men in uniform saluting, shaking hands with civilians, or smiling into the lens. "I love that we've brought so many of them back to honor what they did. But soldiers like your Cal . . . They break my heart. I wonder if he was ever told how grateful the French are for what he sacrificed here."

"It might have fallen on deaf ears," I said to Maribeth. "He was actually awarded a Silver Star, but he disappeared from his home the day he received it. Then he disappeared again a couple months later, the night before his hometown threw a parade for its veterans. I'm guessing being praised wasn't a comfortable thing for him."

Maribeth nodded. "Sad, isn't it." She reached for the jacket hanging on the back of her desk chair. "Every year, this part of France practically shuts down to recognize people like him. The flags, the ceremonies and reenactments, the historical tours . . . Normandy *lives* to remember our heroes, and Cal will never know." She pulled on her jacket and took car keys out of a pocket. "Now—shall we go see where your hero's letters were found?"

There was a construction van in the courtyard of the Château d' Aubry-en-Douve. The tires of Maribeth's Citroën crunched on the gravel as we pulled in next to it. Nate and I got out of the car and took a few steps back to take it all in. It was a noble building. Elegant towers reached toward a still-overcast sky. There were carved stone corbels along the eaves and other decorative elements under the shutter-framed windows and above an imposing front door whose peeling paint in no way took away from its grandeur. Six broad, curved, sandstone steps led up to the entrance.

Maribeth climbed them ahead of us and poked her head in the open door, speaking in French to someone inside. Moments later, we stood in the entryway with a man dressed in filthy overalls. She explained to us that Jean-Marie spoke no English, but that he was heading up the renovation.

"Nate is in construction too," I said to her.

Her eyebrows went up. "Really?" She had a brief exchange with the foreman, then turned back to Nate. "How would you like a tour of the work zone?"

He seemed taken aback and a bit unsure. I realized how seldom I'd seen that look on him. "I don't speak any French," he said, lifting a hand in apology.

The Frenchman rattled off a few words and Maribeth laughed. "He says you don't need to speak French—you speak construction."

"We okay!" the man said jovially. "We okay!" Then he gave Nate a thump on the back and walked away, signaling with his head for Nate to follow him.

"Just steer clear of talking about philosophy and religion," I whispered to him. Nate gave me a look and Maribeth laughed.

While the men disappeared up the stone staircase leading to the first floor, I took a moment to look around. The entryway wasn't large, but it extended fifteen feet upward, its ceiling lined with carved molding. There were no decorations in the mid-renovation space, but the geometric design of the woodwork on the walls indicated where large pieces of art would have hung in the castle's heyday.

A bay window across from the front door gave out onto a lawn that extended to a lilac grove in full bloom. In the middle of the expanse, a colossal oak stood like a weathered sentinel.

"I bet that tree has some stories to tell," I said to Maribeth.

"It's an old one, for sure," Maribeth said. "But honestly, any tree that was standing in Normandy at the time of the invasion would have untold tales to share. What our history books describe is mostly true, but it misses the graphic details of what the boys and men endured after they landed here." She shook her head as her eyes lingered on the scenery beyond the window. "Husbands, fathers, brothers . . . Hard to imagine the chaos and carnage . . ." Her voice trailed off.

"Which is why you do what you do," I said.

"Which is why I do what I do," she agreed. "But you didn't come here for a history lesson. You came to find out where those letters were found. Follow me."

She led me into a room to the left of the entrance hall. It was another tall space, bright with natural light. Stickers were visible on several window panes, indicating that they had been newly installed. The walls were freshly plastered but not painted yet.

"It's a delicate balance, remodeling these historic homes," Maribeth said. "How much of the old to keep and how much to replace with something newer and—given the dampness of our winters—more energy-efficient. The owner here seems to have struck a bit of a compromise." She pointed to the floor, where some strips of the old parquet had been ripped out, leaving the rest intact. "They'll use reclaimed wood to patch it up and you'll never know it happened by the time they're finished."

"Do you know the owner?" I asked.

"Not the new one. The previous one was a local family. They expanded their farm by taking over this one. To my knowledge, they never really remodeled or lived in the château."

I followed as Maribeth walked slowly toward an alcove at the back of the room. "I was driving by here on the way to a ceremony about a year ago—learning the hard way that GPS technology doesn't always get you where you're going on these Norman back roads—and saw the sign out front for the construction company. I'm a bit of a fanatic about these historic buildings, so I pulled over, wandered on in, and met Jean-Marie," she said, pointing upstairs. "He'd found Cal's letters just the day before, so I offered to help track down any descendants he might have, and . . . here we are."

Maribeth crouched down in the alcove, where planks of wood had been torn up, exposing bare floor joists. "There'd been water damage here at some point, and the parquet was warped beyond saving. When Jean-Marie pried up the bad planks, he found the letters I sent to you."

"They were down there?" I looked into the dark space and wondered who had gone to the trouble of hiding them in the floor. And why.

Maribeth nodded. "Given their good condition, I'm guessing the water damage predated them being left here."

I looked from the gaping hole in the floor to the fields extending toward the horizon beyond the alcove's windows. A stone wall bordered a space that might have once held a garden. Its gate hung askew on rusted hinges. I wondered if Cal had stood there too, admiring the untouched beauty of Normandy's countryside, or if he'd been so wrapped up in the fury of war that he'd seen little more than danger all around.

A line from Cal's citation came back to mind. "One of the letters Cal got from the army," I said, "the one that informed him that he was getting a Silver Star . . . It said he earned it in a place about eight miles west of Sainte-Marie-du-Mont."

Maribeth looked up as if gauging the distance. "This would fit that description—give or take a couple kilometers."

"So this could be where it happened," I murmured. "Whatever it was."

I looked around the room again, taking in the simple but grand lines, the arched doorways and delicate details. I tried to imagine the lives that had breathed between these walls—the children, men, and women who had lived under Nazi occupation, as all of Normandy had, for more than four years during the war.

I tried to picture Cal—the Cal from Darlene's baby picture—walking through the front doors on the day the Allied Forces lost thousands just like him. Had he entered as a man or a warrior? Fearful or confident? Healthy or already injured? What had he seen between the place where he'd landed and this stately living room, where the letters he cherished had inexplicably been left beneath decaying floorboards?

Jean-Marie's voice interrupted my musings as the two men joined us again. There was excitement on Nate's face.

"Looks like you had a good tour," I said to him.

He laughed. "Didn't understand a word the man said, but the work he's doing on this place is incredible. You should see how they're replacing stones in the damaged mosaic tile." He turned his attention to Maribeth. "Mind if I take Ceelie upstairs? We'll only be a minute."

She waved us away and turned to speak to Jean-Marie.

Nate's steps were energetic as he climbed the stairs ahead of me, talking over his shoulder. "The amount of work this kind of place requires to bring it up to code is insane," he said. "Plumbing, electric . . . And walls two feet deep—solid stone and mortar."

I smiled. "So when do you start work?"

He smiled back. "Don't tempt me."

We reached the end of a long hallway, where a circular room had been gutted and new windows installed. One of them hung open. "This is what I wanted you to see." He leaned out, looking at a spot next to the windowsill, then motioned for me to take his place. "See there?" he said, pointing.

I leaned out as far as I could and craned my neck. "What am I looking for?"

"A bullet hole. Right next to the sill stone."

I looked down and to the left. There it was. A small hole, maybe a bit larger than a quarter, in the castle's outer wall. "From the war?"

He nodded, a little boy's enthusiasm dancing in his eyes. "Jean-Marie says it still has the remnants of the bullet inside it."

I couldn't remember the last time I'd seen Nate so animated. "War becomes you," I said.

"History," he said. "It's a real thing in these parts."

"If you like history that much," Maribeth said from the bedroom's doorway, startling us, "there's one more thing I want you to see."

The castle's newly renovated kitchen was a stylish combination of old-school charm and modern amenities. It looked to be nearing completion. At the far end was a rustic wooden door framed by what looked like ancient beams. Jean-Marie walked toward it, speaking nonstop, and Maribeth translated as we followed him. "This is the one part of the castle they've left exactly as it was," she said. Jean-Marie pushed the heavy door open and stepped down onto a dirt floor. It was a low-ceilinged, circular room surrounded with rustic shelves on which a handful of old bottles and baskets still stood.

Jean-Marie gesticulated as he spoke. "It's the castle's root cellar," Maribeth translated, trying to keep up with the foreman's explanation. "It was also a bomb shelter during the war, as it's partly underground. Farmers back then made bundles of small branches and lined the outer walls with them to keep shrapnel from getting through."

"*Et regardez*," Jean-Marie said, motioning for us to step into the center of the space so he could close the door. He pointed at a large metal deadbolt, tarnished by time.

"Proof that it served as a hideaway," Maribeth said. "They'd run in here, throw the bolt, and hope the Germans didn't care enough to knock down the massive door."

"Sorry about the trouble getting away," Maribeth said a few minutes later. "Jean-Marie's quite the storyteller."

"Probably what makes him a good renovator too," Nate mused.

Maribeth laughed. "That's more profound than you realize. In my line of work, we call it 'story therapy.' Allowing untold narratives to heal lingering wounds."

We drove in silence toward her office for a few minutes. I thought about Cal and the memories that haunted him. I thought about Darlene and the questions that had robbed her daughter-heart of any semblance of peace or wholeness. I thought of the story-telling my own grief might require, but got stuck itemizing the damaged and dark parts it still harbored.

Story therapy felt like a hazardous exercise to me, no matter how maiming the untold narrative might be.

"There's a gathering at the American Cemetery tomorrow," Maribeth interrupted my musing, pulling up next to our car in the church parking lot. "Nothing as formal as what you'll see at the big events on the 6th, but all nine of my boys will be there to meet local students—it's our big pre-D-Day event."

We got out of the car and she reached into the back seat for her purse, fishing around for an envelope. She took two tickets out of it. "Here—passes to get in for free. It's nothing huge—no dignitaries or fanfare—but you'll get to see some of those heroes we've been talking about."

Nate and I drove back to our bed-and-breakfast in silence. I put on a kettle for tea and got my Kindle from my bag. "I'm going up for a nap," Nate said.

It wasn't the first time the sudden awkwardness had broadsided us. This time it felt taut with unspoken reflection. "Okay."

"Want to go to the cemetery tomorrow?"

"Yep."

Nate dropped his head as if he was contemplating something else he wanted to say. A moment later, with a soft, "Okay then," he turned to climb the stairs.

Chapter 31

The veterans arrived together at the central monument of the Normandy American Cemetery in Colleville-sur-Mer on the morning of June 4th. Maribeth, pushing an elderly marine's wheelchair, led their walk to the place of honor where her boys, as she called them, would be greeted by the students who had helped fund their return to Normandy. There were seven of them in wheelchairs, while the other two held on to relatives' arms as they walked.

They wore jackets and baseball caps adorned with pins and patches that identified the branch they'd served with during the war. They smiled for the cameras of family members and onlookers and joked with each other as they made their way to the semicircular colonnade that surrounded a breathtaking bronze statue honoring the dead.

Nate and I edged as close as we could to the front of the crowd gathering on the raised platform and crouched low so others could see over our heads.

The veteran directly in front of us smiled with unmistakable mischief as he high-fived the man sitting next to him. He wore a black cap with *United States Army* emblazoned across it in gold letters and smiled broadly at the spectators photographing the heroes' reunion.

"Over here, Gramps!" a woman crouching next to me called out to him.

He found her with his eyes and smiled as she raised her camera. "Isn't this a kick in the pants, Gina?" he said in a surprisingly vigorous voice. He sat hunched in his chair, the jowls that framed a formerly square jaw shaking a bit as he spoke. But the excitement in his eyes was the essence of youth.

"Give me a thumbs-up!"

He did as instructed and waited for her to snap the picture, then turned his attention to the official photographer who was walking up and down the row of honored veterans.

"Looks like he's having the time of his life," I said to his granddaughter.

She went from crouching to sitting on the ground and breathed a sigh of relief. "He's having the time of his life at ninety-five, and I'm dragging myself around trying to keep up with him at twenty-nine," she said.

I noticed for the first time the belly she was rubbing with her free hand. "Let's be honest, you're dragging two of you around," I said.

"Right? Whose idea was it to travel to France in this condition?"

I glanced at her grandfather. He was trading laughing commentary with the man next to him. "Based on enthusiasm alone, I'm guessing it was his," I said.

"Yup." She put down her DSLR camera and reached around to her back, stretching left, then right as she took a deep breath. "Hadn't spoken about the war for—what—seventy-four years, and all of a sudden two years ago, he goes to a reunion in San Diego. Then he comes home and tells my mom and dad that he needs to go to Normandy."

"And here he is."

"Two years, one broken hip, and three fundraisers later, here he is."

The crowd quieted down as a tall, elderly woman walked to the

269

podium in front of the half circle of veterans. She wore her gray hair in a short, spiky, and somehow feminine cut and looked to me like the epitome of French class in her shimmering silver blouse and black pencil skirt. A red, impeccably knotted silk scarf completed her look.

She took a moment to scan the attendees with a bright, welcoming smile before addressing them in French. She switched to English after that, her voice confident and warm, her expression sincere. "Ladies and gentlemen, as the Veteran Relations coordinator for the Colleville-sur-Mer American Cemetery, I welcome you here," she said, a vague accent softening her tone. "Thank you for honoring our heroes with your presence. We must always remember what they cannot forget."

She turned partially toward the soldiers behind her and added, "And you who fought to free this land from Hitler's grip, I welcome you with highest honors. We meet today to express our gratitude to you."

The crowd clapped. They clapped for a long time. I realized in a visceral way that I was just feet away from men who had brought both courage and vulnerability to Normandy seventy-six years before, as Cal had, many of them too young to understand the horrors they'd encounter. I looked around at the children and teenagers standing among the spectators and wondered if they could fully understand the price these men had paid for the liberties they took for granted.

Nate hadn't said anything since we'd found our place on the ground, facing the veterans. I glanced at him and found his eyes fixed on one of them. He too was in a wheelchair. He wasn't smiling. He didn't seem to be engaging with what was going on around him. His gaze had the faraway look of someone whose memories were too close to the surface.

Nate caught me watching him. "I think Cal would look like that," he said, hitching his chin toward the veteran in a United States Navy hat. "If he'd come back at their age—he'd have looked like that."

I agreed with his statement. In all the imagining I'd done about an elderly Callum McElway, I'd always seen him somber. Weighed down. Troubled. Though I could recall every detail of the picture of Cal on the farm—the youth and vitality he exuded—there was something melancholy I associated with his name. Whatever had scared him, forced him, or propelled him away from his wife and daughter, had to be significant and dark.

The Veteran Relations coordinator was still speaking, explaining that children and teenagers from local schools had raised money during the year to ensure that organizations like La Belle Génération and Veterans Back to Normandy could assist the heroes returning to France.

"We'd like to invite those students to come forward and meet the veterans whose travels they funded."

The spectators stepped aside as young people formed a line and moved down the row of former bombardiers, rescue swimmers, and paratroopers, shaking their hands and expressing their thanks.

Nate and I drifted away from the crowd by unspoken accord and walked toward the sea of white crosses. The cemetery was not a morbid place, as I'd expected it to be. I was surprised by the sense of peace and calm that rose from its bright-green grass and granite crosses toward a suddenly blue sky.

A paved sidewalk led to a small protrusion overlooking the beach. We made our way there and took the time to take in the details of the map of D-Day landings etched into a stone table. I tried to imagine what had happened in the water and on the sand below us, then stopped myself. It was too brutal—even in retrospect.

Maribeth found us there a few minutes later. "Charles, I'd like to introduce you to two friends of mine. This is Cecelia and Nate Donovan." She patted the veteran's shoulder. "And this is Charles—

decorated veteran who fought in Normandy, earning him a couple of shiny things he'll be wearing on his uniform on Saturday. After that, he moved across France into Holland and earned some more shiny things by getting shot in the butt during Market Garden and sent home."

Charles chuckled and leaned forward in his wheelchair to shake our hands. "Hip, Maribeth. We call it being shot in the hip."

She shrugged nonchalantly and pointed at the bench where the pregnant woman I'd met earlier sat, legs extended, arms wide, in a comically exhausted pose. "And that's his granddaughter, Gina."

A couple children hurried up to Charles, holding out pieces of paper for him to sign. Maribeth turned his chair toward them and pressed its brake on. "This is one of the reasons so many come back year after year," she said quietly to us. "To be welcomed like heroes. Returning to places like these . . ." Her voice trailed off as she turned to look out over Omaha Beach. "More than a thousand men died on this beach alone. There are nine thousand just like them buried here today." She smiled a bit sadly. "Hard to imagine unless you were there to see it for yourself."

Charles had finished signing autographs and said over his shoulder, "It ain't nice to talk about a hero behind his back."

She laughed and turned him so he was facing us and the view beyond the parapet.

"Were you . . . ?" I hesitated. I wasn't sure if there was some kind of protocol about being too direct or too specific with the veterans who came back.

"Did I fight down there?" Charles asked, motioning toward the shore with a gnarled hand. "Not me. Bunch of the guys I trained with did, though." He sat up straighter. "Nah, me and my buddies, we came in from the sky." He motioned for Maribeth to push him closer to the landing map and she obliged. "June 6th, 1944. We were supposed to drop right around here," he said, pointing with a crooked finger at an area between Boutteville and Sainte-Marie-du-Mont. "Sneak in behind enemy lines. That was the plan. Turns out our sneaking didn't exactly work out."

Charles took off his cap and scratched the sparse white hair beneath it before putting it back on. "By the time we got across the Channel in the wee hours, the Krauts knew we were coming." He squinted up at the blue sky above us. "Shelling and flak like you wouldn't believe. Messed us up good."

Nate leaned over the map. I could tell that his mind was on the logistics of such a massive mission, foiled by weather and German counterfire. "So where did you end up landing?" he asked.

"War aficionado, huh?" Charles asked.

Nate looked at me. "I am now." Then he smiled at the veteran. "How far off target were you by the time you hit the ground?"

Charles dismissed the question.

"That's not what matters. What does matter is that I met up with other troops in time for the Battle of Carentan. Now that's a location I can point to on a map."

I crouched down next to him, peering into his deeply lined face. "I'm guessing you have some hair-raising stories to tell."

"Or not tell," Gina said. She'd walked over to us from the bench and was leaning against the map's stone table. She looked at her grandfather sideways, feigning disapproval. "We know about the flight over, right up until he jumped out of the plane, and we've heard about the Battle of Carentan and all that happened after, but everything between those two events—not a word from this stubborn veteran."

"You gotta understand," Charles said, his eyes on the landing map, his voice a bit defensive, "that night . . . It was chaos. And by the time my stick jumped, our plane was flying so fast and so low that we were lucky to make it down in one piece, let alone know where we were. All I did for that in-between time," he said, looking pointedly at his granddaughter, "is figure out a way to stay alive and get back with the others."

I stood and stared at the map as if it held the answers we'd come to find. I'd somewhat narrowed down the location of the castle we'd seen the day before by the town names carved into its surface. "So you were supposed to drop here," I said, pointing. "But you said you overshot your target." I looked up at him and was surprised to see the deep frown on the veteran's face. I tried for a softer tone. "Do you think you were over here? Nearer to Carentan or back toward Utah—"

He cut me off so abruptly and vehemently that I felt a shiver go down my spine. "Why do you need to know that?" The jovial story-teller had been replaced by a combative old man who suddenly had the look of a cornered animal.

"I—" I looked at Nate for support, startled.

"We're trying to get some information about a man who jumped the same night you did."

"He landed near a small castle, several miles off-target," I filled in. "That's why I was asking. Just wondering if you and he might have . . ."

I saw the look on Nate's face change from curiosity to excitement. "Wait," he said, staring at the cap the veteran was wearing. "Charles, were you with the 506th?"

Some of the color seemed to seep out of Charles's face. He took a breath and coughed as he blew it out, so much tension suddenly gripping his body that it made his cheeks quiver. "It doesn't matter!" he said, his voice higher now and strained, squinting at Nate with something that looked like panic on his face.

Out of the corner of my eye, I saw Gina step toward him. "Gramps . . ."

He pointed a finger at Nate, then at me. "It doesn't matter where I landed or what—what—what happened!"

Gina was by his side, crouching down and squeezing his arm

with her hand, using a soothing tone of voice to try to get his attention. "Gramps—hey. It's okay."

But he was not hearing her. "I'm done here!"

Maribeth's wide eyes were skipping from Charles to Gina and back again, clearly as shocked as I was by the vitriolic response. She leaned over his shoulder, "Charles, would you like to—"

"Take me back to the van," he ordered.

"But—" Gina tried.

He craned around until he made eye contact with Maribeth. "You gonna take me back to the van or what?" he barked.

Gina stepped back in consternation and Maribeth put up a hand in a calming manner. "I'll take him back," she said. "The first van is supposed to leave shortly anyway."

Gina looked horrified and contrite. "Maribeth, I'm so sorry."

Charles wasn't done. As Maribeth released the wheelchair's brake and began to push him back toward the parking lot, he yelled, "I got the Krauts—that's what I did! It doesn't matter what happened!" he yelled again as they turned the corner toward the van.

"And that," Gina said, her face red with embarrassment, "is what used to happen every time we asked him about the war. He's been better the last couple of years. That's if he brings up the topic himself and cherry-picks what he wants to tell us. But those two days between the landing and Carentan?" She nodded in the direction he'd disappeared. "Full meltdown—every time."

"We didn't mean any harm," Nate said, shaking his head in confusion.

"I know you didn't." She sighed in a defeated way. "That man back there—at the monument? That's the real Charles. Proud of his service and loving the attention. This version you just saw? For all their bravado, it's a pretty stark reminder that survivors of war are among the wounded too."

Chapter 32

C harles's outburst stuck with us as we continued our visit of the cemetery, awed by the vastness of the memorial's grounds and sobered by its significance. We went back to the colonnade where the day had started to read the maps and narratives flanking its bronze statue, strolled along the Wall of the Missing, then circled back to the path overlooking the beach and found a bench facing rows of white crosses on their manicured lawn.

"Every one of those crosses . . . ," Nate began.

I nodded. "A Cal McElway. A Charles. Brother, father, son, sister, daughter who didn't make it back."

He smiled a bit sadly. "How are those creative juices doing?"

"Flowing strong," I answered. "Overwhelming, actually."

"It's a lot," he said.

"I wonder if Cal would have preferred to die and be buried here than . . ."

"Possibly." Nate seemed to consider it for a moment. "Probably," he amended. "Beats dying alone out in a field in Missouri."

I tried for humor. "Normandy, Missouri . . . ech."

Few things about Nate had thrilled me more when we met back in the nineties than making him laugh. As I shrugged in feigned nonchalance and he chuckled, I realized how fresh that thrill still felt.

"If anything, there's too much," I said on a serious note. "Too many stories. Too many tragedies and untold victories. I'm supposed to be here to add the finishing touches to an essay about Cal and Darlene, but with all this to take in . . . And people like him— wearing their memories on their faces," I said as I noticed the somber veteran from earlier standing up from his wheelchair, with some help, to salute a cross. "It's almost too much."

"Story therapy," Nate said, repeating Maribeth's words as he followed the direction of my gaze. "The veterans may come back because they're welcomed so warmly, but I'm guessing part of their healing needs to happen here too."

The birds trilled in the trees around us. A child in an American flag dress ran between the rows of crosses, her father in hot pursuit. Teenagers clustered around a veteran sharing his memories on a parapet a few feet from us.

"Because their story is given a voice here," I said.

I felt more than I saw the shift in Nate's disposition. "So . . ." He seemed to hesitate as he straightened on the bench next to me.

"Are you about to say something awkward?" I looked at him and he hunched a shoulder.

There was determination under the grin he shot me. "I told you my story," he said. "We sat in a hospital and I imposed it on you. Poor, wounded Nate, forced to run away like a coward because things were so hard."

"Your timing kinda sucked."

"It did." He looked at me sheepishly. "I guess I was determined to get it out."

"You certainly were," I said. I tried to smile to mitigate the darkness the memories were fueling.

"I experienced your cancer as a caretaker. A bystander. But

you're the one who lived it," Nate said. He looked across the cemetery. I could tell he was trying to find the right words. Part of me feared what they would be when he did. Something guilt-ridden fell over his features. "I haven't heard your story. I never asked for it."

Vague feelings began to stir. Fear. Relief. Caution. "You *lived* my story with me, Nate. You went to my appointments. You took care of the house. You managed our calendar . . . You shaved my head when my hair started falling out and you cleaned up my messes. You lived it all."

He shook his head, his forehead furrowed and his eyes intense on mine. "I saw it. I witnessed it. But I was on the outside looking in . . . It's not the same."

His words surprised and silenced me. I tried to unravel their complicated truth—their connection to my pain, my survival . . . and to Darlene. *"Loving can be just as brutal as it is beautiful."*

Tears blurred my vision. "I know it's hard for the caretakers too," I said to him.

He shook his head. "That's not my point."

I sighed and tried to measure the emotional toll a retelling would take. "This may not be the right time to get into it, Nate."

He looked at the neat rows of crosses and Stars of David standing at perfect intervals between us and the reflecting pond. Then he turned his eyes on me with startling intensity. "Or maybe it's exactly the right time."

I didn't say anything as several minutes ticked by.

"Story therapy ain't for the faint of heart," I finally mumbled.

I looked at him. He looked back at me. Then I started to speak. Reluctantly—tentatively—feeling silly for walking him back through what we'd faced together. He kept asking deeper questions, encouraging me to go on. We got to the days right before surgery—the uncertainty I'd felt.

"You were scared," Nate said. "You kept asking me if the

mastectomy and reconstruction . . . if they'd change the way I saw you."

I couldn't help but make a face. "And then you left me."

"But not because—"

"Tell that to a woman who's just had her breasts cut off, put on fifteen pounds, and watched her hair fall out."

The silence between us grated across old wounds. "I left because I'm a jerk," he finally said. "Not because—"

"Every fear I had—other than dying—became a reality that day," I said, interrupting him as tears fell from my eyes. "Just like that." I snapped my fingers. "And every text and lawyer's document after that was just more evidence that I was somehow not good enough anymore. Unworthy and repulsive." I looked him straight in the eye and hoped he saw how torn I was, how torturous my inner conflict between terror and trust. "You added emotional annihilation to the medical trauma. You've explained it to me and I've heard your words, but to be honest, I'm having trouble getting past what it did to me."

He hung his head.

I let mine fall back and stared at the sky for a few breaths.

"I'm sorry," he said. He squinted off into the distance as a muscle spasmed in his jaw. "There's no valid explanation for what I did to you. To us."

"That's why I don't know what to think," I said, finally voicing the hesitation that had hobbled our conversations since we'd started talking again. "We can be in the same room together now. We can travel across the ocean. We can traipse around Normandy on a quest to find a veteran. We can go through the motions of telling our stories, but, Nate, I'm just not sure we can really get beyond what happened. The abandonment. The humiliation. It might be too big." I shook my head. "Sometimes I almost forget—for just a moment—and then . . ."

He looked at me but didn't say anything. We both turned to face the crosses again, leaning back as our eyes followed the visitors walking the cemetery's paths.

The silence felt stifling.

After a couple minutes passed, I sat up straighter and said, "Meanwhile, we have a mission to finish." I hoped my voice sounded more purposeful than wounded. "And crêpes to eat in Sainte-Mère-Église tonight, as per Flo's instructions, so . . ."

"So." Nate stood, something like determined optimism on his face. "Let's go get us some crêpes."

It wasn't until we parked our car and looked up at the church steeple that we realized what an iconic location the bustling town was.

"Wait," Nate said, pointing up. "Is this the place where that guy got hung up on the steeple in *The Longest Day*?"

I looked where he was pointing and saw a mannequin in a paratrooper's uniform hanging from a canopy snagged on the tower. "Sure hope that's not the original John Steele . . ."

"I need to watch that movie again when we get home," Nate said, locking the car.

The *crêperie* was a hole in the wall, a stone's throw from the main square. Gift stores and small snack shops lined the streets. There were tourists everywhere, drawn to the place by its rich history. A small crowd had gathered outside a sandwich place, and I craned my neck to see what the attraction was as we ambled by, but I couldn't see past the cluster of spectators.

When we arrived at the restaurant, we were told in a disapproving tone that people in France don't eat dinner until at least seven o'clock and that we should take a two-hour walk and come back when they opened.

We did just that, finding our way back to more casual interaction as we toured the Airborne Museum, shopped for souvenirs, and took a quick stroll through the church.

The gathering outside the sandwich shop had dispersed a little when we went by two hours later, and I saw a familiar face looking on. Gina sat on a low wall, clearly exhausted despite the smile on her face. I pointed her out to Nate and we walked over, realizing as we did that her grandfather was the man who had gathered the onlookers.

"Telling tall tales," Gina said to me after I sat down next to her. "He doesn't go looking for an audience. They see the hat and the United States Army jacket and—off he goes. I'm guessing those Japanese tourists haven't gotten a word of what he's saying, but they're playing along to get a picture with him later."

Nate leaned around me to address her. "Is he feeling better?"

"Much. His 'episodes'"—she made air quotes—"don't last long, but they sure make an impression."

I pulled my windbreaker tighter. The temperature had dropped significantly since we'd met at the cemetery. "I'm sorry we brought it on," I told her.

She shrugged. "I owe Maribeth a bottle of cider or something for her kindness."

A couple of the tourists who had been talking with Charles stepped away and he saw Nate and me sitting with his grand-daughter. His words and gestures froze. I expected him to ignore us and turn back to his audience to finish the story he was telling. Instead, he lowered his hands into his lap, pressed his lips together, and told the tourists that he had to talk to "those people." He jutted his chin toward us and cracked a small smile.

It took a couple more minutes for him to pose for pictures and sign the pieces of paper his admirers held out to him. Then he rolled his chair over to us.

"Hi, Charles," I said. I tried for a casual shrug and smiled. "Us again."

He looked at me. Then he looked at Nate. He seemed locked in an internal conflict, light and darkness playing across his features. The struggle was so visible that none of us spoke, probably for fear of sending him back into a fit of anger.

For a moment, his hands clenched the armrests of his wheelchair tightly enough for his knuckles to turn white. Then he released them and looked at us as if he'd come to a difficult decision.

"If I'm gonna do this," he said gruffly, "I'm gonna do it right." He hitched his chin toward Nate. "There a place we can talk around here? Somewhere we won't be interrupted by my *legions* of fans?"

I glanced at Gina. Her wide-eyed surprise, I suspected, mirrored mine.

"We've got reservations at a crêpe place right around the corner," Nate said, an electric undertone in the calm of his voice. "I'm sure they can add a couple place settings."

Charles grunted and said, "That'll do." Then he motioned for Gina to come over and push his wheelchair.

A bit stunned, I asked, "Charles, are you sure . . . ?"

He turned and shot me a mock-annoyed look, but there was something gentle—almost resigned—in his voice when he said, "Don't try my patience, little lady, or I'll blow another gasket."

Chapter 33

The *crêperie* held just a handful of tables, all rough-hewn and mismatched. We'd decided that going there to hear more of Charles's story would spare us from the bitterly cold wind blowing through Sainte-Mère-Église that June evening.

A young woman dressed like Rosie the Riveter greeted us cheerily and installed us in a back corner of the already noisy room, where the wheelchair would be out of the way. She handed us bilingual menus and disappeared.

"Well, Gramps," Gina said, her eyes on the selection of crêpes, "you've surprised me a couple times during this trip, but sitting here having a civil dinner with these two after the scene at the cemetery is right up at the top."

"Nobody said anything about civil." Charles's voice was gruff, but there was something soft in his countenance. Not gentle or tender—bruised.

Gina patted his hand. "Old dog, new trick. Give it a try, Gramps."

Nate laughed softly next to me, and I wondered if my face showed the same kind of expectation his did. We'd exchanged a couple looks after Charles's startling invitation to dinner, unwilling to risk saying something out loud that would make him change his mind, and had agreed to let him take the lead by unspoken consent. Now we both sat in the bustling restaurant, sipping traditional, Norman hard apple cider and waiting for our crêpes to arrive.

We skirted the edges of the topic at hand. Gina brought up the weather, and Charles casually commented that it was similar to what he'd experienced on D-Day. I talked about the ceremony we'd attended that morning, and Charles mentioned how surprising it was to see young people so interested in the men who'd fought in Operation Overlord. Nate asked him about the medals Maribeth had mentioned, and Charles told us when, where, and how he'd earned each one of them.

Our food arrived, and still Charles didn't broach the topic we'd hoped to hear about. So we discussed Normandy's scenery, the benefits of a simpler life, and the outrageous kindness we'd encountered so far.

"Makes an old soldier feel like he did something right," Charles said after Nate expressed his surprise at the way the region marked the anniversary of D-Day. We were still amazed as we drove through tiny villages and larger towns, awed by the flags, the re-enactments, the ceremonies, and the gratitude that radiated from the people we met.

"You did do something right," Gina said, looking up from the ham-and-cheese buckwheat crêpe she was eating. "This country still speaks French because of men like you."

"Not to mention how it changed the rest of the world," Nate added.

"Heroes," Gina said, using her fork to accentuate her statement. "Every last one of you."

Nobody said anything for a while. Charles looked pensive, and neither Nate nor I dared risk another outburst by asking the wrong question. So we ate. We waited. Rosie the Riveter cleared our plates and brought us the dessert menu.

"What did you say your boy's name was?" Charles asked abruptly.

I looked at Nate. His eyes were on me, excitement in their depths.

"I don't think we did say," I answered. "But his name was Cal McElway."

Charles's eyes widened imperceptibly. Then he looked toward the ceiling as he gathered his thoughts, folding his napkin and placing it next to his plate.

"And you know him how?" He looked directly at me for the first time since we'd sat down.

"I knew his daughter, Darlene. She died of cancer just a few weeks ago, but she spent the last months of her life trying to find her father."

"What—did she lose him or something?" His attempt at cheerful grumpiness couldn't mask the shaking of his hands or the twitch in his jaw.

"He came back from Normandy wounded in '44," Nate said. "Met his daughter for the first time—she was born while he was deployed. And then he disappeared a few months later."

That seemed to get his attention. "Just . . . disappeared?"

"Poor girl," Gina murmured.

Charles crossed his arms and leaned back. "Doesn't sound like the Cal I knew."

Charles's admission that he knew Cal momentarily stunned me into silence. Nate said, "You knew him?" with a kind of awed excitement in his voice. He glanced at me, then back at the surly veteran.

Charles hesitated for just a moment. "Yeah, but what you're sayin' doesn't sound like him."

"What do you mean?" Gina asked.

"Leaving like that. He wasn't the runaway type. He was the 'stay put and do good' type."

Something electric skimmed over my skin. "What can you tell us about him? Did you train with him? Jump with him? And if you did, where did you—"

Nate chuckled next to me. "Can you tell we're eager to know more?" he said to Charles. "Please—just tell us what you're comfortable sharing."

Charles stared at Nate and me for what felt like an eternity. Then he turned to his granddaughter and said, "Pay attention, honey. I may not tell this story again."

"I'm all ears, Gramps." She reached into her purse and surreptitiously pulled out her phone, tapped an app to open it, and pushed the record button before she laid it on the table. She smiled at me and mouthed, "For posterity."

"If my Cal McElway is the same guy as your Cal McElway—and what are the odds of two Cal McElways jumping the same night in the same place—we met during training in Georgia. The army moved us around for a bit and we got separated, but we ended up in Ramsbury together. That's southern England for you geographically challenged millennials."

"I'm the only millennial here, Gramps, but thanks for the confidence," Gina said.

Charles ignored her. "Those were crazy days," he went on. "Hard work, no rest, and this constant clock ticking at the back of our minds. Tomorrow could be the day. That's what we went to sleep to every night. This constant drumbeat of 'tomorrow could be the day.'"

"How much notice did you get before shipping out?" Nate asked.

"A few hours, but we didn't need them. We were ready from 'go.' Eager, even. Couldn't wait to drop onto French soil and blow those Krauts to bloody hell."

Gina smiled and winked at me. "My grandfather's a pacifist."

Charles gave her a look. "So we get out over water and things turn bad," he went on. "Cal's in the number six spot, a seat closer to the jump door from me. He's focused. Always was. He's got his picture out—"

"A picture?"

"Girl back home. Cute. Too cute for him, but who's to say?"

I looked at Nate. His elbows were on the table and he was leaning in, hanging on every word. I wondered when he had become as invested in Cal's story as I was.

"It was a mess in there," Charles continued. "Mortal fear and a bumpy ride—bad combination. Lots of praying going on, the kind that starts with 'Holy Mother of—'"

"Gramps."

There was affection in the glare he cast her. "You know, one of the things we were fighting for was freedom of speech, Gina."

She patted her belly, smiling sweetly. "And you're free to speak politely within earshot of your great-grandson."

"See what I have to put up with?" he said to me.

"My sympathies."

He looked at Nate. "Sarcastic, this one."

Nate hunched a shoulder. "One of the many reasons I married her."

I looked at him. His eyes were on me. There was something soft and frightening in them. Forcing my attention back to Charles, I said, "Please—what happened when you got over France?"

Chapter 34

The veteran looked out the window to get his bearings.

"We were flying in from that direction," he said, pointing, "and supposed to jump over Drop Zone C, not far from Sainte-Marie-du-Mont."

I caught Nate's eye. "That's where we're staying." I'd never been so enveloped by history before.

"Well, it's not where we landed," Charles said. "The flak began in earnest and it was all our pilot could do to keep us in the air. We had this jumpmaster—Reid, I think his name was. Cool as a well-digger's"—he looked at Gina and caught himself—"rear end."

She nodded her approval.

"Never flinched. Never showed emotion. But that night up there?" He pointed skyward. "We knew from watching him that something wasn't right. The sound of the plane's engines too. Didn't need to be a genius to figure out that the anti-aircraft crap was making us break a few too many rules.

"We jumped when Reid gave the order, but one look out the door and I knew. Too fast. Way too low. Landing alive all of a sudden became a much bigger deal than hitting Drop Zone C."

He reached for his glass and drank. Gina checked the phone

she'd left mostly hidden under her napkin and made sure it was still recording. I understood. This man, who had been reticent to speak of those two days in '44, seemed to have been liberated from his self-inflicted gag order.

"So . . . we jumped." Charles shook his head at the memory. "Me and the sixteen other men in my stick. Right before, though, the plane banked hard, and me and the guys still onboard got thrown around a bit. Thought we were going down, but that pilot . . . heck of a flyboy. He leveled her out while we were thrashing around back there and we jumped as quick as we could. Cal got hung up on the door, but there was no stopping. Every second was another click off-target, right? Had to get down there fast. Barely had time to say a Hail Mary before we were skimming trees."

He took another sip, then sat back in his chair, looking at me. "Your boy. His kid know where he ended up?"

"We were there yesterday," I said, trying to mask my eagerness to hear more. "A small castle . . ." I looked at Nate.

"Maybe seven or eight miles from here."

When Charles said, "I know the place," the hair rose on my arms again. He added, "I was there with him until the 8th. That's when he was carted off to the nearest field clinic and I regrouped with what was left of my unit."

I leaned in. "We don't know anything about what happened at the castle, but some papers that belonged to Cal were found under the floorboards in one of the rooms."

Charles's eyes bore into mine. "Letters?"

"Yes."

"And that picture of his? Pretty girl. Dark hair."

"I— No. There wasn't a picture. His wife had a picture of Cal with his daughter, but we didn't find any with the letters from France."

Charles shook his head. "Always had them on 'im. Left pocket, over the heart. Stared at that picture and read the letters every time he had three minutes to spare."

I reached across the table and grabbed Nate's arm. I couldn't help myself. "So that's where he was wounded, right? In that castle?" I said to Charles.

Nate added, "Can you tell us anything more about what happened between the day he landed and the last time you saw him?"

Charles ran his hands over his face. He kept them there for a moment and breathed deeply. Then he took off his cap and scratched his head with shaking fingers, his eyes distant, his eyebrows drawn.

When he looked at me again, I saw the trembling in his chin, the sheen in his eyes. "I'm gonna tell you what I can," he said. "Just what I can."

Gina's eyes got wider, but she stayed silent.

"That's all we ask," Nate said. I felt myself leaning toward him.

"Your boy got to the castle before I did," Charles said. "I dropped into a Kraut-infested zone and made like a chameleon for the better part of a day. Hiding out in ditches and bomb craters and hedgerows and the like. Listening. Felt like hours, just listening for the sound of Nazi boots. Our soles were rubber, you realize. Theirs weren't. That's how we could tell them apart when they were on hard surfaces, but on wet soil—a whole other thing. Finally stumbled up to this—this castle or something. And this old guy wanders out holding a rifle." He raised his hands, palms out. "I didn't know if he was a good guy or a bad guy. A collaborator or what. All I knew was I wasn't going to die that day.

"So . . . there's a skirmish." He closed his eyes as if he was remembering the details. "His gun goes off when I jump him. I fire off a couple warning shots. Then I perp-walk the old man into the castle and . . . People everywhere. I mean everywhere. Some of them wounded. All of them looking a lot worse for wear. D-Day, right? It leaves a mark whether you're injured or not."

"Cal?" Saying his name out loud felt like conjuring his presence.

Charles nearly smiled. "He was standing there in the living room when I made my grand entrance. A bit roughed up, but same old Cal. Calm as a toad in the sun with all the crazy going on."

I felt Darlene's absence so keenly in that moment that it took my breath away.

"How badly injured was he?" Nate asked.

"Leg, mostly. But the girl fixed him up pretty good."

"The girl?"

He nodded. "Young thing. Real firecracker. That place was full of people from the towns around there, but this—what—maybe fifteen-year-old girl had the joint under control. Her and her little sister. Lisa, I think. She didn't like me much." He looked at Gina and winked, but the levity looked forced. "Must be something about my face."

Gina patted his arm and Charles went on, steeling himself. "Cal and me . . . we thought we'd head out before dawn the next day, if his leg was up for it. Try to regroup with our unit over by Carentan, since protecting access to the town was part of our mission. We figured we'd run across the good guys if we headed that direction."

He paused and I saw his chin begin to quiver again. "This is the part that gets me," he said.

"It's okay, Gramps. Take your time," Gina said, rubbing her hand over his arm.

"It's . . . it's not all clear in my mind after that. The Krauts came back—the ones who spent time in the castle before. The Occupation, you know. Found out later it was for the comms they'd left behind. The girl didn't want them to see me in my uniform. She was scared they'd take it out on the rest of the people if they saw an American with them, and Cal—he was already dressed like one of them farmers. So . . . I got out of sight." He shook his head. "I could barely hear what was going on downstairs, but it didn't sound good. And I—I guess I wasn't thinking straight."

He looked at his granddaughter almost apologetically. "I wanted to be a hero, you know."

"Gramps." There were tears in her eyes too.

Charles's mood seemed to change in an instant. He shook off the hand she'd laid on his arm. "It's what we came over here for, right? Bunch of American kids, rarin' for a fight. Bring on them Nazis!"

His voice had risen high enough that some of the other patrons in the restaurant were glancing our way. Gina gestured for him to keep it down, and I tried to sound calm as I said, "We understand, Charles. It was a horrible time. For everyone. And you were just a kid yourself."

"I was a *man*," he said with such suppressed force that his voice shook. "I was a warrior."

"Of course you were," I said softly, still trying to appease him.

"I was old enough to be a warrior and stupid enough to think I was invincible. I figured, 'Come at me,' right? 'Gimme your best shot, you sons of . . .'" His voice trailed off. "I figured we could take them. Cal and me. Right there in that room full of people."

He dropped his head and rubbed his eyes with the fingers of one hand. They were haunted when he looked up. "Warrior lost. Stupid won." It was a simple statement. It seemed to cost him his soul. "So these celebrations here. They're great. They're fantastic. But . . . war is hell. That's the other side of the story."

Clasping together his still-shaking hands, Charles glanced at his granddaughter. "I think I've had enough." He looked ten years older than he had minutes before.

"Are you feeling okay?" She seemed concerned.

"I just want to go home."

I had to tamp down the impulse to beg him to stay—to tell him we'd come a long way for the story he was abbreviating. "Are you sure, Charles?" I said instead.

"I can't." Tears trickled down the creases on his face. He wiped his nose with the back of his hand. His head was shaking now too, as if the nerves in his body had been overwhelmed by the memories he was reliving.

Nate spoke in a soft but commanding voice. "Just tell us one more thing," he said.

Charles paused.

"Just tell us if Cal was a good man. If he was a hero or a coward."

"His daughter is gone," I added, tears now on my face too, "but I still need to know, Charles. For the sake of her memory."

Gina had pulled on her jacket and was standing behind her grandfather's chair, torn between concern for him and her obvious compassion for us. "Can you just answer that, Gramps? And then I'll take you home."

His shaking increased. His face was flushed, his shoulders slumped, but his gaze was steady. "Your boy Cal was a hero," he said, a suppressed sob distorting his features. "You're looking at the coward he called Buck."

"He knew Cal."

It was probably the twentieth time I'd made the statement.

Nate and I sat at the kitchen table of our bed-and-breakfast, torn between amazement at the connection with Charles and frustration over what we still hadn't learned.

"They were both at the castle," Nate said. "Charles witnessed what happened. And by the way he hightailed it out of there before he got to the end of the story, I'm guessing it was pretty grim."

I nodded. "Grim enough to keep a returning hero from basking in the glory of liberating Europe. Grim enough, maybe, for a soldier whose wife and wartime comrade both considered him a truly good man to abandon the woman whose picture alone seemed to have gotten him through the run-up to D-Day."

"All we have is conjecture based on a handful of facts," Nate said on a sigh, making his wooden chair creak as he leaned back to stretch his legs past the corner of the table. "I hoped we'd know more by the time our trip was over."

"Me too," I said, feeling the disappointment I saw in Nate's countenance and posture.

On a whim, I said, "I have a confession."

A small smile curved his lips. "You really do love Weezer?"

"Not that big of a confession. I brought something with me from the States."

"Okay."

I went up to my bedroom and got the green canvas bag I'd carried over from home. Frustration weighed heavy as I sat across from Nate again. "I thought that maybe if we came to Normandy and learned enough about who Cal was and what he did here, maybe I'd know where to scatter these."

I took the small urn of Darlene's ashes out of the bag and slid it to the middle of the table.

Nate considered my dilemma for a moment, apparently unsurprised by the ashes I'd brought along. "We could go back to the cemetery," he said. "Or to the beach below it."

I shook my head. "That feels like a place that honors fallen soldiers. Cal didn't die over here."

"You could make the case that part of him did."

I let that sink in for a moment. "But not on those beaches. The way Charles—Buck, I guess—described it, it was at the castle that something happened." I groaned and rubbed my eyes. "I hate not knowing."

"Agreed."

"Whatever happened there caused a lifetime of grief for Darlene."

"And her mother."

I frowned. "Not the way Darlene tells it. Not the way Justin tells it. From all accounts, Claire lived in peace. A hard life, for sure. But somehow she found a way back to happy and content after Cal walked out on her."

"Hard to imagine," Nate said, his expression troubled.

I tried not to sound caustic when I said, "She had this verse highlighted in her Bible—I mean *passionately* highlighted—about not holding on to anger. She must have found some way to let go and move on."

Nate's eyes met mine and a delicate, almost imperceptible current bridged the gap between us. It felt like honesty.

"When you said we couldn't get there . . ." His voice was soft and hurt as he shifted to another, equally complicated topic. "When you said we might not be able to get past what I did . . . I know the situation is completely different, Ceelie, but—I guess I want to make it clear that I'm not Cal."

I folded my hands on the table and looked down, unable to answer.

"I walked away, but I came back." He leaned forward. "And I'm not going away again. Not unless you tell me to. I may be the man who bailed on you, Cee, but I'm also the man who came back."

A wave of confusion made me close my eyes. I breathed. I listened to the voice of woundedness hurling accusations at the softening of my heart. Latent fear swelled inside me, fierce and forceful, threatening to snuff out a flickering hint of hope.

Drawing courage from Nate's honesty, I said, "I want to believe you. I do. But— What if something happens down the road that changes things . . ." Dread darkened my thinking. "Or if my cancer isn't really cured and comes back, like Darlene's." It was a thought I'd tried to stifle for months, but there was no escaping its ominous, persistent whisper. "What if it's already growing—somewhere else in my body? What will you do then, Nate? I can't set myself up to be hurt that way again."

Something bruised washed over my husband's face. "I'll stay."

"Really?" I hadn't intended to sound sarcastic.

He didn't look away. He held my gaze with eyes that spoke of self-inflicted affliction and remorse. The talks we'd had—the explanations he'd offered—never could have conveyed the jagged contrition I saw in that moment. It swept across the chasm between us as a nearly palpable energy, past the cremated remains of the friend who had learned too late about the fruitlessness of hate—the bristling, isolating pain of bitterness.

As I looked across the table at the man I'd married when we were both too young to understand the toll and torment of a 'til-death commitment, something primal and powerful stirred:

I felt my posture change.

My determination toughen.

My rebellion against the disease that had assailed us heighten.

Before I could talk myself out of it, I reached across the table and grasped Nate's hand, my own shaking with emotion and nervousness. After a startled moment, he covered it with his, a casual gesture he'd made a thousand times in all our years together. But on that evening in Normandy, it felt like something more. Something present, protective, purposeful, and sure.

"I hate what happened to us," I said, my voice rough with the ache of fear and loss.

Nate rose without releasing his hold and I stood too. We faced each other wordlessly, something electric in the way our eyes met. In the skin-on-skin connection of our intertwined fingers. He stepped close enough that our bodies almost touched and we stayed there, eyes locked, a while longer—long enough for me to be tempted to lean in.

The outside world receded and I saw only Nate. The need in his eyes. The remorse. The certainty and strength. "I'm sorry I gave you so many reasons to hate me," he whispered. I breathed in his nearness, then moved just enough to rest my forehead on the pulse beating in his neck. "You had every right to despise me," he continued. "You *have* every right." His lips were near my ear, his breath gentle in my hair.

He let me rest there, unmoving, something intimate in our barely touching closeness, and I felt my wounded spirit fluttering toward trust.

Before fear's cold defenses could ambush my resolve, I murmured the words I needed to say. "I'm not ready to give up."

Something almost imperceptible softened in Nate. He pulled away—just a few inches so he could see my face—but the distance felt to me like a destabilizing void. I tightened my grip on his hand and added, "I'm not ready to let the things that tried to break us win."

My husband's half smile held a trace of regret but shone with courageous, luminous hope.

Chapter 35

I woke the next morning with a mental clarity I hadn't felt in months. Something in me had flickered back to life as our conversation stretched into the night. It felt bright and buoyant. Hope-adjacent, as Darlene might have said.

Nate seemed to be in a similar mood when he came out of his room—energized and ready to make the most of our last day in Normandy. We decided over breakfast that we'd spend it taking in as much of the history of the area as we could—driving to Juno Beach, then Pegasus Bridge, and then on to Pointe du Hoc, a strategically located clifftop defended and overtaken at unimaginable human cost.

From there, we went on to the only logical place where Darlene would have wanted her ashes scattered.

It was nearly seven p.m. and the construction truck we'd seen two days before was gone. Nate went to the front door anyway, just in case Jean-Marie was inside, but its combination lock was securely in place.

We walked round the courtyard to take a few pictures of the castle for Justin. "So Cal's already in there when Charles finds the old man and takes him inside at gunpoint," Nate said softly, clearly trying to envision the scene. "And the house is full of people who ran here for safety."

"And then the Germans come back, and . . ."

"War is hell," Nate said, quoting Charles.

He got the canvas bag out of the back seat of the car and we walked around the side of the castle to the huge, rugged tree I'd seen from inside when Maribeth had first brought us to the Château d'Aubry-en-Douve. I took a moment to turn slowly, taking in our surroundings, the day's visits to other historic sites generating life-like scenes in my mind. I tried to hear the sounds, feel the emotions, and see the faces that might have been part of Cal's reality on D-Day.

Then Nate and I moved to stand beneath the oak tree. Its limbs—those that remained—were gnarled and weathered, but all but one curved upward from the damaged trunk, a noble insurrection against the ravages of time.

I trailed my hand across the bark of one of the oak's lower branches, wondering, as I had on my previous visit, what it might have witnessed.

"You do realize this is private property."

The voice came from behind us. It was soft, feminine, and had a distinctive accent.

I turned to find a familiar woman standing a few feet from us. She'd just come around the corner, dressed as impeccably as she'd been the day before at the small ceremony in the American Cemetery. Her raised eyebrows indicated that she didn't approve of our intrusion.

"I'm so sorry," I said, feeling guilty and puzzled by her appearance on the castle's grounds.

Nate's fingers clasped mine. I didn't pull away. "You were at the cemetery yesterday, right? The Veteran Relations . . ."

"Coordinator, yes," she confirmed. "Also the owner of this estate. And you're . . . ?"

I felt Nate's grip tighten as he said, "We're Nate and Cecelia

Donovan. We were at Colleville yesterday for the ceremony and—well, now we're here." I heard the smile in his voice when he added, "Clearly trespassing and caught red-handed."

The tall, sophisticated woman took a few steps toward us, hiking her purse higher on her shoulder. As she came closer, I realized she was older than I'd thought when we'd seen her the day before—probably in her late seventies or early eighties. She smiled back at Nate, laugh lines enhancing the classic beauty of her face, but there was still suspicion in her eyes. "And you're trespassing because . . . ?"

Nate looked at me. I stepped forward, dropping his hand and immediately feeling the loss. "Someone we know was here during the war. He . . ." I stopped myself. "Do you know Maribeth Coupey?"

"I do."

I seized on the connection, hoping it would earn us some grace. "She brought us for a visit a couple days ago and—well—we wanted to come back to honor our friend one last time before we leave for home."

"You say someone you know was here during the war." She squinted a bit as she considered our story. "Someone who lived here, or . . . ?"

Nate stepped beside me. He casually draped his arm across my shoulder. I could feel protectiveness in the gesture. "It's a long story," he said.

The castle's owner tipped her head and seemed to be considering whether we were telling the truth. "Long stories require coffee," she finally said. "I happen to know the combination for the front door, and Jean-Marie has a Keurig in that sparkling new kitchen."

When we had our coffee and were seated in the newly remodeled kitchen, I took the letters from my purse. "Maribeth told me these were found here when the renovation began." I handed them to her. "They're addressed to a Cal McElway. We know he jumped over

Normandy on D-Day, and we know he spent time under this roof. We're just hoping to learn more about what happened when he was here. He was never the same after he was sent home."

She took the letters from me as if they were a fragile treasure. Then she seemed to shake off the shock that had stunned her for a moment and smiled at us with a mixture of awe and nostalgia.

"My older sister and I were in this castle on June 6, 1944—it was our family home." She pointed to the oak outside the kitchen window. "And we found Cal McElway hanging in that tree."

Chapter 36

N ate sucked in air next to me. I felt a swirling in my mind and waited for it to right itself. For an interminable couple of minutes, the woman who'd now told us her name was Lise looked closely at the letters we'd brought.

"This one—it isn't addressed to Cal."

"He actually wrote it to his mom. We found it in his old house in Missouri," I said. "One of the many wild goose chases we've been on to find out what happened to him."

She put down the envelopes and folded her hands in her lap, considering us again. There was something gentle on her face now. And also something suspicious—I'd seen it flashing in her eyes a couple times as I'd told our story. "You said you knew him . . ."

I felt myself blushing but couldn't help it. "Actually . . ."

Nate jumped in. "We were talking fast to keep you from calling the cops on us," he explained, raising a hand in apology. "It felt expedient to say we knew him personally, but—"

"But it's actually just his daughter we knew," I said. "She was born while he was over here and . . ." I blinked at the tears blurring my vision. "She passed away a few weeks ago."

I began to tell Lise about the miraculous collection of events and serendipity that had led us to Aubry-en-Douve, but paused when I noticed how pale she had gone. She swallowed convulsively, a disbelieving expression on her face. "I'm sorry . . . a daughter?" It was nearly a whisper. "I was so caught off guard that it didn't register until just now." She shook her head, as if trying to clear it. "Cal had a daughter?"

I nodded. "Her name was Darlene."

After a moment, Lise pushed away from the table and went to stand near the window, a hand at her throat.

There was something in the tension of that moment that I didn't understand.

"Cal was only here for forty-eight hours or so during the war," she finally said. "He was wounded—surrounded by the enemy and unsure of survival . . ."

She turned to look at Nate, then me. "It's my late sister, Sabine, who found him. His canopy got caught on one of the high branches of that tree." She motioned toward the oak. "And it was I who cut it down after we'd gotten him inside. I was a child," she said, "and he was kind to me." Her eyes filled with tears, and she shook her head in confusion. "That he had a daughter . . ." She looked out again, her eyebrows drawn together.

After a brief hesitation, I said, "Lise, why is his having a daughter so hard for you to hear?"

She smiled sadly but remained silent. Nate and I did too, letting whatever ghosts hovered between us find their voice. Lise finally blew out a pent-up breath, as if she was releasing her control over Cal's tale.

"Because he came back," she said. "Because Cal came back."

It was my turn to be stunned. "He . . . what?"

I felt Nate tense. "Cal came back to France?"

She nodded, melancholy and confusion in her troubled expression.

Nate pushed back his chair and took a couple steps away from the table, away from Lise, away from a revelation that was likely as incomprehensible to him as it was to me.

I stood too and stepped toward her. "When?"

"I think it was still 1944. He just—walked through the gates one day in November . . . maybe December."

I shook my head. "He left his wife and daughter behind . . ."

"I didn't know." Her voice was still soft, still incredulous. "I didn't know he had a family."

Nate came to stand beside me.

"Tell us what happened," he said softly. "When Cal came back—tell us what he was like, how long he stayed."

"It's too late for Darlene now," I added. "But we'd still love to know."

Lise closed her eyes and breathed for a while. When she opened them again, she seemed determined to tell his story.

We didn't go back to sit at the table. It never crossed our minds. We stood by the kitchen window as she began to speak of the man I'd spent months trying to track down.

"He walked through the gates with only a knapsack on his back," she said. "I thought I was dreaming and just stood there and stared at him. Then I shrieked for Albert to come see. He must have thought I was in trouble. He came stumbling out of the stables and just . . . froze.

"When I asked Cal what he was doing here, he shrugged and said something like, 'I thought you might want to see a carousel.'" Lise smiled and shook her head at the recollection. "I'd told him when he was here during the war that that was the first thing I'd do when it was over. And that's all he said to explain why he came back. It took a while, but we did make it to the fair in Bayeux. I rode the carousel, oh, probably twenty times. It was the only trip we ever made with Cal."

There was so much I wanted to ask. Seventy-six years of history couldn't be retold fast enough to assuage the deep thirst for answers choking me. "So Cal just . . . stayed?"

"Yes. Albert had moved into the house by then, and Cal took his old quarters off the stables. There were still Americans everywhere in Normandy—headquarters and clinics and troops helping us to rebuild. But Cal stayed with us. If Americans came by, he hid in his quarters or stayed out in the fields. We had firm orders not to mention his presence. He'd come back as a civilian, not as a soldier."

She looked at us, gauging our reaction, and added, "He stayed for thirty years."

I nearly lost my balance, but Nate reached out to steady me.

"Thirty years?" My question was sharp with disbelief. "Three-zero?"

She nodded, and I wondered if the sadness in her eyes was about Cal or Darlene.

"Please," Nate said. "Tell us about those years."

Lise frowned a bit as memories surged back. "For a while, after the war, I'd still hoped that my father would come home from the camps in Germany, but I knew in my heart that he wouldn't. Every day was a struggle before Cal returned. Trying to run a farm—trying to *resurrect* a farm that had been starved into ashes by the Occupation. Most of our livestock was dead. Our horses . . ." She looked upward as the images in her mind seemed to overwhelm her. "The Germans had killed all our horses when they fled on the morning of D-Day. I can still picture them hanging dead from their leads."

Nearly a full minute passed before Lise spoke again. "Then Cal came back," she said. "He walked into Aubry-en-Douve without an explanation. Just a dogged determination to make our lives better. And that's what he did. He worked day and night to help us get the farm up and running again. Crops. Eventually horses. Cows—which meant milk, cheese, butter . . ."

Her smile faded as her mind wandered back to the days after the invasion. "He barely ever left the grounds. Nose to the grindstone, right? I tried to—I don't know—lighten him up. Introduce him to people. But he was . . ." She sighed. "From the moment he got back, the light had gone out of him. He was walled off, reclusive. Much older than his years, but also kind. Helpful. Protective. He never spoke of himself. He never spoke of the war. He never participated in any of the ceremonies or commemorations and would get angry if anyone suggested it." She shook her head. "All those chances to be with other American soldiers again, but he was a ghost when he came back. This farm was his world. And keeping it running—I think it was the only way he could live with his memories."

An owl hooted in the distance. We stood in the castle's kitchen in silence, contemplating the enormity of Cal's sacrifice.

Lise must have seen something in my expression. "This is a lot to take in, isn't it."

"I'm just . . ." I hesitated. "I'm just trying to make sense of it. His returning here and staying for—three decades?" I was dumbfounded.

Lise cocked her head and seemed to realize how shocking her revelations had been to Nate and me. "I suppose it won't make sense until you know what happened before that. When he was here during the war."

"Are you comfortable telling us?" Nate asked, concern for the elderly woman in his voice.

Lise nodded. "Yes—but not here."

She walked across the foyer to the living room beyond it. We followed, and I wondered if Nate's legs felt as unsteady as mine. I looked into his face and saw intrigue and confusion. Something of the awe I felt too, that we were finally—against all odds—getting the answers Darlene had sought.

Lise led us to a spot toward the back of the room and pointed down. "This is where it happened," she said.

I remembered it from our previous visit—an area where some old floorboards had been preserved, while portions around them had been removed. "Cal said so little after his return that I quickly learned to pay close attention to what did come from his mouth. Do you see that darker patch on the original parquet?" she asked.

Nate crouched down and saw it before I did. "These stains?" he asked, outlining an elongated, deeper-hued blotch that straddled several boards.

"My husband and I were contemplating restoring the floors. This was maybe fifty years ago—when I was twenty-nine or thirty. I hated those stains and their reminder. I just wanted to tear up those boards and replace them. The memories they evoked . . ." Lise's gaze had gone distant as she relived the past. "We were standing right here, considering our options, and Cal said, 'History's stains illuminate the future.' It came out just like that. Just those few words and then he walked away." She shook her head. "'History's stains illuminate the future.' What could we possibly answer to that?"

Lise sighed and crossed her arms, contemplating the dark blotches at our feet. "So the floors stayed. We seldom used the formal living room anyway—too many memories, right?"

Her smile was melancholic. Her eyes soft with remembering. "Eventually, my old friend Lucien bought the castle and its grounds from us. By then, the farm was more of a hobby than a breadwinner. My husband and I were doing fine, me as a schoolteacher and him as a civil engineer, and we decided to try city life for a while in Caen.

"But when I learned that our property was on the market again last year . . ." She shook her head. "I couldn't help myself. I've been involved with veterans my whole life," she said. "To love Cal was to love them all. And the prospect of turning this place—the land he saved from the Nazis first, then from bankruptcy when he returned . . . to turn it into an elegant refuge, a bed-and-breakfast for the GIs and their families who come back all these years after the war. It was a 'no-brainer,' as you Americans say."

She pointed at the parquet in front of us. "Those stains had to stay, though. I had Jean-Marie work around them, as they are the essence of Cal McElway's heart." She looked at me, confusion once again darkening her face. "A heart, I now realize, he might have left back home when he returned to us."

"What happened here?" Nate's voice had a somber, awed tone that echoed the turmoil in my mind.

Lise led us back to the kitchen. We sat around the table and she closed her eyes for a moment. When she opened them again, she said, "Cal was a good man. Honorable. Courageous. Responsible. I think it's because he so thoroughly embodied those traits that what happened here on June 7th was such a shattering thing . . ."

Chapter 37

Albert lay on the ground, bleeding from a bullet to the shoulder, and Lise knelt beside him. She pressed her hands to his wound, trying to stem the flow of blood, her face distorted by a sort of silent hysteria. Albert hadn't moved since he'd been shot, but his eyes were open and aware.

Sabine sat not far from them, a hand cradling the side of her face, the imprint of the Wehrmacht's fist already an angry red welt on her cheekbone. The Germans Cal had shot with Albert's hunting rifle lay on the floor in front of her, while a handful of villagers huddled around the injured in their ranks. The rest watched the standoff with tortured expressions that spoke of utter fear and helplessness.

Lise's plea for Otto not to shoot seemed to have gotten through to him. He looked from Sabine to her terrified sister, and Cal saw something in the German's posture change. It might have been the months he'd spent under the girls' roof that gave him pause. Or maybe a flicker of compassion overriding the darker impulses of survival. Whatever it was, Otto began to lower his weapon. His finger never leaving the trigger, Cal did too. Slowly. Warily. Suspicion brittle in the space between them.

"*Vas-t'en!*" Sabine ordered, wiping her bleeding mouth with her hand. She glanced at Albert and Lise, then looked back at Otto with undisguised repulsion. "Leave!" she spat again, pointing at the door.

After a brief hesitation, a muscle pulsing in his jaw, Otto stepped backward toward the entryway. For a moment, Cal dared to hope that the confrontation would end there. That Otto would simply walk away.

Then Buck came lurching through the living room doors, hurling obscenities.

"Buck, no!" Cal screamed, but the shock of the second American's entrance was too much for Otto's nerves. He jerked his weapon upward and something slammed into Cal so hard that it threw him back, his head hitting the angle of the alcove wall behind him. He saw Buck's first shot strike Otto in the chest.

Then the world went dark.

"*Monsieur Cal?*"

It was a frightened voice. A small, shaken, pleading voice. Cal pressed his eyes closed and tried to remember. It took a few seconds for his brain to make sense of the circumstances—for memory to fill in the gaps his mind was skipping. When the image returned of Buck storming through the living room doors, he sat up so abruptly that pain ripped through his synapses. He glanced down. His right arm was badly damaged. A bullet had grazed his chest and blown through his bicep, probably taking pieces of the humerus with it, and someone had tied a twisted piece of cloth above the wound to slow the bleeding. Given the intensity of the pain he felt when he inhaled, he suspected that the bullet had broken a rib as well. Cal attempted to move the injured limb, but the motion made him gasp. When he tried to spread his fingers, they barely responded.

"Monsieur Cal . . ."

He turned his head toward Lise's voice, squinting at the spot where Sabine and Albert had been before Buck's eruption into the living room. What he saw drove the breath from his lungs and brought the details scrubbed by trauma flooding back to his reeling mind.

Despite the pain clawing at him, Cal began to drag himself toward the little girl. Her cheeks were streaked with tears, her face pale, her lips trembling, her red eyes haunted with confusion and disbelief.

She held her sister's hand in both of hers—limp, bloodied. Someone had draped a beige sweater over Sabine's face, but the long brown skirt and scuffed shoes extending beyond its hem were unmistakably hers. The scarlet red soaking through the wool and pooling beneath the fourteen-year-old's body threatened to hurl Cal's mind back into unconsciousness.

"They shot my sister," Lise whispered, her gaze begging for him to come closer yet. She didn't let go of Sabine's hand when Cal reached her. She just leaned sideways into his chest and began to sob.

Something instinctive overrode Cal's concern for his own injuries. He wrapped his good arm around the child and drew her close, nestling her head under his chin, ignoring the pain spearing through the right side of his body.

Albert sat on the floor a few feet away, propped against a banquette as blood seeped slowly through the bandage wrapped around his shoulder. He stared in abject horror at Lise and Sabine. The man whose stoic countenance hadn't slipped since Cal's arrival at the castle looked demolished now-disfigured by a grief so unbearable that his body visibly shook as his tears fell from shell-shocked eyes to leathery cheeks devoid of color.

"You are one lucky mongrel," Buck tossed over his shoulder as he entered the room, stalking to a courtyard-facing window and peering cautiously outside. He looked back at Cal, a cigarette dangling from the corner of his mouth. "No Krauts in sight, but there's no tellin' if they'll come back." He cocked his head. "When you're done playing Daddy, maybe you can get yourself upstairs and keep an eye on the back fields . . ."

Cal ignored him, his attention so focused on the girl whose tears had soaked through his shirt that nothing else could register. He held Lise close until she stirred and pulled away. She hunched her small frame over her sister again, hiccupping on subsiding sobs-an orphaned child mourning the last vestige of her family. Cal scanned the room. There was blood on the floor where the Germans had fallen, but their bodies were gone.

"Dead," Buck said, following his gaze.

Lise added in a raspy, barely audible voice, "Lucien's father . . . and some other men. They took the *boches* away to bury them." There was confusion in her eyes. Shock and pain. She bit her lip and seemed to search for words. "But–I did not let them take Sabine." Her chin quivered as she brought her sister's hand to her cheek, the torment of loss darkening her gaze.

Cal smoothed a hand over her hair, unable to speak. A handful of villagers still sat in the living room, shell-shocked and wan. They neither spoke nor moved. Their eyes were unfocused, their jaws slack, and their shoulders slumped. Beyond despair. Beyond hope too.

Cal shifted his attention to Albert. "You need to put more pressure on that," he said, motioning to the blood dripping down his sleeve. The old man didn't look up. His eyes were on the red pool beneath Sabine's body.

Cal saw more blood on the expanse of floor between him and Albert. "Who else?" he asked the elderly Frenchman. He pointed toward the evidence of injury or death, hoping the old man would understand his question.

When Albert didn't respond, Lise murmured, "One lady, Sylvie, and two *monsieurs.*"

Failure slammed into Cal like a physical force. It indicted and shamed him. It broke him.

"*C'est de sa faute,*" Albert murmured.

When Cal glanced at him, he found the old man's eyes on Buck. There was something hopeless in the sag of his shoulders and the gauntness of his face.

"What did he say?" Cal asked Lise.

"He said it's his fault." She pointed her chin toward Buck, anger flashing in her eyes. "He's the one who made—" She swallowed hard. "Who made this happen."

The paratrooper still stood guard at the window, apparently unfazed by the carnage. "Just did what I had to do, kid."

"I want him to leave," Lise whispered so softly that Cal nearly missed it. He turned toward her and she said it again, more loudly this time. More defiantly. "I want him to leave." There were traces of Sabine in the statement.

"Lise . . . he was trying to protect you." Even to his own ears, the words sounded hollow.

"I want him to leave!" she repeated, this time loud enough for Buck to hear.

He turned from the window, eyes narrowed on the girl, and pointed at her with his free hand. "Hey, you're lucky I was here, little lady!"

"Shut up, Buck," Cal said, fury like acid in his veins.

But Buck had more to say. "Without me and Cal here, you'd all be dead!" He pointed at the few people still in the room. "You Frogs'll thank us later. Just you watch. History will say that we were the heroes here!"

"Shut. Up!" Cal yelled, his voice shaking with the horror of the death he'd been unable to prevent, the devastation provoked by Buck's reckless bloodlust. Anger scorched its way up his throat. He was opening his mouth to excoriate his comrade when a small hand clutched his arm. He looked down into Lise's wide, brown eyes.

"*Crie pas,*" she whispered, pleading on her tear-stained face. "Please—don't scream anym—"

Buck's sneering voice cut through her plea. "And no, it wasn't me who killed your people, little girl. The Krauts did!" He speared a finger toward Cal. "And your hero here—he's the one who shot your sister."

The orange hues of early dawn tinted the horizon. Buck still roamed the castle, going window to window, as if a German attack was imminent. The villagers had no such concerns. Those who hadn't departed under cover of darkness lingered in rooms and hallways, dozing fitfully or staring straight ahead with vacant expressions. The fear that had permeated the space since Cal's arrival had been replaced by something darker.

He'd found refuge upstairs. He sat on the floor in the corner of a small bedroom, the pain in his chest and arm dwarfed by the tumult in his mind. He knew he should be planning his and Buck's next move, plotting a route that would get them to Carentan, but he couldn't get past the paralyzing trauma of anguish and disgrace.

He'd killed a child. He'd killed Sabine.

He could recall it all with stunning clarity, now that his memory had fully returned. Otto's bullet slamming into his chest and arm, the reflexive pull of his finger on the trigger, and his shot going wide as he went down. He hadn't seen it hit Sabine, but there

315

was no doubt in his mind that his rifle had been pointed in her direction. Cal felt pummeled by the realization. Eviscerated. Wrecked.

Several of the men had finally taken Sabine's body to the field next to the woods to bury her. Cal had tried to hold Lise back with one arm as they'd carried the body outside, but she'd torn at his grip, desperate not to lose sight of her sister, and finally pulled free. Albert, who appeared much older than he had hours before and seemed held together only by unsteady resolve, had stepped into the doorway to block her exit.

Lise tried to push past him, but only briefly. The Frenchman said something to her that Cal couldn't hear and she came apart, melting into his chest, sobbing. Albert didn't embrace the girl. He didn't offer words of encouragement or comfort, though Cal could see something loving on his face. He patted Lise's shoulder a bit awkwardly and pulled a handkerchief from his pocket, instructing her to wipe her face. Then he led her out of the room toward the kitchen.

The light of a flickering flame tore Cal away from the morbid memory. Albert stood in the doorway, Lise at his side, their faces lit by the candle she was holding. Albert's arm was in a sling, wrapped in clean bandages.

It took a moment for them to see Cal in the corner, his legs drawn up, his injured arm strapped close to his body to limit movement. One of the village women had splinted it and wrapped it more tightly in the hours since the attack, and the bleeding had slowed to a barely spreading stain. She'd also placed a cloth compress over the deep gash in his chest.

"We want to tell you something," Lise said.

Cal felt his heart constrict at the sound of her voice. He squinted up at the child whose sister he'd shot-whose life he'd altered in an irreparable way.

"You didn't mean to shoot Sabine," she said without prompting.

Something in Cal rebelled at the words. "Lise . . ."

The girl took a couple steps into the room. "Albert says you were trying to protect us." Her voice seemed hollowed by grief.

He shook his head as if the gesture would dislodge the fog of guilt hampering his thinking. "I should have stopped them before they got inside." He felt his nerves fraying at the futility of his words and clenched his jaw against the emotions threatening to overwhelm him. "I never should have let Sabine talk me into-"

"Cal." Albert had never said Cal's name before. It brought him up short. He looked into the elderly man's face and saw conviction there. "*Tu voulais nous aider.*"

"What did he say?" Cal asked Lise.

"He said you wanted to help." She blinked back tears and took a quick breath. "It isn't your fault."

Helplessness gripped Cal's lungs, making it hard for him to breathe. "That won't give you your sister back. That won't-"

Albert interrupted him, his voice firm, and Lise translated again. "You did not mean to shoot her," she said. Then she added, "Please, *Monsieur* Cal. Don't cry."

Only then did Cal realize there were tears on his face, running down his neck into the collar of his shirt. His breath came in short gasps and a groan of utter anguish escaped before he could quell it. He closed his eyes, dropped his head, and tried to control the waves of emotion slamming into him.

He was vaguely aware of Lise's hand tapping his shoulder as he wept, of the springs of the bed squeaking as Albert lowered himself to sit on it.

After the worst had passed, he wiped his face with his sleeve and exhaled a long, stricken breath.

When he was sure he could speak again, he looked at Albert. "What can I do?" Lise translated for him and Cal added, "To help you and Lise. What can I do?"

Albert said something in French that made Lise tilt her chin up a notch. "We will be okay," she said.

Albert leaned forward and motioned for Lise to interpret for him as he spoke.

She did as instructed. "There is bombing everywhere tonight. In all of Normandy, people are dying." Albert waved his good arm toward Cal. "Some of them are soldiers like you, fighting against things that have made our lives . . ." She hesitated, searching for the word, and finally said in French, "*Un enfer.*"

Cal recognized the word. Sabine had used it before. *Hell.*

Albert spoke again, his gravelly voice barely above a whisper as his eyes bore into Cal.

"Sabine was killed because of the Nazis," Lise translated. She bit her lip when it began to tremble. "They are the guilty ones."

"*On survivra,*" Albert said.

318

"We will survive, *Monsieur* Cal." Tears balanced on her eyelashes.

Cal let his head fall back against the wall. He was a soldier. A warrior. He'd boarded that C-47 in Upottery two days ago determined to find, pursue, and eliminate the enemy until France was free of its oppressor. What he had done instead . . . The memories added their disdain to already crippling guilt.

"You must get up," Lise finally said. "Albert will get your army clothes for you."

The old man reached out a hand to help Cal off the floor. "*Merci*," Cal said in French, flinching as the movement increased his pain. He reached for the windowsill to steady himself and looked down to find Lise standing close, one hand in front of her. "You said your mother called it . . ." She seemed to forget. "What did she call it?"

Cal saw the coin she held out to him. "Walking Liberty," he said.

"It was in the pocket of Sabine's apron." She blinked hard. "The one with the daffodils on it." Pressing the half-dollar into the wounded paratrooper's hand, the girl said, "You will take her with you, yes? You and Liberty . . ."

Cal fought the emotions rising in his chest. The trust in Lise's eyes was inconceivable to him. After what he'd failed to prevent. After what he'd done.

Albert stepped back into the room from the hallway and handed Cal the Garand Sabine had hidden on his first day in the castle.

"We must not be careful anymore," Lise translated after Albert spoke.

Cal felt shame burning in his mind, but nodded his agreement. He held the rifle up with his good hand, inspecting it in the light of Lise's candle.

Nearly simultaneously, a shot rang out, debris shattering the glass pane of the window beside him as a bullet lodged in the plaster just beneath it.

Cal ducked out of sight, oblivious to the explosion of pain in his right arm and rib cage. He pulled Lise down with him as Albert flattened himself against the wall on the other side of the window. Only then did Cal hear the voice of a villager outside the castle crying out, "*Non, non, non! Tirez pas!*" and an American voice barking in an urgent, hushed tone, "Get down! Get down! Get on the ground!"

Cal turned his head toward the window and yelled as loudly as he could over the adrenaline tightening his throat. "Hold your fire—we're friendlies! Hold your fire!"

It didn't take long for the medic to declare Cal unfit for battle. The wound to his rib cage was fairly shallow and easily stitched up, but with his leg likely broken and his dominant arm in need of surgery to prevent permanent damage, there were no other options. The corpsman, a young man with eager eyes, told Cal to stay put for a few hours. He'd call for evac and Cal would be taken to the nearest field clinic, then probably on to England and home.

While the medic and his unit took care of the few injured civilians still finding refuge in the castle, Albert included, Buck regaled the newcomers with a tale

of heroism that strained the truth and always seemed
to end with him as a reluctant and courageous victor.

Cal had to leave the room when he launched
into his account for the third time. It wasn't worth
contradicting his story.

Knowing he'd probably be gone before Lise got up,
he asked Albert if he could say goodbye to her. The
Frenchman led Cal to the door of Lise's bedroom. His
gait was slow and weary as they climbed the steps.
He was winded by the time they reached the landing.
Just hours before, Sabine had said, "Daughters need a
father." Cal wondered if the old man had what it would
take to care for a growing, orphaned girl.

"Lise," Albert said as they entered her bedroom. The
girl stirred under her covers, then twisted around and
squinted at him. She frowned sleepily when she saw
Cal standing there too. The fragility in her eyes, the
sadness and the need, nearly undid him.

Cal moved to sit gingerly on the side of the
bed and reached into his pockets, taking out every
remaining piece of candy and chewing gum he'd carried
over from England. "I wish I could give you steak and
fries," he said to her, noting again her sunken cheeks
and pale coloring.

Lise's eyes widened when she realized he was
wearing his uniform. "You are leaving?"

Cal nodded. "I am."

She moved so fast it startled him. When her thin
arms came around his neck and she whispered a soft,
"Goodbye, *Monsieur* Cal" in his ear, he felt a piece of
his spirit begin to break-an intractable fissure, life-
bending and marrow-deep.

"I want you to keep this," he said, pulling away to press the coin back into Lise's hand. "Liberty is walking." He took a moment to compose himself. "And she is determined and brave."

"*Comme toi?*" Lise asked. "Like you?" she said in English.

Cal dropped his head. His eyes shone as he fixed them on the seven-year-old again. "No, Lise. Not like me. Like you."

Chapter 38

There were tears in Lise's eyes as she recalled their goodbye. "I didn't ask him to come back. I knew Albert would take care of me—find a way for us to keep living without Sabine. And we did, for those months before Cal returned. It wasn't easy, but we had enough."

"You didn't have any family to take you in?" I asked.

"Not really. I had some distant relatives. In Saint-Lô, mostly. But well over seventy percent of the city was destroyed during the Allied bombings and . . . their lives were blown up too. Those who didn't die likely went into survival mode just as we did, without much thought for the rural cousins they never saw."

"How did you do it?" I asked, astounded that a little girl and her elderly guardian had managed to survive unaided for so long.

Lise smiled at the memories. "We were creative. And the people of the village, the people we'd welcomed in on the worst day of our lives, showed their gratitude to us in many ways. The men worked in our fields with Albert, then with both him and Cal. We were given chickens and I sold their eggs. We planted large gardens and sold our produce at markets. I learned to barter for flour and yeast and made breads—I actually got quite good at it."

"But you were only seven," I said.

"Nearly eight. And eight in 1944 is not eight today. We had lived four years under the occupation, the three of us. Three years without our mother and over a year without Papa. I was young in age, but with us survivors . . . Our lives can't really be measured in years." She stood. "Come with me."

We walked out to the backyard again. Night fell late in June in Normandy. It was nearly nine, and still the sky was light.

"I saw you looking at the tree when I arrived," Lise said to me. "I wonder if you saw this too."

She led us to the lilac grove on the outer edge of the grassy expanse, where pieces of scaffolding were stacked. My breath caught as we followed her around to the other side.

In the shadow of a tree in bloom stood a white, marble cross.

"It looks just like the ones in the American Cemetery," I murmured.

"That was the goal," Lise said. "A hero's resting place."

Nate read the inscription on the stone. "How did he die?" he asked.

"As quietly as he lived. He went to sleep one night and didn't wake up. The doctor assumed it was his heart. He was, I think, somewhere in his fifties."

"Young," I said as emotions broadsided me again.

Nate peered more closely at the cross. "No date of birth," he said.

Lise shrugged. "We never knew what it was. He never told us. And in those years after the war when so many were moving, returning, or still missing, nobody thought to register or become legalized, so . . ."

I took a couple steps closer and crouched down, noticing for the first time the small, silver frame embedded in the center of the cross. It was a picture of Cal and a young, dark-haired woman standing close. He smiled a bit cockily at the camera, his arm draped around her neck, while she laughed, her face upturned and luminous.

"It never left him," Lise said. "Not when he was here during the war and not after he came back." She smiled wistfully. "He carried it in his breast pocket every day he lived. It only seemed fitting to make sure it stayed with him in death."

"The woman he left behind," I said under my breath.

Lise smiled a little sadly. "All these years I thought it was a girl-friend from before the war. Maybe someone he'd lost. I imagined that he'd run back to France, at least in part, to get over her. But I never thought that she was still alive. That she was his wife. And now, to think he had a daughter too . . ."

I stood up and took a step back. The cross appeared to be lit from the inside, its gleaming white a stark contrast to the shadows of the lilac grove behind it. I thought of Darlene—of her mother too—and couldn't help the anger that bubbled to the surface. A fierce protectiveness rose in me, a posthumous defense of my dearly missed friend.

"How could he leave a woman who loved him and a daughter who needed him for—" I caught myself. There was nothing I could say that wouldn't be insulting to Lise.

"Perfect strangers?" she completed my thought. There was no rancor in her tone. Only sadness. "Unrelated people he'd only known for a couple of days under the worst of circumstances?"

Nate spoke before I could answer. "I think it nearly killed him." Intense emotions played across his face. "Leaving Claire and Darlene . . . I think—" He ran his fingers through his hair in a gesture of frustration. Or maybe it was compassion. He tried again. "What if he was so sure of his unworthiness that he convinced himself he was doing them a favor? That after shooting Sabine, he had no right to be a father and husband—no right to find happiness in raising his own child?" He stood there, hands on hips, his eyebrows drawn together as he tried to understand the reasoning of a man who had lived decades before, burdened by the kind of guilt he couldn't fully grasp. "What if he believed that a life in exile was the just penalty for the horrors that happened in this castle that night?"

Lise shook her head. "And yet he was a father to me," she whispered. "He was young—just a few years older than Sabine—but in every way that mattered, he became my father."

Her eyes lingered on the castle for a moment, then drifted over the open fields framed by the gate in the stone wall, and on to the lilacs whose fragrance permeated the air around us. "This is where we found Cal the day he dropped into our lives. He'd crawled from the oak toward this grove, probably trying to get out of sight." She stepped forward to lay a hand on the white cross. "This is where Cal's ending began, where he entered a world so complicated and violent and upside down that good could not emerge from it unstained."

She looked at me, mourning on her face. "I knew that the Cal who returned to us was just a shadow of the Cal who'd rescued us. And now that I know all he chose to leave behind—the grief that sacrifice required . . ." She covered her throat with an unsteady hand.

The moment felt sacred. I let it breathe, standing next to Nate in solemn reverence for the wounded veteran who lay beneath our feet.

After some time, Lise wandered closer to the broken oak that somehow still radiated majesty. She caressed its bark with her hand and looked up toward the place where Cal had landed all those years before. The air was cool and I hadn't dressed for nightfall. Nate opened an arm toward me and I stepped close without hesitation, leaning into his warmth.

Lise's voice was barely above a whisper. "Thousands of American soldiers died on D-Day." She turned with tears in her eyes. "But how many of those who survived essentially died too? They just went on breathing for a few more years, like Cal."

"And Buck," I said, just as softly.

Lise straightened at the name. "Buck—" She shook her head in disbelief. "Do you know him?"

"We do," Nate said.

"Lise," I began, remembering the commemoration at the American Cemetery, "you've met him too. You shook his hand at the Colleville ceremony yesterday."

We found Charles in his wheelchair, sitting under the wing of a B-26 Marauder displayed in the Utah Beach Museum. He'd dressed up for the occasion. His uniform looked crisp, his medals meticulously aligned on his chest. He saw Nate and me coming and looked ready to bolt, but Gina saw us too and made a bit of a statement by deliberately depressing the brake pedal on his chair.

I got down on my haunches next to him, unconcerned that neither Nate nor I were dressed for the cocktail party. Lise was known well enough in these parts that she'd gotten us in at the entrance. I knew she stood behind me, listening.

"I told you I was done," Charles said gruffly.

"I'm not here to beg for more stories," I assured him. I'd spent the night thinking about what I wanted to say to Buck, the warrior whose memories were so filled with honor and shame. And I'd spent it grieving for Cal—for the self-inflicted exile, the atonement he'd chosen for what he'd done during the darkest night of war. I still ached for the strapping young man standing with the woman he loved in the old photo he carried with him, looking into the lens with a smile entirely devoid of unworthiness and pain.

As I crouched by Buck's chair and took his hand in mine, I prayed he could feel the healing pulsing through my veins, feeding hard-won hope with every inhaled breath and exhaled sigh.

"I know what happened," I whispered, looking at him with all the compassion I felt.

He scoffed. "No, you don't."

"I do, Charles."

His jaw tensed as his eyes hardened. They locked with mine—defiant and scared.

"Otto." It was all I had to say. A brutal softening descended over Buck's features. Capitulation. Guilt. Relief. He stared at me as if his worst deeds were written on my face, accusing him—condemning him.

"I—I was young," he stammered.

"I know you were."

"I was hopped up on adrenaline and booze. I didn't know what I was doing," he said, half-groaning, half-pleading as he reached toward me with shaking hands.

"I know," I said hurriedly, pressing my fingers over his. "I believe you—I do." I tried to infuse my expression with gentleness. "And, Charles—Buck—there's somebody here who believes you too."

I rose and stepped aside. Charles's eyes darted around, then settled on the tall, elderly woman who stood, hands clasped in front of her, smiling at the veteran. There must have been something about her—something in her big brown eyes—that pierced through Buck's defenses to the memories beyond.

His face crumpled and he reached blindly for Gina. She squeezed his shoulder, frowning in confusion. Lise took a few steps and knelt down in front of the weeping veteran.

"Buck," she said softly, taking his hand in both of hers. "Buck," she repeated when he kept his eyes averted, tears streaking down his face into the starched collar of his shirt. "Buck." Her voice was firmer now. Coaxing.

Charles's gaze took an eternity to rise to meet hers. When it did, she leaned in close enough that he could see the forgiveness on her face. She held up the Walking Liberty coin his friend had given her and smiled at the recognition in Buck's eyes.

Then she pressed it into his palm and said, "Thank you, Charles Mancuso, for liberating France."

Epilogue

L ise and Buck were still talking when we left the museum. We wandered toward the dunes lining Utah Beach, past several monuments honoring the American soldiers who had landed there seventy-six years earlier.

After we found a spot overlooking the water and sat on the sand, I tried to wrap my mind around the journey that had led us to this place—the choices and discoveries and surprises and planning and dumb luck that had pieced together the bridge between past and present, between lostness and a fullness that took my breath away.

Nate sat quietly beside me, and I wondered if his musings mirrored mine.

"'History's stains illuminate the future,'" he said in a pensive tone after a couple minutes had passed.

I looked at him. "Quoting Cal?"

"I am."

"Because you agree or . . . ?"

"Because I want a future," Nate said. Boldness and hope washed over his face. "And because I'm feeling particularly courageous right now."

I smiled. "I guess it's a contagious thing."

We sat close enough for our arms to touch, facing the sand and water where so many lives had been sacrificed to change the course of history.

"I told you what Darlene said about courage, right?"

"I don't think you did," Nate said, frowning as he tried to recall.

"The opposite of courage isn't fear. It's resentment," I paraphrased.

He let that settle for a beat. "Dang, she's good." There was warmth in his voice. "You think she got her philosophical savvy from the father she never knew?"

"Maybe she did." I pondered the father-daughter dynamics that had brought us to this place. "Both of them died after a lifetime of resentment," I said to the man whose vulnerability and strength had been constants in the past few days. "Cal at himself and Darlene at Cal."

I looked at the sliver of sun shining a trail of light from the horizon to the water's edge. I wasn't sure how to formulate what I wanted to say. "Resentment is exhausting. And corrosive. I just—I don't want to live that way."

Nate said nothing for a while. Then he repeated, "I want a future with you, Cee."

I smiled. "So you've said."

"I want a future that is brave."

"Brave," I repeated. Testing the word. Savoring its power.

"Brave like Darlene," he continued, "the woman who laughed through her cancer and kept on loving others until the day she died." He looked directly at me. "Brave like the survivor who asked her nearly-ex-husband to go with her to Normandy when his stupidity and selfishness had caused her so much pain."

I was caught off guard by the impulse to disagree. This man who'd flown to Normandy with me on a whim was more the man I married than the one who'd walked away. His abandonment had inflicted agony—the kind that might still take a miracle to undo—but after months of a livid, debilitating resentment, I understood how my cancer might have broken him too, and how fragile we already were before it even struck.

I reached for Nate's hand but paused before I touched it. I thought of the rejection that had upended my life, my outlook, and my self-esteem. I remembered Claire and the forgiveness she'd chosen. And I considered the man sitting beside me, whose penance since we'd reconnected had been sustained and sincere.

The tips of my fingers brushed the top of Nate's hand, jolting us both. He turned it over and laced his fingers through mine, his grasp sturdy and sure. The enveloping warmth. The roughness of the callouses on his palm.

It felt like coming home.

I looked up into my husband's face. "Those monuments behind us, they're a testament to the brutality of war," I said. "It nearly destroyed this part of France. Entire towns bombed off the map, civilians massacred—all in the pursuit of freedom." I hunched a shoulder. "But France came back. It built on the ruins. It let its stains illuminate its future, and look at what this beach is like today."

I hitched my chin toward the teenagers sitting around a bonfire a few feet from us and the man walking back to the parking lot, a towel-wrapped child in his arms. "I want that, Nate. I want a re-building kind of brave."

I thought of Darlene's brick-carrying gnome—of the restoration she'd sought as she overcame then succumbed to her cancer. It felt right to have left her ashes in the ground next to the cross that marked Cal's life of wounded sacrifice. Nate had dug the shallow hole with his bare hands and gently tucked the urn into the moist Norman earth before covering it again—a father and a daughter finally reunited, despite the many decades of their joint but distant pain.

The sky was fading to a golden red as small waves swept onto the sand of Utah Beach. "Stay here," Nate said, startling me as he got to his feet, kicked off his shoes, and strode to the water's edge. He seemed to be looking for something specific and walked back and forth, picking up and discarding, over and over until he was satisfied.

He returned to our spot in the dunes with two fairly thick sticks and sat down next to me again, tearing up a couple tall reeds.

"Finally putting your Boy Scout training to use?" I said, confused by what he was doing.

He gave me a look and started to bind the sticks together with the reeds. When he was done, he moved to a spot at the edge of our dune and planted his makeshift cross in the sand.

Then he faced me, his hands on his hips in a determined stance. "The crosses in Normandy are as much about courage as they are about death," he declared. "And you know what, Cee? Survivors deserve crosses too."

I blinked at the tears suddenly blurring my vision. History, hope, and healing saturated that moment.

But Nate wasn't finished. "I never learned how to carve letters in Boy Scouts, but if I had, this cross would read: 'A hero stood here. Cecelia Donovan. Born in 1977. Fought cancer in 2019. Beat the beast in 2020. Lived in that victory for the rest of her life.'"

My smile was tremulous. "That's a lot of lettering for such a small stick," I said. "And it really ought to read: 'Nathanael Donovan fought by her side.'"

The light in his eyes dimmed. "But then he walked away."

"And then he came back."

He nodded and quietly repeated, "And then he came back."

From the void in my heart where Darlene would always live, I heard her voice, hoarsened a bit by the toll of overcoming, say, "*Puff out your chest, girlie. Own this victory.*" I looked up at the sky and hoped she was watching.

"I know that the last few years weren't great," I said after a moment. "Even before my diagnosis. And I know that you and me being so strong in some weird way made our 'together' weaker . . ."

I let my mind drift back over the decades I'd spent with Nate. It was all so complex. So natural and joyous. So messy and mundane. So prone to damaging, indiscernible change.

"I want a future too," I finally said. It was a simple statement. Clear-minded and earnest. Powerful enough to mark an end. And a beginning.

Pulling out my phone, I found the old Bryan Adams song Nate had played at O'Hurley's on the night we first met. I stood and propped it against the cross he'd made—a memorial to our complicated, intertwined grief—and held my hand out to him, mouthing the words as they began to play.

"*Look into my eyes . . .*"

Nate exhaled and hung his head.

"*And you will see . . .*"

I lay a hand on his shoulder and he looked up.

"*What you mean to me.*"

He hesitated only a moment before taking me into his arms. It felt breathtakingly familiar and startlingly new. I leaned into his embrace without reservation, wrapping my arms around his waist as he pulled me closer still. And we began to sway.

"So . . . ," he whispered a minute or so later, tightening his hold, the warmth of relief in his voice. "Are you saying . . . ?"

"Yes."

"Okay." I could almost hear his lopsided grin when he added, "And does this mean . . . ?"

I pulled away just enough to see his face, to reach up on tiptoe and let my lips brush his. The contact jolted me. A rush of recognition tinged with mystery. Caution and desire dueled in my mind, but it was love—the kind that aches, endures, and somehow still believes—that coaxed a reborn courage from my grief.

As I stared into the sureness of my husband's steady gaze, a leaden darkness fluttered toward light.

"I want to be us again," I said to Nate—to the man who had fled and the man who had returned. "A new us. A *reconstructed* us."

I heard my sweet friend say, *"Give time the time it needs,"* and added—just in case, "But you have to understand that I need to take it slow. Slow enough to wrap my mind around everything that's happened." I sighed. "Slow enough to crawl back into this body I don't recognize."

He swallowed hard as something galvanizing flashed across his face. His breath brushed warm against my skin. "You take the lead," he said. He seemed to hesitate, then added sheepishly, "But just so you know, I've been carrying your ring around ever since you gave it back to me. So when you're ready—whenever that is . . ."

I smiled and nestled in, pressing my scarred survival closer to his steady strength, and said, "Hey, Nate—shut up and dance."

A Note from the Author

Iam a three-time cancer survivor.

Just over two years ago, I awoke in the hospital and listened dumbfounded as my surgeon informed me that the mastectomy I'd chosen to *prevent* a recurrence had actually revealed several malignant tumors. I was at a loss—battered and disbelieving.

It took a while for it all to sink in. Nights were the worst. Prognoses seem harsher after dark. Rosy denouements more difficult to envision. Yet in those days following surgery, the same gentle voice that had whispered serenity to me as I'd made the decision to go under the knife was still there. I heard it in the kindness of nurses as they worked to steady my pain and ease my fears. I felt it in my GP's hand on my arm, as she came by early the first morning to sit by my bed and pray for peace. I sensed it in the Christmas lights and carols, dimmed by pain and uncertainty, but still radiant with the promise of God's overwhelming and sufficient love.

Survival is miraculous. It is also torturous. The weeks I spent waiting for pathology results and a treatment plan were hard. And even when the tests finally came back with optimistic conclusions, I couldn't fully celebrate. I'd been staring death in the face for so long that I didn't know how to look away.

When I began writing *Fragments of Light*, I knew I wanted to explore the unspoken consequences, emotional and physical, of breast cancer. But I also wanted the novel to be about "brave"—the kind that shows up in so many ways, under so many circumstances, in so many different lives. The first voice I "heard" was Lise's. A seven-year-old daring to be hopeful when her world told her to be scared. Then I heard Ceelie's. It sounded an awful lot like mine, at times, but without the anchors and buffers of a sustaining faith. I thought Nate would be her bulwark right up until he chose to walk away. His determination to earn back Ceelie's trust surprised even me. Then Darlene entered the story. She breezed into Ceelie's hospital room unforeseen by this author. And she transformed the novel's trajectory.

A serendipitous invitation to be the translator for *The Girl Who Wore Freedom*, a WWII documentary filming in Normandy, completed my cast of overcomers. As I witnessed the expressions of veterans standing on the parapet overlooking Omaha Beach, reliving the day that changed the world's history, and as I heard them recount their memories surrounded by the citizens of a liberated France, Cal, then Buck, entered my imagination.

I let the elements of *Fragments of Light* steep for a while and wondered what bravery would really look like for the war survivors, the cancer conquerors, and those who loved them if they didn't have the kind of faith that fosters peace—that heals the natural resentment of suffering, failure, abandonment, and loss.

Claire wasn't in my planning for the book. But she became the anchor point I was hoping for. *"Cease from anger, and forsake wrath"* isn't just the sentence a fictitious character underlines in her Bible. It's a life-enhancing and life-restoring invitation to take back the reins torn from our grasp by the perpetrators of harm. It's an exhortation to turn our gaze from the inflictors of our pain to the promises of the One whose love bandages the most maiming of our wounds.

I wondered—could the faith of a woman bruised in marrow-deep ways yield generational healing simply by the power of the verse she chose as her survival guide?

I believed it could. And in my mind, it did. I envisioned Ceelie later going back to Claire's Bible to consider the other verses Darlene's mother had underlined—the admonishments and covenants that had given Claire's broken life a sense of serenity and meaning.

I like to think Ceelie found God there. And an even deeper, more lasting kind of healing.

Acknowledgments

M y deepest thanks to those who breathed life into *Fragments of Light*.

Those who inspired:

A huge *merci* to the warm-hearted people of Normandy for rekindling my love for France, the land of my childhood. You may be its most compelling ambassadors.

To Jean-Marie, Dany, and Flo, for reminding me of the extraordinary power of open-armed kindness. *Votre amitié m'est précieuse.*

To Team Tom, for making me feel welcome despite the frantic pace of Staff Sergeant Rice's anniversary adventures on the soil he liberated.

To Denis, for allowing me to tag along (in a WWII command vehicle!) with Tom and members of the 101st Airborne as you retraced his D-Day steps.

To Francine, for opening your family's photo albums and bringing history to life as you recounted all that happened in your château in 1944.

To ninety-two-year-old Albert, for letting this stranger hear your story and witness your tears when we met on a sidewalk in Carentan during the reenactment of its liberation.

To *The Girl Who Wore Freedom*, for inviting me to be your translator as you filmed the documentary in France.

To the American veterans and French survivors of the German occupation I met in Normandy, for the life-changing and novel-inspiring impact of looking into your faces and watching the memories dance in shadows and light in your eyes.

To Mom, for traveling with me to the seventy-fifth commemoration of D-Day and for being just as deeply moved as I was by the people I love.

Those who healed:

Words are insufficient to adequately thank Drs. Steven and Noemi Sigalove for saving my life and rebuilding my future.

Dr. Ferris, for caring for this oncology patient with uncommon compassion.

Dr. Chang, for performing a miracle with the lymphedema surgery you pioneered.

Susan C., Jamie O., Nikole C., and Claudia B., for the extraordinary kindness, the laughter, the relief, and the expertise.

You all were God's answer to my most fervent prayers.

Those who empowered:

I wouldn't be writing these thank yous were it not for Becky Monds, my editor. You understand my heart and breathe life into my novels. Thank you for walking alongside me for the third time with your trademark enthusiasm, calm, and incomparable mastery.

Chip MacGregor, my agent. Your expertise is well established in the publishing world, but it's your kindness and dedication I've come to appreciate most. Thank you for finding this novel a home.

Thomas Nelson, my attentive, highly-respected, and standard-setting publisher. I am flabbergasted, blessed, and grateful to work with you.

Discussion Questions

1. The original title of the book had the word *brave* in it. How do you see each of the principal characters demonstrating bravery?
2. What do you see in Ceelie's thinking and decisions that are a consequence of surviving breast cancer and having a mastectomy?
3. As Nate tries to repair their relationship, what does he say or do that eventually makes reconciliation possible?
4. What do you see in Nate and Ceelie's story that might have led to their estrangement even without her cancer?
5. Looking back, what might have preserved Nate and Ceelie's marriage?
6. What do you think motivated Cal to abandon his family two months after getting home? And what do you think motivated him to leave his farm and return to France?
7. Is Cal a hero?
8. What made it possible for Lise to honestly thank Buck for fighting in WWII?
9. In what way did the verse *"Cease from anger, and forsake wrath"* change Claire's life?

10. How can a person realistically *"Cease from anger, and forsake wrath"*?

11. How might Darlene's life have been different if she'd understood sooner that "the opposite of brave isn't fear—it's resentment"?

12. What do you see as healing moments in Ceelie's journey?

13. How do you see Nate and Ceelie's story playing out in the future?

About the Author

Author photo by Carrie
From Photography

Born in France to a Canadian father and an American mother, Michèle Phoenix is a consultant, writer, and speaker with a heart for Third Culture Kids. She taught for twenty years at Black Forest Academy (Germany) before launching her own advocacy venture under Global Outreach Mission. Michèle travels globally to consult and teach on topics related to this unique people group. She loves good conversations, mischievous students, Marvel movies, and paths to healing.

Learn more at michelephoenix.com
Instagram: shellphoenix
Twitter: @frenchphoenix
Facebook: AuthorMichelePhoenix